Advance Praise for *River Meets the Sea*

"Brilliant and inventive, *River Meets the Sea* is elegantly told in heartrending poetry. Moorthy's protagonists, Chandra and Ronny, feel familiar in their search for meaning and belonging, even as they grapple with the implications of race and masculinity. With exquisite prose in which water becomes just as much a character as Chandra and Ronny, *River Meets the Sea* flows smoothly between the protagonists' histories, the forces that propel them, and their inevitable meeting."

— Francesca Ekwuyasi, author of
Butter Honey Pig Bread

"Rachael Moorthy's writing is driven by an innate creative curiosity, interrogating history, identity, and the human condition, and always rooted in deep artistic and moral convictions."

— Lee Henderson, author of
The Road Narrows as You Go

"Deeply poetic, fluid, and dreamlike, Rachael Moorthy's prose, much like her characters, is more than just the sum of its parts. She transports readers to a time and place thoroughly lived in, with characters that carry powerful memories and stories. An excellent debut!"

— Ajuawak Kapashesit, star of
Indian Horse

T0035102

River Meets the Sea

A Novel

Rachael Moorthy

ANANSI

Published in Canada and the USA in 2023
by House of Anansi Press Inc.
houseofanansi.com

House of Anansi Press is committed to protecting our natural environment.
This book is made of material from well-managed FSC®-certified forests,
recycled materials, and other controlled sources.

House of Anansi Press is a Global Certified Accessible™ (GCA by Benetech)
publisher. The ebook version of this book meets stringent accessibility
standards and is available to readers with print disabilities.

27 26 25 24 23   1 2 3 4 5

Library and Archives Canada Cataloguing in Publication

Title: River meets the sea : a novel / Rachael Moorthy.
Names: Moorthy, Rachael, author.
Identifiers: Canadiana (print) 20220488444 | Canadiana (ebook) 20220488452
| ISBN 9781487011420 (softcover) | ISBN 9781487011437 (EPUB)
Classification: LCC PS8626.O5975 R58 2023 | DDC C813/.6—dc23

Cover and book design: Alysia Shewchuk
Cover image: Photo by Nick Moore on Unsplash
Typesetting: Lucia Kim

*House of Anansi Press is grateful for the privilege to work on and create
from the Traditional Territory of many Nations, including the Anishinabeg,
the Wendat, and the Haudenosaunee, as well as the Treaty Lands of the
Mississaugas of the Credit.*

With the participation of the Government of Canada
Avec la participation du gouvernement du Canada | Canada

*We acknowledge for their financial support of our publishing program the
Canada Council for the Arts, the Ontario Arts Council, and the Government
of Canada.*

Printed and bound in Canada

For Papa (Ron Young), and my father, Balan,
whose riveting lives inspired this work of fiction

1

The River

qiqéyt (New Westminster, Canada), 1946

chóxw
Go down to water.

Stó:lō came rolling up in waves. The mouth of the river roared open. My muscles tensed stiff as cedar, as silver water swelled to swallow me whole for being a left-handed bastard, and for the bad thing I'd done to Widow Belyea. She was right to say I was a savage boy with bad spirits tangled up inside of me.

"Leave it to Cuddy Wifter to open the gates of hell!" Vince's craggy voice ricocheted off the river.

Clay splattered against our sun-bronzed calves as if the earth itself were protesting. I followed his lanky strides as he raced to higher ground. We dove into the long grass and clutched the dry tuffets as the earth laughed beneath us.

My thoughts collapsed into a single clear entity, as if I'd lifted a stone out of rippling water: It was all just water. Water falling out of the sky, water flowing in the river, water pooling in my eyes, droplets collecting on my tongue, my skin, my hands. The language of water was how my mother called out to me.

ACCORDING TO CHILDREN'S AID, my birth mother was a Canton Alley lady of the night with an insatiable itch. I didn't believe a word of it. Children's Aid was a pack of no-good, lying child-stealers. They scooped me up as a toddler. No birth certificate, just a mouldy diaper and cradle cap, tied to the front porch by a leash. Brought me back to the orphanage to delouse me before shipping me off to my first foster.

My father was every drunk on the streets of New Westminster. One of countless shell-shocked shells of men staggering down the quay, a flask on each hip and a lady of the night for each limb lost on Vimy Ridge. He was Irish. Maybe Dutch.

I looked for my mother in every woman I saw. She was the one carrying milk crates, all ebony victory rolls and freckles. The one in the apple orchard with terracotta skin and a chipped grin. I saw her in the faded *Soldiers without guns* posters at the motorcycle club, dressed in flannel and a welding helmet that looked like Napoleon's bicorne.

I knew that my mom, whoever she was, was soft and strong, the way a mother should be. A gentle current carrying her child through this awful world. Not like Belyea, or the nuns at the orphanage, who were erratic and sharp as a midsummer hailstorm. Every time I was down at the river, swaddled by the soothing taffeta of liquid, I felt my mother: the force of the torrent and the pacifying sweetness of water, searching.

That morning, at high water, Mrs. Belyea had melted into a mirage of my mother. The window glow ironed out the deep lines in her face, and refracted early sunlight spilled into her eyes: sparkling polygons of gold and river green. Her silver hair was dipped in shadow, turning it raven black. She hummed along to "Moonlight Serenade" as she buttered hot rye bread.

Then she stepped away from the window and turned back into her sea-hag self.

"Use your right hand. No devil's grip in this house." She clocked me in the back of the head with her cold, flour-caked hands.

I'd been in her care for two long years and I was still buck-fisted and feral, still teeming with bad spirits. Mrs. Belyea took to fastening my devil arm behind my back with a ripped apron. But even a year later, using my right hand still felt wrong and inverted, like looking at life through a mirror. It took me eons to finish a meal.

I swallowed down the last globule of honeyless porridge

and was tossed out onto the porch with my foster brother, Gordon, a mouth-breathing darling with ever-crusted blue eyes. The whole church was gaga over him because he had a hole in his heart: "Oh, isn't he a walking miracle, proof of the living light?" — simply because he hadn't died. Dressed in these dreadful short pants that itched worse than nettle leaves, we walked around the corner of Edinburgh Street to the motorcycle club in what was called back then the DL, the District of London. I kept my bucket for candle-fish and snakes buried beneath a crawl space at the club, wrapped in one of Mrs. Belyea's arm-tying aprons.

I clutched the collar of Gordon's knit pullover. "Say anything to Belyea and I'll skin you." She'd give me the belt if she found out I'd been skipping church all this time, so I waited until we were out of sight to make a run for it.

Gordon craned his neck towards the sunlight, rocking back and forth on his heels as the Lacey girls, all chinless and browless, with dishevelled mops of ash-blond curls, came around the rose hedge.

"Come along, scamp. Leave the devil to his mis-chief." The eldest, Deloris, flashed me a sardonic grin. She grabbed Gordon's sleeve, tugging him along.

Then I was off. Bucket at the hip, weaving in and out of the Ambrosia and Gala trees, tumbling over the thorny thicket surrounding thin strips of marshland. August air was all blackberry and salal. The smell of fermenting fruit and skunk cabbage sat heavy in my lungs as I brawled through the brambles. The long grass grazed my knees. Nearly stepped on a toad before I reached the swing bridge that soared over Stó:lō, the river. The opalescent moon was still visible in the melting blue sky.

Every time I came up to the swing bridge I felt anchored. The brawny bottom chords, the intricate steel webs, and the great red trusses were like a staircase leading up into heaven. Below the bridge, docked tugboats slept. Salmon fishers and watchmen flocked, laughing, drinking, storytelling.

From the bridge, I saw Vince and Jagger down by the boats, chatting with Ray. I scaled down the slanted silt rock, met by the reek of the bank and the booms that I loved—the familiar stink of wet cedar, metal chains, and rotting candlefish.

"If it ain't Cuddy Wifter." Leaning smugly against the base of Ray's tugboat, Vince tossed me a wedge of fry bread. Sundays were bannock days. Ray liked to experiment with berries and perennial herbs: blackberry and wild violet, salmonberry and sage. I sank my teeth into the fried gold, dappled with orange and purple berry confetti. The bannock dissolved against the roof of my mouth and churned gummy between my teeth. I recognized the thick sweetness — taste of earthy blueberry with blackcurrant at the core.

"Salal for sure...," I said, sucking a crumb off my pinky finger. "And..."

"Cloudberry." Ray nodded. "Rare. Found 'em in a bog."

"Huh." I let the floral flavour evaporate on my tongue. "It's like...cream."

"Like a cloud." Ray grinned.

"Any catches?" I asked.

Ray shook his head and groaned. "Dry spell, eh. Salmonberries are small and pale. Creator's up to something. I can feel it in the tempo of the river...Ground feels moody. You cubs'll catch more candlefish in that bucket of yours. Not a good year for sockeye, sad to say."

"Rats." Jagger folded his arms.

I smothered my second piece of bannock with sun-softened butter and looked down at the river rushing by, trying to see what Ray saw. The closer I looked, the more convinced I was that I could see it, too. I believed in Ray and the river more than I'd ever trusted the blue lace agate forehead of that pastor with the facial veins or the gilded pages of his so-called holy book.

"Ts'ahéyelh Xwe...xwelá...ah, lost my words, eh." Ray laughed, sad and low. His hooded eyes were like silver crescent moons. I studied Ray's Tuscan-brown skin and straight black hair. He stood his right leg up over the rail of the boat and stared off into the endless silver. A story was coming.

"Once, we found an octopus at the booms in Burrard Inlet, the colour of old socks," Ray began, between swigs from his red canteen. "Well, it was a hexapus, to be true, on account of it only had six tentacles. I met a river pig who said that a few miles east of the sawmill a fellow he knew had fallen off the dock into the water and was seized by the creature."

Ray latched onto my neck with his warm, leathery hands. I tried to pry them away, failing to hold back my laughter.

"The hexapus dragged him farther under. Deeper, deeper, deeper. Infinite black. Luckily, the logger had his hunting knife in his boot and managed to sever two of the beast's prongs, pry himself free of the suction-cupped grips of death, and swim to the surface. You never know what's down there...deep, deep down."

I imagined being pulled down into blackness as my lungs filled up with water, the light at the surface disappearing. Vince leapt in, pulled Ray's hands off my neck, and swam me up for air. We collapsed in a fit of laughter, water coming out of our eyes and mouths, the spray of the river misting our faces.

"I thought octopuses came from the sea." Jagger scrunched the vacant space where his eyebrows belonged. His snow-white hair glittered beneath the radiant sun.

"Right you are," Ray said. "But this river flows into the sea. And things end up where they don't belong all the time. Ain't that right, you delinquents?" He smirked as he offered us each a sip from his flask.

Jagger took a swig, then spat it back out over the

starboard edge and into the water. Vince and I shook our heads at Jagger's tenderness and fought each other for the liquid fire. We knew that one day we'd both be like Ray, that we'd drink whiskey like water, so we gulped it down without wincing, even though it stung our throats and we hated it.

People who spend their lives around water start to become like water themselves: fluid. Soft and strong at the same time. Ray was firm in his fluidity, steadily flowing like Stó:lō. Unlike Mrs. Belyea, whose temper was chained and precarious like the log booms. So the first thing I'll say is always go down to water. Wherever you end up, find the water and go down to it.

Ray raised anchor to return to the river. We thanked him for the bannock and raced down to the bank. The three of us darted over the compacted silt, past the brilliant tugboats and the Chinese fly fishers, until we reached the ceaseless rows of chained cedar logs. They floated end to end on the surface of the silver river, like packages upon packages of hot dogs.

Vince stood proudly in the U-shaped crotch of the sycamore maple, clasping onto the rope swing we'd made from the ruins of an old tugboat. He always swung first, letting out a war cry as he soared over the bank. He became a small bird, disappearing into the Cascade mountain range along the horizon. The loud, throaty puffs of a nearing Big Mike train swelled in the distance.

Then he let go, his feet hit the slick cedar logs, and he hightailed it, skidding over the booms like a skipped stone.

Jagger and I scrambled up the side of the maple. The rope was tough, tearing the insides of our hands until they were raw and glazed pink. It burned when I took hold of it — but when I was swinging, it was like I was wearing that ghostly, inside part of myself on the outside. For a moment, every thistle of hair was going in the same direction. I was there. I was real.

When my heels hit the booms, greasy and wet like candlefish scales, I had to run like hell or I'd fall between the spaces and drown.

We took turns swinging until our arms and legs throbbed. Then we waded in the river and caught candlefish with our hands. I filled my bucket to the brim with the slick little buggers. Jagger flipped over a rock and found three red racers, brown snakes marked by the ribbon of red that ran down their backs. He picked up the fattest one and held it up to his sunburned face as it wriggled, revealing its red thread of a forked tongue.

"Give it here." Vince reached out his scratched-up arm.

Jagger reeled the snake back. "There's two others."

"I wanna try something." Vince snatched the snake from Jagger. He held its small, wriggling body firmly in his right hand. With his left, he pulled the switchblade out of his pocket and sliced the snake's head clean off. Its gaping, soundless mouth fell softly into the silt.

I cringed, chewed on the inside of my cheek.

Jagger kicked Vince in the shin. "Why'd you do that for?"

"You could have killed the smaller ones," I said.

"Oh, don't snap your caps, tulips. It's a stupid snake."

I felt sick but figured Vince was closer to manhood than I was, so I shoved that feeling down and followed him. Watery clay splattered the backs of his legs as he ran past the fly fishers and the tugboats. We rose up to the bridge, the echoing tufts of a steam train growing louder and louder as Vince laid the headless snake on the tracks. The smell of steel and rust hung in the air as the carcass, a small brown tube, rattled on the sleeper.

"Come on!" Vince yelled.

We slithered down to the base of the bridge and crouched beneath the tracks. As the big black train surged across like a shrieking dragon, we cradled our heads between our knees. Intermittent screeches cut into my ears, bounced off my teeth and skull, while pebbles and white stone dust gathered around our feet.

The ground settled and the sound faded. As the train vanished down the track, we hiked back to the top to see what was left of the snake. It was flat, a piece of fabric.

Jagger tilted his head. "It looks like suspenders."

"Kinda, yeah," I agreed reluctantly.

Vince kneaded his stomach with his knuckles. "I'm hungry."

And so it was off to Leichenberg's orchard.

"SWEAR TO GOD, LOTHAR Leichenberg's a myth. We've never seen him. Not once." Vince whacked the blackened base of a bronzed-leaf Ambrosia tree with a stick. "Crown rot... They need to get rid of this one."

We moved to the heart of the orchard.

"I mean, there's gotta be someone... who picks all this?" Jagger gestured to the apple-filled canopies.

I shrugged, and we climbed to the treetops. The tree and I worked together — I could feel the energy pouring out of its limbs and bark, telling me where to grab on, leading me to the next branch as I worked my way up to the top. I perched between the highest branches, where streams of skylight spilled through the holes between the leaves and all I could see above me were clouds.

The orchard was splashed with a medley of crimson, gold, and pale green. The florid smell of Earligold, Gala, and dewy green leaf enveloped everything. Only Earligolds and Galas were ripe for harvest: the Earligolds yellow-green and sour, the Galas yellow, marled with cream red, tasting of sunlight with brown-sugar undertones. I dove down to the lowest branch and shook, sending a cascade of ripe Galas to the ground with a soft thud. Jagger held up a glossy crimson apple, nearly the size of his head. Perfect for a wrestling trophy.

It was always down to Vince and me. Jagger was mopey and brittle as milfoil. He gave in quickly and shed tears often. Made me grit my teeth to powder.

"You pigeon-chested hood!" Vince's lanky tentacles wrapped around my belly like a hexapus. I reached around his hips, and then we were doing a sort of silly waltz.

"Take that, Cuddy Wifter!" He kneed me in the gut, and the cloudberry and sage bubbled up through my chest and into the bottom of my throat.

I stuck out my right foot behind Vince's heel. He toppled backwards with a snarl.

I straddled him, giving him sharp shots to the kidney until he elbowed me in the nose. "Nose punch of death!" Vince crowed.

Hot blood streamed out of my nostrils. It stung, but the fight wasn't over. I pressed Vince's shoulders down into the earth and leaned over his face. We were two magnets, repelling — my arms and core flexed with fire as Vince arched his back. Blood trickled down from my nose into his mouth.

"All right! All right! You win!" Vince tapped out.

I let go, and he rolled away, wiping my blood off his lips. Jagger tossed me the trophy. I winked at Vince, let my nose bleed onto the shellac skin of the Gala, and took a bite: the gory tang of victory.

"You sick Mick," Vince scoffed and shook his head, brushing dirt off his clothes.

"I might be Dutch," I said between bites of blood Gala.

"Fat chance. You're Irish. You've got black hair and you leap like a goddamn leprechaun."

"I think he looks squaw," Jagger said, picking an Earligold. "Like Ray."

"Ah, shut the hell up with that." I rolled my eyes.

"Well, you do get real brown." Jagger held his alabaster forearm up to mine: russet brown like sliced apple left out in the sun.

"My mom's Irish and my dad's Dutch, or something else. Either way, I'm white like you," I barked.

"Still don't explain how you get so coloured-like," Jagger said.

"It's called a tan." I shoved Jagger, and he fell backwards, warbling like a chicken. "Look at my eyes." I clasped his narrow neck. "Blue as the Atlantic...Injuns can't have blue eyes."

"Hey!" Vince cut in, shoving me off Jagger.

"Mrs. Belyea told everyone at church that your mom was a whore," Jagger said.

Then I had to beat him up all over again. Palm flat on the base of Jagger's frail neck, pressing his freckled nose into curled black apples and the thick, split roots of a Gala tree, I noticed the tiered, cantaloupe seashell bracket of what looked like bright orange coral. The splash of sunshine bursting out of the heartwood was Chicken of the Woods. I shoved Jagger to the side, gathering the fan-like fungi into the hem of my shirt.

"Hey! You hoods! Get the hell off my property!"

We whipped our necks around to see a hunched figure lumbering towards us, a gun hoisted against his hip.

"Guess Lothar Leichenberg ain't no myth!" I yelled as we blitzed out of the orchard, all back on the same team, the life force of the river surging through our bodies.

"I GOTTA HEAD HOME," I said when we made it back to the DL. If Gordon had gotten there before me, I'd need to explain myself.

"All right, Cuddy, meet me at the swing bridge at sunset," Vince winked. "Bring cigs."

"Yeah, yeah. If I can get away from the hard-boiled hag... Later, Jag."

"See ya, Cuddy."

I floated past the wilting rose hedges, tinted bronze with rot, on the outskirts of Dublin and London Streets, past the motorcycle club, and arrived back at the aged house with the wraparound veranda that was decaying slowly from the underside. I treaded up the steps, quivering hands pocketed around my fragile mushrooms, and slid through the door, begging to go unnoticed.

"Ach, Ronald, there you are." Widow Belyea smacked

me on the back of the head, a thick pain. I'd swear she had a plank of cedar for a right hand. "Eh, why'd Gordon come home alone? And why is your shirt stained?"

I looked down at my orange-tinged shirt hem. "Mrs. Prime's tabby was on the roof of the chapel again."

"Well, that is hardly your problem, is it? That negro-loving lesbian is too old to be taking care of an animal. She can barely take care of herself, non?" Up close, Mrs. Belyea had veiny, almost translucent skin, eyelids streaked with purple lightning. Her body was as weathered as a woman's of sixty, though she was only thirty-seven. "Gordon needs someone to look after him."

I strained every muscle in my face holding back an eye roll.

"Well? Go chop wood for the stove." Mrs. Belyea returned to dicing carrots with a violent intensity.

I pulled a face at the back of her head before folding my mushroom haul in a dry dishrag, which I concealed in a thicket of overgrown holly outside. I ought to have been more grateful, I know, but I hated that woman to the soles of her hag feet. She earned her living from fostering. There were six of us: me, Gordon, three girls who have melted into a single, indistinguishable entity in the eye of my memory, and Pat. I didn't care for anyone in the house except Pat. She fluttered around the place, her face round and glossy pink as a cherry blossom. Whether she was slipping out the window to tangle tongues with her most recent suitor, taking me skating, or sneaking into my room with a pocketful of butterscotch candies, she brought spring freshness with her.

Met by the spasmodic cluck and warble of the chickens in the yard, I hauled the axe towards the chopping block. I lined the wood up on the pine stump and hacked it into smaller pieces, startling the chickens into a fear-trill.

"Ack, that's not how you chop wood, Ronny!" Belyea clucked from the kitchen window. "I'll show you."

I groaned and contemplated throwing the axe through the window as Belyea thundered out onto the veranda and over the dying grass. She rolled up her sleeves before seizing the axe from my hands. I stood back as she lined up the lumber on the pine, right hand on the log. She struck the stump in a single ham-handed swing, breaking the wood unevenly. What looked like the tip of a raw frankfurter flew into the dirt.

Then the screaming started.

"Look what you made me do!" Belyea fell to her knees, her hand a sperm whale spouting blood instead of water. The chickens erupted into chaotic alarm cackles. She hollered for Pat, dousing the grass and wood in maroon, her wide, flat arse tilted to the heavens as she fumbled. "Where is it? Where is it?"

The corners of my mouth split open with laughter.

Belyea's index finger was curled up between the toe of my scuffed-up oxford and the base of the pine block, but I refused to say a word. I clutched my gut to stop it from rupturing as my eyes welled.

Pat came toppling down the steps with her hair tousled, cornflower-blue blouse half-unbuttoned. Her meatball beau, Bobby or something, came plodding behind her.

"Ma! What happened?" Pat trilled.

"Ronny happened!"

Before I could blink, I was in the air, flying backwards across the front yard. The back of my head thrashed against the side of the chicken coop.

"Billy! He's a kid!" cried Pat.

"It'd be a civil liability to let the beast live."

I could have held my own against the fathead if I hadn't been so wrung out from swinging over the booms and wrestling Vince. There was so much noise, and the back of my head stung. I stayed crouched by the coop until Mrs. Belyea, Billy, and Pat drove off to the hospital in Belyea's automobile.

THE LILAC SKY HAD deepened to a staid plum, with sashes of pale tangerine bleeding through. The chickens had settled and my ears had stopped ringing, so I stole a few cigarillos from the denim jacket Pat had left draped over the banister, shovelled bread pudding into my trap, fastened a rag of chicken into a sack, and split.

The air was calm and warm. I was running, lost in thoughts of my neck being lined up on the pine block when Belyea came home, and wound up in an alley criss-crossed by clotheslines hung with vibrant linens of crimson and fuchsia. Like decoration, oil, salt, and fragrant spices sang in the air, followed by a sound like nothing I'd ever heard. Glittery and gold like honeycomb or seafoam candy dissolving in a hot cup of maple tea. I forgot who I was, what I was doing. I just had to find the source of that sound.

A milkwoman with dark sienna skin and a cerulean headwrap glided past me, and I followed her like a charmed cobra. The way she looked — graceful and dignified, holding the empty milk crate like a sceptre — didn't match up with my foster mother's crude descriptions of dark-skinned folks. The saccharine sound coated the air as we crossed a gaggle of coloured teenagers playing soccer. The woman nodded at a passing Chinese shopkeep and grabbed an empty blue crate from the stone steps where the singer perched. He plucked a wooden guitar and breathed into a small wind instrument that I didn't recognize. His angelic voice soared over the clotheslines, into the sky, dipping into the river before flying back into my ears, like a boomerang that had scooped up all the beauty in the world before delivering it to me.

He stopped playing when he noticed me gaping with swollen eyes and bloodstained calves. "What you after, alley mutt? Never seen a harmonica before?"

I jolted, spine stiffened.

"Cat got your tongue, alley mutt? Where you from? You sure is one weird lookin' white boy." He cackled, revealing a big, off-white smile.

"Oh, Angel." The milkwoman shook her head. "You know it ain't right to talk like that."

I didn't know what to say, so I just ran. Towards the thin strip of blue, faintly visible along the horizon. As I made my way to the tracks, Vince's sinewy silhouette was visible below the bridge. A visit from the child stealers was on the horizon, and Belyea was going to put me on the chopping block with her four-fingered grip, but God, the story was good. I was going to tell Vince and we were going to laugh until everything made sense again. I picked up a dead twig and ran towards him.

"Hi-de-ho." I tossed the stick at Vince's neck.

"Well, would you take a gander at that," Vince said. "Escaped the hag?"

"You won't believe what happened."

"What?"

I handed him a cigarillo. A feathery ache spread throughout my chest as the inconsolable laughter took over. I clutched my gut, desperately sipping air to stop myself from chucking up apples, blood, and bread pudding. "Sh-she…okay, she started ragging on me for how I chop wood, yeah? 'I'll show you how it's done,' she says." I puffed up my strained cheeks, stuck my arse out, and tilted my nose up in my best Belyea impression. "And then…and then…she chopped off her own finger!"

Vince's cynical eyebrows softened to neutral, then lit up with cock-a-hoop delight. "You're kidding me!" His low, serrated howl pierced the air as he propped himself against a tree. "Wish I coulda seen her face!"

I keeled over, holding my ribs, my entire body wrapped in the plume-pang of laughter. My insides felt like they were going to come apart and leak out from beneath my fingernails. Tears seeped out of my sockets, mingling with the glaze of sweat on my skin. "My face hurts… Damn, my face hurts so much…I'll get licked over this… but it was worth it to see…"

Suddenly Vince swooped down beside me and placed his hand on the earth. "You feel that?" His face sharpened, razor-blade eyes looking intently into mine.

"Feel what?" I sat up, rubbing my face with the clean half of my palm.

"The ground…it's shaking."

"We were laughing, you daft moron."

"No…I swear…Look at the swing bridge!"

The grey-pearl water frothed like saliva as a swell of silver waves barrelled in the river. The swing bridge swayed back and forth like a red uvula in the throat of the

Creator. The bridge's scarlet trusses collapsed and I studied the braided rivers of my palms, a dizzying array of tangled lines and crosshairs. Drupelets of sweat ripened on the fingertips of my ever-indigo-tinged, ever-dissident left hand, curled to cup the waxing moon. These were ancient hands, labyrinthine as mycelium, hands that looked like they belonged to a barnacled old sea dog rather than a young fry around eight. In the salmonberry light of dusk filtered through long grass, I was struck by the sight of my hands: callused, bruised, and immemorial.

2

The Sea

Snʊ'neɪmǝxʷ (Nanaimo, Canada), 1977

———

தண்ணீர் நினைவை; தண்ணீர் கனவுகள்.
Water is memory; water is dreams.

Between the lilac-like plumes of the oceanspray and the back steps of our pink townhouse in Nanaimo was a shadowed space that smelled faintly of sugar cane. Cumulus and cream, the flowering shrub looked like a cloud that couldn't fly. This is my earliest memory of a home, though every so often, under the spell of the cascading blossoms, I was visited by daydreams of impossibly clear, blue water, scintillating in gold light. Sand like white diamonds, the scent of coconut. Being pulled out of cool turquoise before being thrust into the atmosphere, then caught again, by a pair of large, cinnamon-bark arms.

The answer to the question of where I come from is a complicated one. Vathany says I dove into the world on a merchant ship departing the coast of Ceylon, a black drop in the heart of the Indian Ocean. Sick of the Sinhala Only Act that enveloped the teardrop-shaped island like an invasive plant, my parents packed their whole lives into two tweed suitcases and boarded the boat, unaware I was budding in my mother's belly. Vathany, the willowy daughter of a Tamil rice farmer, had assumed that her half-brother's boat caught a net of bad kawakawa that didn't agree with her and that the kithul treacle Appa kept bringing home was making her fat.

Her water broke beside a vending machine. It was a stroke of luck that Appa had just completed his nursing diploma and the ocean liner had medical personnel on board. They gathered around my mother, enchanted by her Lakshmi aura. She claims she didn't make a single sound during labour, but when she saw me, a baby with indigo-black skin like a charred eggplant, she screamed.

Out on the vast jade sea, Appa confessed that, despite his tolerable date-palm-jaggery shade of brown, he was part kāpil, a descendant of the Bantu tribe brought to the island as slaves by the Portuguese colonizers.

Appa had gotten his paws on two one-way tickets to England the instant he was accepted into the University of Liverpool for his master's. He completed his postgraduate degree when I was three, got a job as a psychiatric nurse overseas immediately afterwards, and we moved to a terraced townhouse on Vancouver Island. I don't remember a thing about living in England, but my parents took away certain linguistic and cultural artifacts. French fries were *chips*, underwear were *pants*, and they developed a taste for cow's milk and mutton. Vathany started eating with a fork and knife, while Appa continued to eat with his hands. Beneath the stained glass of a stone cathedral in drizzly old England, Vathany found a new deity. When she learned of how the snake spoke in Eden, like Manasā the nagini, Vathany couldn't unsee the parallels and added Christianity to her increasingly tangled web of spirituality, which at the time included folk Hinduism and Theravada. The teachings said that life on Earth was suffering, and after iḻam was ripped away, its quartz beaches blackened with the blood of every last one of her male relatives, she could confidently say that it was. To love her homeland was to be hog-tied in a coconut grove and labelled a terrorist, so she had to rip that love out of herself.

When we got to Canada, Vathany begged the universe to cut the malam aḷḷum, to crack open and reveal its divine powers to her in a plain, tangible way. The next day, a group of Jehovah's Witnesses knocked on our door, and that was that. Ever since, she spent most of her time at the Kingdom Hall, which was where I assumed she was as I slipped into the living room to watch cartoons one morning when I was seven. Appa's waterbed snores oozed from the cracks around the master bedroom door.

He worked nights as a psych nurse in our coastal town of whale falls and mill workers. I teetered on the armrests of our old cornflower-blue mohair sofa. It was a canvas for my imagination, transforming into snow-capped alps, a carrack ship scouring an aquamarine coast, a castle tower wrapped in wisteria. That day, it was a tightrope stretching through broken clouds into a vast, rust-red canyon.

With the turmeric-salt tang of fried chakodi between my teeth, I looked up at the TV rabbit ears glinting beneath a halo of sunlight. The screen flashed from pale-skinned shampoo ballerinas twirling underwater to diamond-eyed Californians surfing barrels. I knew all the commercials by heart.

An unfamiliar three-toned jingle sent static down my spine. I leaned into the screen: this world had the soft glow of morning light, a backdrop of blurred greenery, and spring birdsong. A vanilla man with a rhythmic whistling snore slumbered in his swaying porch swing. Hard cut to silk-like coffee pouring into a mug held by a lithe white woman with a Chiclet grin. She floated onto the porch, holding the cup beneath the man's L-shaped nose. A stream of steam wafted up into his hairless nostrils, and he woke with a gleaming white smile that mirrored hers.

I flopped off the sofa, feet over my head like a Slinky, and shuffled from the shag carpet to the crumb-iced linoleum floor of the kitchen. I geckoed up to the countertop, mindful of the dappled bananas and swarm of fruit flies. As I rummaged through the cupboards, a loud tangle of smells assaulted my nose: Ceylon cinnamon, dried turmeric, cumin, fermenting dosa batter. Finally — a pale blue tin of ground coffee.

I slid the blue tin from the dust-caked shelf and pulled the plastic lid from the container. The coffee was almost as dark as my skin. It smelled rich and chocolatey. I licked my finger, pressed it into the powder, and brought it to my mouth. As soon as the soap-dirt taste hit my tongue, I spat into the sink drain and chugged down a glass of tap water, shuddering. Clearly, the coffee machine was an important step. I placed a scoop of the coffee grinds into the sieve, filled the machine with water, and pressed the button. It glowed red — a good sign.

I darted back to the TV and slipped into the screen, shedding my black skin and emerging as the peach-hued boy I knew I really was. Icicles formed on my skin as I ascended a frozen Himalayan peak. With blue fingers clamped around my piolet, I hoisted myself up into the snowy abyss. Beads of sweat crystallized into a crown of ice. When I summited, I tossed my piolet in the snow and roared, wrapped in a chrysalis of cloud. A deep growl sliced through the echo trail of my voice. Panting, I turned, met by the ravenous snarl of a sabre-toothed tiger. The tiger roared again, revealing its bloodstained fangs before slashing my forearm. I scanned the snow for a fallen slate of ice or a plank of wood, something to snow-surf to safety.

The coffee maker beeped and the room quickly thawed back into reality. Kitty was on her haunches, hissing at me from the arm of the sofa; a fresh gash on my arm. I grabbed Appa's Liverpool mug from the drying rack and, with shaky hands, I poured the searing hot coffee, splattering the counter. I stirred in three heaping spoonfuls of rock sugar and a splash of cream.

Appa lay in the centre of his red waterbed in his white undershirt, his furry chest exposed. I crept over the silverfish-laden carpet, tightly clasping the mug, steaming liquid sloshing back and forth. From the edge of the bed, I studied Appa's face. Broad kāpil nose, so wide you could cross a river on it. Billowy tear troughs beneath impossibly round eyes — eyes that, even when closed, held so much kindness. Skin a rich, cinnamon-bark brown, several shades lighter than my own.

I knelt on the waterbed, certain he'd wake to the smell of fresh coffee with a serene and silent smile like the man on the TV. The yellow stains would lift from Appa's teeth as he took the mug from my hands. But it was difficult to position the coffee under Appa's fallen tree of a nose with his face turned up to the ceiling. My arms were getting tired. I leaned in...

Appa's eyes bulged out of his round russet face.

"Eṇakku tayavuceytu utavi!" He shrieked as he looked down at his chest, singed beneath his soaked undershirt. His eyes darted around the room in a panic, before locking with mine.

I dropped the coffee mug and bolted, burst through the screen door barefoot, no time to lace up my Chucks. I grabbed my blue fishtail skateboard from beneath our mailbox and scaled the front steps, kicked and pushed against the hot pavement, feeling the pebbles tear into the bottoms of my feet as I pumped down the block. Cool, briny air beat against my face as blood pooled under my leading foot.

I ROLLED UP TO the whipped-butter house with the porch at the end of the block, wedged my board under my armpit, and tiptoed over the unkempt jungle of grass and dandelion skeletons, careful not to step in any of Dr. King's sun-baked surprises. Jill believed her German shepherd's shit was natural "fertilizer for the earth."

A mild, earthy smell was knotted in the air, growing stronger and sweeter as I approached the front step. The pale yellow paint was peeling up the sides of the house. I rapped my fist on the door.

"Little Moon! Gee whiz!" Rocky emerged from a cloud of smoke. He swivelled his head back into the hazy house and called, "Jill!" He coughed. "It's Little Moon!" He sloped out onto the porch, closing the door behind him. "What's the skinny, Chan Lennon?"

We bumped fists. Rocky was a lanky guy with tightly coiled ebony hair and sleepy eyes. He tucked his unbuttoned paisley shirt into his corduroy bell-bottoms, combed his faded Black Panther pick through his teased fro, and popped a squat on the bottom step. "Well?"

"I'm toast. Spilled coffee on my dad."

"Zoinkers!" Rocky's soulful laugh billowed.

I sighed, ripped a handful of grass out of the earth, and tossed it back into itself. Rocky wrapped his noodle of an arm around me and knuckled my noggin, his sterling peace ring scraping lightly against my scalp. "You can kick it with us until your dad goes to work. He'll forget all about it by the time he's back from the cuckoo's nest."

"What's cracking, Little Moon?" Jill's blond eyelashes were see-through in the sunlight. She held a script in her right hand.

"Chan Lennon spilled coffee on Pops this morning."

"Well, shoot." Jill laughed. "We were just going to head down to the lagoon to practise my lines, maybe watch the sun go down. You wanna help us out?" She grinned and flipped her thumb through the script.

I nodded, picking up my board.

"To the sea!" Rocky shouted as he leapt off the porch.

I skated after them like a little quail.

—

WE MOVED THROUGH THE thicket and the auburn arbutus trees, scaling the driftwood at the mouth of the lagoon. A baby-blue bicycle was hoisted up into the branches of a big cedar tree on the top of the biggest sea stack. No one knew how it got there. The ocean was velvet blue, and the tide was high. Jill, Rocky, and I climbed to the top of the stack. The galling cry of seagulls rose and collapsed like the waves against the rocks.

I held onto an arbutus branch. Prose fell out of Jill's mouth like water, but I didn't understand a word of it. "Is that even English?"

"Barely," Rocky quipped, returning to the script. "'Temp-or-al royalties he thinks me now in-ca...in-capable; confederates'—I need a break from this." He chucked the pages to the sand.

I let go of my branch and picked up the book. "'So dry he was for sway—wi' the King of Naples to give him anal tribute.'"

"Shoot, you read pretty good, Moon Boy!" Rocky snatched the book from my hands. "'Anal tribute.'" He chuckled.

I raised my arms above my head as the ocean devoured the sun and felt the magic inside of me. The tide receded slowly as the moon reeled it into itself. Wafts of sweet August blackberries at their peak ripeness rode the waves of the wind. My feet grew numb in the cold sea air. Creamsicle sashes bled into the sky, and I knew that Appa would be leaving for his night shift.

We scaled down the face of the sea stack and made our way back to the Flower Power House as the sky turned a million different colours: melting blue to salmon roe. I said peace to Jill and Rocky and skateboarded back to my little pink home at the end of the street. The condo was warm, and I could smell halibut and turmeric simmering on the stove. From the entryway, I saw the bottom edge of Vathany in the bathroom light.

"Chandra?" She turned to me as I reached the top step, her pupils dilated in the harsh fluorescence. She grabbed my forearm and sucked her teeth. "You got so dark in the sun."

I yanked my arm away.

"You should thank the skies you were born a boy. A girl this dark?" Vathany dipped her skeletal hand into the nearly empty jar of fairness cream from Sri Lanka, painting her fine nose and high cheekbones with the diluted bleach. "A girl this dark would never find a husband." She pulled me into the bathroom and lathered me with the lightening balm, the sear of white burrowing into brown.

I left the coldness of my mother for the warmth of the kitchen. As I stirred the lumps of caramelizing white fish in the yellow curry sauce, which was starting to char at the bottom, I noticed the sabre-toothed tiger lurking beneath the kitchen table. The fish reassembled itself and began swimming around the pan, a golden mahseer. The walls fell away, and I was back in the canyon. Nothing could interfere with the world inside of my head, and that made the world outside of it sting less.

3

The River

qiqéyt, 1947

⁓

Mrs. Belyea said the quake was my fault. Said I'd angered God with my antics and my overall left-handed-bastard existence. I held back the impulse to spit in her face, saliva pooled in my cheeks. She returned from the hospital with one less finger and twice the contempt for me, which seemed only to grow over the following year, in time with my lengthening limbs.

After the black clouds dissolved, the temper of the air changed within a breath, the land stilled, and the water went back to calm: patches of light, crisp and glinting. A blanket of panic-stricken candlefish was left to rot under the pale sun, a log driver still hadn't been found, and I started looking at my hands real close. I also started writing backwards. Every time I put my pen to paper, it felt like moving through sand; the resistance in my right hand gave me a headache. When I did finally manage to write something down, the cursive I produced was so hideous I nearly died of embarrassment. What was a strikingly still summer bled out like stained glass, turning the trees from vibrant green to gold and burgundy. All the earth's colour and life drained out. The sun had retreated into hibernation, leaving us with stinging grey and, soon, nothing but rain, rain, rain. Flowers and leaves wilted and disintegrated into the mud. The apple orchard turned into bare branches and shrivelled black apples; squash caved in and decayed the way Vince, Jagger, and I withdrew into ourselves. We spent our time at the booms in a wordless, overcast trance, looking out into the river.

On November 11, a ceremony was held at the community cenotaph. War memorials were draped in crimson poppies, which veterans and churchgoers wore over their hearts. This was one of the only times we saw the Cyclops in broad daylight. Jagger's father took out his glass eye when he slept. Permanently sauced ever since he returned from the war, he'd wake up wailing about the Frogs or the Huns, the empty eye socket was healed over, but remained an open wound. Today, he staggered towards the stone memorial, clad in his midnight-blue service uniform. He held his cap to his chest and traced the names of the fallen men he had known. His glass eye was unnaturally green, and the pupil didn't dilate.

"World's going to hell in a handbasket." He laughed, then walked through us as if we were air, straight towards the nearest joint with a patina of smoke and whiskey.

We made it down to the docks just before the log drivers and fishermen stopped their work for two minutes of silence. The bleating trumpet of the "Last Post" ricocheted off the surging, silver Stó:lō, where Ray's boat rocked and creaked. The carking of a raven pierced the air.

"Xwis7elánexw," Ray said. "Moon of the howling winds and shaking leaves."

"More like moon of howling stomachs and shaking fists," I quipped.

"You walking growth spurts ate me out of oolichan oil this autumn. Ought to consider the scarce months, especially during the abundant ones."

"Vince ate you out of oolichan oil." Vince's concave, clay-crusted cheeks went red, and I instantly regretted my comment. We were all hungry, but Vince was insatiable. He ate handfuls of clay from the riverbank just to quell the stomach pangs.

"Damn, Cuddy, you're whiter than me all of a sudden." Jagger held his near-translucent forearm up to mine.

Ray stood glassy-eyed, looking out at the river. "Ah,

well." His melancholy was contagious. I sighed. "What's eating you?" Ray griped, angry almost, as if he saw something dangerous in me.

I tried to order my words to match my thoughts. "Missing my mom."

Vince raised his eyebrows. "You've never met her."

"You shut the hell up." I caught worries like hiccups. Worried she'd been swallowed up by Stó:lō, or Children's Aid had her trapped under the floorboards. Worried she'd never wanted me. Worried for myself for being unwanted, an alley mutt with bad spirits, ancient hands, and strange, changing skin.

"Possible to miss someone you've barely been around. Also possible to barely know someone you spend every second with." Ray let out a deep throaty sigh. "Carry that missing with you, but don't be looking back all the time. Makes you bitter. Traps you. You've got to keep moving forward, like Stó:lō." He paused. "You know how long this river is?"

"Hundreds of miles?" Jagger folded a tendril of white hair behind his ear.

Ray shook his head, and a black tress fell over his right eye. "Nearly a thousand. It stretches all the way to the Pacific Ocean." He reached over the edge of the boat, gliding his hand over the current.

"Hey…" Vince stood up from the rail. "I've been wondering why you're so set on calling it that, even when everyone else says this is the Fraser River. Even says so on the sign."

"Yeah, you made us look all" — Jagger made a series of erratic hand gestures — "at school."

Ray turned to me with searching eyes. "What's your name?"

"They call me...uh, Cuddy, but you know, it's Ronny Belyea...Ronald...kind of. Before that, it was something else, I guess. Not sure what, something Dutch." I dodged Ray's gaze, looked at the sun-splashed starboard deck instead.

"Names are complicated, wouldn't you agree? Just 'cause most folks call something one thing, don't make it what it is. Or do you mean to tell me you've grown fond of Belyea?" Ray scratched his eyelid and grinned. "You don't look like no Ronny Belyea."

I sucked my teeth and scowled.

"Whatever he looks like, it gripes my cookies," Vince said.

"I'm gonna flatten you like a snake on the tracks." I lunged at Vince, but Ray's canoe paddle of an arm corralled me to the stern.

"Ignore Hungry One. His bark is bigger than his bite. Before I was Ray, I had another name, but it was taken from me, and now I've lost it. Before Simon Fraser came, stole a canoe and some women, and decided to name the water after himself, this was Stó:lō. Lhtakoh.

ʔElhdaqox. The Fraser River? That's like you being Belyea's boy."

Vince's stomach growled so loudly we all tensed. "Well, if we're all going around calling things what we wanna, I say this river's name is Vince."

"Easy, glitterati," I said.

"Enough ragging." Ray gestured to the lot of us with his flask. "One of you clay guzzlers tell me a story."

Vince threw his head back and groaned. "But you're the storyteller."

Ray exhaled all the stale air from the pit of his belly. "Anyone can tell stories."

"Not me." Vince swung around the mast pole before leaning against the rail.

"Me neither," Jagger echoed, following Vince's movements like a shadow.

Thunder growled and a big charcoal cloud enveloped the sky. As the November rain came pelting down in bullets, the river looked almost black.

I held onto the mast with my right hand, opened my palm to cup the raindrops in the other. "See these? Angel tears. The heavens weeping over fallen and forgotten soldiers... and alley mutt foster kids."

Vince fake-coughed into his hands. "Gee, you're a sensitive little tulip, aren't ya, Cuddy? Angel tears my bony backside. Ain't no angels crying over you or me."

I lunged for Vince and Jagger interceded, shoving me

into the mast, sending a sharp pain up my spine to the back of my head.

I pounced on Jagger and started pummelling him. "Vince, you hungry enough to eat this sewer rat?"

"Vince!" Jagger squealed. "Get the fairy bastard off me!"

My closed fist hovered above Jagger's quivering upper lip. "Don't call me that!"

"Don't talk to him that way!" Vince's wiry body leapt onto my side.

"Ho! Easy, cubs!" Ray pried us apart. "You're nearly right, Ronny, but these tears are from the clouds laughing." He stood his leg up on the rail of the boat, and we gathered around him, little balls of unbridled, seething rage.

"Laughing?" I pressed my throbbing side.

"Mm-hm. Clouds watch us fatheads fighting over stupid things like this, they laugh so hard they piss themselves."

And then we were all clutching our bellies, laughing until we melted into tears.

"You gotta find ways to laugh, boys," Ray said. "It'll help you survive."

THE RAIN STOPPED AND the sky parted. Light hit the water just right and it glittered white gold. We left the boat and ran down to the booms. I waded in the river up to my ankles and felt the current's force against my skin, closed my eyes and imagined being swallowed whole by Stó:lō, dissolving into the water.

I watched from the bank as Jagger swung from the rope. He held on much lower than Vince and I did, and his swing lagged. He fumbled down the logs with his brittle bow legs and gossamer balance. I nearly stopped breathing as I watched him nearly fall into the river. Jagger returned to the shore looking bleached out.

"You all right?" I asked.

He froze, pale as ice. Then he fell to his knees, lurching up clear puke onto the silt. "There's a body under the booms."

I looked up over the horizon, scanning the river and the booms where Jagger had swung. Then I saw it: oblong, bloated, and green. The body was wedged between two logs, arms reaching out for a saviour that never came.

I ran back to the fishing boats as fast as I could, but the sand was sucking up my speed. With heavy legs, I leapt onto the dock and leaned over the starboard rail. "Ray! Ray! Jagger found the log driver!"

Ray spat out his pipe. "Stay put." He waved me away as he untethered the rope. The bleat of his horn pierced the air, and the boat ripped the black surface of the water until it was white froth.

Something grazed my shoulder and I jolted. Vince had been right beside me the entire time. We ignored

Ray's orders and ran back to Jagger, panting. We watched from the bank as Ray and two other fishermen hauled the ballooned body up from beneath the logs. My stomach churned at the smell of death, but I ignored Ray waving me back to the shore and waded in to get a closer look. The limp, lifeless body of the log driver was all puffed up and verdigris like a sea creature. His lips were black and pulling away from his teeth.

4

The Sea

Snʊ'neɪməxʷ, 1979

⁓

"Tell me the colour of water." Appa straddled the surf-board, his soft, sinewy hands cradled around mine. "Cup it in the palm of your hands and notice how it appears colourless to the human eye in small quantities. Look out and watch as its tint thickens, becomes a deeper blue as the depth and quantity increases. The blue hue of water is an intrinsic property, caused by the selective absorption and scattering of white light. Water is not blue. Water is colourless and every colour all at once."

Late spring, after I turned nine, Appa strapped his seven-foot surfboard to the roof of our white Volkswagen Westfalia van and we swerved along the island's grav-elly back roads. He smoked cigarettes the whole way down the coast to Tofino; the stench of tobacco and body odour seeped into the fabric of the seats and made me want to ralph all over the black vinyl. Vathany and I rolled down our windows and let the cool ocean air dilute the stench.

We stopped frequently, whenever Appa was called to touch a particular part of the earth, and eventually, for ice cream. Appa parked the van, and I slid out, feet hitting the dirt with a hard smack. I could hear blue behind the trees and wanted to run straight through the dense forest until I saw the ocean.

A man with sleek black hair, jutting cheekbones, and bronze skin worked at the ice cream stand outside the Tla'amin Convenience Store. He was nearly the colour of Appa but with sharper features and without Appa's wiry hair.

We wandered up to the counter with our hearts set on waffle cones, the warm, sweet, golden grooves like honey paper. My attention quickly turned to the kaleidoscope of colours behind the cold glass. I pressed my nose against it, enticed by a two-toned ice cream.

"I want tiger."

"You're sure?" The man flashed a crooked smile.

I hated the taste of citrus and of black licorice, but that was irrelevant. I liked the way the black stripe tangled around the pale peach. And I loved the name. Vathany chose mango sorbet, and Appa chose mint chocolate chip to wash down his cocktail of prescription meds, the ones that helped with his shakes and nightmares from a war called "civil" that seemed to be anything but. We licked our cold cones as the salty summer breeze complemented the sun-baked cedar of the picnic table. Jurassic ponderosa pine and Sitka spruce grazed the heavens.

The fat sound of a guzzling truck cut into the peace. "Dirty ragheads! Fuck you!"

The red flag with a starry-blue saltire in the back window shrank as the truck sped away. Appa grabbed Vathany's hand. She didn't finish her ice cream, and I didn't understand how she could neglect something so delicious. My father swallowed another pill.

We got back in the van and drove until we reached Cox Bay. There are places dotted along the west coast of Canada that look almost tropical, places where the ocean is a pale cerulean and the golden sand wraps around the towering sea stacks.

"When we lived in Gurubebila, we surfed at two local breaks: Plantation Point and Coconut Point. October to May was the season." Appa smiled, transported back to his homesands. "The sand is white, glitters like crystals, not beige and flat like this."

Although I'd never seen a horizon like that before, it sounded like home, or close to it. The sand like packed sugar beneath the opal sky.

"White sugar and brown sugar," Appa said. When he

smiled, his eyes turned into crescent moons. "This beach is like a widowed Gurubebila."

"Ceylon is like this?" The moody sky and deep teal water made me feel slow and pensive.

"In some ways, it is like this, but it is so much more colourful . . . more electric. The sand, the ocean, the trees — everything is rich with colour. The air smells of salt, coconuts, and cinnamon. And, of course, it is never this cold."

Vathany shoved a bottle of coconut water in my face. She drove to the other side of town for it, drank it by the litre, swore it was the elixir of youth. To me, it tasted like Froot Loops and urine, wasn't worth the extra years of life.

"I hate coconuts. What about a cola?" I cocked my head at the sight of a little sculpture made of stacked stones.

"A cola?" Vathany sighed. "First he tells me he's a vegetarian, now he asks me for a cola? What black magic did you conjure this voodoo child up with, Sam?"

"Enough, Vathany. Kids like sugar, kids like animals. You cried for a week when your uncle slaughtered your favourite goat."

"Aashika. That goat's name was Aashika, and I loved her more than I've loved a single human being."

"Oof, an arrow to the heart." Appa clutched his chest and reeled back.

"I knew Aashika. I played with her daily. Chandra doesn't know the market fish or pepperoni."

"What animal does pepperoni come from?" I asked, struggling to pull my calf in through the leg of the black wetsuit. It suctioned onto me like a boa constrictor. "This is suffocating me."

"It has to be like this, Chandra. It grows in the water." Appa tugged harder as I resisted. "That's another thing about Eelam — you don't have to wear a wetsuit there."

"I want to go there!"

"Stop filling his head with these coconut-blossom dreams of Ceylon. It's a cemetery. We are lucky to be here."

Appa's face dropped, dragged down by the weight of Vathany's words.

I pulled my arms through the restrictive wetsuit, and Appa gingerly zipped up the back but still managed to pinch my neck. I furrowed my brows, then caught a glimpse of myself in the reflection on the Westfalia.

"I can *diiig* this!" I said, running my hands over my slick neoprene stomach.

Appa grinned, hoisted the board on his head, and walked out to the water. I imagined Vathany had looked the same when she carried water basins through the rice fields back in the forbidden place that my father called Eelam, my mother called Ceylon, and most others called Sri Lanka.

The water prickled like tiny needles as it leaked in through the ankles and collar of my suit. Then it engulfed me whole. I made the swift decision to piss in my suit. The warmth travelled all the way up.

Appa paddled me out into the choppy, teal water where I could still stand and the waves were about a foot high. He held the board as I lay flat on my stomach and kept checking behind him. "You need to watch the water. Watch it rise above the horizon... Here it comes!"

He sent me surging through the water like an arrow. "Dig, dig, dig!" he chanted as I pulled the water with my palms. "No fork hands!"

I closed my fingers so I could cup the water. I stood up, wobbly-legged, way too far up on the spongy board. I didn't weigh enough to topple over the front of the board, but instead crumpled off to the side. That was called pearling, which I proceeded to do, over and over again. Briny ice water filled my stomach like a frozen, nauseatingly over-salted broth. It seeped into my nose and ears and eyes.

I faced the shoreline, shivering with frustration. "Appa, can we go ba —"

"Paddle!" He thrust me forward.

I felt the wave surging beneath me and paddled my heart out. Then, I popped up, remembering to keep my core flexed and my legs loosely bent. I rode the tiny, undulating wave into the shore, feeling like I was flying.

After that, I was hooked. Every wave I caught was a victory. Each time I pearled or bailed was easier to shake off because now I knew what it felt like to surf. My arms burned as I dug into the water. It was alive. I could feel its pulse as I glided over the surface of the sea.

Evening fell over the horizon like a velvet drape. The waxing crescent moon became visible above the Sitka trees as we warmed our pink palms over a fire Appa made.

"If you're ever upset, Chandra, you should go to the sea," Appa said, handing me a toasted marshmallow, golden brown.

"Why?" I popped the marshmallow in my mouth: a caramelized pillow of sweetness.

"Because it reminds you of how small you are. How your problems aren't as big as they seem." He looked up at the black-azure sky, ridden with white stars.

"What are stars made of?"

"The sun is a star," Appa said, not answering my question. "And we are made of the dust of stars."

"But what makes up the stars?"

"They're exploding balls of energy…atoms, I guess. Most of those stars are already dead." He nodded up at the sky, smiling at me in a way I didn't understand.

"So they're like angels?"

He laughed, revealing his straight, off-white smile. "Sure, you could say that. It all depends on what you believe."

—

THE NEXT MORNING APPA and I surfed while Vathany looked for God in the sand. The sky was a charcoal overcast, ominous and epic, like it wanted to devour us. I caught five waves in a row. I was discovering the sweet spots of the board and my centre of gravity.

We spent the afternoon racing tiny crabs we found under rocks. I tried to find one of every colour: dark purple, olive green, brown, grey, pink, white, and red.

"What makes the crabs different colours?" I asked Appa.

He laughed. "You are so curious about everything. I suppose the same thing that makes people different colours: மெலனின் ... I forget the English word. It's an insoluble pigment."

I was about to ask him another question when I fell and scraped my leg on a barnacle-covered rock. Scarlet blood streamed down my chilled calf.

"But we all bleed red." Appa chuckled. "Just rinse it off in the salt water. It cleans."

I bit my tongue and hobbled over to the water's edge, cleansing myself in the tide. The purifying sting confirmed to me that the ocean really did cure everything.

On our way back to Nanaimo we stopped at a pet store in Coombs. It smelled of wood chips, earth, and sweet birdseed. There were calico kittens in large, open cages, iguanas, bunnies, a blue parrot, lime-green budgies, and a marmoset that roamed freely around the store.

The marmoset was silvery brown with a scrunched-up face and big ebony eyes like a doll's. He was latched onto a cat tree, being accosted by two teenage boys who were buggin' out. One with a shaved head and the other with a mullet, both wearing cut-off T-shirts. They swivelled around the cat tree, trying to scoop the marmoset up, but he squirmed away from them, into the small cat house, chirping from the blackness.

"Come on!"

"S'no use." Mullet shrugged and held his middle finger up to the marmoset.

When they moved on to pester the parrot, I crept up to the cat house. The monkey crawled out cautiously and scampered to the top of the cat tree. I stayed still, extended my arm.

"Say 'tits,'" Mullet barked at the parrot. "Say 'Ungawa, Black power.'"

"Hey, Jesse, look." Scalp nudged Mullet, nodding in my direction.

The marmoset took tentative steps towards my open palm, grabbed onto my fingers with both of its little paws. It ran up my arm and onto my shoulder.

"Blood brothers," said Scalp.

"Blacks are related to apes." Mullet laughed, then turned back to the parrot. "Ungawa! Come on, Ungawa!"

My face went hot. I wanted to duck-dive under the wave crashing over me.

On the drive home I felt like a shaken can of soda pop, thrumming in the space between my chest and my lips. I clenched my jaw, grinding my teeth for two straight hours. After we passed Qualicum Beach, one of my baby teeth popped out like a kernel of popcorn. I tongued the sour, metallic taste of the tender place where my tooth had been.

"Throw it out the window," Vathany said.

"But it's *my* tooth!" Hot tears and snot sluiced out of my aching face.

"What use do you have for a tooth?" She reached back, snatched the tooth from my hand, and tossed it out the window.

The moment we returned home, I grabbed my skateboard and zipped over to the Flower Power House. Staying still was painful when I had so many questions. As I wandered up to the lawn, a sound that could only be described as electric water washed over me. It pierced like lightning, rippled like a lake under rain. I leaned languidly over the banister.

"Hey, Moon, how were the waves? Did you love it? You gonna abandon us to be a Ukee bum?" Jill turned to me on the porch swing, docile and sleepy-eyed. She was draped over Rocky's torso, rising and falling in time with his slow breath. She lifted her body so that it was slightly more upright, crossed her uncrossed legs.

"What's this music?" I rested my board against the steps and crawled up to the porch, trance-like.

"Isn't he the grooviest?" Jill handed me the album. The cover was all splashes of colour, a coffee-skinned man with a cloud of black hair, like Rocky's. "And he's left-handed."

"What? Like it's a magic power or something?" Rocky scoffed, nudging Jill off him as he combed his fingers through his fro. "You should grow your hair out, Moon." He ran a thick, shea-buttered palm over my scalp.

The house was full of sweet clouds again, so they made me wait on the porch. I sat in the splash of light, surfing the chord progressions. Jill came out with a pitcher of sun tea and some blackberries, copies of a new play wedged under her armpit. I sprawled on the chipped cedar and watched the shadows move across the wall, tried to catch them. She handed me a script, and I shed my skin, trading my problems with someone else's for the rest of the evening.

THE NEXT DAY, APPA and I went swimming. He wanted to make sure I could contend with the white kids before signing me up for summer swim club. Taught me everything he knew in a diamond-shaped loop: Long Lake, Green Lake, Lost Lake, and Diver Lake. He wrapped sugar-laden space food in our towels and shoved them to the bottom of his red duffle bag so Vathany wouldn't see the metallic blue and red wrappers of our vending machine stash. She was pulling her eyebrows out over how chubby I was getting that summer. And blacker.

Appa couldn't have cared less what I looked like. "Beautiful thoughts make a beautiful person," he said, half-joking, as he washed his meds down with cola and a toaster strudel.

Vathany wrung out the damp tea towel in her hands and whipped him in the butt with it. Appa kissed her chiselled cheekbone, spackled with faint vitiligo, before swinging the bag across his body. He rushed ahead on his cherry-red bike, putting metres between us. I pedalled as fast as I could, panting, barely keeping up.

I couldn't see the end of Long Lake. Clabbered brown sand and a wood pier stretched into vast blue that looked like a discount version of the sea. The water sure glimmered, though — light filtered through an aquamarine gemstone. Appa and I leaned our bikes against the trees, pulled off our shirts, and ran to the lake's edge. A school of perch scattered as I waded in, digging my toes into the soft sand.

"Did you know people steal sand from Eelam?" Appa said.

"You're lying." I splashed him.

He grabbed my wrist and shook his head. "Am not." He splashed back. "Beach theft . . . It's a real thing."

"How can someone *steal a beach*?"

"Humans do…all sorts of strange things." He rubbed his head in a circular motion, chuckled softly. I pictured bandits shovelling trucks full of pristine white sand under the moonlight and vanishing before the sun arrived.

I learned my rākkeṭ kappal at Long Lake. Appa squeezed my arms in a tight streamline, my shoulders suction-cupped around my ears. He propelled me forward, and I launched my rocket ship out into space. Blasting off, I heard his voice in my head: *Squeeze your ears. Look down. When you lift your head up, your belly sinks!* I kept my eyes fixed on the perch and the reeds dancing in the lake bed as I glided forward, making it a little farther every time, thinking about stolen sand. The more I learned, the more cluttered my brain became and the less anything made sense.

Green Lake was sandless and named for the brilliant jade hue of the water. The bottom was filled with a colourful array of eroded stones.

Appa stood waist deep in the emerald lake, his furry chest covered in water pearls. "Watch this," he said, humming "American Pie" and slowly submerging himself until bubbles came out of his nose.

I started humming along between inconsolable giggles, lowering my face into the water. Sure enough: bubbles.

"Always, always blow air *out* when you're underwater." Appa said this over and over. "Always. But if not," he warned, "hold your breath."

I held onto his shoulders as he dove down, stretching our lungs, exhaling small reverse sips of air. I pointed to a calico stone and he grabbed onto it, walking along the drop-off until my chest was pierced and tight, aching to explode. I let go of his shoulders, propelling out of the water to suck in the sweet air.

There was a monster at the bottom of Lost Lake, vinyl black, nestled in pine. The water was ominous and overtaken by the reeds.

"Imagine there is something gross on your foot and you want it off," Appa said, flicking off his loafers in demonstration.

Every time I felt a reed graze my leg, I imagined the tentacles of a ravenous sea monster and thrashed as quickly as I could.

"No, okay, no — not like that. Fast and little. Flick, flick your feet!" He scooped me up by the armpits and clasped onto my feet. "Like this!"

I kicked and kicked, away from the clutches of whatever lurked beneath, knowing that the faster Appa was satisfied with my strokes, the faster I would be safe, out of the bewitched black water.

Diver Lake was, ironically, shallow. Shallow and still. The chameleonic surface reflected the forest. At Diver Lake, we floated, waded, and looked inward, sometimes spending an hour in silence, just staring at the water, breathing in time with the ripples.

"Many swimmers...many athletes...they overlook the importance of union. The marriage of movement and breath, but it is...everything. The ability to be *here*." Appa flicked the water. "It is our connection to the divine."

He was talking about that God thing again. That thing Vathany called Jehovah, or whatever. They were always on about the great unseeable that was in the water and in the air. The thing that was holding everything together.

"But how do you *know* it's there?"

"I'd be a liar if I told you how to *know* anything. I don't think you can ever *know*. But you can always look closer. Feel..." Appa dragged his fingertip gently over the water's surface, slowly submerging his hand, then his entire body.

I tilted my head, chewed my lip. Traced my own fingertips over the sleek skin of the lake. Then I slipped in, let it pour over me like cool silk.

5

The River

qiqéyt, 1947–48

⌒

The Sunday after we found the missing log driver, I went to church rather than the river, only to find that it was full of corpses. The skeletal, blue-skinned pastor raked strands of white hair across his veiny forehead, which extended several degrees north without going properly bald. "Through Christ, we conquer death," he intoned in a voice so hymn-book paper thin I felt I could break it. His thread of an upper lip quivered; sweat pooled at his armpits.

Behind him, the gaunt and gaping marble Jesus peered into my soul with pupilless eyes. Corpses. Corpses everywhere.

"Here." The boy beside me nudged me with his elbow

and shoved a plastic goblet of burgundy juice and a crumb of stale bread into my lap.

The pastor raised his hands. "The blood and the body of Christ."

All I could think of was the body in the booms. My stomach twisted and burned. I stood up from the pew, heavy in the head. The thick stench of floral perfume and body odour shrouded everything. My breathing got real shallow, and then everything went black.

I woke up with my face covered in a glaze of cold sweat and the blue-tinged blur of the pastor hovering beside me. He handed me a glass of cold water and tears started falling out of my face like water through an opened valve. The pastor prayed with his hands on my shoulders.

That week I fought the persistent urge to beat up Gordon. The threat of being sent back to the orphanage loomed in the overcast air, a piercing whiteness on the horizon, so I made my best efforts to repent. As the days grew darker, I tried to use my right hand and let my river dreams stay buried deep down in my candlefish bucket under the motorcycle club. But even after enduring coffee farts and monotone preachers in the pews, everything was still flipped, inverted, and I was still left-handed. Still thirsting for the river. I craved the pine and the uninterrupted skyline, the light that danced across the water.

And then, Jagger found an air gun.

"Let me see it." Dried clay on the corners of his mouth

and fingertips, Vince snatched the gun. It was an old Daisy Model 25 with a wooden pump handle and a really long cocking blended into the front of the trigger guard. "Any BBs?"

Jagger shook his head. He had a green bruise on his collarbone and dried blood on his lip. The Cyclops must have had a particularly bad spell.

"I can get some." Vince was holding the gun with that venomous look in his eyes, the kind he had right before he sliced off a snake's head or stomped on an oolichan.

The school bell rang. Vince shoved the gun into Jagger's gut and we shuffled inside.

Fluorescent lights hung from the rafters of each small, white classroom. My teacher, Miss Swan, was a reed of a woman with giant black globes for eyes and oily silver hair. She looked and moved like a candlefish. She rarely sat down at her small wooden desk at the front of the class. Instead, she wriggled around the room like she was being carried by a current — from the blackboard to the boy's row, across the back wall, finally halting on the left side of the room by the window before continuing the cycle.

We rose to sing "God Save the King." My skin itched, not just because of the anthem's moth-eaten melody, but because the King of England was the last person on earth who needed saving.

As I copied sentences down, I imagined sailing the

world with Ray. As the lesson transitioned to history, his gruff voice hung around in my head. *Best to stay sharp-eared, critical.* He'd suck his teeth, waving his pipe in my face. *The best stories aren't written down — can't be. Least not properly.*

What we learned seemed full of holes. I knew, for example, that the Second World War had killed Mr. Belyea and made Jagger's father lose his mind. I knew that it made Ray prefer the company of water to people, and the soldiers hadn't all been white men like the posters showed. The wars hadn't left a scratch or bullet shell on Canadian soil, but they had left New West fragmented and fatherless.

I was imagining an army convoy bursting the walls of the classroom, right into Phil, my towheaded nemesis, when Miss Swan called on me. Glowing white like a beacon of hell from his corner of the room, Phil made an array of contorted faces in my direction. I felt a sharp twinge in my chest, gritted my teeth, and carved my nails into the edges of my desk. Contemplated picking the thing up and throwing it at him. Wondered if he'd explode into a white dust cloud, like chalk.

My nerves settled as Miss Swan described our task: "Including the past, present, and future tense, write an original story."

The story I wanted to tell settled in my skin and flowed out of my fingertips, my mind polished as an alcoholic's decanter. The problem was getting the enormity of it all out into tiny words. A blind sailor named Shell was hurled into a silver sea in the middle of a lightning storm. He couldn't see, but he could hear sonar, the way whales do. His ship nearly went down in the storm, but as he clung to the mast, he sang for help, striking a crystal note that even sirens couldn't reach. That's how he befriended a young whale called Snow. And Shell sailed the seven seas on his back, sustained by a diet of kelp, clams, and mackerel. I could smell the salty stink of the whale; I could feel his cold, wet skin beneath my bare feet. I knew the constellation of barnacles on his back.

Miss Swan stood up from her desk, clutching our stories to her chest. She held my paper up to the ceiling light. Everyone was about to know how smart I really was.

"This is all... backwards," she said with a scowl, her thin brown lips curled upwards.

"It ain't." I folded my arms.

"Yes, it is. Look."

llehS fo yrotS ehT
.selahw yb desiar yob dnilb a

Phil snatched the paper from my desk, and the rest of the class huddled around him. "Slow as molasses, just like his brother."

"He ain't my brother!"

The ceiling was closing in on me. The walls were snickering. My heartbeat hastened. All I wanted to do was run back down to the booms and swing. I looked over at Deloris Lacey, reticent, her curler-made ringlets already limp and falling out. And then there was Phil: pure evil, intense, and as white as the walls.

Something in me quaked.

I ran to Miss Swan's desk, lifted the globe that sat there, and chucked it at Phil. He ducked, and the globe smacked Jagger in the back of the head. His busted lip reopened to spout purple blood down his neck. Then Vince was on top of me, whacking me in the side of the skull. I broke loose of Vince's hold, prying off the thicket of limbs, and ended up standing on top of a desk waving Jagger's gun.

"Get down from there this instant, Ronny!" ordered Miss Swan.

The sound, the colour, the light — it all melted into a marbleized swirl. All I could hear with any clarity was "They're gonna hang him before he's twenty-one!"

AFTER DETENTION AND THE STRAP, I sat on the front steps of the schoolhouse with Gordon, who was smearing his palms yellow with dandelion ligules. He smelled of sour grass.

"Come on, Gordon, let's go."

He looked up at me, batting his impossibly long, dark eyelashes, clumped together with sleep. His button nose was so round and precious, begging to be clocked. I swallowed my savage impulses and started towards the weak, early sunset. Gordon shuffled up off the steps and trudged home behind me.

The quake had claimed the lives of two river pigs and destroyed the magnificent swing bridge, yet Mrs. Belyea's decrepit veranda was still, somehow, intact. It creaked menacingly as I made my way up the steps. I sat down at the table in silence.

"Where've you been? I was worried sick about Gordon." Mrs. Belyea folded her four-fingered hand behind her back and wrangled Gordon towards her with her other arm.

Pat sat at the dinner table with her head cradled in her hands. Her swollen eyes had shrivelled up and near disappeared into her face, which looked like a wrung-out towel. Two new dark-haired fosters continued eating in silent synchronicity.

"Can I be excused?" Pat asked.

"You haven't eaten a thing," Belyea barked.

"I don't fancy meat loaf."

"Oh, you fancy it just fine or you wouldn't be dating it."

Pat folded her arms and stopped herself from saying anything more.

Belyea gestured to me. "Don't let your food go to waste, or I'll send you back to the orphanage and swap you with a grateful child. Eat."

She rapped me on the shoulder, and I flinched, nodded. The pogey was spread thin and I was hungry, yet food was the last thing I wanted. I closed my eyes and tried to replay my movie reel of funny moments: Mrs. Belyea knocking over a vase with her wobbly arse, startling herself at the sound of shattering glass, then farting loudly. Gordon crying over losing his shadow. The church ladies wearing those stupid hats that looked like roadkill. But the log driver's bloated blue corpse kept appearing. Out of habit, I raised my left hand.

"No shit-grabbers under this roof."

"Sorry." I hung my head and squeezed my fork, cold silver digging into my callused right palm.

Beautifully timed, Gordon broke out in a squawking fit, a thing he did on occasion. Pat rose from the table and flew to her room. Mrs. Belyea thundered after her, quaking steps shaking the entire house. This would go on for hours. I got up, grabbed a biscuit, and shoved it in Gordon's screeching mouth. The dark-haired girls, still chewing, turned to face me as I slithered out onto the back porch.

The sky's colours had darkened and intensified. As the sun disappeared into the river, ribbons of soft yellow and harsh violet curled in the atmosphere. I sprinted to the rope swing and climbed to the top of the tree. A cool clay breeze whipped me in the face as I gripped the rope, and the rough strands stung my palms as I swung out into the cloudberry hue. I launched myself into the air, a chilly glaze washing over me as every hair on my body stood up. Under the open sky, swinging forward into the atmosphere, I felt the damage of the day dissolve like the sun slipping into the river.

THE TIME OF LITTLE FROGS, when wildflowers laugh colour out of the cold ground and Creator's grace spills into every conversation, struck me as the perfect time to steal back Jagger's gun. Pacific bleeding heart burst out of the earth along the edges of thawing blue streams where the frog's croaking crested. It was a calm spell, when the apple blossoms blanketed the streets like pink snow, though the sight of streetcar-flattened frogs upset me. Tiny tadpoles thrust into being, only to be immediately crushed the moment they grew legs by the cruelty of life on land.

I picked the sleep crust from my eyes before wrangling Gordon under the magenta cupula of the magnolia tree outside the schoolhouse. My long cotton sleeves and pleated pants were suddenly much too short, and they were wearing thin in the crotch and armpits. My mouth tasted how salal stank — sour and rancid. I'd overslept again and missed handover with the Laceys, so Gordon was my dead weight accomplice for the undertaking.

I scaled the building to the ground-level window that Miss Swan absent-mindedly left unlocked. I removed the screen and slipped into the vacant room, less threatening now in its emptiness. The teacher's desk was riddled with papers and tea rings. I pulled open the drawer, retrieved the BB gun, and nearly shut the drawer before noticing the spearmints. Grabbing a much-needed handful, I escaped like a light going out.

"Come on, Gordon!" I tugged him out from under the asylum of star-shaped flowers. He folded his knees, plopping back to the ground in defiance. Placing the BB on the ground, I heaved him up by his armpits. Again, he sat down, this time reaching for the gun. The snug knot beneath my breastbone turned into a sinking stone, throwing off the gravity of my thoughts. My rational, thinking mind moved at a banana slug's pace compared to the weightless, flittering impulses that swept up and took me over.

I held the barrel of the BB to Gordon's head.

He jolted to his feet. "Bad spirits! Ronny! Bad spirits!"

I aimed to the right of his shoe, hitting the blossom-blanketed earth. Gordon yelped and swerved around the magnolia trunk. I lifted the gun and pulled the trigger again. He shrieked, and the weight of what I'd just done spread its black wings over the moment.

I'd shot Gordon straight in the ass.

I raced down to the riverbank, reed sweetgrass brushing against my skin. The water gleamed, glinting with soft spring light. I paused to pluck a handful of thyme leaves and chive stems and shoved them into my mouth. The slap of fresh, oniony herbs failed to drown out my acidic anxiety. One of those Earl Grey–guzzling bible thumpers with the bird's nest hats would surely find Gordon and bring him back to Belyea.

In the distance, I spotted Jagger and Vince. "Jagger! Jagger! I got your gun!" I scrambled to the booms, nearly tripping over my feet. A seagull squawked in the distance, sending a shudder down my spine. I was going to be sent back to the place I hated more than Belyea. I panted, offering the gun to the air. Vince swiped it out of my hands with a smile, then handed it to Jagger.

I flipped Vince off as I hobbled down to the bank to float. Still shaking, I dug into the rocky clay with my fingers and anchored myself against the ice-cold current. The water ran over me like the chilled edge of a smooth blade. I was bad. What I'd done to Gordon was bad. I launched off the silt, leaping into the atmosphere like a flying fish before diving under the surface. I held onto the edges of a large, submerged stone, my legs floating up behind me like a kite. I screamed into the rushing silver, shouted as loud as I could, but the water absorbed the sound, turned it into a soft bubble.

When I came up for air, Vince was mid-swing, looking like a miracle of physics as he eclipsed the sun. He dropped with a thud, ran like hell along the logs like a BB headed straight for the opal water.

Jagger swung after like a cheap replica. He held onto the rope too low and swayed over the booms with fraying force. One minute he was capering down a log; the next he disappeared between the rows. Evaporated like morning mist.

My heart thumped in my ears. Vince's hollering crescendoed as he straddled the booms, clambering over the rolling logs, reaching desperately between the gaps where Jagger had fallen and trying not to fall in himself. Vince shrieked for help, shrieked at me to help, shrieked at the sky to do something. I ran towards the logs, but the breadth of the cedar booms had multiplied, become infinite. We were searching for a needle.

The log drivers came, and while everyone around me was shouting, I couldn't make even a single sound, as if the river were still absorbing my screams.

When I saw a pale, limp arm flopped over the edge of a boat, I heaved. The acid-onion taste of partially digested thyme and chive covered everything. The moment became slow and thick like fog. A flash of Jagger's face, porcelain and serene. He looked asleep.

"Get on out of here." A police officer with a chiselled jaw and the build of a phone booth waved his black baton at Vince and me, crouched in the reeds. "This ain't a scene for children. Get on home to your mothers."

"He's our — he's my…" Vince sobbed.

I touched Vince's back and he crumpled into me, melted as if he'd left his body. He sobbed the whole way home. I wanted to cry, but the tears wouldn't come. A flurry of cherry blossom petals swirled in the spring breeze.

EVERYTHING WAS HAZY ORANGE, like the summer heat. I was back in the dilapidated building with ivy crawling up the sides, sitting in a painful metal chair that felt like abandonment. I shuffled in the hard little seat, which chilled the backs of my legs while somehow simultaneously making my arse sweat. What I remembered as unnaturally bright white walls were now yellowing, but the same deflated woman sat at the front desk. A few coils of hair had escaped her neatly fastened bun, deep trenches had formed under her eyes, and the forehead wrinkle, merely a hint before, had now been firmly etched.

"You're not good enough for the name Belyea," the widow had said, swift and searing as a blade. This scene hung around in my head like a persistent cold. I had been determined not to cry, but when Children's Aid arrived to pick me up, I bawled so much that blood vessels popped in both my eyes.

Now another woman entered the room. She had grey skin, feathered white hair, and a beak-like nose, painted faintly yellow by the glow of my files. She looked like a seagull. "No birth certificate," she squawked, sifting through my papers.

"I know." The tired woman at the desk yawned. "They just guessed."

"This bit true? With a dog leash?"

"Hush…" The tired woman rested her chin on her hand. Her jaded eyes glazed over as she blinked, eerily in sync with the ticking clock. She yawned again and nodded.

"Him? Him's one? He don't look like one…though now that I see it here…"

Hard to tell what you can really remember, and what's simply been told to you so many times you think it's a memory. Every time I was in the orphanage, the dog leash came up. It was the most prominent detail in my file. The front porch, the dog collar, and the dish of water. The bruises crawling up my legs, the full, unchanged diaper, rancid and moulding. The whisper of another place, a secret somewhere for "ones like me," whatever that meant. Seemed like they thought I should be thankful for the lesser of two evils.

The seagull woman rifled through my files as if they were puzzle pieces that could be matched together and made sense of. But the tired woman, seasoned in the chaos of abandoned children, knew that they couldn't. There was no such order to be found, and to believe in such a thing was utterly delusional. My last name — made up. An educated guess based on the hearsay of my first foster's ex-landlord. My birthday — pulled out of thin air by Children's Aid.

I saw the glimmer of hope drain out of the seagull woman as she closed my files. She took me under her wing-like arm and sadly ushered me inside past the green doors.

THE BOY WHO SLEPT beneath my bunk had skin like a toad: an already unfortunate face covered in painful-looking pink-orange welts. Said his skin was soft as a baby's bottom when he walked in here, and now it was like a sea hag's arse, greasy and covered in barnacles. Said it was from all the lard.

All we ate were lard sandwiches. Every day. Bread that tasted like sawdust slathered with pig fat. If you whined about it, you got no food at all for your main course and a licking for dessert. I started compulsively running the back of my hand over my face to check for bumps. I might've been the pond scum of society, but at least I didn't have any papules. I closed my eyes and imagined I was eating golden bannock and candied salmon down at the river. I was real good at sailing out into my thoughts, at watching the movie screen in my head. Sometimes, though, memories would slash their way in like a kraken thrusting its tentacles through my daydreams.

We recited empty prayers to an empty sky and were summoned to the plain eating hall by bells, like cattle. There we sat in the uncomfortable metal chairs, hunched over the cold table, and ate our lard sandwiches, chewing on the sides of our teeth and avoiding our tongues so our stomachs would fill up without having to taste the stale bread or the revolting fat. A lard sandwich may be better than a dog leash and a dish of water, but it's still a lard sandwich. I craved golden butter, dark meat, and freshly baked bread, and I didn't understand why some people could have them but not me.

The worst days were Fridays, when prospective parents would come by Children's Aid to look at the young ones. If you were doe-eyed, snow-haired with round cheeks, and under the age of five, you had a good chance of getting picked. Me? Slit-eyed, dark-haired, and nearly ten? I was a flea-ridden raccoon with a missing leg at a dog pound. Yet a dumb part of me still hoped someone would choose me.

On my twenty-eighth Friday, I stood there gritting my teeth as infertile Christians scanned for the perfect orphan. A clean, middle-aged woman gravitated towards a boy with skin white as milk and eyes bright and round. He looked like Jagger: pure. And he clearly favoured his right hand, using it to stack some blocks. On sight, this woman knew that *he* was her little blank canvas. Her little angel dealt the wrong cards. With shame, I looked down at my left hand, tinted blue from the tying.

Six full moons had passed since I was in a proper home. The white light on those nights kept me awake. I returned to my room, teeth on the brink of shattering, and punched the bed frame, then the wall. The thunder of my knuckles smacking against the plaster spread throughout my entire body. It hurt good. My left fist throbbed, allowing my jaw to unclench. There was a dent in the wall that I'd get licked for later, but I had discovered that pain temporarily shut off all the other thoughts, and then a rush of release would wash over me.

I lay down on my bed and stared up at the ceiling. The cheap metal frame dug into my bones. When I looked down I saw my pigeon chest. I had a real violent hankering for some freshly fried bannock and the smell of the river.

I sat up to look out the window. It was midafternoon, though cinder fog had swallowed the skyline. In the weird limbo between chores and supper there were no shadows to chase, no rain to turn the windows into kaleidoscopes. So I was just looking.

After a while, I noticed something new: a wooden ladder on the side of the building. The window slid open with naive trust, and the moody smell of rain, cedar, and wilting maple leaves invited me out. The ladder creaked and swayed with each step. When I was a little more than halfway down, it swung all the way to the left. My stomach twisted and I held my breath as the ladder smacked abruptly into the branches of the big maple tree, shocking my whole body.

I gave myself a shake and hopped off the ladder, now a mere leap from the pavement. Then I ran out into the achromatic November sky and down the empty street, a wild, left-handed bastard on the loose! I ran as fast as I could, past all the churches and the decaying doorstep pumpkins, until I got to the heart of downtown.

Lines of fancy cars scintillated along either side of the street. I was drawn to my reflection in the window of a sky-blue Chevrolet. Although I was as pigeon-chested as ever, I looked older, more handsome. Almost like somebody with a family. Somebody who mattered.

Through the glint of my smirk, I noticed that the window was a quarter rolled down. Too narrow for a well-fed man but not for an emaciated orphan on a diet of lard sandwiches. I sleeved my hand through the opening, scraping it against the glass and car frame, and bent my arm at an impossible angle, twisting my torso until I was able to reach the window crank. After two challenging turns the rest was cake, and I opened the car door to find a plump wallet resting in the glove compartment belonging to some posh schlub with coiffed blond hair and a weak jawline. I tossed the ID on the road and shoved all the coins and banknotes into the pockets of my sagging pants. Over thirty dollars — enough to buy a brand new gun and ammo. If I'd gotten the BB back to Jagger in time, he'd have been shooting pellets instead of swinging over the booms.

I glided down the aisles of the nearest toy store, past the model horses and the noggin-sized lollipops. I wondered if the people in the store could sense the bad spirits in their midst, danger coming off me like musk. But with the Crosman Marlin Cowboy in my hands, I felt like I was thirty dollars myself. I glittered down the street, aimed my baby at the street lamps, and shot out each light one by one. Shattered glass fell to the streets like dying fireflies, electric bursts of gold. I had raised the barrel to the last light at the edge of an alley when I heard music — *that* music. I froze, and then followed the sound through a labyrinth of vibrant alleys. The damp smell of piss and liquor grew strong and then faded once I found myself on an open street. I was on the edge of that magical little district, where angel man and the colourful folk lived. They were called the coloureds in white society. Even as a left-handed orphan with skin that took the sun, I was taught not to associate with them. But colourful made more sense because of the way that place was painted. All vibrant fabric, fascinating faces, and flavourful food.

A group of young girls sporting stiff pigtails jumped rope around a radio. They sang over the music in rich, melodic voices.

"You gotta problem?" The smallest girl with the biggest hair dropped her end of the rope and stared straight at me.

I looked down at my hands. "You sing nice."

The small girl's dagger-like air softened somewhat. They all regarded me with wary eyes.

"Not too many white folk come 'round here," said the darkest of the three. She was the kind of pretty that makes the air thick and roseate, the kind with a magnetic pull that starts between your legs. Lips full enough to break your heart.

Something told me I wasn't allowed to think that way about these girls. I hadn't quite learned all the rules, and none of them made sense to me, but skin colour seemed less important for people who needed a dollar. I lingered in the awkward stalemate, eyes fixed on the swan-like neck of the darkest girl.

"Well, maybe he ain't all white." The third girl, who had impressively big teeth, circled me. She held her arm up to mine. "He's got skin darker than me."

"Yeah, but so what, Liz? You high yellow." The smallest girl laughed. "So he's a tanned white boy." And then they all laughed.

"I don't know what I am, or where I'm from."

I shrugged. "They call me alley mutt... Wait, you know a man named, uh, Angel? Sings like... like..."

"Honey butter?" Liz revealed her bunny teeth with a grin.

I nodded, snapped my fingers.

"You talking about my cousin? Angel Hayes?" The girl who stopped time looked directly at me.

"Could be. He's the best singer I've heard in my whole life." I chewed the inside of my cheek, avoiding her eyes, shoving my hand in my pocket in case my body decided to betray me.

"Everybody say that... Even Zenora. Makes James Marshall quiet." The smallest girl giggled, whipped Liz with the rope.

"You know where I can find him?"

They shook their heads in unison.

"They call him Angel 'cause he floats," Liz said. "Lives in the clouds."

I was formulating a plan to find the man and the music that would save me.

"All right, alley mutt, we'll tell Angel you looking for him," Liz said. "Well, maybe we'll see you around... Careful, though, Italians catch you around here, they might not like it."

The girls turned back to their rope, and that was my ticket out of the conversation. I had enough coins left to catch a trolley to the quay in New West. Took some time before arriving at the edge of Stó:lō. I could never blame the river for Jagger's death. We were careless and arrogant in the face of something so powerful. I heard the familiar rush of the river, my mother's voice, and felt at ease.

I found Vince thrashing a white sturgeon against a rock. "No way in hell you caught that yourself," I harped, wincing at the sight of the mutilated fish, the size of a small porpoise.

"Nah, it washed up dead... Wanted to use its spine as a sword." Vince rinsed his hands in the river, wiping them dry on his shirt.

"Sturgeons don't have spines."

"Never you mind." Vince shook his head. "Ah Jesus, Cuddy, there you are." He pulled me in for a stiff hug. "You could come live with me and my brothers," he offered.

"Kid stealers would never let me do that." Truly, I didn't know if they would have cared, but I didn't want to sign my life over to the gang just yet. After Jagger died, Vince got tossed out of school for beating up Phil and moved in with the Clark Park gang led by his older brother Stanley.

"Ray's docked," Vince said, and we ran to the boat.

"You're gonna get a hell of a licking breaking out of the orphanage," Ray said.

"Need my freedom to feel real," I explained.

That seemed to be enough for Ray. He gave me a small sack of bannock and canned salmon. I scarfed it all down right there on the bank until my gut swelled, nearly burst out of my skin. I was terrified the nuns would confiscate it. I knew I'd get lashed when I returned to the orphanage. After that it'd be off to another foster home. I looked out at the metallic river, the Elysian pairing of cakey bannock and salty salmon on my tongue, longing for my mother. For another earthquake. For Angel Man's music. For something to come and shake everything apart.

6

The Sea

Snʊˈneɪməxʷ, 1979

⁓

I swam in sunbeams. The ceramic tiles of the outdoor pool caught rivulets of light. Rays ricocheted into my goggles; my lenses sliced them into a cathedral of microscopic rainbows. I laughed in bubbles, a faintly echoing fizzle that streamed out of my mouth and rose to the surface. Suspended weightless in the water like an aerial silk acrobat, I loved the slowing thrum of my heart. My mind, usually caught in webs of thought, was untethered.

When I popped my head out of the water, all the noise rushed back in, an assault on my senses. I clutched the grooved pool ledge and flicked my feet the way Appa taught me.

"Right on, fish boy, you swim good." Coach Lee, a Taiwanese tower of a man, held out his big, tanned hand for a high-five. My hand met his with a wet slap, and then I got back to work, kicking until my legs turned to liquid fire.

Coach Lee turned to Appa, who sat in the bleachers with a proud, regal spine. "Man, solid kick technique he's got...He swim before?"

Appa nodded.

I trembled on the white blocks, feeling betrayed that Appa hadn't taught me how to dive. The aqua-blue water was dangerously far away. Panic set into my chest.

"Hands, head, body, legs!" Coach Lee said in his crumbly way, the words loose and falling apart, as if it was no big deal. As if I wasn't about to smash my head against the side of the pool, crack my skull, and bleed to death.

I gritted my teeth and shot an angry glance at Appa. I turned back to Coach Lee and nodded, took a shallow breath, then leapt in like a show seal: headfirst, my arms plastered to my sides. Water flooded up my nose, and my head tweaked from the blood rush. I popped up, involuntary tears melding with snot and water.

"You're all right, kiddo." Coach Lee seemed to come from some other realm where pain did not exist. Even at rest, his eyes smiled. He reached his oar of an arm out to me. "Grab on, dude." Then he reeled me over to the pool's edge. "Tuck your chin in more and lead with your fingertips. Hands, head, body, legs — got it?"

I assembled myself into a streamline position, ears squeezed firmly between my arms. Pearls of cold water on my body turned warm in the heat, flattened into streams and ran down my skin as I hovered on the block. Coach Lee counted me down and I abandoned all technique, leaping forward like a flying squirrel. My body hit the water with a slap. I came up, stinging all over. Electric and ready for more.

VATHANY SAT AT THE dinner table with her arms folded, her plate of okra and lentils untouched. I ignored her shaming eyes and devoured my meal. The coalescence of sharp salt, toasted fenugreek, and sweet coconut milk soaked into the rice.

"The coach said Chandra was a raw talent. Fastest boy in his division."

"You said he can't dive," Vathany hissed.

"Yes, but that's a small thing…He'll learn."

"You eat more in one day than my whole village ate in a week." Vathany yanked my plate away. "If you ate some meat, you wouldn't be so ravenous."

"I won't. It's cruelty to children!" I protested.

"Well, what about fish?" Vathany groaned.

"Fish *is* meat, moron." I face-palmed, pulling back my plate. My spine stiffened — I realized my mistake as her back-of-the-head slap was already in motion.

Vathany turned to Appa. "This cussing Canadian — fat even though he only eats rice — is *your* son."

My lip quivered as Vathany poured my curry down the sink. I wondered why she couldn't love me as effortlessly as Appa did.

The loud smell of coriander and clove cut through the silence. Appa squeezed my side, pug-dog eyes lit up with glee. "My boy, the fastest swimmer on the team."

THAT SUMMER I GREW GILLS, could hold my breath forever. I'd wake up to the sun spilling in through my window, then skate down to the ocean and kill time, sometimes running lines with Jill and Rocky until swim practice. I craved that neon-blue water, the first dive, bursting out of the water in a stroke of butterfly, the underwater streamline competition.

The secret to being quick was listening to the dry bits — all that boring technical stuff that the other kids zoned out for. I could tell they weren't listening to Lee when I lapped them. They dragged their feet, thrashed their necks around to breathe. Not me. My arms stayed sealed over my ears, my head locked down, following the cherry-red centre line. I sipped and exhaled air efficiently, a swift roll keeping my ear to shoulder; my pull was strong and thorough, and I never, ever, ever stopped kicking.

Waiting for the rest of my lane to finish the set, I bobbed up and down in time with the rhythmic splashes and frothing white water, did the odd somersault and came up for a citrus-twist of air. Someone on deck had peeled an orange... a svelte woman with teased snow-blond hair. She looked like the women on Vathany's beauty product labels. She spoke to Coach Lee. Behind her, a boy with a shock of lemon hair and freckle-splattered skin tugged at her shorts. He threw his head back and groaned with his entire body as he marched into the change room.

"Hey, fish! Caught a guppy that can keep up with you." Coach Lee called out in his booming Valleyspeak.

Here was another light-skinned boy about to pull my pride from under me like a riptide. Slender yet superior in size, my competitor slipped into my realm, sending tense ripples around me. His eyes of an ever-elusive undecided hue reflected light like the water. He looked like he wanted to punch everyone.

Coach Lee squatted down; his long, squid-like limbs loomed over the cement deck, red whistle firmly between his teeth. This meant it was time. Gripping onto the grooved wall, I waited for the whistle blast, ready to hold my breath for eternity if that's what it took.

Shriek of the whistle and I arrowed into the blue satin tunnel, pumping my legs until my quads burned before melting into the liquid void around them. The faint rush of bubble streams whipped past me — something slithered by, brushing the side of my body. I jolted back into separation, my synchronicity stifled. *Don't look up...* *Don't look up...* I caved, came up for air before hitting the flip-turn line. The light kid, already there, perched on the ledge of the pool.

"I'm usually better." I tried to mask my laboured breathing but ended up gasping for air. I wanted to shatter the cement.

"First place, Tony the Tiger! And Chandra in a close second!" Coach Lee held out his fist; I pounded in reluctance with an eye roll.

Tony shrugged, and beads of water fell from his forehead. "You're still good." *That*, I thought, *is what a lie looks like*, and took note of it.

"That's the spirit, Tiger."

Tony hopped back in the water. "You like superheroes?"

"Love 'em."

"You look like the Green Lantern."

Coach Lee had us swim the flip-turn flags down to the other end of the pool. We otter-swam the flag lines back before dolphin-diving under the lane ropes, holding our breath as far as we could, just like I did at Green Lake with Appa. Without the rest of the swimmers cluttered around, without whistles or clamouring coaches, the pool returned to a still, gelatin-like state. We launched off the wall into the infinite calm and quiet, and it was somewhere between the lane ropes, in the liquid haven that drowned everything else out, that he became my closest friend.

ON A LANGUID MIDSUMMER DAY after practice, Tony hopped out of the pool before lane takedown. He was going to watch the Great International World Championship Bathtub Race that took place in Nanaimo every year.

"Tell your parents to meet us there!" he said.

I cycled home on an inhale, rushing past the blanket of bellflowers and daisies that was the Flower Power House's front lawn. I ditched my swim bag at the bottom of the stairs, thumped up to the living room, and rifled through the couch. I ripped off the cushions, hoping to find some spare change that had trickled out of Appa's pockets during one of his drug-induced slumbers. The first gleaming coin caught my eye from the couch lining. Within a few minutes, I found over six dollars — more than enough to buy a ticket and a pink cloud of candy floss. I shoved the loot in my pocket and grabbed my skateboard.

A pastel crowd bustled towards the docks. A girl with thick-rimmed glasses like television screens around each magnified eyeball held a colourful bouquet of balloons. I handed her a penny and gestured to the big, aquamarine balloon that scraped against the sky. She gawked at me like I was a deep-sea creature that had emerged from the ocean floor before handing me a balloon of partially deflated green.

The bronze smell of suntan lotion, candy floss, and brine wafted up as I shoved through a thicket of wide-brimmed sun hats and sunburns. At the water's edge, the sea breeze beat against my face and the tubbers tended to their ornate bathtub boats, which dipped and crested in the temperamental sea. My favourite was a pink tub with shark's teeth painted on the bow. I figured Tony would dig the round neon-green tub with the simple white sail. I kept checking over my shoulder for him like a twitch. My legs were numb from cycling, swim practice, and skating. I salivated at the smell of salt, starch, and butter floating from the popcorn stands, my stomach burning with hunger. A man in a ruffled blouse and a pirate's hat emerged onto the docks, wielding a plastic sword. A warm glow enveloped me as I waited, eager for my friend to arrive and for the race to begin.

"Ugh! He's going to stink up the whole beach!"

The air around me grew thick and viscous. I swivelled to face a buck-toothed teenager in a windbreaker. My throat constricted.

"Maybe he's here to take a milk bath in one of the tubs." The girl on his arm wore ineptly applied lip gloss and otherwise bleared into a replica of every intimidating teenage girl I had ever seen.

"Careful, Sambo, Blacks can't swim." He nudged me. "The bottom of the ocean is lined with dead slaves."

"That's no biscuit lip, Jeb. That's a fresh-off-the-boat Hindu. Can't you smell the difference?"

"What are you smoking? He's way too dark."

Consumed by the same frozen panic that took over when I was diving off the blocks, I watched my shrivelled green balloon fly up into the atmosphere and disappear into the clouds. I stood stunned for some time before working up the will to push past the gleeful crowd at a glacial pace. Salt and spun sugar lingered in my nostrils, making me want to hurl. I could feel my own Blackness, like being coated in algae. I wanted to leap out of my skin. In a haze, I threw my board onto the cement and kicked and pushed, tears caught somewhere in my throat. I held my breath until the pressure built up inside my chest, like it was full of leaping sand fleas. I was going to either puke or shatter into a million pieces.

When I got to the lagoon, I quenched my lungs with the healing, briny air. At the sight of the vast midnight blue, my shoulders lowered. Rocky and Jill were there, noses buried in their scripts, running lines for this summer's Shakespeare by the Sea performance.

"Moon?" Jill had wilted primulas braided into her hair and a painful-looking sunburn on her cheeks. She floated over to me and ran her eyes over my face, searching for a story. "What is it, Little Moon?"

I tried to swallow the shame down, but it overflowed, bubbling up through my throat and leaking out of my eyes.

"Hey now...gee whiz," Jill said softly.

I hugged my knees into my chest and buried my face in my legs.

"C'mon, que pasa, my man? Oi! Give us a smile," Rocky prodded, tickling me under the armpits.

I squirmed away and let out an angry, muffled "Mind your potatoes!"

"Peace, Moon, peace."

"Sorry," I groaned, flattening the tears with my fingers and painting them over my skin.

"Okay...whoa...no more of that. Sounds like you need to be somebody else for a little bit." Rocky threw himself over a piece of driftwood as if it were a chaise longue. "I love my father!" His deep, theatrical voice reverberated.

I smirked.

"Is that...is that a smile? Houston, we have a smile!" Rocky lifted me up, his ash-brown arms offering me to the pale, tracing-paper sun. Jill cheered and whistled. I studied the gradient of colour from my arms, to Rocky's, to Jill's. When we were acting, it didn't matter that we were all different shades.

I stepped into character like slipping into a different skin, a different world. Like putting on a cloak — one sleeve at a time, making slight adjustments before understanding where the seams were meant to settle around my shoulders. Soon enough, I was Valentine. He took long strides and stood with his chest puffed out like the peacocks at Beacon Hill Park in ritzy Victoria. Jill, now Proteus, had taken out her braid. Rocky played every other character, using an array of voices and postures.

As we sang our lines from the Broadway musical of *The Two Gentleman of Verona*, the deep ache in me subsided. Our voices soared over the choppy sea. A few kite-surfers coming inland put their boards down to whoop and applaud. Rocky curtsied and bowed.

After the dragon fight in act two came to an end, we went down to the water, painted pink and gold by the setting sun. The tide was high and getting higher. We rinsed the characters off and remembered ourselves. I waded in from my ankles to my knees until it got deep enough for me to dive under entirely. The underwater drum in the sea was fierce, like God's heartbeat. It was the next best thing to Appa's arms.

I SKATED HOME UNDER a maroon sky. I pulled the unused tub race ticket out of my pocket, shredded it, and threw it to the cement before closing the front door behind me.

Vathany was a menacing blur in my peripheral view as I went to run a bath. While the water ran, I paused in front of the mirror and gave myself a good, hard look. My skin was so black it was nearly blue. I had gangly arms and legs but a protruding potbelly. My nose was thin and distinguished, what would have been a redeeming feature if it didn't so strongly resemble Vathany's. My eyes were big and sad like Appa's.

I ripped my gaze away from my reflection in disgust and slipped into the scalding water. If my skin could have turned red, it would have. I scrubbed myself with soap and baking soda until it was raw. I towelled off, feeling like I was covered in Velcro, and retrieved the lightening cream from Vathany's cabinet. I lathered myself from head to toe with the thick, snot-yellow paste. It smelled like bleach and lemons, and oh, how it burned. I went to bed on an empty stomach, comforted by the sting.

That night, I was in a pink bathtub in the middle of a dark, volatile sea. I had no oars. I thrashed my arms, paddling and paddling until my muscles throbbed. Just as I was about to give up, a woman emerged from the water. Her skin was vivid blue, a rich pigment I'd only seen in my dreams, and she must have been a hundred feet tall. As she reached out her arms, they turned into rivers, braided channels of silver. My tub rocked in the waves, the salty taste of brine entangled with sweet splashes of fresh water. The meandering river carried me to a place of stillness, where the water was pale jade on one side and deep midnight on the other.

I jolted awake at the first trill of morning birdsong and scampered to look in the mirror. My chest sank at the sight of myself — just as dark as the night before. Only now my skin was parched and covered in a constellation of welts on my forearms and thighs. I hung my head and dragged myself out of the room.

Appa came around the corner in a peacock-blue sarong, singing. He scooped me up with his fuzzy brown arms. "Sollunga, son! What happened here?" he asked, brushing his hand over the sores.

I shrugged.

"Oof, you're getting heavy." He laughed, setting me down on the shag carpet.

I ran my hand over my empty stomach, which gurgled quietly. What a feeling: to be skin to skin, pain rising in you like hot oil, yet the other person has no idea. Appa popped on a Bob Marley record and the room was painted with split-toned gold and teal — a warm, grainy filter washed over everything.

7

The River

Scəẃaθən; xʷməθkʷəẏəm, səlilwətał, Sḵwx̱wú7mesh
(Delta and Vancouver, Canada), 1950

From first light until night swallowed the sky, Lilah shrieked like her insides had been set on fire. I was no stranger to tantrums or tempers, what with the orphanage and Gordon, but never had I heard a shriek quite like hers. Thought it would shatter the smudged farmhouse windowpanes if it didn't crack the earth open again first.

"Ach du lieber Himmel...my brother didn't cry so much when the Wehrmacht put a gun to his Kopf." Tobias, my new foster father, grit what was left of his mercury teeth.

Tobias Urslack was from a place in Austria called Fehring. He had a face that blended into his neck like a giant tube. Tubeias. He lived on a plot of farmland out in the sticks, on the opposite side of the river.

On my first night in the house, over a meal of salt potatoes and red cabbage, his wife, Violet, told me a story about a boy who'd fallen between the booms in the Fraser River. "What's the sense in a tragedy like that?" She spooned green purée into the yowling infant's mouth. Lilah swerved her face away in sputumy dissent. She'd been born to crack, they said. Whatever spirits had her were worse than my own.

Violet sighed. Blue veins crawled up her fingers and arms like a network of meandering streams. "So, what are you? Some kind of Italian?"

"Dutch, I think."

"Last name is Young? Where that come from?"

"It ain't a real name. It's made up." I shrugged.

"Never seen a Dutchman with black hair..."

"Irish, then."

"Irish? I'm Irish," she said. "Well, I mean...I was born here, but my mother was from Brandon in County Kerry. You're too brown to be Irish, though, I —"

"Halt die Klappe, Frau," Tobias groaned.

At that point, I didn't care whether my mother was Dutch or Irish. Hell, by then, I didn't care if she really was a call girl or an addict, so long as she was alive with two arms to hug me. All I hoped, in that moment, staring at Violet's translucent forearms, was that my mother had a bit of colour to her so I wouldn't have to see her veins.

TUBEIAS SPENT THE FIRST few days after my arrival showing me an endless list of chores that I was responsible for now that I lived on a farm. He was probably seven feet tall, with hands the size of a plough. It took him two steps to get from the house to the barn, while there I was, hauling my trash-born candy-ass through the rows of oat and wheat as the waking sun turned the sky a million different colours — ribbons of claret burst into orange flames, melted into half-churned butter, bloomed into cornflower blue, all before settling on an ugly overcast. I squinted. Couldn't tell if it was going to rain; it was one of those constipated skies that could go either way.

I wasn't used to the cow-shit smell of a dairy farm, where, under the great elm on the highest part of the hill, I could overlook a distant glimmer of the river's south arm. In the District of London, the streets were riddled with glass bottles, crushed cans, and cigarette butts. It smelled of log booms, salt water, and candlefish. On the farm, there wasn't a butt on the ground, but the air was smoggy and shitty. Across the river, I always felt like I was moving towards something. Like I had a future of some kind, if I could just claw my way out of the thicket and get to clear water. But here, out in the boondocks, I swore I was going backwards in time.

I took to imagining, drifted off to the sound of heifers mooing and chewing their cud. Soon I was off on my own clipper ship, sailing the Silk Road. Water, teal-tinged and clear as glass. Soft, yellow sand. Stopovers with bananas as big as my arm and sweeter than golden syrup. Sometimes, the shadows moving across the barn with the hours of the day would morph — the menacing tentacles of a hexapus, ready to pull me under into the turquoise-black ocean. Then I'd be thrust onto a ship sailing over a stormy sea with a band of bastard pirates — not mangy scoundrels with rotting teeth or missing limbs but suave, sparkling seamen, adorned with the treasure they stole, feared and envied by all landlubbers. Finally, I'd find Mom. Give her some gold to get her out of the brothels.

After the calves were all nursed, I filled the feeding trough with grain and let the heifers graze for a while. I pulled my stool up on the right side of the great white cow I'd named Moby-Dick. Moby-Dick was a mad kicker, always gave me trouble. I placed the milk bucket beneath the great white cow without a breath, the shitty-silage air heavy in my lungs. I squatted down slowly, didn't want to startle her, but Moby let out a great whale-cow moan. She started to tap dance around the bucket, swishing her tail. I ducked as she thrust her hind legs at my face.

Tobias's cows were all mad kickers — touch 'em the

wrong way and you'd get a hoof to the forehead. I'd learned that the hard way. Completely mashed up my nose, shattering any shot of being on the silver screen, or getting properly adopted. Not that I was any Cary Grant before. No, the new crooked beak wasn't doing me any favours. The fear that Mom wouldn't recognize me if she saw me trickled into my head. I had to shove those kinds of worries down deep, else I'd be paralyzed.

Moby let out a muffled moo as she settled down. I bent down slowly, careful not to disrupt the peace. I looked down at her feet. It was as if the bottom of a cow had turned to steel: four flat, identical hooves. I imagined what it'd be like if human hands were so equal as I pulled down on her leathery teats: *left hand, release, right hand, release, left again.* White rods of milk bolted into the pail.

Despite Belyea's best efforts, I was still left-handed as Lucifer. It didn't matter, though, on account of Tobias was carrying on with switching me, so I'd be right-handed in no time. At the dinner table, he tied my left arm behind my back with a lasso.

You'd think it would be easy to use your right hand when a lasso is searing into your flesh and your circulation is cut off and you haven't eaten all day and there's fresh-baked bread on the table, but it seemed my demons were fixed. I wondered if Mom had given me up on account of the fact that I was ailing with bad spirits.

The white whale started to trundle and whine. I must

97

have been all tangled in my thoughts and pulled a little too hard. Her tail swished as I straightened up to pet her. Her piss hit my tongue, hot and yeasty. I vomited in the hay. Violet had warned me not to milk with my mouth open. Whenever Tobias drank his lager out on the porch she'd wince, shake her head, and say, "Beer tastes like cow piss, don't I know it."

Now I did, too.

THERE WERE THREE FIST FIGHTS in my first week at my new school. I was in all of them. The first time, a kid called me "bastard." The second time, a ginger said I smelled like cow shit. The third time, I frothed up with insoluble rage and kicked a glossy, well-behaved blond in the shins for reasons I still can't remember. My brain felt like it was flipped backwards all the time now, and I'd realized it had something to do with my hands.

I dreaded school, but I loved the bike ride there. I had a clementine-coloured Schwinn that Vince "found" on the side of the road and gave me, a little too easily, some sapless Tuesday when I was in limbo at the orphanage. "This way you can get across the bridge," he'd said.

When I was on my bike, cycling past the acres upon acres of undulating farmland and tall grass, it was like I was sailing over an ocean of gold. Every hill was a wave, and I sailed so fast that I couldn't smell anything but cold. I'd let go of my handlebars and imagine I had wings instead of hands, spanning the air, ready to fly up and out of the valley, above the horizon and away from the shit, behind the clouds where the colours stayed hidden. For a moment, the world couldn't hurt me.

I failed the first semester with flying colours and set fire to my report card in the barn. Eventually, I stopped going to class altogether. I'd leave the farm after milking the cows, lock my bike up near the school, and jump the train upriver like coho coming home in the spring.

"Don't be late home," Tobias would say every single day, each word like the lash of a whip.

That day, I ditched my bike in the old, grooved bike rack made from a cedar tree and ran down to the station, managed to catch the boxcar by the skin of my teeth. Hopping trains was like taking a cold shower; the rush of river air rinsed the shit smell clean off my skin. By the time I landed on the other side, I was met with the fresh salt tinge of the ocean.

I walked from the tracks to the gang house near Clark Park on the east side of Vancouver, lost in thought. All that time, I remained dogged on that music, on Angel Man's alley. I sifted through the film reel of my mind, trying to recollect lyric fragments, or even just a few morsels of melody, but all I could remember from all those years ago was how the music made me feel. Before I knew it, I was wading through the knee-high wild weeds on

Vince's front lawn, kicking over an empty glass bottle. I rapped on the rickety front door, and it swung open with a loud creak.

"Cuddy!" Vince always looked like he hadn't slept in days. His tear troughs were swollen and purple, swallowing his already disproportionately small eyes.

His brothers were all doped up and scheming, and that left us free to do as we pleased. We shot the shit as we crossed residential neighbourhoods and industrial zones, flashes of sound and colour. Half an hour later, we were in a different world. Our calm, crooning river communion was replaced by the clatter of the trolleys and automobiles. Language bended in all different directions, carried by different strands of the rich, polyrhythmic jazz that flooded the air. We bummed around diners, our diet consisting of cherry pie and cigarettes. Days on the river were growing less common now that we'd discovered how to sneak into the nabes. Vince didn't see Stó:lō the way I did, and that was a barrier between us. After Jagger drowned, kid felt robbed by life, and now he was taking back what it owed him, stealing anything within the reach of his sticky mitts. He'd show up at the nabes with his pockets full of candy bars, ginger beer, and yo-yos, things he'd been too flat for in the past. If he wasn't glomming, he was grifting. He'd flash devil-may-care grins at the ticket booth girls who were easy to barter with, and when that didn't work, we'd slip in through the alternate exits or the bathroom window, slithering into Technicolor flicks at every small cinema in town: *Lady Luck* at the Orpheum, *Sunset Boulevard* at the Castle, *Love Is a Headache* at the Revue.

We meandered through Vancouver alleys, dizzyingly following that ribbon of silver on the horizon, taking wrong turn after wrong turn, trying to get to the sea. On the way, we reached the jewel-toned soutache of double base, double Dutch, smoked-paprika-bay-leaf, and claret-red opium poppies trumpeting out of the concrete of the East End. *Always a racket out there*, the bulls would say, but I felt swathed and rocked by the bustle. The array of rare, royal pigments in the fabrics draped over the clotheslines like an ode to a peacock, the acrobatic aroma of tantalizing spices tumbling into the air.

"Would you hurry your candy-ass." Vince rolled his pebble-eyes, sparking one of his pickpocketed lighters. "Or do I gotta hold a flame to it?"

I lingered, longing for those liquid honey harmonies, for the music, so plum and so gold. But all I'd found loitering around the crucifix-shaped intersection where slaves escaped America through the Underground Railroad were identical doorsteps, the quarters where Black railway porters slept, and the streets where wops patrolled. The colony stretched all the way to the southern edge of Chinatown, near the brothel area where

Children's Aid said they'd scooped me. I could walk through it no problem, but what I wanted was a way in.

Somewhere between the jump rope and jambalaya, staggering through a colourless Park Lane under empty laundry lines and blossoming elm, Angel Man swung around a wooden lamppost and re-entered my life before my optimism could wilt white with the opium poppies.

"Alley mutt? Knew I'd see you around." What was it about that voice that made my entire body relax into a smile? Angel Man had his guitar swung over his shoulder, and he shoved his black-cherry harmonica into the pocket of his corduroys. "Heard you was looking for me."

"Vince! Vince! This is the best singer I've ever heard. The one I told you about."

Vince took some tentative steps towards us, sizing up Angel, who wasn't tall but carried himself in a way that elevated him. He had sleepy eyes and full lips that looked like they were welling up with song even when his mouth was closed.

"Oh shoot, alley mutt. What you want? I don't have any money. Well, I do have some, but damn, I need it...the way you need a bath...Whewoy, you smell like somethin'."

"It's the cows," I sighed.

"Cows? Where you got cows hiding around here? A speakcowsy?" Angel Man laughed, a sound so thick, sweet, and resonant that the air caramelized around me.

"What kind of music you play?" Vince pursed his

non-existent lips, flicked his dying lighter on and off until the gas quit.

"You milk bags wanna talk music? Shoot...come down to Vie's with me. Maybe she can deep-fry the stink off you."

THE INTOXICATING SCENT OF chicken plunged into hot oil and dusted with salt commanded the air. Vie's Chicken and Steak House was crackling with colour, the walls splashed with loud, primary reds, yellows, and blues like an inflatable beach ball. Everything was an upbeat, harmonious improvisation.

"Well, ain't that timing? We're fresh outta crackers," snapped a man who was my height but twice as thick. He had muscles like the log drivers on the booms and the biggest eyes I'd ever seen.

"Junior, that ain't no way to speak to guests, ya hear?" a harp-like voice called from the kitchen.

"Yes, ma'am...You know I was only teasing!" Junior rolled his eyes.

"Don't you be rolling your eyes at me, nephew. Melanin-deficient folk get hungry, too." The voice grew louder as a woman came out of the kitchen, wiping flour on her apron. "My name's Zenora," she said. "Go on, have a seat now." Though she wasn't the owner of Vie's, then, Zenora Rose Hendrix was the heart of the place.

We sat down at an oil-cloth-covered table. Sweet Lord — the chicken was breaded in what I can only describe as salt-frosted gold. It melted in my mouth, revealing tender white meat. The hot, cakey, golden clouds called biscuits sent me to another realm, and the cook had somehow made peas, mushrooms, and salad taste like heaven.

"Alley mutt? You crying?" Angel Man said.

"This is…" The medley of deliciousness dissolved on my tongue. I could hear a rhythm so smooth and voices so rich and soulful they were like dessert for my ears. My body ached to get up and dance. "So damn good. What music is this?"

Junior's orb-like eyes lit up. "That there's Cab Calloway." He put his mop down and came over to our booth. "Jive."

"These boys want to talk music," Angel Man said.

"For real?" Zenora asked and sat down. "James always says he wants to come up here. Walked in on the kid using a broom as a guitar the last time I saw him, but I told 'im folks don't listen to the blues up north." Now all of us were seated in the booth, sipping sweet, sparkling colas. "Where you boys from?" Zenora's kind eyes sent a shiver through me.

"New West." I shrugged. "Live on a farm downriver these days."

"Downriver? Hmmmm…a right tumbleweed." She

leaned back to study my face. "You 'mind me a little of my grandfather."

"Your grandfather? Ain't he a little young for that?" Angel Man chuckled, revealing chicken-filled teeth.

"Ain't he a little *white* for that?" Junior howled.

"Paler, sure...but the same hue...same bones."

"Puh-lease, Zenora, this boy is white as salt." Junior chirped, pointing at my forearms.

"Ain't no such thing," she huffed and held the bottle of salt up to my arm. The iodized crystals looked impossibly white next to my tawny skin.

"Well, I'm the colour of bologna." Vince lifted his arms to the light.

Zenora, Angel Man, and Junior rose and rolled in rivulets of laughter that swaddled the room in joy. My shoulders lowered, my heart opened.

Vince looked at Zenora the way he'd looked at Jagger — an expression of deep, earnest appreciation. When Vince smirked at someone with the left side of his mouth, and his eyes got all searching and sentimental, that meant they'd struck him to the core, and that meant he'd pull out his switchblade on anyone who dared try to harm them. Cold and destructive to almost everything that crossed his path, Vince offered every atom of his soul to those he decided to love. Two scoundrels like us latched tightly onto anything loving when it crossed our paths, even if the sentiment wasn't quite reciprocal.

Zenora made everyone feel loved simply by being in her presence, the way Angel made my pain dissipate the first time I heard him sing a sugary riff.

"Oh, shoot, what's the time?" I said.

"Four thirty," Junior said.

"I gotta go!" I turned my pockets inside out and threw some change onto the table. "We'll be back...I want to talk to you more about that jive music." I locked eyes with Junior before dragging Vince out of the joint.

We hustled out the door and sprinted towards the train tracks. The corners of my mouth were salty and stinging, and my eyes watered as I trudged up the hill. *Shit, shit, shit.* I slipped past the ticket booth, sifting through the sparse crowd of gents heading home. The black compartments of the train began to chug past. I chased the slowly accelerating locomotive, reaching for the ladder. The force of the jump jolted my body as I latched on.

"Vince!" He stood on the platform, waving me away as he pulled a cigarillo out of his pocket. His words were drowned out by the thunder of the train. All I could make out was "Don't die, Cuddy!"

The sun was already nesting behind the gnarled canopy of oak as I cycled up the hill to the farm. The muscles in my legs burned, as if they were about to rupture through my skin, but they kept pedalling, propelled by searing fear. I entered the barn glazed in sweat and grease. The reek of fresh cow-pies and stale hay filled my nose.

Tobias was yanking on Moby, meaning he'd milked the whole herd by himself. He muttered something in his guttural German as the old whale-cow tap danced, lifting her hooves and bellowing with so much power she could have blown the rusted tin roof off the aged, wooden barn. Tobias clenched his teeth and seethed. He stood, wound his leg up, and booted the poor cow straight in her swollen, pink udders. I felt the kick in my own pelvis and wailed in pain with her. Tobias snapped his neck around to face me, eyes unflinching, and strode over the hay, which crunched softly beneath his shit-caked boots. The leather whip clasped firmly in his right-hand grip, he grabbed me by the collar of my shirt and threw me into the hay.

"*Schweinhund.*"

The hay scraped against my face like the bristles of a steel wire brush. The lash of the whip had the glacial bite of water beneath ice before turning to the pure burn of a blue flame. My body convulsed, and I cried out in time with the hollering cows. But after a while, the sharp prickle of the hay turned to soft down feathers, and I was able to focus on the space between the lashes — the brief absence of pain. I activated the movie theatre in my head: dark bodies moved spineless like rivers, spindling in time with the ever-shifting sugar of the layered melody. I was safe, surrounded by laughter and cornbread in Angel Man's alley with the crew from Vie's. I found jive.

8

The Sea

Snɵ'neɪməxʷ, 1982–83

⌒

December's new moon darkened day at the hem, making it indistinguishable from night. I woke to the roar of the vacuum and the unmistakable floral-laced sulphuric scent of elderly white people. The Witnesses froze as I entered the living room, eyes locked on my skin: the mark of Cain. Every winter, a time that was sleighbells and candy canes for other families, I'd wake to a house full of freaks in frumpy, ill-fitting sweaters tidying our home until it sparkled. They would leave a tin full of bland Danish biscuits and jam thumbprint cookies, most of which would inevitably go stale and be thrown out.

Shovel in hand, Appa crammed three cookies into his mouth, chewing through a smile before he fastened his winter coat. It was time to dig the Volkswagen out of the avalanche.

"Happy Not-Christmas!" he called from the bottom of the stairs, the winter wind whirring in.

I pressed my cheek to the chilled window glass, licking cereal-milk dust out of my bowl, and watched Appa scrape dense ice off the van, glad to be warm and inside. Vathany thundered into the room with a snap and a thud. Despite her feather-light frame, she moved through the house like a Seneca gun, slamming doors, drawers, and windows.

"It's not a gift." She chucked a white envelope into my lap. I peeled open the envelope, which was labelled *Son* and filled with cash. It wasn't a gift, though it was wrapped like a gift and arrived on Christmas...

Vathany picked up a neglected grapefruit half from the kitchen counter and spooned the pink flesh out of the rind. On top of eschewing caffeine, team sports, and national anthems, Witnesses weren't allowed to celebrate birthdays or holidays. But hers was a fluid faith with an affinity for loopholes. She urged Appa to work on holidays because he earned double (and because the hospital put on a turkey dinner). I was sent to Jill and Rocky's.

"You should eat standing up. It boosts your metabolism." Vathany licked the serrated edge of her spoon, dappling the cat-hair-laden linoleum with pink juice before continuing into the winter garden.

I looked over at the couch, soaked in the stench of Appa's cigarettes and post-shift body odour, ridden with silverfish. Tiny, tapered, alienesque bodies wriggled up and down the tobacco-stained seams, undeterred by the Witnesses' cleaning. Vathany lived in her head, and I imagined it looked something like the state of our home. I'd never seen her pick up so much as a broom and dustpan. She let the house pile up with clutter, let the cellar spiders and the silverfish hang around. She spent so much energy fussing over every millimetre of her physical appearance, she was left little time for anything else. My lodestone skin created a diamagnetic field between us, and I had come to accept that we would forever be two poles repelling.

I watched my morning toons, all snowfall, sugar plums, and Santa Claus. Even the commercials were gift-wrapped with candy canes, jingle bells, and Christmas glee. I envisioned myself as some rendition of the blond archetype that starred in every single one of the specials, imagined my biggest problem was something outside of myself... that there wasn't enough Christmas spirit or something. After that I bundled up and made my way to the Flower Power House.

The air was cutting cold and dense with brine. Winter wind lashed my skin as I slid over the black-ice-coated streets. My feet eventually sank into the thick blanket of snow on the front lawn with a satisfying crunch. The smell of cinnamon, gingerbread, and mulled wine seeped towards me, and the thrum of psychedelic Christmas rock swelled as I came up the steps. I pulled off my red mittens and lifted my fist as the door swung open.

"Merry Christmas, Little Moon!" Jill pulled me inside, into the warmth of their home.

Trailing jade, Peperomia Hope, and string of nickels hung from macramé plant hangers, filling the room with lush green leaves. Along the wall was Rocky's record collection, and in the corner was his cherry-red guitar. The teakwood table was draped with garlands and an orange-and-white geometric tablecloth. A mountain of green vegetables, beets, and white rolls encircled the sweet potato turkey — Jill's ingenious creation. The chipped gravy boat was filled to the brim with gelatinous cranberry sauce, and the butter dish held a pool of liquid sunshine thanks to the warmth of the room.

"Watch out for the fart bombs, my man," Rocky chuckled, waving a Brussels sprout at me before popping it in his mouth.

Rocky's parents lived across the border in Seattle, and he said he'd see 'em when he saw 'em. Jill's parents had grown increasingly devout over the years, and she said that Catholicism had sucked all the joy out of the holiday, which was originally Yule, anyways, the pagan festival of light. "The cognitive dissonance is out of this world, Moon, out of this world," she said. Jill told her folks she was with Rocky's folks for the weekend, planned to go down to their estate tomorrow for a sullen afternoon of post-Christmas depression, brysselkex, and tea.

But tonight was all light and love to combat the lack of it outside. We piled our plates high and sat around their little tree. The sweet potatoes tasted like cake, the golden sweetness and soft, spongy texture melting in my mouth. Every year I marvelled at how something so perfect came straight out of the dirt and was still way better than any gas-station candy bar. We unwrapped our gifts with sticky cranberry fingers. A tambourine for Rocky. Mala beads for Jill. A copy of *Electric Ladyland* for me.

"You're gonna love this one, Moon Boy." Rocky popped the record on the player. "This one's called '1983...(A Merman I Should Turn to Be).'"

"Mermaids are for chicks."

"Nah, Moon. Anything's for anybody." Jill smiled, sinking into the loveseat.

The song sounded like the lagoon. Seagulls calling and whirring wind. Guitar like rippling tidal pools and swelling waves. That Christmas I learned that there were sounds that leaked into your soul and made you glitter from the inside out. Ones that were so true they almost scared you. Made you wonder if your thoughts leaked out and travelled on the wind. Or maybe your experiences, your pain, heartbreak, joy, and love, were universal...no matter how different we all seemed. We swam in the song, listened to it again and again. Then another time, and just once more. Submerging, shivers running through me.

Rocky sucked the crumbs off his fingers and picked up his guitar. He twanged the strings along to the aqueous sounds like he was running his hand through water. I reached out to pull a string and he winced, pulled the guitar back, a flicker of irritation in his eyes. "Moon, brother, you don't touch someone's instrument while they're playing!"

My eyes widened.

"Here, I'll show you," he said, softening. "I'm not so good, but I can give you the basics."

He showed me how to hold the guitar and I mirrored him.

"That feel right? Try to strum."

I combed the strings and nodded.

"Shoot, you play Hendrix style! Righteous."

By the end of the night, I'd eaten and laughed so much that my whole body was reverberating with joy. So much joy that it ached. Jill sent me home with some pie for Appa and a vibrant red poinsettia for Vathany. As I slid home over the ice, tiny snowflakes formed flurries in the wind, brushing past my face and settling on the petals of the poinsettia. I stopped in my tracks and looked around at the white blanket shimmering in the warm glow of the street lamps like magic dust. All that crystallized water, a frozen sea.

AFTER THE HOLIDAYS, I was assigned the seat next to Indra in History class. Indra, whose shirt had yellowed at the pits, who hadn't got the memo about bleaching her upper lip hair like the white girls. She smelled of cumin and body odour.

"Gag me with a spoon," I groaned, reluctantly gathering my books. I sat on the edge of my desk, leaning as far away from Indra as I could. I felt queasy and light-headed. Each cell of my skin tingled with brownness, everyone's eyes on the pair of us.

Our granola teacher stood at the front of the room and proceeded to recite a Dr. King quote, one of the vanilla ones about peace, unity, and dreams. Rocky had warned me about how they never failed to omit the bits about exploitation, rioting, and the evils of capitalism.

"Call them on it," he said, "and crackers'll go full Red Scare on your ass and flag you as a threat."

The teacher locked eyes with me the entire time she spoke, peppering the lecture with the Underground Railroad, even though it didn't fit.

With the metallic sound of the school bell, I booked it out of the classroom and over the gum-spackled cement of the basketball courts. The pretty white girls huddled by the hoops flashed me a smile. Indra sat alone beneath a sycamore maple, eating her fragrant lunch using flatbread rather than utensils. When the white girls laughed, I imagined they were laughing at Indra's long braid and ill-fitting clothes and unbleached facial hair. I didn't understand why she wasn't even trying. Her refusal to blend in was making it worse for both of us.

I met Tone and Stu on the chipped blue monkey bars, where we hung upside down, in that weird space between child and teenager, swaying back and forth like pendulums as blood rushed to our skulls. From our vantage point we could see the high school we'd be attending in a year.

Stu jabbed my right oblique.

"Batman. Batman would win in a fight for sure." Tony interceded, straddling the edge of the bars.

"Dream on...He's barely a superhero. He's just a rich guy with cool toys." I could hear the eye roll in Stu's voice.

"You wanna die right now?" Tone backflipped off the bars, and I jumped down after him with a heavy thud. We booked it over the cold, wet grass. Stu grabbed Tony by the neck of his shirt and they started grappling, laughing as they shoved each other. The smell of dewy grass, sweat, and soil wafted up. Stu had Tony's right arm twisted behind his back when I noticed Indra behind them, staring at me.

"What do you want?" I furrowed my brows.

She lingered, fidgeting, before striding towards me. She said something in her language, as if to confirm that we were on the same team. Indra's long, dark braid and the high, Carnatic pitch of her sarod-string voice filled me with slow, burning rage. I wanted to go underwater and scream.

"I don't speak Hindu," I said in a voice so hard it could crack a coconut shell. I couldn't bear to look at her.

She tried again, louder this time.

How do I explain the events that followed? The tempest inside me turned everything into a melted blur. It was a small action, unfolded in a whip of time, yet the memory of it has stretched over my life.

"Kick rocks," I said and shoved Indra to the grass with the weight of my frustration.

She looked up at me with her sad amber eyes, mud splattered all over her jeans. I felt a twinge beneath my sternum, as if the blow had landed on me.

AFTER SCHOOL, THE BOYS and I skated down to Sandcastle Centre. The mall caught light in a hypnotic way. All the glass sent beams of white light bending and refracting across the space. We flocked to the smoothie bar, where I ordered a sixteen-ounce Buzz Monkey: espresso, low-fat yogurt, banana, and whey protein. It sat like cement in my stomach, but I still felt hollow.

"Trade you a chicken strip for a sip." Stu pushed his grease-stained cardboard box towards me.

"Chan's a vegetarian." Tony placed his hand in front of the carton.

"Oh. That like, an Indian thing, or a gay thing?"

"I'm not Indian." I gritted my teeth.

"So a gay thing."

I turned to Tony. "This kid really has a death wish, hey?"

"He's Black, you royal idiot." Tony defended, and I lowered my shoulders.

We cruised around the shopping centre, passing clusters of cool teens from the nearby high school, and then Caroline Ford and her clan.

"What's cracking, Caroline?" I chirped.

She and her friends looked like a pack of Lite-Brites, with their teased side ponytails, cyan mascara, and electric-pink lip gloss. The way their bodies curved, budding out of their spandex and conveniently unzipped windbreakers, made me dizzy.

"Not much." She winked. "You?"

I held my breath and bolted away without giving her an answer. The bench by the water clock was free, so I planted my butt and started counting pennies.

Tony and Stu came howling around the corner, clutching their drum-tight stomachs. "Real smooth, Chandra," Stu said. Their laughter boomed and reverberated off the high ceiling.

Shaking, I looked down at my worn-out jeans,

Superman shirt, and tattered sneaks. "I need new threads."

"You need to learn how to talk." Tony's face was stained red with joy. "But yeah...I really want one of those jackets, the denim ones."

"Okay, fags," Stu griped.

"Caroline Ford just winked at me."

"You're both a bunch of fags...always talking about girls..."

"That doesn't even make any sense," I pointed out.

"Stu never makes sense," Tony said.

"I miss the old days. The no-girls-allowed days..." Stu dug his hand into the water clock, fishing out a toonie.

"Doesn't want girls around? Who's a fag now?" I splashed Stu in the face. Tony scruffed up his hair before getting off the bench.

We bought ourselves some new high-tops, and Tony got a sick jean jacket. I watched him pull his arms through the sleeves and wished I looked like him. When I saw my reflection behind him in the mirror, I got a fright. I'd imagined I was getting whiter from the skin bleaching, but my skin was stubborn, remained black as midnight. And despite countless hours of swimming and surfing, I was swathed in puppy fat. My tightly coiled and textured hair resembled a Jheri curl from all the humidity, chlorine, and sun.

Glowing under a halo of light, a neon-green

windbreaker caught my eye. "Gnarly." The light, soft fabric of my new jacket felt like cool water as I slipped into it.

We rolled out of there fresh as ice.

"EARTH TO DREAMER." Coach Lee dipped his foot into the pool, splashing me in the face.

"Don't mind Chandra, he's in love again." Tony nodded to Caroline, who sat cross-legged in the stands with her white brick phone in her lap.

"What's it to you?" I smiled to myself, dunking under the water. Crystalline bubbles escaped my nose and rose to the surface, like locusts leaving my lungs.

I swam so fast, Caroline's eyes on me, hers on my mind. I leapt off the white blocks like I was powered by electricity, streamlining all the way to the wall. I pulled through the neon-blue water, holding my breath for as long as I could, kicking and pulling. I didn't need to breathe, not with Caroline Ford as my girl.

Mid-set, my body burned all over and Indra's face appeared in my mind. I felt an immediate twinge beneath my breastbone. Figured the feeling would fade, but instead, it intensified. I swam faster to shake Indra out of my head.

"Righteous, dreamboat! You just shattered your best time by two seconds!" Coach yelled.

After practice I wriggled my tight jeans over my damp legs and caught a glimpse of my reflection in the steam-coated mirror. My midsection was a nebulous blob. No chiselled abs in sight. My face really was round like a full moon. I splashed some hard water on my face and sucked in my gut, glancing over at Tony, who slid his new denim digs over a sculpted six-pack. I envied his strong jawline and perfect skin. I pulled up the band of my underwear and zipped my new windbreaker over my flab.

That night, the blue-skinned woman rose, pearls of ocean cascading from her great, grooved forehead. She glowered at me as her arms became silver rivers. My pink bathtub was picked up by the current, and I arrived at the juncture of two-toned seas. A voice called out in a language that I knew but didn't speak. I faced the slate of midnight blue: Indra flailed in the dark sea, thrashing her arms against the choppy waves. I reached for her hand, but every time I clasped onto her, my guts would twist and I'd lose my grip.

I woke up drenched in foul-smelling sweat, feeling like I hadn't slept at all.

FRAGMENTED, BARELY TRUSTING THIS new self to balance on my skateboard, I kicked and pushed tentatively on the way to school as the cinder-rose sky turned blue. I spent the day like I was on the blocks, avoiding eye contact with Indra. After practice, I skipped dinner and skated over to the Flower Power House.

"Ooooh, shoot, Jill, come here," Rocky called. "Who is this child?"

Jill came into the living room from the kitchen eating a bowl of ramen. "Look at those electric threads! Give us a spin... Come on."

"Are you eating with paintbrushes?" I said.

"Didn't have anything else clean." Jill shrugged. "You want some?"

"Already ate," I lied, kneading my stomach with the side of my fist. There was something soothing about hunger pangs. An ethereal feeling of emptiness.

"Well, since you're a man now and everything, you want to try this?" Rocky passed me his joint. "Might give you an appetite."

"How old are you now, Moon?" Jill asked.

"Twelve."

Jill took a concerned bite of ramen.

"There's worse ingredients in Pop Rocks," Rocky said.

"One hit." Jill pointed her paintbrush chopsticks at Rocky with a sternness I wasn't used to.

"All right, Moon. So you know how when you're acting or singing you gotta really engage your diaphragm?"

"Yeah, 'course."

"That's it. But this is real important — before you inhale the weed into your lungs, you want to draw the smoke into your mouth, ya dig?" Rocky sucked the air into his mouth, real theatrical-like, looking like a puffer-fish. "Now take a breath, man."

"Mixes the dense smoke with the oxygen-rich air," Jill said, taking the joint from Rocky and following suit.

Rocky let air out like a smoke-breathing dragon. "Results in a more flavourful puff."

"All right, you hippies, let me try it already." I snatched the joint, which smelled like sweet wood. I sucked the smoke in, held it in my mouth for a good while, then breathed it in with the ocean air. It came back out like a cloud.

"Dang, Moon...you're like a weed prodigy," Rocky said.

"I know how to control my breath is all."

I slipped into a forest-green haze. Rocky and Jill were talking about taking off to Goa, something about walking the ancient yogic path. We puffed and passed and danced to Bobby Brown, then lay languid on the floor.

I clutched the deep piles of the stained shag carpet. "So many memories here."

"You're a sensitive flower, Little Moon," Jill said.

I clenched my teeth, sat up. "Am not."

"Ain't nothing wrong with it," she said.

"Means weak. Means gay," I snapped.

"You become one of those gay-bashing jocks, full dis-respect, my man. That attitude ain't welcome here." Jill gestured out towards the road.

"All the queers I know are tough as nails, but that's beside the point," Rocky said, running his fingers through his fro. "Only thing you should hate is hate, Little Moon."

But I was already high tide with hate for gentle things.

WHEN THE SECOND SNOW melted to reveal Indian plum, bleeding heart, and skunk cabbage, Tony and I filled the gap between school and swim practice playing Rambo tag in a row of residential scaffolding. We climbed up the half-constructed homes and scaled the skeletons of the buildings with cotton candy–like insulation oozing out the sides. Once in a while, we'd lose our foothold on a ledge and scrape our legs or elbows, maybe sprain an ankle — nothing too critical. Coach gave us fist bumps when we came to practice all dinged up; meant we were teaching the body to heal and regenerate. Meant we could handle pain like men were supposed to. Dangling from the floorboards, a surge of adrenalin rushed through my entire body that was almost as good as being in water.

My West Coast town was one of sand-caked scalps, unkempt hair, and callused feet. Kids with coral-scarred shins, barnacle-bruised arms, and rose-coloured skin from untreated sunburns, like this kid Cody I had wrapped in a headlock.

"Indra and Chandra stinking in a tree, K-I-S-S — Ow, let me go!"

I coiled my arm, toned from two-a-day swim practices, around his chafed, red neck. "No can do, space cadet. You're at the mercy of the black mamba."

He smelled like pit sweat and canned meat. The March rain hardened to hail, pelting bullets of ice on the temporary tin roof as Cody backed himself farther into a corner of pine planks.

Being Black was no cakewalk on the Canadian West Coast, but getting slumped together with the ragheads was just insulting. As a dark-skinned, coarse-haired kid from a half-Tamil, half-secular family, I was shunned by the cashew-skinned, silk-haired Indo-Aryans as much as I was by the Confederate-flag Codys of my area code. I wasn't Indian. Didn't speak their languages or pray to their gods.

"I'm not Hindu, dig?"

Cody tapped out. I kept my arm wrapped firmly around his neck for another second before releasing him.

"Now float," I said, kicking up a cloud of powdery dirt, which billowed at Cody's feet as he fumbled out of the half-built house.

"You're not Black, either! I saw your parents! They're fresh-off-the-boat Hindus!" he shouted before disappearing into the ice rain.

Tony and Stu whooped and heckled, throwing handfuls of gravel out the empty doorframe.

At practice later that afternoon, I dove into my chlorine chrysalis of chemical blue, shedding the skin of the day. I swam butterfly until the never-ending reel of being called "biscuit lip" and "Sambo" dissolved like the trail of bubbles behind me. I smacked the wall, thrusting my left elbow back before launching into a slick streamline, soaring along the red line.

Suddenly, I felt the dreaded hand-graze on the bottom of my foot that meant I wasn't swimming fast enough. That girl with the huge hair, already much taller and broader than I was, was gaining on me in both speed and strength. Drove me wild because I had no gas left to give.

Thirteen was the year we found our strokes. Three of us from A-group got scouted for winter club: Tony, the girl who wore two swim caps over her unruly hair, with an endearing face I could never forget and a ridiculous name I could never remember, and me. That meant Olympic-sized indoor pools, matching evergreen team suits, and an honest-to-God shot at being swimmers for real. Tone was duckweed, growing daily; his arms, now freakishly long, served as sculling oars. He could swim on one breath, too, something I still hadn't mastered. And he was lean and cut, unlike me — stunted and stocky. Fly was the only race where I had a chance at beating Tony, who was seeded ahead of me in every event. Though I was a swift freestyler, Tony had a good six or seven inches on me and flipper-like feet twice the size of mine. There was no technique on the planet that could compensate for my lack of height. But with fly? I became one with the infinite blue around me and swam like nirvana was on the other side of the pool. Like if I hit the wall fast enough, I'd transcend space and time. Lake swimming with Appa was a relic from a past life.

Draped over the edge of the sofa after practice that evening with milk in my eyes, like Coach Lee taught us to soothe the burn of the chlorine, I felt a sheath of soreness spread over my quads and shoulders. I thought of Rocky, who'd taken me under his raised fist since my family first landed in Canada. He'd taught me about the power embedded in my melanin. The narrative. Fast on our feet because our ancestors had outrun their oppressors. Smooth under pressure with eloquent tongues like the great MLK. Giving up Blackness would mean giving up the only brotherhood, the only sense of identity, I had. That thought was unbearable. When I wasn't swimming away from it, I had this panicked feeling that someone was on to me, that I'd be found out. As for what I'd be found out for, well, I still didn't know exactly.

I sat up and poured more milk into my eyes. Leaning my head back, I traced the grooves in the skip-trowel ceiling as milky tears trailed down my cheeks. I called out for clarity: "Were our ancestors slaves?"

"What are you on about?" Vathany lunged into the room in her metallic spandex leotard like some sort of space woman.

I turned my attention to Appa, who had just grumbled awake from a cat nap. "Appa, are we Black?"

"We're from places that no longer exist, and that aren't worth remembering," Vathany snapped. "Nations are a sin." She gestured to the thick stack of unopened *Watchtower* pamphlets on our tea-ring-and-crumb-covered coffee table.

Appa shifted his gaze to me and leaned in, speaking softly. "Your mother is from Eelam, the upper crust of what was once Ceylon, now called Sri Lanka."

"But what does that make me?" I groaned.

"A teenager who is too curious about everything," Appa chuckled. His impossibly round cheeks bloomed and blushed pink.

I glared with a rage and intensity only afforded to people in their thirteenth year of life.

Appa's shoulders lowered, and he emitted a staggered exhale before speaking. "In Sri Lanka, the Sinhalese call Eelam *Tamils*, like your mother, Black, but don't tell her I told you that. I am what some call a *Kaffir*, like the lime." Appa chuckled again. "Something of a mixed breed, or a mutt. Part Bantu slave, part Vedda, part Portuguese colonizer…God, who knows what else? I was adopted, you know. They said my father was a snake charmer. Not a good one, it seems, since the snakes were what killed him. Did you know a cobra bite can kill a human in minutes? And my mother…They said my mother lived in a cave and worshipped the cult of the dead. Perhaps that's how she met my father, ha! But you, Chandra." He grabbed my upper arms, and I realized both how much broader than Appa I had become and likewise how much frailer his grip. "You are Canadian. You don't know anything else."

Unsatisfied, I felt the lunar pull of my skate deck at the front door, an orbital lure outside the rings of Appa's murky answer.

The coral light of dusk spilled over the damp earth. I felt a sharp shift within my chest; an acrid loom of change hung around my mouth like unripe tomato. The cusp of spring smelled of high water and blooming lavender. I was quick to anger, couldn't sit still. Manhood was rising on the horizon like an oncoming wave, and it made me mean, restless, and competitive.

"What's with you?" Rocky asked.

I could feel him trying to make eye contact with me, but I ignored him and kept plucking a watery riff on my guitar. All this time I'd been called Black, and that alone was a hard enough truth. Now I had to solve for x and try to understand the obscure algebra of what it meant to be Black. Rocky was Black, that was for sure, but his skin was bark brown while mine was piano-key ebony.

"All right, all right…Moody Moon today. I can dig it." Rocky strummed a harmony that synced with mine like spring tide and a new moon.

"Ooooh, check these copacetic Casanovas! Sounds dynamite." Jill came crooning onto the porch, Dr. King limping after her. He wheezed and drooled all over the place, and I knew doggy heaven was right around the corner for him. Pained me to see it.

Rocky stopped playing. "Whatchu got there?"

Jill was clutching something in her lap. "Excavating some relics from Papa's chest."

Her grandfather had died the weekend prior.

Rocky reached out and took the newspaper clipping. "'The Kanadian Klowns Konklave... The South's band of KKK halfwits has fumbled its way to British Columbia dressed like kiddos in pillowcases...' Your granddaddy write this?"

"Mm-hm... I've got radical blood flowing through my veins." Jill swiped the article back and kissed it, then Rocky.

"Good, we're going to need that radical blood this weekend. Red Power's protesting against the logging in the old-growth forests up in Ukee."

"The KKK came here?" My heart fell to the soles of my feet.

"Not for long," Jill said.

Rocky's nostrils flared. "Long enough to lynch my great-uncle Frank." He crinkled his broad nose, put his guitar down, and pulled back from Jill. "Canada ain't all rainbows and Underground Railroads."

"Hey baby, you know I didn't mean it like that." Jill placed a gentle hand on Rocky's thigh. He flinched at first, then melted into her. They kissed and I wanted to throw up.

"I like to imagine those clowns watching us twist tongues from a jail cell." Jill's face was flushed red, her dark blue eyes dilated like she was hunting prey.

I stopped plucking my strings, placed my palm on the sound hole. "What's Red Power?"

"Like Black Power, but for American Indians," Jill said.

"First Nations and Native Americans, Jill, this ain't India." Rocky lightly shoved Jill away and turned to me, revealing his big, chipped teeth. "Look, Moon, this land — all of North America and South America — it was stolen by Europeans. The same ones who took people like you and me as slaves."

My stomach twisted. I folded sheepishly into myself, clamping my legs firmly together, hoping that Rocky couldn't see through my melanin into the tangled web of my ancestry. That he wouldn't know that, despite how black my skin was, I wasn't American Black.

"Think about it. What language we speaking?" Rocky asked.

"English." I shrugged.

"Where'd that come from?"

I paused quizzically, searched the thinning fog for an answer, and scoffed as it came to me. "England."

Rocky nodded.

"And in South America, Columbus and his merry

men from Spain raped, pillaged, and colonized their way through the land," Jill said under her breath. She nervously braided a tress of her hair, failing to mask the sting of Rocky's sudden coldness towards her.

"And that's why they speak Spanish there," I said, in time with my own realization.

"Right on. And me? I'm part Seminole and Cherokee on my mother's side. Native American." Rocky's shoulders were proud, his eyes stern, as he said this.

"What? I thought you were Black."

"I am," Rocky said.

I had more questions now than I'd arrived with. Though Nanaimo's unceded sands and Sitka spruce–laden lands belong to the Snuneymuxw First Nation, I didn't pay it much thought at thirteen. Like with the great coastal mountains visible along the horizon, I saw only the snow-capped peaks and thought little of what ancient life was beating, volcanic, underneath.

"Black has no nation," Jill said, leaning into Rocky.

He softened and pulled her onto his lap, kissed her neck. "You *are* some jive-turkey, radical girl, ain't you?" They were getting so close and breathing so hard, like they were about to eat each other.

"I'm gonna split." I slid off the porch swing, swung my guitar over my shoulder, and grabbed my board.

"Later, skater." Rocky bumped my fist without breaking eye contact with Jill.

"Peace, Moon." Jill flashed her fingers in a V.

I skated home wrestling my thoughts, comparing my face to Jimi Hendrix's, which was why I forgot to swerve around the pothole right in front of my house. It launched me off my board, palms first, onto the cement. My guitar twanged against the pavement. I looked down at my raw, bleeding palms and wanted to shatter the ground, wanted to fight the whole world. Instead, I clenched my fist and hammered it into the side of my thigh.

A pair of hairy brown arms helped me to my feet. "Ten points." Appa grinned. "I think that tumble earned you some watalappan."

I brushed dirt off my damaged guitar. "I hate watalappan," I seethed, shoving Appa's arms away, even though all I wanted was the taste of cardamom-spiced coconut custard, even though all I wanted was to be held by him.

"You hate watalappan?"

"I just want this fixed." I plucked at my guitar strings, all now brutally out of tune.

Appa took the guitar from my hands. "We'll take it to get fixed, but you have to come to the store with me first."

Appa's car reeked of second-hand smoke. I flicked on the classic rock station: Hendrix. I kicked my feet up on the dashboard, rolled the window down, and disappeared, surfing the sound waves of his guitar. Music had that rinsing effect, like water. And Appa was good at silence. He gifted me space to feel, knew there was a conversation going on in my head, and trusted the words would come out when my thoughts were aligned, like the tide with the shore.

In the beer-bottle-glass-and-pothole-filled parking lot all but one of the street lights were burned out. Underneath the dull fluorescence sat a set of strong shoulders that would have been entirely eclipsed by the shrub of black-cherry hair cascading over them had they belonged to a non-swimmer. The girl with the face and the nerve to graze my foot in a race pace sat on the curb in front of the liquor store with a curved spine, posture so poor Vathany would have regarded it as a sin. The girl touched — but did not pick — the weeds emerging out of the cracks in the pavement. The jingling front door swung open at the hip thrust of a tanned man with the same strange face, holding two six-packs of beer. He nudged her in the back with his knee and handed her a case when she got to her feet.

In the burning white hum of the freezer section, I hid behind Appa's swollen frame, afraid of being seen by one of the pretty white girls from school. He reached for a package of hot dogs, now a household staple that he'd once believed were made of dog meat. He also threw a few packages of tofu dogs into the red cart.

I retrieved the cold, firm plastic. "I don't eat these anymore."

"Why not?"

"They're non-food, all refined oil." Nothing to help me slash my times or the band of black blubber I was trying to free myself from.

When we got home the TV was on. Kitty pounced over the banister and meowed. I scooped her up in my arms with my bruised palms. Vathany burst out of the bathroom, a newly opened pot of fairness cream in her hand. She liked to bleach herself to the sound of the news. Forecast said spring snow. Then, the image of three Black teenagers who had been beaten to death in Toronto flashed onscreen. Tattered yellow police tape flapped around the bloodstained street, intercut with burning crosses and clips of Dr. King's assassination. Then something about the Snuneymuxw Nation and thousands of filleted chum being dumped in the ocean.

I polished off my bowl of spinach, broccoli, eight egg whites, and watercress, debating whether I deserved a side of black-pepper rice. Ultimately, I decided against it and reached for the remote, flicking the channel away from the news, and my hunger.

TONY WAS MY BEST FRIEND, but in a bruised way. I found it harder and harder to look at or be happy for him. His lighthearted, golden demeanour was as tall and effortless as his trim, toned body. His mind was never weighed down or darkened by the petty vanity that permeated mine. Meanwhile, I'd eliminated nearly everything from my diet to reduce my aerodynamic drag. People flocked to him like pill bugs to a beach fire, every deck mom and daughter serially swooning over Tonyboy and his ocean eyes. Locker room talk swirled about our team's best swimmer, even though our times were within milliseconds of each other. Worse was the way he wasn't aware of any of it. Or was it that I saw myself rippling out in his inverted reflection? The stocky, dark afterthought that made him even more beautiful in comparison.

At regionals Tone and I sat hip bone to hip bone, centre lane champs. I don't remember the ribbons or the feeling of getting a best time. What I remember is the Powell River kids to my left and right in the semis leaning so far away from me their butt cheeks barely scraped the edge of the bench. I was Moses, parting the rednecks. I couldn't stomach anything before marshalling and felt as though I'd accomplished something with my emptiness. The fact that I'd shed weight meant more to me than the fact that I'd shed time and was right on Tonyboy's heels.

It was the free final — the most important race — and we were next on the blocks. The top three finalists got to go on to provincials. I sat in the outer lane, steeped in chlorine, knees knocking and teeth chattering. Two other boys sat on the bench with Tony and me: a kid from Saanich and one from Cowichan Bay.

The lady in marshalling with feathered hair huffed and muttered to herself, "Didn't realize this was a southern state."

I turned to Tony, who hung his head. Powell River had scratched from the race. All four swimmers. Tony told me he'd heard the boys in the bleachers, heard them say they didn't want to swim in the same pool as a — he couldn't fit his mouth around the word. By the way he strained his lips, I could tell that he understood. The power of that word, even unsaid, had a visceral effect on me. Sure, the shock had dulled, but I was not and would never be numb to the sting of it. A black stone sank to the sandbed of my chest, and I was thankful to have Tony in this moment.

"Don't sweat it. Pow-Riv are a bunch of hicks anyways," said Lane Five as he tucked his mane into a faded Cowichan Bay swim cap. The ends of his hair were bleached white from chlorine.

"Yeah, bet they're all related," scoffed the bald Saanich boy, all cystic acne and teeth.

Laughter soothed the burn for the briefest of moments. But it leaked back in with the pre-race silence. The cold crawling up the backs of my thighs from the damp bleachers made me shudder. I still hadn't eaten and could taste acid in my mouth.

Tonyboy was in the middle lane, seeded to win. Saanich was taller and leaner than I was, a genetic advantage. Cowichan Bay was consistently a few milli-seconds ahead. I stared down at my short, black legs, shivering with adrenalin.

The marshal ushered us to the diving blocks. The pool, untouched after its hour of rest, was cerulean Jell-O. Turquoise scales spread up my dark legs, wrapped around my torso. My hands and feet grew webbed.

Beep. *Soft arch of foot against the gritty white blocks.*

Beep. *Take your mark — squeeze your ears with your shoulders, don't let any air in, tuck your chin into your chest, lean ever so slightly forward.*

Beep. *Fly — propel your body into the air, glide into the water, dolphin kick, dolphin kick, dolphin kick, kick, kick, kick. You don't need to breathe.*

Flickers of light. Goggles slowly filling with a thin layer of water. Exhaling white bubbles into infinite blue, I followed the thick black lane line at the bottom of the pool, swam without a single sip of air. Swam, swam, swam, smacked the touchpad, whipped my head out of the water, quenched my lungs with sugary oxygen. I looked up to the glowing red numbers on the score clock.

I'd shattered the meet record. I'd won.

9

The River

Scəẃaθən; xʷməθkʷəẏəm,
səlilwətał, Sḵwx̱wú7mesh, 1952

Junior started sliding scratched records in with our
bills at Vie's. First, it was Cab Calloway. Then, Duke
Ellington. After that, he hit us with Count Basie and
Charlie Parker. Artists we never heard outside of Angel
Man's alley — or Hogan's Alley, as folks call it these
days. The music filled me with a kind of fire cloud. Sent
lightning strikes through my system, raising my blood
sugar and frequency. Made me feel like I could see more
wavelengths of the light spectrum. Beatings from Tobias
were brutal but uncommon, and the hard coating wasn't
enough to make my life miserable now that it contained
the undouseable wildfire of jive.

Every time Vince and I stopped in for chicken

and records on our way between Clark Park and the beach, Zenora gifted us a story. She told us that during Prohibition, Vie's Chicken had doubled as a speakeasy. When the blue of the day was overtaken by the indigo night sky, all the thirsty railroad workers and immigrants from around Hogan's Alley would float on down to Vie's. Hell, I could see it. I looked around and pictured the place bursting with life, liquor, and jive.

Vince used up all the dough we rattled from phone booths to buy a record player. His brother Stanley and the rest of the gang were usually out hustling or rumbling with the Italians during the day. During those sweet hours alone in Vince's basement, we practised jive. Enchanted by the way jive dancers moved — swift and weightless, like Siamese fighting fish in water — we memorized the names of the steps: chasse, accordion, flamenco, Wurlitzer, swizzlestick. We danced until our entire bodies were drenched in sweat and every muscle ached and glittered.

First, we learned to count on a simple six-beat sequence. *1-2-3-ah-4-5-ah-6.* Then we learned the rock step. *Left foot step back, right in place.* It was like rocking back and forth on a boat. Easy enough, and hypnotic as hell when we did it to the beat. I just visualized being on Ray's deck.

Then it started to get a bit trickier with the triple step: *Left, right, left. Chasse, chasse.*

"You're doing it backwards," Vince said, squinting and running the back of his hand over his stubble.

"No, I'm not... Well, I was doing it on purpose." I touched my own hairless face, hot and flushed. Shit-grabbing habits die hard. I was a goddamn mirror for the whole universe, it seemed, inverting everything.

"Oh, like being the girl?" Vince fluttered his eyelashes mockingly. His hair had started to curl ever since it started appearing on his face. Sparse, wiry hairs reached out of his neck and chest. The odd zit, too. Not me. I was the same Ronny, only stretched out over my bones like elastic.

"Well... yeah, I guess. Someone's gotta be the girl, else we're a pair of queers."

"Well, you don't have any facial hair, so I guess it fits."

Vince held his hands out to me, smug grin plastered across his face. He started to dance, fumbling foot leading. There was a warm, gold security in the air, that pure glee I'd only ever felt at the booms. Dancing made me feel like I was a river myself: free and flowing. I was a good two inches taller than Vince, so it was easy to spin him. He twisted on his feet like a ham-handed ballerina. Eventually, our footwork smoothed out. We closed the practice with a botched catapult, sopping in sweat.

"Jesus. If anyone sees us, they'll think we're a couple," I said. We were still holding hands.

"I'd slit their throats before they had a chance to think."

I wheezed with laughter. It was like this dancing was witchcraft.

"WHERE YOU OFF TO, SCHWEINHUND?" Tobias asked as I stepped out of the house on a cool, bright Saturday.

"Library."

He grabbed me by the cuff of my shirt. "Don't you dare lie to me in my own home."

"I ain't, I swear."

He let me go with a skeptical eye. The electricity of violence jolted from his fingertips, and the after-sizzle in my skin didn't lift until I was on the boxcar, flying over the river.

I'd developed a routine. Skip school to jive, dash home to milk the cows, practise moves while I shovelled the cow shit. It would have been quite a sight to see — a wire-thin alley mutt covered in shit, jive dancing for an audience of cows. But, in my mind, I wasn't in some shit-smelling barn, nor was I a scuffed-up alley mutt. I was a dark-skinned, white-toothed Jive King, the type on the posters at the cinema. I'd go to bed every night with my legs all jittery, eager to wake up into a new day, to hop on the train back to the Clark Park house to dance with Vince.

When I arrived that night Vince had a shit-eating grin on his face. "I've got a surprise for you. Follow me."

We walked down Granville Street to the cinema, and Vince pulled two tickets out of his pocket.

"Shoot, you paid? You spent real dough?" I snatched a ticket out of his callused hand. "How civilized."

Vince pursed his lips. "Nah, stole 'em out of some schnook's ragtop."

"They always leave the roofs down!" I snapped my fingers. "Forbidden fruit." Countless times while strolling through the heart of the West End, I'd see an unattended Cadillac Coupe deVille or Rolls-Royce and fantasize about driving it off to Harlem, where the jive was alive and there was never any rain.

The sound of sugary giggles behind us caught our attention. Two glitterati-looking skirts: one was willowy with gold eyelashes, a glossy victory roll hairstyle, and skin so fair it looked like it'd never seen the sun; the other had cashew skin, a classy chassis, and a pearl choker that looked real easy to lift.

"Hey, sweetheart," I chirped like a reflex, expecting nothing more than an eye roll. Instead, they smiled. A spark jittered down my spine, filled me with a tangle of adrenalin and pride.

Vince took the lead, speaking to the pearls more than the dame attached to them. "You dollies wanna see a flick?"

Around this time, I had started looking at girls a lot. To my surprise, they started looking back. The gang always had dames lying around the house, but they were the damaged, loudmouth types. Ones who had been in foster care like me. They drank and swore and painted their eyelids with hideous blue eyeshadow like the Canton Alley call girls. One girl named Molly who we all called Mouse told me that if I wanted to become a man, all I had to do was let her know. But I didn't want anyone from the gang house. I wanted a West End girl out for a flick after Sunday service. One with maraschino-cherry lips, skin clear as holy water, and ribbons fastened in her silken curls. One with a Colgate smile and a cardigan tied around her drum-tight waist. The church tried to pry the girls' eyes away from ducktail-haired degenerates like Vince and me, but that only made us crave each other more. All those girls saw were suntanned boys with cigarette smirks, stolen leather jackets, and bodies chiselled from dancing and freight hopping. Boys their white-handed, argyle-vest-wearing kind couldn't take in a rumble. Reflected in the glint of their bright eyes, I saw possibility. A way to my own gleaming white colonial house with blue trim and an Ambrosia tree. And a ballroom, just for dancing.

We sat front row at the matinee. The unspoken pact was that Vince had Pearls, and Goldie was mine to court, but as always, both girls were locked on Vince. Even though Vince wasn't the least bit handsome, his impenetrable coolness drove the rich girls wild.

I leaned in close enough to feel the heat coming off Goldie's neck; her perfume was harsh and floral. She was facing Vince, whose eyes were fixed on the screen. She kept flicking him in the back of the arm and blaming it on Pearls. So I tried flicking Goldie, first feather-light on her shoulder, then firmer on her thigh. She either didn't notice my advances or was ignoring them. I was nothing to this girl. Nothing more than a danger kiss. A slumber-party story. Something to make her dull life momentarily interesting. Eventually, I gave up on the girl and dove into the world onscreen: Harlem jive.

DAYLIGHT SEEMED UNNATURALLY bright when we left the darkness of the cinema. Pearls draped her arm around Vince's shoulder as we strode past the ticket booth. "You hepcats wanna get a sundae with us?" I was surprised the choker was still around her neck.

"Nah, we're going home." Vince brushed off her perfect arm.

Home? Instead of scarfing Neapolitans drizzled in hot fudge with two glitterati knockouts, Vince wanted to go home to a decrepit basement full of drugged-up hoods with nothing to eat besides canned beans?

I held onto the base of a cherry tree, feet stuck to the pavement. "Ah, hell, come on, Vince. I'm pining for ice cream, and these dollies are easy on the eyes."

Vince just shook his head. "You coming or not?"

I leaned towards the West End angels, but how the hell would I handle myself without Vince? "Sorry, ladies, we'll see you around."

Their deflated shoulders suggested they were unfamiliar with rejection. On the way back to the gang house I kept thinking about how we'd messed things up with those girls, but that regret dissolved as soon as we started dancing.

Vince pretended to be the girl again, and I laughed. "I'm gonna close my eyes and pretend you're pretty."

But Vince's hands were cold, thick, and tough as leather. He smelled like cigarillos, sweat, and a faint glaze of Four Roses. I pictured the girl from the cinema, her gold eyelashes shimmering in the light... Then I imagined Angel's little cousin with the swan neck and the perfect skin, and I felt a pair of lips on mine.

My eyes popped out of my skull as I shoved Vince off me. "What the hell?!"

Vince laughed. "I'm just *messing* with you, tulip."

"You're a damned queer." I wiped my mouth with my forearm so hard I nearly tore my lips off.

As soon as the words left my mouth, Vince seized up. His silver eyes became razor blades, and he put his fist in his pocket, grabbing onto his switchblade. "Don't ever call me that," he said through clenched teeth.

In Vince's face I saw my own reflection, the same

blind rage that took over anytime someone called me a bastard.

We parted sorely that night. As the train jolted to a halt at my stop, I was still shaken up, but I made my mind up that Vince was just playing a trick on me. That was all. And it wouldn't happen again. By the time I got back to the barn, I'd already forgiven him.

TOBIAS WAS IN THE STABLE, lashing the hell out of Moby-Dick. She wailed like crazy, her big white body rippling, kicking helplessly in the corner of the barn while the monster whipped her. Her enormous eyes pleaded with mine, begging me for help.

Tobias noticed her gaze and quickly turned his head. "Schweinhund..."

I swung my arm to hit him, but he grappled me down to the sharp hay. Soon, he was going after me with the horsewhip again. A blue-white fire consumed me and I noticed the teeth of a pitchfork glinting in the hay. I went limp, and the moment Tobias let up, I seized the pitchfork.

"Take that, you Hun!" I screamed and speared him through his foot.

"Sheiße! I'm going to kill you! I'm going to kill you!" Tobias shrieked. A black-cherry lake of blood formed in the dirt. I could see the tendons in his foot sticking out like bits of chicken liver.

I ran out of the barn into the chill night, still stinging from the lashes. I grabbed my bike and pedalled towards the river as fast as I could. The bitter air smacked me in the chest and made it hard to breathe. It leaked into my ears and made my jaw throb something awful, but I knew I couldn't stop. I wasn't ready to see Vince again yet, so I decided to wander past the docks and look for Ray's boat. I felt like my heart and lungs were going to fold in on themselves. All I wanted to do was leave my body. Swing out of it. Run off the booms and plunge underwater.

Like a maniac, I started jiving in the moonlight. A few frenzied kicks and swizzlesticks with the wind. On the edge of the docks, I danced in the darkness, flailing my lanky limbs to the whir of the river current. I lindy-hopped until my lungs lifted back up and my heartbeat settled.

Up ahead, I saw the dim lantern glow on Ray's docked boat and felt a light flicker on inside me. I dragged my bike up against the dock gate, hooking in the front wheel and handles as best as I could. Sloshing water and the wooden creak of the dock echoed as I ran towards the butt of Ray's boat. I stopped, breathed, then rang the bell.

"Huh? Who's it?" Ray came out, grunting, rubbing his haggard face. In the orange glow of his lantern I could see his skin had liver spots now, and his hair had gone completely silver to match Stó:lō. Shadows pooled in the deepened lines in his face. He blinked and squinted in my direction. "Who's there?"

"It's Ronny."

"Ronny... Ronny?!" He hauled me onto the rocking boat. "Jesus. You look like hell. How skinny are you?"

I opened my mouth to speak, but my throat grew tight. I felt all the water in my body rising up to my lower eyelids as my heart anchored in the bed of my chest, so I just shut my mouth, sat down, and stared.

"Ah, well," Ray grunted, pulling a flask out of his chest pocket. He took a swig and handed it to me. The boat rocked softly as I chugged down the liquid fire. Swig by swig, the liquor took my mind off everything. I looked out at the white stars reflected in the water.

"Saw Seelkee in the swamps a few weekends ago," Ray said.

"Ah, that ain't real." I stabbed my tongue against my cheek, pursed my lips.

"Sure as hell is. Rose out of the murky water, a black serpent with two hideous horse heads, intricate red scales. Pray you never meet one. And if you do, don't you dare turn your back, or you'll puke your guts out."

A chill ran up the backs of my ears. "Tell me the hexapus story again," I said, looking into the depths. The silver half moon rippled in the black water like a ribbon in the wind.

"Musta told you that story a hundred times. Jagger's favourite."

"Jagger's dead," I said, immediately sorry for the bite in my bark.

"Yeah. Yeah, he is." Ray seemed to understand. "Ho-hum," he sighed. He stood up, still limber enough to raise his leg over the rail.

He told me the story, the same way he'd always done, as if it were the first time. Instantly, I fell asleep.

THE NEXT MORNING, Ray gave me a cigarette and some bannock for breakfast before kicking me off the boat. I told him I'd be back sometime, but neither of us knew when that would be.

I hopped the train down to Hogan's Alley for a meal, thinking about how the hell things between Vince and me could ever go back to normal. An army of pigeons loomed on the power lines, dropping shit bombs on the laundry below. Maybe I'd take a polar bear dip down at Kits to soothe the lash wounds, settle my nerves a bit. Hell, I'd stabbed Tobias with a pitchfork. My head was a tangled fishnet.

"Eh, bianco!" I felt a sharp bullet in my neck. The skinny wop who'd thrown a rock at me had two thick-necked friends with him. In their pressed zoot suits they closed in like pinstriped vultures.

A high-yellow girl with coarse hair fastened into a bun froze like a stunned deer, a soccer ball clasped between her hands. The ball dropped and rolled when the Italians waved her inside her house. The Indian woman pulling fuchsia fabric off the clothesline abandoned her laundry and followed suit. This alley was wop territory, after all. Without Vince or Angel Man by my side, I was a lone alley mutt in the wrong neck of the woods.

"Fellas, I ain't gonna be any trouble, just passing through."

"Empty your pockets, snow." The skinny wop flipped out his switchblade and held it to my throat. "See that bloodstain on the blade? That's from one of yours."

I hadn't been jumped into the Clark Park gang yet, but I was always with Vince, and that was all his enemies needed to know. This skinny guy was talking shit, but I turned my pockets inside out anyway. I was fourteen and scrawny as a lamppost. Coins jingled as they fell to the uneven pavement. A thick-neck with a scar bent down to pick up the change. I kicked him square in the mug, leapt over him, and blitzed into the burnt umber of daybreak.

"Oi!" The Italians clamoured behind me as I booked it towards the deep red horizon.

I arrived at the gang house in a glaze of sweat. When I stopped moving, it pooled on my upper lip, in my armpits, and in the trench of my spine. I took a seat on the front steps, vibrating, and pulled out a cigarillo. Jive music oozed out of the house and into the street, somehow matching the orange-red of the day. My heart smashed like cymbals in a quick-tempoed swing song. I heard the chortling of Vernon and Lyle, the older Clark Park cats, the clanging of bottles, the cackling of girls. It was just after sunrise and the party was still going strong. Every night, folks would drink cheap beer, moonshine, rye and seven, and what we called panty remover. Everybody smoked, and a few of the big wheels did cocaine and heroin, but I learned real quick not to mess with that stuff.

Mouse came bursting out the door for a light. She nearly flew off the steps, her makeup smeared. "Ronny? The hell you doing out here? Shoot…were you here all night? I didn't think I drank that much…"

"Had a run-in with the Italians this morning."

"The Eye-talians? Shit." Mouse crouched down beside me, her breath hot and smelling like alcohol and dope. "You all right, baby boy?" She gave me a slobbery kiss on the cheek.

"I'm fine." I shrugged her off.

"Mouse? Get your tight little ass back in here!" Stanley stuck his ostrich-like neck out the screen door. "Ronny? What the hell are you doing out here?"

"Jesus, you lot give a warm welcome." I massaged my temples.

"Ronny's here?" Vince clambered in the background.

I was dragged inside for a drink, and the day quickly escaped. The big wheel disc jockey Red Robinson made an appearance that night, so Vince and I decided to show off our jive dance moves.

"Hey, Mouse, give me your scarf!" Vince said.

Mouse obliged, tying her pink scarf around his lodge-pole pine of a neck before pulling a tube of liquefying lipstick out of her purse. "Pucker up." She glided the tacky, melting red all over his thin lips. Laughter flooded the house.

When I was dancing, I felt that same sensation of being snapped into my body I got swinging over the booms. Like I was suddenly real.

"Wooo! Them's ducky shincrackers!" Red Robinson whooped, slapping his thigh with his ham shank of a hand before taking another toke.

Just as we were feeling real good and alive, Jessica, a rickety bottle blond in need of a meal, came shrieking down the stairs. "Somebody better check on Billie!"

The whole group of us scampered upstairs. I hovered over Vince's sharp, damp shoulder. Billie was in the bathtub, blue skin and white lips, limp as a dead snake, with a needle in his arm. Soon, a squad car arrived, and John Law was lugging his lifeless body away.

At the end of that night, Stanley and his squad of zooter degenerates pummelled the living hell out of me against a chain-link fence in Clark Park. I moved in with Vince and his brothers with a cracked rib and two shiners, bluer than my eyes. Suppose I took Billie's place in the gang.

10

The Sea

Snʊˈneɪməxʷ, 1986

In bronze September, I got a postcard in the mail — a painting of a lithe, long-haired, honey-ring-skinned man with four arms sitting in a lotus above the ocean. He held a pink seashell in his left hand.

> *Hey Moon,*
> *Arrived safe in Goa. Never seen such a gorgeous*
> *coastline, for real. Palm trees taller than pine.*
> *Cows just lying on the beach. Water like blue glass.*
> *Jill sends her love and says make sure you read*
> *more than you smoke.*
> *Power,*
> *Rocky*

By the time Jill and Rocky left town, I was sixteen and way over Caroline, who'd hacked off her long blond hair. I'd been locking eyes with this girl Paula, total stone-cold fox. She had that Valley girl tangerine skin and crimped, snow-blond hair up in a high side ponytail. She traced her thin lips with high-voltage lip gloss — a loud blend of galactic pink and purple. I had swiped Tonyboy's spot in centre lane and in the hearts of the deck bunnies. University scouts lined the bleachers at practices and meets. I kicked and pulled, watched the bubbles seething as I stared at the red line. Flip turn, streamline. Kick, kick, kick.

After swim practice, we took to smoking weed, got off Stu's older brother, in the dilapidated buildings where we used to play Rambo tag. It made everything hilarious.

"Chan, do the Shakespeare thing again," Tony wheezed. Smoke billowed around his face, which had turned azalea pink.

I perched on a heap of concrete and took on the shape of Lavatch, slapping my own ass. "'It is like a barber's chair that fits all buttocks; the pin-buttock, the quatch-buttock, the brawn-buttock, or any buttock!'"

"That's high art," Tony declared.

I snatched the joint from him, toked, and exhaled a cloud of smoke. "No, that's *high* art."

Tony and Stu crumbled in a current of laughter, clutching their stomachs as tears ran down the sides of their faces. I clicked my heels and cartwheeled. We shot the shit for hours, laughing ourselves sober, at which point we skated to the gas station in a lucid purple haze.

What happened next was Stu's idea, but he'll tell you it was mine. Our skateboards and crushed Slurpee cups were upturned on the pavement, baking in the sun. Our jeans were cranked down to our ankles: two full moons and one new moon, shining for all Nanaimo to see. It was all adrenalin and the nickel-saccharine aftertaste of diet sour cherry as the cool, crisp rush of traffic lashed our bare backsides. Until the sound of a wailing siren swelled.

"Fuck," Tony said.

He and I hiked up our pants, grabbed our boards, and blew that Popsicle stand. I swerved around the corner and glanced back to see Stu in spaz mode. Pants still around his ankles, platinum shag hair flying everywhere. He'd tripped, fallen flat on his face, his bare ass up in the air, surrendering to the cops like a white flag.

Caught between laughter and tears, Tony and I kicked and pushed through the suburbs of Nanaimo, past the kaleidoscope of turning maple trees — bright green leaves bursting into flames of crimson, tangerine, and lemon yellow. We skated over the crunch of leaves, swerving over potholes, gasping briny, putrid air. The smell of rotting whale flesh chased me home, waxed along the cove, waned in the curve of my cul-de-sac. A dead whale had washed ashore on the weekend. I felt like I might hurl on the hot sidewalk.

Tripping over my unfastened shoelace before conking my face on my front door, I groaned into the house, skateboard deck tucked under my armpit. I massaged my throbbing nose bridge, gently closed the door, and ran a damp palm across my chest to calm my pulse.

Vathany'd recently met a Tamil woman at Kingdom Hall she called Auntie, but no one could clarify how we were related. Auntie could not have been more than four foot ten. Her features were warm and round. She dressed in bright colours — bougainvillea fuchsia and peacock teal — and wore a red putu in the middle of her forehead, which looked to me like a globule of dried blood. Auntie had taken two war orphans of indeterminate ages named Moorthy and Bagira under her wing before fleeing the bloodstained beaches of Jaffna. They were staying with us in our already limited space for an undefined period of time before settling somewhere east near Toronto, where there were enough Tamils to be considered a community.

Moorthy had alarming sea-green eyes, camel-brown skin, and a mop of thick black hair that had fallen out of his scalp in irregular lunar mare patches from stress. Bagira was brittle-boned and fine-featured, with vitiligo that wrapped around his neck like a white vine. They spoke broken English in high, Carnatic voices. Both were timid and mild-mannered and reminded me painfully of Indra.

Their visit prompted Vathany to start speaking in tangled tongues and deep-frying everything. As the TV droned in the background, we would sit across from each other in the living room, drinking boiling-hot tea in the searing summer heat. I could feel the layer of oil in the air, the grease leaking into my bloodstream, and the undulating tambura twang of whatever creole they spoke irritated me. It sounded like they were riding over hilly terrain on horseback after inhaling helium. The shrinking space, segregating sounds, and unbreathable adipose air led me to avoid home altogether.

As I came upstairs, the smell of frittering fish croquettes made my stomach twist. Appa was asleep on the couch, his protruding belly rising and falling with each whistling snore. I turned the stove down, scraping the black ash of singed mackerel and potato towards the edges of the pan, soothed by the cloud of warmth and suddenly seduced by the sin of salt and fat.

Vathany jolted out of the bathroom. Her staticky, box-fried hair rose above her head like the dorsal fins of a lionfish.

"It was burning," I said.

"Stop yelling. You'll wake him."

"Oh? This is yelling, got it. So, like, what do you call the Sri Lankan seagull screech y'all keep me awake with every night? I'm about to report you to the landlord for violating noise ordinance since everyone else in this ancient apartment needs hearing aids, apparently."

"I'm awake, it's fine. Hush." Appa sucked his teeth and rolled his eyes, bloodshot and tired. He combed his thin wisps of black hair, yawning with all of his body.

As we gathered around the coffee table, I stared intently at Vathany's angular face, caked in powder. She pulled at her clotted eyelashes. I turned to Appa. Thick rings framed his sad eyes, and dark blotches had formed all over his weathered skin. He had the defeated demeanour of a failed freedom fighter.

The doorbell rang, And I looked over my shoulder to see the white and blue bonnet of a police car. *Drag.* Cold sweat pooled in my pits and under my nose. I was going to ralph my heart up into the Jehovah's Witness cookie tin, still pulsing with a slosh of stale shortbread and questionable thumbprint jam biscuits.

Appa cocked his head and rose to answer the door, an inconvenient but refreshing sign of life. Standing there was the great blue omniscience that somehow knew where I lived. My father flinched at the sight of the fuzz, collected himself, and offered the officer a fish croquette, which he declined with an upturned nose. Fuzzy had a red face crammed between a bushy, brown chevron moustache and one long eyebrow. He shoved himself inside our home and up our stairs, painting everything with a cruel, corporate aura. He sat on the edge of the sofa, shovelling his mouth full of stale shortbread. White crumbs gathered in his moustache, which seemed to have gained sentience. I hadn't eaten any creature who swam, walked, or flew since I was young enough to believe our oceanspray bush was a flightless cloud, but given the choice between a fish croquette and a Witness biscuit, I'd've reconsidered.

The fuzz looked at me, then at Appa, and softened his manner. "Your son and his buddies were flashing their bums."

Righteous.

Appa raised an eyebrow and coughed. "Sorry?"

"Mooning people. On the highway. In Canada, that's a crime. Public indecency." The cop placed his hand on his gun, and I stiffened.

Appa turned to me. "So...you're into that sort of thing?"

I thrashed my head no. "We were just messing around." I made eye contact with the sentient moustache, channelled my most articulate sitcom voice. "Sir, I sure am sorry. It won't happen again."

Fuzz frowned at my compliance. His crumb-blossomed moustache went on and on about the merits of integrating into society, about morality and what to do with bootstraps (the thing about bootstraps that everyone forgets is you have to have them in order to pull them up). When he issued the hundred-dollar fine I held back all the profanities available to me. Figured I deserved an Academy Award for the smile I donned as I handed him last year's envelope of unused Not-Christmas money. He sealed the interaction with a clean, blue-door slam.

Vathany reached across the sofa and whacked me on the side of the head. I had expected that. What I had not expected was the speckle of stardust under her jaw, the first signs of damage from all the skin bleaching. Her hair, once shimmering black, was now limp, yellow, and fragile. She was thin. So thin that I didn't fear her striking me a second time, figured her hand would shatter like glass. Hers was a beauty that looked painful to maintain. A limp celery stick curling itself into translucence.

"What kind of example are you setting for your cousins?" Vathany squeezed my neck with her brittle fingers before clicking out of the room.

"They aren't my cousins," I muttered under my breath.

I braced myself for Appa, a wooden smack or a strong word, but instead, he laughed. A deep, low laugh. He clutched his globe-like belly, which had doubled in size over the past months, and his eyes welled with water. I searched his face for stories of his youth — for tales of mango-liqueur chugging, elephant tipping, or peacock riding. Of challenging other men to cinnamon-snorting contests. He smiled at me and placed his hand firmly on my shoulder, as if to say, *I get it.*

"She is right, though. You have to be careful with the police. Looking like you...born where you were, you can't get away with what your friends do."

My father usually kept his stories to himself, but with Moorthy and Bagira around, Tamilian creole spilling out of the cracks of the makeshift guest room, tales started to uncoil and serpentine out of the seagrass basket of his memory. How we dark-skinned Dravidians were seen as inferior to the Indo-Aryans, who considered themselves adjacent to white Europeans. That's why they hated us.

"Even Gandhi was a racist twat." Appa swayed back and forth, sucking his teeth before telling me of his adopted brother, who was as dark and reckless as I was, and who drowned in a shallow shoal after a coconut fell on his head. "Coconuts kill a lot of people, more than leopards." They also sustained life on the island.

Appa spoke, mostly, of secret surf breaks: white sand beaches like pulverized diamonds and perfectly peeling crystal barrels enclosed by baobab trees. He also spoke of the day he woke up to them painted red with Tamil blood.

"Stop talking about Eelam." Vathany fanged venom from the rear of the bathroom. "It's not real."

Her way of coping was to seem charmed, a split-consciousness ready to strike when necessary. She changed her hair and skin colour, speech patterns and belief systems — at first believing she could box-dye the memories out, eventually realizing that wasn't possible. You can shed skin but not memory.

WE SWERVED AROUND THE burgundy cedar roots that had broken out of the concrete roads in protest. A family of black-tailed deer crossed our path, gnawing leisurely on dandelions, completely unfazed by our presence. Tony drove his '72 Civic tentatively, like a whisper, over the dirt road. Now that he had his licence, we road-tripped at every opportunity. My eyes were drawn sharply to a large, painted red fist on the side of a dilapidated white building framed by sweetgrass, the golden buds dancing in the spring breeze like scintillating stars. Above the blood-red fist were the words *LAND BACK*.

"Can't believe I had to pay a hundred bucks for mooning hicks," I moaned.

"Dude, you got fined?" Tony had one hand gingerly on the steering wheel, the other in his lap. His legs were so long they came up to his chest, like he was driving a clown car.

"Yeah… Wait, you didn't?"

"Nah, man."

"Stu?"

"Don't think so."

"That's whack."

"For real, especially because it was Stu who told the cops where you lived."

"He fucking what?"

"Yeah. Cops caught him and immediately asked where his Black friend lived. Kid folded like a tent."

I stifled my anger, saving it for the water. And for Stu the next time I saw him. We were on our way up island to get a taste of the thirteen-foot swells that graced a discreet local jewel concealed by the giant old-growth cedars on rez territory. Tony'd heard tales of white surfers having their tires shanked by aggro Natives, but the prospect of catching a rare, glacier-blue river-mouth wave was worth the risk.

"Stole their land and now their waves." Tony's stifled chuckle was laced with discomfort. A thick cloud of tension billowed between us.

We parked on a small patch of dirt where the shoreline was visible, suited up, unstrapped and waxed our boards. A surfer with long, ebony hair and cheekbones carved from granite emerged from the water. His hawk-like eyes narrowed at the sight of us. We nodded a silent acknowledgement and kept our distance as we paddled out through a lattice of red kelp. He and the other local-locals bobbing in the swell had dibs on the waves. We knew that.

The long-haired rider surfed with an unmatched fluidity, carving the generous river-mouth barrels with celestial artistry. This guy was so in his element, so connected to the waves, he barely even noticed anyone else was in the water. I felt goofy and alien in comparison, with my stiff and calculated technique. Even Tony, who surfed laid-back and stylish, looked out of place next to him and the other rez surfers, who seemed to know this particular break like it was a close relative.

This place had an enigmatic energy that I couldn't get enough of. The giant cedars and the pulsing ocean tangled with the jade river current. Nature dominated the space in a way that was enticing and made all buildings looked feeble. But the territory felt bruised, too, for reasons I didn't fully grasp. I sensed that I had to be properly welcomed into this landscape, and I hadn't been. My sesh, though full of clean, uncrowded rides, felt wrong.

DURING SWIM PRACTICE THAT EVENING, I was still thinking of the river-mouth swells on the rez, dreaming of open water. The chemically neon pool and plastic, potted trees that framed the tiled decks just didn't do it for me. How would it feel to surf Appa's crystal breaks? Peach moonstone sand, uncrowded aquamarine water, and curved coconut palms. What was the ache of losing that?

Post-practice, Tony and I rolled up to my suburb, the car windows rolled down to allay the reek of chlorine, BO, and brine. My skin was dry as sandpaper from the combination of seawater, sun, and harsh chemicals. As we neared my home, it became clear that the elephant-like sound of the Kanvidutumbu flute and tambura growing louder and louder was not merely the intrusive elevator music in my head.

"Here's fine!" I cranked open the door of the car while it was still in motion.

"Whoa, dude! What the hell?" Tony brought the car to a screeching halt.

A sinking panic seized my chest. "Thanks for driving me!" I slammed the door and bolted into my backyard.

Appa sat beside the boombox, blaring Tamil tunes like it was no big deal, drinking hot black tea under the sweltering sun with Auntie, Moorthy, and Bagira.

I cut through their circle, unplugging the boombox in a fit. "You can hear this all the way down the street!"

Moorthy and Bagira sat frozen in their folding chairs. I followed their gaze towards the sliding back door, where Tony stood, eyes wide, holding my dripping swim bag. "You forgot—"

"Thanks." I yanked my bag from him, avoiding eye contact, and stormed inside to collapse on my twin-sized bed. The smells and sounds of Sri Lanka, or Ceylon or Eelam or whatever the hell it was, seeped into the fabric and the walls of our home. I felt a deep, festering disgust towards my own skin, towards the strange culture I came from that even the land itself had rejected.

I changed my clothes, grabbed my skateboard, and headed straight for the Flower Power House. My trucks were loose, making for a sloppy tic tac and a near-devastating slam after what should have been an effortless ollie over a tree root. I picked up my board and rolled up to a *For Rent* sign wedged in a well-watered and trimmed lawn. The realization that Rocky and Jill were still in Goa slapped me in the chest. I threw my head back and groaned before cruising down to the lagoon.

The water was a cold blade, but I craved the sharp cut of the freezing waves. The coldness, the quiet, and the immeasurability of the metallic sea offered me clarity. I wished I could unbecome. That I could be formless, colourless, weightless. I thrashed and kicked underwater, swimming as far as I could without breathing. My eyes burned from the brine, a murky blur. I screamed underwater, tasting salt water and kelp granules. The pressure in my lungs swelled, and I broke the surface, inhaling the ocean air. The sky was the colour of ripe cantaloupe, the waxing gibbous moon nestled between smoky blue clouds. My lips and fingers and toes tingled until I felt nothing at all.

"CHANDRA WILL TEACH YOU how to swim," Vathany said, the softness in her eyes hardening when they met mine.

As enraged by my dark-skinned delinquency as she was enamoured by Moorthy's mint-green eyes, Vathany had thought up a fitting retribution. There was nothing I would have rather done less, and in normal circumstances I would have told her to kick rocks, but Moorthy and Bagira, gangly and awkward in their ill-fitting clothes, had lost everything save for their own lives. And I'd been an ass to avoid them. Least I could do was teach them how to swim. Just had to make sure we went early so I didn't run into anyone I knew.

Bagira's legs were too short for Appa's bike, but he adapted by standing as he pedalled. Moorthy took my old fish skateboard, which he could barely ride. He was mad pigeon-toed, and his balance was shaky. I was worried he was going to swerve into the street, which, thankfully, was relatively empty at sunrise on a Sunday. The two communicated in their psychedelic-delay-and-fuzz-pedal language. Something between a trumpet and an electric guitar. Bagira gestured to the back of Appa's bike, which Moorthy clasped on to. Then Bagira pedalled with impressive strength, given his reed-like limbs seemingly void of muscle. I kicked and pushed slowly beside them as we made our way down to Green Lake.

We rested the bike and our boards on a moss-covered rock and removed our shirts. I was envious of Bagira's jutting ribs and hip bones. Both boys came from my supposed homeland, but neither looked remotely like me. Least of all Moorthy, with his light skin and mesmerizing eyes. I waded into the cool silk of the water, instantly relieved. The boys stood planted like totem poles at the water's edge. Despite hailing from an island ringed by white sand beaches and surfable breaks, Moorthy and Bagira were petrified of water.

"Come in!" I splashed in their direction.

Bagira flinched and shook his head with a nervous smile before crouching down in the calico pebbles. Moorthy sighed deeply and let the water graze his toes before taking a tentative step into the lake.

"Cold?" I asked.

"It's like the North Pole." He shivered, gasped, and gripped firmly onto my arms.

"You can touch the bottom here. It's not deep." I laughed, trying to pry his fingers off me.

Moorthy hollered in a primal, convulsing fear, digging his sharp fingernails into my skin, grasping tighter. His small, lithe body felt dense as dolomite.

"Just trust me," I said. "I won't let go."

After some minutes of resistance, Moorthy gingerly released his grip and lay back in the water. I held the back of his neck, and he clasped firmly onto my left wrist as I pushed his spine up to the surface of the lake with my knee. He remained stiff as a surfboard. Vibrations of fear reverberated off his skin, which had already darkened from the sun. But with time, he became lighter, breathing into his stomach, lifting it to the sky. I towered over him, watching the tension leave his chest and his eyes, large and jade with flecks of gold and aquamarine, scintillating like the light on the water's surface.

Finally, he surrendered, let his head fall back, and lightly closed his eyes. A serene smile crossed his face. He didn't even notice that I had removed my hands, that the water was carrying him, that he was floating all by himself.

11

The River

xʷməθkʷəy̓əm, səlilwətał, S̲k̲wx̲wú7mesh; qiqéyt, 1954

⁓

The ducky shincracker was a redbone and a regular at the China Pheasant, which had been a speakeasy during Prohibition. The bulls hated it, always lurking around hoping to pinch some ossified dame or dick. Everything was stained a scarlet vermilion under the dimming lights. She twirled to Dizzy Gillespie like a handkerchief caught in a gust of wind, sinewy black hair gummed to the sweat on her neck and forehead. Big teeth and eyes like crystallized honey, begging me to put down my Four Roses on the rocks and jive with her.

Hell, I'd given her the wrong idea by staring.

The dame stopped jiving and came stomping over to

the bar. "Hey, Valentino, ain't you that hood that won that big gold trophy at the Jive Swing Jive?"

I stayed fixed on my drink and didn't answer.

"You bet your dollar he is." Vince's callused meat-hooks clamped down on my shoulders, and his lanky frame clad in a sharp charcoal zoot suit skated between the shincracker and me.

"You two finks are wearing the same suit?" she scoffed. In the light I could see the globules of sweat like translucent marbles on her upper lip. The scent of cigarettes seeped out of her pores, growing stronger as her perfume faded.

"Why do you think we bought them?" Vince wrapped his eel of an arm around me and winked. "So every Jack and Jane in this joint knows who my guy Ronny here belongs to."

Vince wanted me to jive because I'd been in a sour space all day, and he knew I'd feel better after I danced. I, too, knew that dancing would help lift the wet stones off my chest, but I didn't feel like dealing with this dumb Dora, buzzing around me like a mosquito. Junior had said she was the gem of the joint, and that seemed probable. I could tell by the way she flung her clammy little arm out at me, demanding I put down my drink, that she wasn't used to rejection, but I wasn't in the mood.

"Hey now, Ronny, don't be a cold fish." Vince's eyes seared into me like switchblade incisions beneath his black brows. Suddenly, the whole bar was nagging me, so I took her sweaty hands with an eye roll and started jiving.

Vince was right to make me dance. It was instant, and I hated to admit that. Hell, my blood was glittering in my veins and all my worries dissipated. I lowered the girl to my left in a dip and then pulled her back upright. The song changed starkly, so we shifted our tempo. This ducky was a damn artist, couldn't deny that. She had long, slender gams and was swift on her feet. I raised both my hands and turned her in a three-sixty spin, then let go with my left hand and we stepped apart — the accordion ballroom drop. She catapulted into an aerial, whirling around in air like water before floating back to me, a smooth and sexy flingy flung and a honeycomb. We locked eyes and I realized I hadn't been leading — parabolic sidecut to neckbreak butterfly — she was the rope swing flying over the river, and I held on for life, hoping she could air step me all the way out of my skin, sling me outside of myself.

I lifted Ducky up onto the cherrywood bar top, the pink chandelier light like a halo behind her glossy face. Her warm brown arm cascaded towards me like spring rain. The bartender sucked on his teeth and shook his head but didn't say anything; he knew Vince and I came as a pair. I took her hand and leapt onto the bar. We beamed, revealing our big off-white teeth to the whole joint, and started twisting, gliding, swizzle-sticking. I was feeling good. Glitter in my veins good. I glanced down and saw Vince finishing off my Four Roses with a smug look on that ugly, slit-eyed mug of his. God, I loved Vince. Loved him so much that I just wanted to kick him straight in his hood-rat face. Wild how wearing fresh slacks and dancing your arse off can make you feel brand new.

The song came to an abrupt halt — the looming space between tracks on a record. For a second, I was left with the raw pit of myself: an apricot's hard and grooved endocarp marked by an unbearable yearning. If my mother was alive, if she really did work a street corner in Canton Alley, I might have passed her dozens of times. Hell, she could walk into the China Pheasant right that moment.

The windowpane behind Vince clouded with drupelets of white mist, blooming like snowberries around the shape of the rain. Through the milky haze I made out the blurred figure of a robust man in a dark outfit and a helmet, some cop strolling past the joint looking for trouble, no doubt. He scraped a flowering of water droplets from the window with the side of his hand and peered inside. Then he rapped his baton against the glass and shouted at me to get down. Fat chance. The next track started, so I started jiving again. Swizzlestick, twist, swizzlestick, twist. The zoot suit made me slick and invincible. On top of that, I had those bad spirits inside me, always beckoning.

The bull burst through the door, sopping wet, skin

red from the rain. "Hey you, get your greasy ass down from there!" he hollered, panting already from taking five steps. Too many maple-glazed sinkers and not enough real-life chases in his career.

I grinned and twisted harder, swerving to the beat like my bones belonged to it. Say what you will about being a bastard orphan who can't read, but it'll make you quick on your feet.

"I mean it, hood." He reached for my ankle.

"You gonna make me?"

He smiled from the middle of himself. "I sure as hell am, you smart little bastard."

The blue feather in Vince's fedora rose as he stood to his full height, as if he could see my next move reflected in my eyes.

I transferred my weight to my right foot. His jaw felt like a stone wrapped in soft rubber against the laces of my oxfords. I dove off the bar, leaping onto the sawdust-covered floor. Gravity hit like a hammer to the bones.

Vince and I tumbled out of the China Pheasant like a snare drum, paradiddle speed. In the distance I heard the fat flatfoot struggling to blow his whistle. We wove through familiar back alleys, sauced and howling at the moon. Wound up in the gut of Little Italy, the damp cement gritty beneath our heels; the smell of piss and warm carbonara confused the air.

"Boy, you got some moxie! Right in his face!" Vince

tilted his head back, tears falling out of him like thawed fear. "You're gonna get yourself hung, you hear me, juvie?"

"I'm gonna get us both hung."

We crumpled in laughter so hard our faces felt stretched and our eyes were stinging. Vince held his arm out to me and we started doing the Wurlitzer. He pretended to be the gal and we transitioned into a sunset combo; then he sugar-jumped and rolled his ankle on an empty glass bottle, fell flat on his ass. We fractured, laughing even harder. My stomach was going to come apart, and I felt like I could sneeze right out of my zoot suit, maybe even out of my skin. My knees buckled, and I let my head fall on Vince's shoulder. My breath came back slowly, in paper-thin wisps.

Vince's finger was lifting my jaw. He leaned in. I could feel the heat radiating from his face, but then he jolted to his feet, grabbed a beer bottle, and smashed the bottom to shards. I knew what that meant. I tracked his gaze, slit eyes hidden beneath his brows, stern face turned to stone. He started walking away from the street lights, towards a short, shadowy figure chain-smoking by a Dumpster.

Micky.

Two weekends prior we'd been bumming around Kits Beach after a jive, sauced and rowdy, chasing a burst of impossibly vibrant pink as it moved across the horizon. We were so transfixed by the flamingo-fuchsia sunrise, we didn't realize we'd crossed territory lines. Micky materialized out of the air, strapped with a gat, and told us to beat it. Vince was sick in the head and got off on a rumble — all the more if he'd had a drink. Mouse, a true Clark Park girl, hocked a loogie at the Italian, and a big glob of cigarillo spit landed right on his cheek. Micky called her a dead hoofer. Mouse and the rest of the gang split, so it was just me and Vince, suddenly surrounded by six Italians. Miraculously, we scrambled out of there — concussed, with cracked ribs, shiners, and a reason for Vince to clip an Italian the next time they crossed paths.

Vince stalked towards Micky with no hesitation in his stride. From the swiftness of his step alone, I knew. I got to my feet and dogged after him, gut twisted, unable to breathe, hoping Micky was strapped so we'd have an excuse to split.

"Hey!" Vince shouted, deep and throaty.

Micky looked up. We were in his territory, but he was unarmed and alone. I felt sick. Micky ran for it, his short legs desperate, flailing. Vince ran after him, long and fast as an arrow, with spidery gams and elastic arms. My stomach felt like it was on fire. Awful metal taste in my mouth.

Vince hooked Micky, his arm like a big lasso, and picked him up by the ass of his pants and the collar of his shirt.

Micky yelped and wriggled. I couldn't bear to look, but I couldn't leave Vince, either. He lowered Micky down to the wet ground and dragged his face along the pavement, scraping the skin right off. Micky shrieked like the screeching wheels of a freight train. In the circle of yellow street light, I could make out the sashes of crimson-black blood glimmering on the pale cement and the fine ribbons of flesh dangling from Micky's face.

Vince let out a black-hearted cackle. "Ronny, look at this. His face looks like goddamn spaghetti!"

Micky quivered, angel-hair strands stained in blood, and hollered in Italian. "Ait…uami! Aituami! Mi sta uccidendo! Mi st—"

"You roll up your traps or I'll clip you." Vince was itching to snap Micky's neck.

My throat tasted of unripe apples and sandpaper. I hoped the cops would show up so we could amscray.

But it was just us and the moon.

There isn't anything to say after you've watched your best friend kick a kid out of his body. All I could think about was how only an hour ago, I was staring at the ducky shincracker's big teeth, how we were jiving and laughing, how Micky was smoking, and now he was just a stiff in the gutter.

"ADAM AND EVE ON A RAFT," Vince said as he tossed a nickel at Zenora's new server and sat down next to a fat man with an azure bruise crawling up his chin.

It took me half a Danish to recognize the cop I'd given a shoe sandwich to last night. I turned to stone in my seat. Didn't know how to tell Vince without making a fuss, so I nudged him with my elbow.

"Whaddya want, Ronny?" he snapped loud enough to make everyone in Vie's turn and look. The cop glared at me, at my sweaty suit, at Vince in the same suit, with bloodstained sleeves.

"Go," Vince whispered.

On my way out I slammed my hip bone on the door. I turned a corner and hid behind a Dumpster, crouched down on the damp pavement, and watched the navy-blue blur at the end of the alley haul a pale, lanky figure into a squad car. I waited there for some time before standing up, legs and arse burning like hell.

I finally made my way out of the alley and smacked right into another flatfoot. A towering cop about half the width of the other one. A thin river of piss streamed down my inner thigh.

"Who are you running from?" The cop had huge blue eyes and a dapper grin.

I tried to compose myself. "Nothin'." I could taste my mung mouth, enough to make a maggot gag.

"I recognize you."

Bile boiled in my gut.

"You won that big trophy at the Jive Swing Jive!" He snapped his fingers. "You defy physics on that floor, a real

179

ducky shincracker. Don't think I've ever seen someone dance quite like that before."

"Thanks." I looked down at the faint smudge of blood on the toe of my left oxford.

"You know, there's a big jive competition down in Southern California at the end of the summer…"

"Fat chance I'll get to Southern California. I don't have any lettuce," I called over my shoulder, making my getaway.

"The Royal Canadian Navy's set to port there at the same time."

"And?" Who was this uppity elephant ear? I turned back around, brows furrowed. The sky was pearl white, sun and cloud all blended together.

"Name's Hank."

I sized him up, reckoned he'd be a decent grapple. Freshly trained and full of hope, not jaded like the fat one.

"They take all kinds as recruits. Negroes, Indians, hoods… You've got fast reflexes, you're agile, and you're tough." He handed me a little blue leaflet.

"Thanks, Hank… for the sermon." I put the paper in my pocket and walked away.

My head throbbed. I needed to tell the gang what happened to Vince. Stanley would know what to do. So I ran, weaving in and out of Gastown, over the sopping-wet grass of Clark Park. I busted through the white door of the gang house and stormed into the kitchen.

"They got Vince!"

Vernon and Lyle looked up from the table where they were eating bologna and jelly sandwiches.

"What are you on about, Ronny? It's nine in the morning," Jessica said, blowing cigarillo smoke.

"He killed that wop," I panted.

Stanley came into the kitchen, a towel wrapped around his waist. It was the first time I saw Vince in his face. Stanley'd already heard all about it — he'd been Vince's call. The cops had been waiting for Vince to do something like this for a while so they could finally get rid of him. I collapsed into Stanley and cried. Felt like I was suffocating in my skin and just wanted to tear it off.

After I wept myself dry, I fell asleep on the couch for ten straight hours. When I woke up, it was confirmed. They were going to hang him.

"When?"

"Monday," Stanley said.

"Jesus..." I got up and walked outside to the front porch. A sliver of yellow was attempting to poke through the swirl of white sky. I vomited over the rail, right into the dormant azaleas, until I was flashing up nothing but clear, bitter acid. My eyes felt swollen, bloodshot. My head rang something awful, and I was absolutely parched. I turned on the garden hose and drank straight from the ice-cold metal end. I wiped my mouth and told Stanley I was going for a drink.

He nodded. "Just keep in mind we all oughta lay low for a while."

The white sunlight stabbed my eyes as I made my way to Coccola's for some Four Roses. When I got my drink, this Jack Teagarden song that really griped my kidneys started playing in the background.

"Hey, look who it is! Valentino!" It was the ducky shincracker with the teeth and the legs and the cigarillo breath. "Come jive with me."

"Not now," I said and ordered another drink.

"Come onnnnn…" I shook my head and resisted as she pulled my arm. She leaned on me then, and the reek of fermented smoke webbed across my face.

"Scram," I snapped.

She slapped me so hard that the liquid in my head sloshed around. Everyone in the bar was looking at me, wondering if Ronny was gonna flip his lid. But I needed to stay low for a while.

But then she said it.

"Bastard."

I took a piece of ice out of my drink and chucked it at her, told her she looked greasy. Before I knew it, some thick-shouldered fatheads with a hankering for a brawl were circling me like mosquitos. They dragged me out of the bar, and I knew they wanted me to throw the first punch. Maybe they'd kick me right out of my body the way Vince kicked Micky out of himself. A crowd gathered around our huddle like a ribbon of fog in the blinding white daylight. All at once the whiskey hit me and I figured I'd just give in to the beating. I could use a good sting. I took a few sharp blows to the ribs from the side, felt knuckles kiss the back of my head, before crumpling to the cement.

With that, everyone went back inside. I bit the inside of my cheek, felt my eye sockets pooling with grief. I tried to hold the water in as I stomped the bloodstained cement of that cursed city. Vince was a vise in the centre of my chest cavity. A memory reel played of Jagger and Vince and me, the three of us running over the booms. Suddenly, both disappeared into the river. And didn't come back up. While my bad spirits kept me alive, kept me alone.

A painful itch took hold of me, each cell of my skin aching for things to go back to the way they were even just days ago. I wanted to be lifted up by two great arms and carried over the clouds. I wanted to see Ray but knew I would splinter like a weak-trunked tree in a storm. It was a gnawing pain, this yearning, left me feeling like the only resolution was to escape my body, to dissolve into the space around me.

So I rolled up to Mouse's house. She pulled me inside, kissed me all over. I fell on the bed and let her climb on top of me. She was pale as the overcast sky, rivers of tawny freckles all over her body. I didn't like the feeling of her lips, or her rickety hips, but the warmth of her skin, the soft parts, the love she pressed into my skin with each kiss, that I bathed in.

PALE SUNLIGHT LANDED ON my face when I woke up, dehydrated and pillow-eyed.

"Can you pass me my pants?" I asked Mouse. My mouth tasted like iron and arse, like hot garbage marinated in Four Roses. She rolled over and handed them to me. A leaflet fell out onto the bed.

"What's this?" she asked. "Hot broad from the bar?"

"Navy stuff."

"The navy? You?" Her laughter, crested in sincere disbelief, got right under my skin.

"I've been hand-selected, actually," I snapped. "And I'm going there today. Gonna go jive in Southern California."

She broke into more laughter, thin pink lips parted, button nose crinkling. "The navy ain't for dancing."

I pulled away from her. "Well, shoot. Wish I'd known that." I buttoned up my pants and gathered my things.

"Hold on, Ronny, don't be such a fruit."

"Watch your tramp trap." She stopped dead in her tracks and stared at me. I knew I'd said an awful thing, but I didn't feel like I was in control of myself. I felt like a watcher, floating above all this madness. "I'm in a bad way. They're hanging Vince tomorrow."

"What?" Mouse looked lifeless as a mannequin as

I delivered the news. The light drained from her face; her thin lips uncurled.

I was full to the brim with my own sorrows, so I turned away and left. I went to the river.

Ray's boat rose and rippled in the choppy current. From my vantage point on the bank, Ray, who was a deep, autumn cherry brown from the sun, was significantly fatter and more hunched over. No one to split the bannock with, I reckoned. He'd let his hair grow long as a woman's. Now it was silvery white instead of ash grey. I watched the boat bob in the distance, wrestling the desire to go to Ray and lay my troubles on him.

Instead, I went over to the rope swing and threw the broken length out into the air. I climbed behind the base of the tree and traced the rough, satisfying texture of grooved bark, took out my switchblade and hacked off the frayed wreck that remained. The rope fell into the silt. I ran down to the water's edge and kicked the river. Water droplets ricocheted off the silver surface, rippling into infinity.

12

The Sea

Snʊ'neɪməxʷ, 1986

～～～

The first fall that Bagira and Moorthy had ever seen was one of vivid colour, torrential downpour, and merciless wind. Even in the calm aftermath of October's rage, the threat of storms and rip currents loomed in the suspiciously silent sea. The mirror-skin of Green Lake, the dark teal foliage of evergreens interrupting the skyline, and the eel of fog slithering serpentine along the treeline all looked the same: opal, silver, charred-turquoise mist, melded in one moment, suddenly separate again in another. The landscape was a shape-shifter, a trick of light, freezing in time before vaporizing into nothingness.

But it was dry enough to get a beach fire going. The flames matched the bronze leaves of the turning maples.

I felt safe, concealed by the enveloping wetsuit and hood and the veil of the fog. There weren't many swimmers at the lake in late fall. Only the odd navy vet or open water Olympian. And one Black(ish) kid teaching his two Tamil not-cousin-cousins how to swim because you can't teach lessons at the pool unless you work there.

My old wetsuits and booties fit Moorthy and Bagira's fine-boned frames like a glove. My new suit was looser than I remembered, allowing the algid water to pool generously in it. I shivered, my upturned palms yellow. Bagira and Moorthy floated serenely on the metallic surface of the water, an array of fallen leaves framing them in a striking protection of copper and red. We dove into the cold, penny-and-blood-drop sea, streamlining towards shore. Bagira thrashed his head straight up out of the water to breathe, which he did every second stroke, sending his legs and torso perpendicular.

"Keep your head down. When you lift it up, you sink." I demonstrated, floating on my back, heaving my head up, and sinking. Red leaves pooled over my submerged face.

THE VAN SWERVED AROUND a hillock of cement, ripping my headphones out of my Walkman. At Appa's sharp break before the detour sign, I conked my head against the window glass. An autumn storm swell had swept over the flame-red coast, wind torrenting swarms of leaves into the air like an atmospheric river of fire and tearing out oaks from the roots. The tree-root-laden and power-line-plowed roads remained uncleared. Sand fleas batted their wings in my chest and up my throat, and stomach acid brewed into my mouth, as I hunched in the shotgun seat. I unbuckled in the pool parking lot before we came to a full stop.

"Eat something," Appa said, thrusting a freckled banana in my direction. Its honey-like fragrance alone held too many carbohydrates.

Indoor meets smelled like jarred fear — enclosed spaces, sterile white tiles, chlorinated water, controlled air, and sweaty, high-strung swimmers. I longed to cut a hole through the tiled ceiling, an opening so that the lungs of the indoor pool would be flooded with fresh air and light. But there wasn't so much as a skylight or a window, just a viewing deck, behind which was a café full of calorically dense non-foods.

From my lane, I found four brown faces blurred in the crowd. Paula was also there. She'd tagged along to the meet with a group of older deck bunnies. They laughed loudly near our team banner, constantly looking over to see if we were looking back, which we did, but only out of the corner of our eyes. I ran my hands down my rib cage, counted each bone.

"Water'd turn orange if they jumped in," said Tori, the backstroker. She was loud and funny, tomboy pretty.

A girl we'd all had a waning and waxing crush on for at least a season.

The breaststroker with the Herculean shoulders and the weird name laughed beside me as she tucked her giant, dense mane of black hair into her two swim caps. Our elbows brushed at the lane rope as we both slid our goggles up. We turned to face each other, too close for two people who didn't know each other's names. I was captivated by her small, enigmatic face. She had dark blue hooded eyes, a sharp, angular jaw, and high cheekbones. Her olive skin deepened to a rare terracotta in the summer but was white now. Name another activity where you regularly graze the bottom of someone's bare foot or get your ass whacked by a focused backstroker, but that's just how it goes in the water. Swimming with someone could mess with your mind and make you feel a type of way about them.

Tori was right about Paula and her crew, of course, but there was life aquatic and life on land. I was enchanted by the world of pretty deck bunnies — girls who stayed dry on the edge of the pool and seemed to live in the air itself. Illusory creatures that were all around me yet out of reach. Surely, they'd be the antidote to everything if I could just swim fast enough.

Be cool, I thought, as we eeled through marshalling like a collective.

I was handed my time card and an audible whisper escaped from the thick of the crowd. "Dude, that's the

Black kid with mutant lungs, the one who swims without breathing."

"Heard he's a cloudburst."

"Whaddya mean?"

"Kid snaps. Gets real mad."

"Heard the cops went to his house."

Reality thickened as my feet met the cold, damp pool deck, contrasting with the humid air. I climbed up onto the blocks and scanned for Coach Lee. I pulled a fist to my chest, kissed my peace fingers, and held them out to the crowd.

"Merman X!"

"Merman Luther King Jr.!"

Be cool, collected. No false starts. Tell your entreating heart there's no harm done.

I felt the power in my body surge to the surface of my skin. The gun went off, and so did I, launching into the water: dolphin kick, dolphin kick, kick, kick, kick. Chasing after a moving target, not the touchpad or the wall, but something else, something intangible. If my legs didn't feel like they were going to disintegrate, I wasn't kicking hard enough. I pulled the water and roared out what was left of my oxygen, sending spirals of bubbles into the infinite blue. Nailing the flip turn, swiftly inverting with wings of rushing water, I pushed off the wall and flew. Torpedoing through the atmosphere, I chased after that thing. Pressure built up in my lungs until they felt heavy enough to sink me, but I wouldn't cave.

At the touch of the wall, I threw my head up out of the water, took a sweet sip of air. My body flooded with fresh oxygen as my eyes turned to the scoreboard. I'd added milliseconds to my best time, securing first place by only half a second. I took my cap off and plunged underwater to mute the clamouring crowd. I was angry, certain that I'd swum faster. Until I got that thing, whatever I was swimming after, I wouldn't be satisfied.

After receiving my medal at the podium, I fist-bumped and high-fived my way out of the pool to where Paula stood, shivering by the bike racks. She looked like she was about to freeze to death in her sheer blue blouse. "You killed that race."

"Thanks." I ran Rocky's Afro pick through my hair.

"You wanna come get milkshakes with us?"

I eyed Appa, Auntie, Moorthy, and Bagira, beaming in my direction from the edge of the parking lot. Pretended not to see them or the warm drink they were holding for me.

THE TEMPER OF THE AIR was placid and so was I, sitting in the mint-green cushioned seats of the sixties ice cream parlour. The chipped, salmon-coloured walls had been immortalized during an era when I wouldn't have even been allowed inside. There was a jukebox and a big framed and autographed poster of Elvis. Rocky'd eye-roll at any mention of Elvis, who stole Otis Blackwell's music. I wasn't going to sour the mood, though, not with a bunny brushing her shoulder against mine.

Paula ordered in an octave range much higher than her normal voice. "A cherry-chocolate twist with whip, please." Refined sugar, artificial flavourings, and saturated fat. Pure body fat.

"Uh, the low-fat peach freeze." I shifted in my seat, trying to ignore the chlorine itch and tingle that crawled up the sheath of my skin.

Paula looked at me through mascaraed lashes. "Damn, you're dedicated."

Guy goes vegetarian for the ethics of it, he's a pussy and a socialist. Guy eliminates nearly everything from his diet, including animal products, for a cut physique? He's a dedicated athlete.

"Low-fat tastes like feet," Paula's older, gorgeous blond friend said and licked the whipped cream off her maraschino cherry.

"You know what feet taste like?" I said.

The bunnies laughed, and Paula leaned into me, pressing her bare thigh onto my hand.

We started going together for real after that weekend. Dating Paula was nice because she mainly just talked about herself. Listening to her picket-fence problems helped me forget all about mine, and I melted into her cloud palace world where the pain was painted rose gold. She knew next to nothing about the world outside Nanaimo or its history, and that was a relief to me. Her parents were always bickering over little things, which she speculated was because they didn't truly love each other. Romantic love wasn't something I'd ever thought about until that point, or, at least, hadn't thought to distinguish from the other kinds of love and admiration I craved. Whether Vathany and Appa loved each other seemed irrelevant; they were two shipwreck survivors on the same floating plank of wood. My parents mostly liked to stare out into the sea in silence, and I'd always regarded that as a conversation. When they spoke with words, well, they argued. Over the ethics of eating meat. Whether I should bleach my skin, or whether educating me about my heritage would radicalize me into a terrorist. The difference between a terrorist and a freedom fighter. How many painkillers Appa should take, and if he should mix them with the Sertraline.

Paula's parents argued over things like deseeding tomatoes or drizzling grilled nightshades with butter or cold-pressed olive oil. Whether to raise their kids Catholic or Protestant (a difference that was imperceptible to me). Her father's father fled the Adriatic Coast to evade the Fascists and settled in Burnaby just outside of Vancouver. Though he was born and raised in Emilia, he was Sicilian, and therefore considered Black and uncivilized in the north. North or south, Italians were white, I argued. All-Canadian Tonyboy was Tuscan, after all. But Paula clapped back with a sawtoothed "no"—to be Sicilian was to be "dark white," even when her father, Luca, was the stock photo that came with the picture frame. Even though he looked and sounded like the carbon copy of every patriarchal archetype in every TV special I'd ever seen. Aside from the perils of being "dark white," Paula was constantly being compared to her older sister, Jesse, who was a senior at our school and in the running to be valedictorian. Her mother warned her father that this rivalry was going to make Paula resent Jesse, but what neither of them noticed was that Paula was more worried for Jesse than anything. Jesse washed her hands upwards of thirty times a day. Sometimes she pulled out her own eyebrow hairs, and if you looked closely, you could see the gaps, the gaps, the gaps.

Paula wanted to run away to San Diego, fan palms, piazzas, and Parmesan, where she wouldn't have to deal with icy Canadian winters or ignorances.

"Let's bail this skid town, move to Little Italy," she said, nestled into my chest.

"That'd be rad," I replied.

We escaped into a tie-dye paisley haze of endorphins. A blur of cherry cola ChapStick, warm, downy skin, and neon daydreams of sandy California beaches. I'd ditch her for West Hollywood once we got to the Embarcadero, where I'd find a Hollywood starlet. That's who I was going at it with in my imagination. I kept my eyes closed, occasionally blinking open to glimpse the flash of a bracey smile, a tousle of fine blond hair, crimps straightening out. I knew, deep down, this fantasy was fragile.

A CHARCOAL SEA OF storm clouds blanketed the sky, but the air was warm. The biting lurk of winter had dissipated, and a sudden heat sent spiderwebs of lightning across the horizon. Skating to school against everyone's advice, I nodded along to my new Run-DMC cassette. The collar of my denim jacket was popped and Rocky's Black Fist Afro pick was wedged artfully in my hair. I did a clean backside flip to impress the freshmen girls, who'd gotten hot, and the older, blonder bunnies behind them. Tony and Stu leaned against the red bike racks, windbreaker-clad backs exposed.

I fought the urge to pull the band of Stu's tighty-whities over his thick head and pounced, shrieking karate kiais while pretending to choke him out with my skateboard. "Black lightning strike! Hundred-dollar indecency fine, all because of your slow ass! Hi-ya!"

Tony bit his lip, tucked a gold curl behind his ear. "C'mon, let it go man, s'been weeks."

"Tony, I'm about to break his knees."

"What was I supposed to do?" Stu pried my hands off his ostrich neck.

"I don't know, not rat out your homie?"

"Be cool, Chan, be cool." Tony placed his hands on my shoulders.

I hated that Tony was defending Stu. Had it been the other way around, Stu would have already been ass-up in a Dumpster.

"Fag." I glared at Stu, hoping he'd get a fleeting gust of courage and look me in the eyes, just so I could see him flinch and look away again. A vein of white lightning bolted across the horizon, and we took that as a signal to get indoors.

Stu just kept looking at his feet. "Peace. I said I was sorry, all right?"

"Your mother." I left him hanging and strolled off, grinding my teeth.

I was still seething when I got to class. I took my seat by the window and slammed my binder on my desk. Everything seemed louder and more irritating than usual — the hardness of the chair, the height of the desks, the sound of Bertrand clearing his throat every two seconds. I was ready to jump on top of the desk and go totally feral.

I spent the rest of class hungry and lethargic, longing for a power outage. The weather outside thickened and intensified. Rain pelted down and I immediately regretted skateboarding to school, angrier still that it was my own dumb defiance that drove me to ignore the forecast. With the rainfall came a hollow pit in my chest, and something felt wrong in my body, like a loose screw or fraying wire. The world had a monochrome filter over it, so I used the small magic I had available to me and teleported: Turquoise waters of secret beaches, Olympic-sized saltwater infinity pools that overflowed into the sea. I surfed Big Sur, Supertubos, the North Shore of Oahu, Fiji, Tahiti...met golden surfer girls. In my daydreams, I had light eyes and skin, a perfect body: chiselled as stone.

I slipped out of my daydream, rain splattering against the portable's tin roof. Paula flashed me a smile, revealing her silver braces. "Earth to dreamer," she said, her lip gloss smeared on one of the brackets.

I winked back, wiping the drool out of the corners of my mouth. The tension in the air made me hot enough to forget about the hellish weather.

IN DRAMA WE WERE allowed to move around, and I dug that. Aside from Tony and me, the class was mostly girls (which was why I took it, I told myself), a few squares, a cluster of thespian skids, and the rest were flamers. All of them took it way too seriously. None more so than Kenneth, a kid so flamboyant he was competing with the sun. That afternoon he was wearing the most ridiculous pants I'd ever seen — olive gold with long, ribbony threads all over them. He looked like a shag lamp.

I smirked. "Far-out pants."

Ken stuck out a pierced tongue at me. I could never understand why white kids like him chose to make life harder for themselves by dressing like that. Like our drama teacher, Mr. Sparks — or Sparky — who had a prominent Adam's apple that quivered as he spoke and wore bright colours and patterns that never matched. Today it was a pale blue paisley button-up and pen-red plaid slacks.

While Sparky squeaked on about how to breathe (from your diaphragm, not your chest), the threads of Ken's lampshade pants dangled in front of me, hypnotic.

Back and forth.

I tracked the swaying ribbons like a cat mesmerized by yarn.

Back and forth.

I reached into my pocket and pulled out my lighter, igniting the little orange flame.

Back and forth.

I held my lighter up to Ken's butt, and the thread of his pants sizzled up instantly like a wick. One string caught, and then another, catching fire like dominoes. Within seconds, his backside was in flames like Hendrix's guitar.

A trail of smoke billowed in the air behind Ken as he

ran, shrieking, out of the drama room. Choking on my own laughter, I chased after him down the hallway in figure eights, trying to smother the ass-inferno with my physics textbook. A flash of blue paisley and red plaid charged out of the theatre wielding a fire extinguisher, and a cloud of white foam billowed over Ken's butt. I thought I would rupture my spleen laughing.

THE SCHOOL SECRETARY TOLD ME to shut up because it wasn't funny. But it was so funny. Every time I almost stopped laughing and caught my breath, the image of the flames engulfing Ken's pants, the way he ran like a Looney Toon, the white foam on his ass would resurface and I'd start laughing all over again.

The phone rang, piercing. I had the sinking realization that the school was going to call Appa and Vathany. That put a pin in my laugh attack, just in time for the principal to pull me into his office.

Mr. Latimer reminded me of a walrus. He had an island of hair in the middle of his pink balloon head, round, unremarkable blue eyes, white eyelashes, and a white moustache that eclipsed his top lip. He was shiny in a way that principals often are — sitting in an office filled with stacks of unopened school supplies, never *really* knowing what's going on in the hallways. Like with the teachers who stared at female students' chests, or the ones with the stale curriculums who never stood up from their desks, it seemed to me that someone should have intervened before it got to this point. That, surely, the way we treated each other was more important than handing in our homework on time or getting good test scores, but no one stepped in, and so we were angry at the world and we took it out on one another.

Mr. Latimer unfolded his hands and groomed his colonial moustache before opening his mouth. "You know what I see when I look at you?"

I clutched onto the soft flesh on my lower abdomen, then my lower back. I felt almost nothing other than hard bone and relaxed.

"Talented athlete, popular kid, decent student...tossing his life down the shitter. You have a sense of humour, son, and that's good. But every time you're in my office, it's over something stupid. I read your file."

I held back an eye roll, looking around the office. Either Latimer had the same type of tea every morning, or he still hadn't disposed of the Earl Grey wrapper from last week. I'd been in here last Tuesday for mouthing off to my history teacher. After I got kicked out of class, I used Paula's friend Flossie's brick of a phone to dial the school number from the hallway. I put on my best corporate voice and told the secretary there was an emergency and I needed to speak with Mr. Alexopolous immediately. When my teacher ran down to the office to take the call, I went back to the classroom and told him over the phone that the medical results were in, that he had a terminal case of being a giant Greek dick. The class busted their guts laughing, and it was worth every second.

"All this jack-assery means you're on a fast track to expulsion, which I really don't want to do," Latimer said. "I'd rather not go through the paperwork. Unless you turn your act around and stop wasting your talents, you're going to end up just another thug in a jail cell. Or dead. That's right, high school is a bit like daycare, and no one's going to be looking out for you when you get out of here."

I just shrugged, but I could feel the sand fleas leaping.

"Mr. Sparks seems to think pretty highly of you. He says you'd make a great actor if you tried. In fact, he begged me not to expel you."

Actor?

"Not everyone can get up in front of a crowd. And not everyone who can get up in front of a crowd can entertain people, either."

Huh.

Pulled under by a swift and vicious current, I saw a reel of Appa and Vathany's lives. The countless ways getting kicked out of school would mess me up. Disastrous outcomes surfaced in my mind like a pod of orcas leaping out of the surf. How grave their dissappointment would be. Appa and Vathany had made it clear that I needed to into medicine or law, despite not having the grades or work ethic for either.

I was overtaken by the sharp, searing feeling I got standing on the blocks before a race, only this time I had no water to dive into. I held my breath and dug my nails into my wrist. My mind swung from one vine of possibility to the next, wondering what humiliation Mr. Sparks had in store for me.

Mr. Latimer sent me back to drama class. I scanned the room as I entered, my eyes darting to Tony, who bit his tongue and hissed through his teeth with laughter.

From the opposite side of the room entered Ken, now clad in his gym shorts. He locked eyes with me, and his chest and cheeks puffed up with words he'd never say.

"How, uh...are you, Ken?" Sparky stood with an open script resting in his hands, paisley shirt tucked into his plaid pants.

"He's on fire," I quipped.

The room swelled with laughter.

Sparky glared, then paddled into a soliloquy: "'Our revels now are ended. These our actors, as I foretold you, were all spirits and are melted into air, into thin air —'"

I snaked in for the ride, a reflex — "'And, like the baseless fabric of this vision, the cloud-capp'd towers, the gorgeous palaces, the solemn temples, the great globe itself, yea, all which it inherit, shall dissolve and, like this insubstantial pageant faded, leave not a rack behind. We are such stuff as dreams are made on, and our little life is rounded with a sleep.'"

Sparky squatted like a yogic frog, placed his script down, and slid off the edge of the stage, striding into the aisle where I stood. "You know Shakespeare?"

The eye of my memory transported me back to the lagoon with Rocky and Jill. I loomed over the edge of the sea stacks, silver water beating against the rocks.

"Nah." I shrugged.

"Read this." Sparky grabbed the tea-stained script and offered it to me.

I took the script.

"'Now I arise.'"

Held it up to the light.

"'Sit still, and hear the last of our sea-sorrow. Here in this island we arrived, and here have I, thy schoolmaster, made thee more profit than other princes can, that have more time for vainer hours and tutors not so careful.'"

My tongue surfed the rhythm; my lips traced the words. It was muscle memory. I didn't vibe with the head bust Bard of Avon, held up and heralded by bourgeoisie who would have spat on low-born Shakespeare in their day. But I dug Shakespeare, that elusive dude. And damn, there was something psychedelic about the rhythm of the words, like an electric guitar solo or a barrel wave.

"You didn't stumble over a single word." Sparky's

resonant head voice filled the theatre even when he spoke softly.

"I can read? Tony, I can read!" I leapt onto Tonyboy's lap.

The class rippled into laughter.

"You've got great lungs, a loud voice," Sparky said.

The approval of the room was intoxicating.

"And you certainly love attention."

"Attention loves me back." I somersaulted off Tony's lap, ending in a striking viper pose.

"I won't argue with that. I'll see you at auditions for our production of *The Tempest*."

A dormant part of me awakened from hibernation, something rising from within the deep den of myself.

"For real?" Ken scoffed. "His punishment for committing arson is a role in the play?"

"Arse-on." I pulled my lighter out of my back pocket, flicked the flame in his direction.

Sparky snatched the lighter away. "I didn't say he'd get a part, but he will contribute to the production in some meaningful way. Chandra, channel that energy into your monologue."

"Watch your back, Fancy Pants." I pointed at Ken.

The room's laughter crawled up the back of my neck, seeped into my pores, and filled me with a feeling of invincibility, a quiet promise of power. Command of the room, centre stage.

— ⁓ —

I EXHALED A STREAM of white bubbles into the electric blue.

Bore us some leagues to sea; where they prepared

Flip turn. Streamline. Dolphin kick. Pump from the chest.

A rotten carcass of a boat, not rigg'd,

Kick, kick, kick. Pull through the infinite cyan, through space and time.

Nor tackle, sail, nor mast; the very rats

Flip turn. Streamline.

Instinctively have quit it: there they hoist us,

Fight the pressure building in the lungs. Stroke faster. Pull past the hips.

To cry to the sea that roar'd to us; to sigh

The harder you kick, the sooner you can taste the air.

To the winds whose pity, sighing back again,

Smack the wall. Depleted lungs replenish with decadent air.

Did us but loving wrong.

I came home soaked in my chlorine ever-reek. For once, my first thought wasn't about food; instead, I pulled the script out of my bag and went over Prospero's lines, sleeving into character the way I entered water, each memorized line a stroke. The aching sting of a stolen homeland stretched out. I felt relief as the thick band of anger around my chest vaporized, bolted out through my fingertips. The clouds thundered in time with my hastening pulse; the silver sea swelled at my command.

To act is to melt into air, into thin air, like the baseless fabric of vision, the cloud-capped towers of thought. So when I was waiting in the wings of the stage to audition weeks later, I was a formless spirit. Until I embodied Prospero, driven only by the illusions of the island, my kingdom of turquoise waters, sparkling quartz sand, and towering coconut palms. The shelf of anger on my chest billowed out, thundered across the stage.

We are such stuff as dreams are made on, and our little life is rounded with a sleep.

The dismissal bell punctured the air and I bit my lower lip. If I'd had eaten lunch, I would have lost it as I walked towards the bulletin board to find out whether I got the part.

13

The River

*x^wməθk^wəy̓əm, səlilwətaɬ, Sḵwx̱wú7mesh; qiqéyt,
1954–55*

I queued at the naval recruitment office behind a long-haired leviathan with overactive sweat glands for what felt like an eternity of stink. An overcast sky glared through the windowpanes. The relentless brace of November's wind-up winds rattled disrobed choke-cherry and dove trees. Ray called it the month to put your paddle in the bush, and indeed, every inch of me desired to rest. But there I was, defying the season's message and raising my oar to high water with the rookie cop's tattered leaflet crumpled and rain-smudged in my sagging back pocket.

After an eager interrogation and some talk of a wig chop, the chrome-dome recruiter spread his lap to show off his pleatless Ivy Leaguers and welcomed the smelly giant with a stamp.

Then he took one up-and-down scan of me, shook his head, and said, "Too skinny. You'll blow away."

He waved me out without knowing I'd seen Vince drag a wop's face on the sidewalk like he was grating Parmesan. Without knowing I'd taken a horsewhip to the back and stabbed a man with a pitchfork. Without knowing how fast or agile I was, how I could move. I shredded the threadbare leaflet and let the fragments fall in the gutter. Sail off into a new life? What a crock. I had the sudden sinking realization that I had no place to sleep. Going back to the Clark Park house without Vince would gut me. Vancouver felt like a festering wound on a bum limb that I needed to hack clean off.

I stopped in at the China Pheasant for a drink and stayed until they forced me to agitate the gravel. The sky was a haze of topaz as I paced the streets, avoiding Italian territory and the Clark Park crew. Didn't think they'd clip me if they found out I was trying to leave, but they'd beat me to my senses. Every crow squawk, blues hum, raccoon shuffle, and trashcan twang made me twitch. Anxious for daylight, I didn't know how much longer I could keep my eyelids open, but I kept on walking, drawn to well-lit areas like a moth. But now it was all black sapphire under the street lamps, and I felt the miles in my gams as they seized up over a rustle in the brittle thicket. Fragile twigs snapped under my feet as I made my way to the water I knew.

Sleeping boats rocked, chirred, and jingled in the river. It had to be three thirty in the morning, the veil between night's oblivion and daybreak's heed at its thinnest, and I could no longer feel my dogs. Creaking across the dock, I ran my numbing hands along the boats until I felt a rounded wooden stern under a faint film of frost. Leaning in for the unmistakable whiff of cedar, I knew this boat. The only boat on the docks with a handmade cedar strip stern. I hauled my rickety ass over the wet rail, climbed on deck, pulled a fishing net over me as a blanket, and curled up. Engulfed by the smell of rotting candlefish on ice, I tried and failed to transport back to a time before all this.

I woke to harsh overcast and a pang in the shoulder. "What in Coyote's name you doing here, eh?"

I jolted up, tangled in the net. Ray hovered over me, prodding me with a fishing rod, his carving knife held to my neck.

I flung my arms up. "Ray, easy, it's me! It's Ronny!"

Ray kept his knife raised. "Thought it might be you... had to be sure. Stand up. Let me look at you."

As I rose, all the blood rushed away from my head, and I stumbled, nearly plunging into Ray's knife. I clutched onto the rails of the boat.

"You look worse than the last time I saw you."

I looked up. "Christ. That's off-colour..."

"You got no colour. You don't have to hang around with Jagger's spirit all day."

"Well, you look old," I chirped back.

"That's no way to talk to someone holding a knife."

"That's some hair," I said. His hair was pure white. Straight as fishing line, it sparkled in the light.

"Figured now that I'm old and talking to river spirits, I might as well let my hair grow out. Nah, to be honest, I just can't be arsed these days. You want something to eat?"

I nodded. "Ain't nothin' sound better in the whole world than some hot bannock."

"You're making the dough." Ray tossed me a mixing bowl and gestured to the flour.

Bannock was a simple fry bread, but Ray had his own twist. I hesitated, then realized I'd watched him do it so many times of course I knew how.

"Not bad technique." As I folded the dough, Ray nodded, then cracked open a beer and poured a few splashes into the batter. "This is my new thing."

"Never say no to beer."

"Well, you've changed."

"For the worse. Aren't you gonna ask me where I've been?"

"Nope, and I don't want to know, either, so you can keep your escapades to yourself."

The crackle of the bannock frying on the stove and the sight of the river was like a sliver of Fiddler's Green. I took a quenching breath and felt my shoulders lower.

"You can tell me where you're going, though," Ray said.

"I...I'm going to join the navy."

"Now, that's great news. That's real great."

"But I'm too skinny. Figured I'd bum around your boat for a while and eat bannock until I whale up."

"'Whale up.' That's some wordsmithing."

"Hey, I always wondered...Where's your family?"

Ray's silence was loud. The grooves around his eyes and mouth had deepened. We ate our bannock and looked out at the river, flowing as always. She just kept rushing forward no matter what.

"Some people believe that our ancestors live here. The Stó:lō. I kinda thought that was all nonsense, like the white man's heaven and hell. Until Jagger's spirit started hanging around my boat." Ray rapped the side of the cabin with his elbow. "Was he always this sentimental?"

"Jagger? Biggest tulip I've known in my life." We laughed.

Before I left, Ray told me to get the hell onto a navy cruiser. "You're landlocked," he said. "That'll make you loony, lead you to drugs, or worse. Look, I don't pretend to know where you came from, and truth be told, it don't mean a damn thing to me. Far as I'm concerned, we all come from the same Creator. Fine not to know, just don't say you're something you're not. But I will say that you...you've got water blood, that's for sure." He gave me a sack full of bannock. "Now go on, get out of here and have your adventures. You know I'll be here. Dead or alive, I'll be here. Me and the ghost of this little asshole." He whacked the cabin again and revealed his off-white smile. "Just remember not to look back, 'cause the current's not carrying you in that direction."

THE STRENGTH OF THE STÓ:LŌ undertow rushing through my veins led me right back to the recruitment office.

"If it ain't the Cloudwalker with nine lives... My stars, look at those shiners. So, what are you waiting for? Get in there."

I hovered outside the door where the rookie cop stood with a thinning stack of flyers. "A meal, Hinky, a meal. The navy cats said I'm too skinny for their water gang."

"The name's Hank. Figured they might say that — fat floats." He patted his alderman and chuckled. "We've gotta get some steak and taters in you, get you pumping some iron... That'll take care of that pigeon chest."

What'd Hinky have to be so chipper about in November? "Cut the apple butter," I scoffed. "Steak... iron... You think I got the bees for that?" Suspicious. Everything about this man was suspicious.

"I'll pay for it."

"Ah, go climb up your thumb, Hinky. What do you want from me, huh? I won't dish anything on anyone. Just club me to death like you lot love doing if that's what you're after."

"It's Hank. I only want to help."

"Why the hell would you want to do a thing like that?"

"'Cause quite frankly, I'm sick and tired of seeing all you young guns clipping each other and hanging before the age of twenty-one. I take no pleasure in it at all. I was afforded privileges in my life, loans from God. I'm here to extend a loan to you."

I studied the truth in Hank's wide, ringless eyes. This was an earnest, decent man. Or a whack job.

"I'm real sorry 'bout your friend, Ronny."

I said nothing, sucked the rage back into my tear troughs. Hank handed me a flask, and I took a swig, let the sweet burn of the rum coat my whole mouth.

SNOW FELL ON A brilliant December day and I had saxophone in my step from hearing Ornette Coleman play at the Cellar. Powdered sugar glazed the streets only to melt within minutes, as did the rich timbre of the horn when I entered the confined space of clanking cast iron and grunting men that reeked like a distillation of the giant I'd queued behind some weeks ago. In this house of metal, men, and mirrors, I met my full reflection for the first time in years. The gun staring back at me was taller and lankier than I remembered, like a broomstick with a head. His chest caved in, with a few wiry black chest hairs in the canal. His limp arms dangled beside his body like spaghetti. Hell, it was probably a good thing I didn't know how I looked or I wouldn't have had the gumption I did in a rumble.

Save for my skeletal frame and gnarled aqueduct of a schnoz, I wasn't hard to look at. Stern, hooded blue eyes, smooth black hair, a strong jawline, and a smirk that dames went crazy for. Didn't have much to gloat over in life, but I could say I never once had a pimple, despite all the greasy soul food, cigarettes, and alcohol. My complexion was clear and light, nearly white in winter, but boy, did it hold onto colour — a deep cherrywood tinge took hold of my face in the summer. I was never translucent pale like Hank, peach cream or tangerine like a Californian. Easily as pigmented as Zenora's redbone nephew Junior, I was darker and browner than high-yellow Liz. I tried to place myself among the faces I'd known, but truly, never in my life had I seen a grown man who had a map quite like me.

"You done fawning over yourself, Cloudwalker?" Hank said.

We started with the free weights — dumbbell curls and flys. Then we got to the bench press, leg press, squat press, deadlifts, and medicine balls. I wasn't the strongest, but I wasn't weak either. I had the endurance of a river otter.

"You sure got a strong heart there, Cloudwalker." Hank shook his head as I finished box step skipping for thirty minutes straight, barely a mist of sweat on me. "All that jive dancing did you good."

I smirked. "It's from outrunning the fuzz."

"Well, no wonder you're so damn skinny. Let's get some grub in you."

Hank's kindness was paired with power, something that was unfamiliar to me. He drove me to his house in the cop car, and the whole time it felt like a trap. My ass hovered above the seat, my hand above the door handle. At any moment, he was going to jerk the car around, cuff me, and put me behind bars. We cruised down the streets, folks gawking, tentative with their steps when they saw the car. I liked that feeling, that icy, clean power. A silver rush of invincibility.

Hank's place was as unspectacular and tempering as his face. No yard or nothing. It was modest, uncluttered, and spotless. I stood in the glowing white sterility and realized I liked it an awful lot. Everything had a place. The order made me feel relaxed, clear-headed, happy.

Hank handed me a glass of milk. "Guzzle this down. Here, have a roll while you're at it. Don't be shy with the butter." The refrigerator clunked shut.

I leaned over the counter, chugging down the milk.

I scraped a thin wisp of butter out of the dish and spread it on the roll.

"Christ, more butter than that. No wonder you're such a rake. How often you eating a day?"

"Uh...once. Sometimes twice."

"Jesus, you need at least three square meals. Lots of butter, lots of honey, lots of fatty meat. White sugar, white bread, and white rice...Bathtubs full of rice, you hear me?"

"And bannock?" I said, shoving a thicker dollop of butter inside the second roll, met by a sharp, hot ripple in my lower intestine.

A quizzical look took hold of Hank's map. "You get on top of that and you'll be on a ship by Christmas."

"Or sinking one." I scarfed down the rest of the white dough. None of this bland food held a candle to the biscuits at Vie's. My palate had grown accustomed to oil and spice and nothing short of gold-crusted, cakey, salty heaven.

But then, after a few bland rolls, an incredible thing happened. My appetite groaned awake like an emaciated bear exiting hibernation. I salivated as Hank grated cheese over the red potatoes, buttered the carrots, and simmered lamb in cream.

"I've never had lamb before," I said, eagerly leaning into the table, breathing in the warm, savoury fumes.

"Never had lamb? It's the best meat. You gotta just

drown it in this —" Hank slid over a dish of green jelly that looked like something straight from outer space.

"What is it?"

"Mint jelly."

I winced.

"What, you going to stop trusting me now all of the sudden?"

Slathering the gorgeous seared lamb with the revolting-looking jelly got me emotional. Hank was something else, ruining a piece of meat like that. I carved my knife into the soft flesh, which fell away from the bone. Hank watched avidly as I took my first bite. Two loud, juxtaposing flavours somehow paired together deliciously — a damn polyrhythmic bebop in my mouth.

SPRING CAME AND I SHIRRED eggs in hollowed-out cubes of ham, served it over Vie's pepper rice by 6 a.m., before meeting Hank at the barbells. Most nights, I took the tram to Vie's for the special. Zenora offered me a fat discount on account of what happened to Vince.

In Angel Man's alley, folks rose in love to look out for each other, with the tenacity of a gang but without the threat of violence. The crowd took pride in giving until it ached, and that emptiness, I imagined, was the cavity from which the divine music, the Elysian flavours, and the cosmic capacity for compassion flowed.

"Good that you cleanin' yourself up. Good for you getting outta here. They jackin' up the prices on everything here," Junior huffed as Cannonball Adderley's alto sax mellowed our swing steps over the freshly mopped linoleum.

"Maybe I can chip in," I said with a spin. I turned to Zenora, her heart-shaped face huddled over the counter in thought. "Let me pay for all the chicken and grits at least."

"Where you gon' get the bees from, huh? You gon' steal it? I don't want that. Nah, it ain't your dollar that's gonna save us, Ronny. Ho boy, it ain't about a dollar at all."

"I could ask Hank—"

"Hank? The cop?" Junior laughed, and I caught his pain as it echoed over the blades of the ceiling fan.

"Don't you lose sleep. We bounce back." Zenora placed her hand on my upper arm. "Shoot—you got some guns on you now there, Ronny," she said with a wink.

While I fattened up double-time, the alley's inner voice was diminishing, slowly eroding under the acid of some ominous force. What started as one boarded-up record shop soon became a deserted speakeasy with shattered storefronts. Then the cigar shop was gone.

The next time I was at Hank's place for lunch I asked him, "Why is it that out of all the neighbourhoods in Vancouver, they chose the East End to hike the cost up in, huh? All it's near is the train tracks."

"That slum?" Hank shrugged. "It's a blight on the city."

The suddenness of his words, the wrongness of them, put me off my food. "So the plan is to just plow through the whole joint? More talent comes out of that alley than the whole of Vancouver."

"C'mon, Ronny, I got nothing against dark meat, you know that, but they're different. Out of control."

"Out of control?"

"Ah, Ronny. Your youth is pure. You'll learn."

I went down to the water. Jostled buildings on the waterfront lent a glimpse of the sea. The city had started to feel like an infected place, like damaged lungs struggling to breathe. The anger in me settled when I got to thinking about Stó:lō. It made no sense that someone would try to own, tame, or name a river for themselves. I stared out into the ash-emerald ocean and disappeared into the surf, losing myself and all my burning questions in the endless chromatic green.

Weeks later, the folks in Angel Man's alley emerged from a walloping winter singing loud as ever, their spirits a tribute to the sturdy timber their homes were made out of. Tri-coloured tulips trumpeted out of the earth to announce spring and I caught a glimpse of myself in the speakeasy's sparkling new window — thicker and more threatening. Wiping a crumb of breaded chicken from my lips, I couldn't help but smile, got so distracted by this new version of me that I had to run for the tram.

Re-entering the recruitment centre twenty pounds heavier, I locked eyes with the recruitment officer and saw my future reflected in his face as he traced the muscles in my arms, the breadth of my chest, the Angel Man's Alley tenacity in my eyes. Just like that, I was on a ship.

14

The Sea

Snʊˈneɪməxʷ, 1987

—

"Way too flat, Caliban." Ken crossed his legs, tilted his head to one side. "The delivery of these lines is crucial. The audience needs to grapple with your internal conflict. You're communicating in the colonizer's tongue, remember?"

I stood onstage, a sheath of soreness over my muscle tissue. "Sorry," I sighed and dove into my tired blood, swam into the trenches of my chest cavity, searching my veins and lungs for some dormant burst of energy, only to come up empty-handed. I gave the lines:

"'You taught me language, and my profit on't
Is I know how to curse.
The red plague rid you
For learning me your language.'"

221

I was melted air, subsisting on dreams. The light-headedness, dry mouth, food cravings, and fatigue from swim practice had followed me to rehearsal.

"Thanks, Ken. I'll take it from here," Sparky said. "Overall, we're in good shape. Opening night is when?" he asked the cast.

"Three weeks," we answered in unison.

Sparky called me over, crouched downstage in a yogi squat, impressively limber for his age. "You know, I've been teaching drama for nine years."

Spare me.

He slid down from the stage. "I was in the professional theatre circuit in Vancouver. Dabbled in screen acting for a bit, too. That's a different medium. Did you know they film many Hollywood movies right in Vancouver?"

"For real?"

"Yep. Hollywood North. Tough industry to break into, though. It's like a grimy, out-of-order toilet in a five-star hotel. Far from glamorous, worse than squatting down in a forest. But that's not the point. People imagine it's wonderful, and imagination is more powerful than reality."

The metaphor wasn't doing him any favours. All I could picture was Sparky shitting in a bush. "Huh."

"Some say film is a more realistic style of acting, but I'd say the opposite. Especially commercial acting. You're barely allowed to blink. But when you get paid, you get paid. I still get money for the coffee commercial I did back in seventy-five, can you believe that? They replay it all the time. All I had to do was sleep in front of a green screen while my fake wife — who was a model, not even an actress — brought me fake coffee. It only took a few hours. Between takes I ate chocolate croissants. Not a bad life, getting paid to sleep and eat chocolate croissants."

I looked closely at Sparky in the slant of the stage lights. The outline of his younger self, etched firmly in my memory, fell perfectly over his face. "I know that commercial! That was you? Tried to wake my dad up with coffee and spilled it all over him." Flashes of memory splintered into a fit of laughter. "Why the hell did you quit to become a teacher?"

"Kept forgetting I was in my own body yet kept having to prove my individual superiority while being in a room with twenty replicas of myself. And no one in that industry eats, can you imagine? You start hacking yourself to bits."

That I could.

"Made me flaky," Sparky continued. "Had to cancel on friends and family to go to auditions, most of which I didn't book. Square-jawed white men are a dime a dozen. Not like you. I've seen a lot of actors in my time, and you've got captivating stage presence. Not everyone has that. Spellbinding movement, that voice, and, well, your skin. I won't lie. The performing arts are very visual."

"That why you cast me as Caliban, then?" I straightened my spine, zipped and unzipped my faded windbreaker. "'Cause of my skin?"

"Caliban is the concealed heart of the play. An anger like Prospero's would have been too easy for you to perform. It's less layered. I wanted to push you past your obvious gifts to see where you could go, where I know you can go."

THE WINTER STORM CLOUDS moved east and, with them, Moorthy, Bagira, and Auntie to their settlement in Toronto. Hard-packed sand glittered like a field of burnt sugar under a rising salmonberry sun, red-orange and ripe enough to eat. After rehearsal, Tony and I treaded water in silence, side by side, past the towering sea stacks, ignoring the calls of the seagulls, focused only on the horizon. We gauged the conditions: low tide, perfectly peeling barrels, fifteen waves per group with nineteen-second periods and minimal chop. Beauty. The water stung like frozen nettles as it seeped into my boots, flooding my wetsuit. Colder than usual, but we had to get a taste of the winter swells that had swept Nanaimo's coast. I was surprised by how much I missed Moorthy and Bagira, vanished from my life as quickly as they had appeared.

My shoulders burned with lactic acid as I dug towards

the lineup. The freak swell presented a difficult paddle-out, but God, was it ever beautiful. Tangerine sashes singed the melting blue sky. The kelp-saturated water looked like gold broth filled with black soba noodles. A wave travels away from the area of wind that created it, forming a string of swells. The wave trains have smaller waves in the lead and the rear; the big waves are at the heart of the pack. That's where we were headed.

A ridge of liquid rose above the gold lip of the horizon. I aligned myself with the newborn wave as it cascaded towards me. Dug my arms into the water hard as it crested. Felt the water surge with life beneath my feet as I popped up, perfectly positioned. I envisioned a quick bottom turn — I'd hug the wall and ride the wave all the way to the sandbar. Slip. Pearl.

Smacked in the face by ice-cold green crush. The dulcet hum of underwater ear pressure drummed my temples. I broke the surface, humiliated, with a gut full of salt water.

Tony gained a lead. He rose over the shoulder of a wave and dropped in, his powerful legs bent, wet hair plastered to the nape of his neck. He carved balletically as the wave peeled, rotating his torso in the direction he wanted to go, and pumped away from me.

I gripped the rails of my board to duck dive beneath an oncoming wave — cold, sparkling green, underwater hum.

—

ON THE RIDE TO swim practice, the tang of ocean hung on my lips, brine dust crystallized on my skin. Should have caught those waves. Should have been Prospero.

"There'll be other waves." Tony took a bite of a double chocolate muffin. Simple carbs, trans fats. "If you wanna catch some of 'em, though, you better start eating, dude."

"Shut up." I rolled my eyes.

In the change room I was met by a cloud of shower steam. The scale was nestled behind the lockers in a nice, isolated back corner. I stripped down and stood on it.

"Chan?" Tony's voice echoed from the pool deck.

I nearly slipped and smacked my head, jolting off the scale.

"Jesus, still not changed yet? You have any spare goggles?"

"No," I said.

"Better check the pot of gold."

While Tony went to loot the lost and found, I pulled on my Speedo, catching sight of my waning reflection. My bones popped out at all angles, but I still wasn't lean enough, or at least, not in the way I wanted to be. I couldn't see the fat, but I could feel it all over me. Like it was braided into my bones. Not white or billowy but ink black, intricately woven into the marrow.

I met Tony on the pool deck, the gaseous reek of

chlorine permeating everything, and sailed past the use-less, gumby-looking lifeguard I would have paid to see save someone.

"Nada." Tony sighed. "Swimming blind today."

When we forgot our gear, Coach Lee had us swim without it (with the exception of Speedos).

"Use mine." I passed my silver TYRs over to Tone.

"Mighty heroic of you, Chan." He took the goggles skeptically.

Warm-up without goggles was total cake, followed by a few mellow kick sets. I dolphin-kicked, pumping my chest down, undulating my torso as bubbles fizzled over my skin. The pull set was more of a challenge; after a while, my eyes felt like they were soaking in vinegar. In a way, I liked the sting.

By the middle of the eight-by-one-hundred individual medley on pace time, my eyes were bloodshot. Glimpses of choppy white water were intercut with harsh fluores-cent light. By the seventh set I was a wreck, missing the wall at turns and kicking into empty space. I inhaled warm water up my nose, which felt like snorting wasabi and soap. Then — smack — conked my melon straight on the wall. Felt like a baseball to the teeth, and I couldn't tell if the nickel tang I tasted was blood or chlorine. I pulled and kicked as hard as I could, until the lactic acid burned so bad it felt like my muscles were going to tear right out of my skin.

Every time I came up for air I heard whistle blasts, but I was nearly finished my last set. I reached, reached, reached — suddenly, I was being reeled backwards. Something had a strong hold of my leg.

"Let go." I splashed, erratic. With my head out of the water, the throbbing and stinging came flooding in, like the pool had been diluting the pain.

Tony froze, his calm stillness a mirror for my tantrum. "Chandra, hop the hell out of the pool."

I looked down and saw orange-red blood spouting from my face. I pulled myself out of the pool, and an unearned muscle ache spread over me. When the beak leak stopped, my body felt like it was full of sand. I slipped in and out of the tiled room — long pauses of black, flecks of fluorescent light, and splashes of water. I still had seventy-five metres of the set left. I rose, staggering over to the blocks.

"Oh no, you're not getting back in the pool. Not after that gusher." Coach pulled me back, guiding me to a yellowed plastic deck chair. "Park it."

"I'm fine."

"Like hell you are. You're not getting back in the water." He clasped my arm, his hands moving up to my shoulders. "Shoot, how skinny are you? You eating?" He handed me a protein bar. Chock-full of chemicals and calories. "Here."

"I'm good."

"Eat it." Coach tore open the package and held the bar up to my mouth.

I didn't want to make this a thing, so I reluctantly bit into the bar, planning to grind it against my molars before quickly spitting it back into the wrapper when Coach turned his head. But the velvety cocoa, vanilla nougat, and peanut melt cloaked my tongue in fatty, sugary goodness, dripped down my throat, leaving a thick trail to linger between my teeth. Shivering in the flimsy plastic chair, I felt plumes of guilt billow inside me. All the hard work and dedication — trashed. Phantom fat swathed my stomach as my teammates finished with a fly set and a slow cool-down, their toned arms and tapered torsos undulating in the water.

As I entered the change room, my feet hit the tiles with a wet slap. Droplets of water coated the bathroom stall, which reeked of piss, sweat, and chlorine. I made a fist and punched myself in the gut, kneading it upwards in a J motion, Heimliching myself until I hurled into the toilet bowl. I took a long drink of cold water from the fountain before making my way back out on deck.

I couldn't risk losing the deep grooves in my six-pack, my quad separation, the feeling of being made of steel, of being protected. The less of me there was, the less of me there was to target.

WHEN I GOT HOME, I found Appa passed out on the couch, curled up with an empty six-pack. He looked like a browning banana, skin speckled with liver and sunspots. His gut was swollen from all the fried food and stress. His hair was fine, disintegrating wisps. The smells of body odour and booze tangled with turmeric and cinnamon had seeped into our carpet.

Kitty's craggy meow slit the silence as I slipped into the bathroom to take a long, painful look at myself in the pale yellow light. I was incurably dark. Skin like pitch. My eyes were bloodshot, starred with popped vessels. I wanted to gut myself like a fish or a fruit and free myself of desire. Burn the blackness out of my skin, chisel every ounce of fat off my frame.

I opened the cabinet under the sink to retrieve the fairness cream. I lathered myself, then went into the kitchen covered in invisible flames to down a litre of ice water with lemon and cayenne, gritting my teeth as I passed the bruised berry that was my father. I wondered if pain was contagious.

Sprawled languidly across my bed, stinging and seething over the sloppy surf session, shit swimming performance, and, worst of all, being cast as Caliban, I ran my hands up and down my rib cage, counting bones until I felt slightly better.

The ringtone of my lime-green brick phone siphoned me back into my room. "I don't want your Girl Guide cookies."

"Don't make this harder than it needs to be." Ken's

voice was just as snide over the phone. "Your place or mine? I'm near Sugarloaf Park."

I ran my palm over my face, folded over my bed frame in frustration. "Yours."

FANCY PANTS DID NOT live near Sugarloaf. He lived way, way out on the rez. Only an eleven-minute drive if you had a car, which neither of us did. An hour by bus. I lurched as the bus swerved around the uprooted back roads, the robotic hum and screech of the engine like a fork on a plate. I was livid with Sparks for casting me as Prospero's slave. Racist. Everyone agreed that my Prospero monologue had been the best. My voice was the loudest. My anger the most terrifying. Flossie could act, sure. Her monologue was interesting, but it didn't make any sense for a pretty blond bunny to play the fierce king. If I had to be a slave, why not Ariel? Shapeless and graceful. Why Caliban? With a physical exterior so excruciatingly hideous it was only matched by his internal ugliness.

Ken was stage manager. Our character analyses couldn't be done during school time. Part of the punishment (or "restorative justice," as Sparky insisted on calling it) was in organizing them on our own. Whack call.

A cool whip of cedar air lashed my face as I stumbled off the dreadful bus and onto the road. "You take that every day?"

Ken rolled his eyes. "Peasant wagon too proletariat for you, Hollywood? Expecting a limo?" He crossed his arms around himself. "I don't actually live here, and I'm not from here, cool? Just staying with my aunt and uncle for now."

"How come?"

Ken didn't answer. I stopped asking questions, but I didn't stop having them. Like what was a well-dressed white kid doing living on an Indian reserve? Why'd he have a Native aunt and uncle? Why'd he live with them for now? What was behind the heaviness in the way he'd said *now*?

The house was small, simple, smelled like leather, cane sugar, smoke, and sage. It was weakly lit and cold as a refrigerator. I peered into Ken's room, which looked too lived-in and characteristically Kennified to be as temporary of an accommodation as he made it out to be, but I wasn't about to pry further. His room was full of beads — strings, feathers, beads, and beaded feathered things on strings. On a makeshift sewing table were the pants I'd torched, still on the mend.

"Want something to eat?" he offered.

I was famished enough to lick the congealed day-old grease or burnt egg-white film from an unwashed frying pan, but I didn't deserve a calorie. For thousands of reasons. One of them being that I'd lit a kid's pair of handmade pants on fire because I was bored and because he was different.

I shook my head. Ken shrugged a *suit yourself*. He left

the room briefly and returned with a plate of spherical, toasted fried bread, with a golden, gleaming crust that peaked like the Cascade mountain range. The cakey white dough revealed itself in the broken parts. And there was jam — a kaleidoscope of orange, ruby, and pink-red with drupelets intact, spilling slowly over the edges in thick dollops onto the plate as Ken sunk his teeth in, sending a breeze of sugar molecules up into the air and right into my nasal passages. The berries were so, so fat. Saliva pooled in my cheeks.

"You...look like you want a piece."

"Smells...dangerously good."

"Here, weirdo."

I reached out to accept the proffered plate, my eyes skidding, the back of my thighs sweating.

Somewhere between gobbling Elysian mouthfuls of golden bread and sticky-sweet jam and underlining Caliban's lines, long after we'd spoken about anything in our shared reality, I heard Ken say, "I got kicked out, okay?"

"Ah," I said, with a lacklustre nod.

"It's fine. You and my old man would get along great. He'd dig your fruitcake jokes."

Wish I could tell you I came around then and there. That I saw past Ken's perfectly pale skin and recognized his pain of being othered as my own, both of us finding peace in pretending. That I wrestled with my ebbing and flowing rage, the one that couldn't comprehend why someone would choose to stand out when they could so easily blend in, and tamed it into the recognition that it wasn't a choice, that I wasn't looking at the margins closely enough. But instead I swallowed it all down like shame and held my breath.

"Damn, you were really hungry, hey?" Ken's voice anchored my meandering mind, clean as the plate I'd licked.

"For real, you could put some of that jam on an old shoe and I'd eat it."

Ken's laugh echoed from the narrow hall as he went to the kitchen. "Salmonberry and peach, biatch."

Expecting judgement but receiving none, I felt calm as I ate. I devoured one piece, and then another, until the sweetness stuck in my throat and the cakeyness of the bread expanded in my stomach. Fuelled, we tossed our magazines on the floor — mine were all *Freedomways*, *Thrasher*, and *Guitar World*, his were all *Vogue* and *Seventeen* — picked up our scissors, and got to it. Slitting glossy pages from the spine, dismantling indexes, and collaging a chaos of magazine clippings, we reconstructed the pieces until they made sense, tumbling into talk about *The Tempest* as thin shreds of coated paper fell to the ground.

Be not afeard; the isle is full of noises,

"Cavaluna. 'Moon calf.' Son of Sycorax; the witch that controls the moon."

Sounds, and sweet airs, that give delight and hurt not.

"Black magic. Caliban means cannibal. Caliban means Black! Also, codfish?"

"Caliban means human being."

Sometimes a thousand twangling instruments

"He's half-fish, half-man."

Will hum about mine ears; and sometime voices

"Sycorax has blue eyes! Remember? Blue eyes!"

"He's Black."

"Black people can have blue eyes."

That, if I then had waked after long sleep,

"Savage. Miranda calls him 'savage.'"

"Colonizers call every Indian a savage."

Will make me sleep again; and then in dreaming,

"I thought you said he was Black?"

"Indians can be Black, too."

The clouds methought would open, and show riches

"Craves freedom."

Ready to drop upon me, that when I waked

"Would rather live in dreams than in his fucked-up reality."

I cried to dream again.

We stood back to admire the character study we'd created.

"Damn."

"Damn."

THE CALM CARRIED INTO the next morning, cold but bone dry. I put cane sugar in my tea and ate papaya salad for breakfast without guilt. I hopped down the creaking stairs, the sound of Vathany slogging through an aerobics video in the basement following me out the door.

In the silence of the change room, I felt the full weight of my fullness. The pool scale taunted me, but university scouts were in the bleachers and I had no time to dwell or sour my mood with a weigh-in. I dove into chemical-blue panic, but the nauseating discomfort subsided shortly after warm-up. I felt solid. Powerful. Present. My technique, which in the last weeks had been sloppier than a B-lane swimmer in the outer lanes, suddenly locked into place. Sugar and refined carbs weren't supposed to work this way, but I was no longer dragging my feet, no longer feeling the fingertips of the swimmer behind me brushing feather light against my toes. Instead, I was lapping the entire lane. Preserved salmonberry sweetness had pierced the winter lull, dense and wet-cold like sea glass, and I was swimming like I was half-fish.

After practice, the sky was unnaturally bright. Flossie and I were going to run lines. Her house was in a ritzy part of town; it looked like an American suburb, all white-picket-fencery and trimmed hedges. Too many cars to fit in one garage.

Flossie opened the door, popping a gum bubble with her tongue. Manicured hands pulled me upstairs to her sacred room, which smelled like chemical berries and aspartame. We ran our lines one and a half times before she straddled me.

"The cool thing about dark skin is you can't see hickeys." Her warm, pink lips and small tongue sucked on my collarbone as she draped her legs over my lap.

I tried to distract myself from the thick spell that was spreading over me, pulling me under like a riptide, by studying the details of her equestrian-themed bedroom. "You ride horses?"

"Only black stallions."

We tried running lines a few more times, but it was impossible, with the horse decor, the grease-stained pizza box diffusing the air with the orgasmic smell of cheese and dough, and this platinum blond I shouldn't touch, enchanting me in her tight jeans. So perfect, so powerful.

OPENING NIGHT WAS WARM enough to skateboard without a jacket. The first evidence of spring emerged as trumpeter swans, with grey goslings nestled in their wings, swimming inland before toddling across the roads. Rose-gold light poured through the trees, which were covered in a few velvety buds. The cherry blossoms would bloom soon. I'd started eating and secured the interest of a local, mainland, and prairie swimming scout.

Appa had wanted to wear his red sarang to opening night, but I told him not to come if he did. I was on edge, knowing that people would see Vathany and Appa, brown as cinnamon. Vathany in her Lycra, with her bleached hair and painted face, Appa with his ill-fitting jeans and thick desi accent. The veil would be pulled back to reveal a complex truth, naked in the lights of my high school auditorium.

I dug my costume — turquoise fish-scale tights and billowing blouse. And Flossie *was* Prospero in her tapered crimson gown. In the stuffy green room, I watched as she dabbed her face with beige foundation.

"Think this is my shade?" I joked, nervous energy adding to the heat in the room.

"Can I put some on you?" she asked.

"Hell naw."

Flossie pushed me onto the ledge of the vanity and leaned towards me. Her dress was corseted and low-cut; she had a mole right above her cleavage. I was suddenly real aware of how revealing my tights were.

"This is whack," I said, closing my eyes, imagining myself finally transforming into the person I knew I was inside. It was uncomfortably humid, and my butt was sticking to the counter as Flossie dabbed my skin with a makeup sponge, covering my entire face in foundation. Sweat formed on my upper lip beneath the thick film.

"I turned Chandra white!" she crowed.

I opened my eyes, swivelled to look at my reflection. It hurt my chest to see what was mirrored back at me. The thick cream covering my face didn't look right. Not with my coarse hair, or the sudden jolt of dark brown where the makeup ended and my skin began. No matter what I did, no matter how many blond girlfriends I had, no matter how much I surfed or swam or read Shakespeare, I was never, ever going to be white.

"He looks like a potato." Paula, an ensemble member in all black, seemed taller and more powerful than I remembered when she swept into the room.

"All right, Prospero, Caliban, in the wings! We're about to start!" Ken shouted into the green room.

My pits pooled with sweat. Fuckin' A — I still had the makeup on! I grabbed a rag and rubbed it off, leaving my face covered in light blotches and streaks. I stared into my reflection, readjusted my costume over my lithe body. If anyone had a problem with the shade of my skin, or my parents, it was they who were ugly, not us. Not Caliban. I told myself this over and over, trying to force my mind to believe it. But I kept thinking about the cast headshots plastered on the wall. Flossie looked like a porcelain angel against the black background. Even Ken looked crisp and distinguished. My face blended in with the nothingness, and all that was visible was my teeth. A disfigured wretch, the forgotten shadow: Caliban.

As we took our places in the wings, heavenly light poured between the maroon velvet curtains and I realized this was the last time I'd walk through the portal to this other world. The last time I'd slip into scaled and enslaved skin.

Words and tears flowed out of me like water. My lines were not lines but a truth that I kept deep in me. All I needed to do was speak it. Acting wasn't about me at all, and that's where I'd been getting it all wrong. It wasn't about Shakespeare, or Sparky. It was that oneness, like staring out at a vast ocean, knowing that within were quadrillions of vigintillions of water droplets. That we are all composed of such water droplets. That everything in the universe is really just tiny, tiny droplets. And in those tiny droplets are even tinier atoms. And within those atoms are three linked Möbius strips reflecting everything that has ever happened. There it is, clear as glacier water: the futility of human undertakings. Separation is the grandest illusion of all, and until we realize our ultimate unity, we are destined to suffer.

And so a part of me died staring up at the spotlight beam, the illuminated molecules of dust dancing in the air. I felt a profound calmness. My entire body was relaxed, like waking up in the summertime after a deep sleep.

THE FLOATING TIMELESSNESS CARRIED me off the stage and into the repurposed cafeteria, where a gaggle of ninth graders stood plastered against the wall, their conversations coming to a halt as I entered the room.

Sparky came down the stairs from the tech booth and approached me, his impressive wingspan outstretched. "Finally didn't drop your lines."

I turned to Ken, his dense black eyebrows that had once been singular were now tweezed apart. "Thanks for hammering it into me."

"Yeah. Anyways, you were good. That was really good," he said, sincerity in his eyes where the snideness normally rested. "I still hate you." Ah, there it was.

"Fair enough, I set your ass on fire."

"I mean, I hated you before that. You're kind of a massive chode."

I wrestled the urge to clap back with a "Thought you liked chodes." That would have proven his point. Instead, I said, "You're cool, Ken."

"You, too. And you're a good actor. But I still hate you."

Flossie swung her arms around me, scraping the side of my face with the thorny stem of a yellow rose.

I stared into the heart of the rose, entranced by the way the creamy yellow petals folded in on themselves. I tore away from her and floated towards the white island of hair in the middle of my father's terracotta head.

"Too long," Vathany sighed, sipping a diet cola from the vending machine. "It would have been better if it was shorter." The bones in her face were carved out under the harsh fluorescent lights, and her chest caved in so much she looked concave, a hollowed-out whelk shell.

I swiped the cola from her hand and took a swig. She smacked me on the back. All Appa could say was "Good."

"Chandra?" A contralto voice soared over my shoulder.

Sparky had his arm dangling over a stout, silver-haired person with a peachy complexion. I studied their jade mala beads, thin wrists, and the palpable sheen of their wine-coloured lipstick but was unable to place their gender.

"Mo. Mo Sitka." They reached out their hand to meet mine. "Brilliant. Absolutely brilliant. You've got a great head voice, striking authenticity — good cheekbones. Difficult to find in a young actor. Difficult to find Black actors on this white island. I run the Phoenix, the theatre company at the University of Victoria. Would love to have you audition."

As they spoke, my headshot came into focus. Teeth, just teeth. My skin blurred into the black background. I remembered who I was. What I looked like. That my path was fixed and clear. I wasn't going to keep playing make-believe for the rest of my life.

The warm, golden haze of unity started to dissipate. Time was water. The more I tried to hold on to it, the more the moment slipped away, liquid pouring through the spaces between my fingers as if through a sieve before evaporating entirely.

15

The River

kw'ótl'kwa (the sea), 1955–58

White water frothed up like parting clouds to reveal the sea wolves, ascending slick from the emerald surf. The pack glided in from the docked ship, shedding ocean undercoats as they set foot on land in the form of men. The sailors had a quiet, elemental strength in their shoulders, a storm-quelling peace in their eyes. Ray's peace.

Soon, I'd be one of them, I thought, molting memory — if only I could stop wreck-diving into the troves of my mind for sunken moments to polish and reconfigure, instead of keeping my ass glued to the goddamn chair.

Having dropped out of school early, and on bad terms, I never did learn how to sit still. I wriggled in my seat, waning in and out of the lesson, catching only fragments.

I chewed the insides of my cheeks, slapped myself in the quads, and straightened my spine.

"Stop drifting off," I whispered to myself. The recruits around me glared.

The admiral droned on about the anatomy of naval boats, the differences between types of combatants and ships in the fleet, monochrome as the overcast sky. Without meaning to, I slipped into a sea of clouds on a three-masted ship with billowy sails, wind beating against my face, sunlight flickering on the body of air like gold…

And just like that, class was over. I snapped back into the room and looked down at my pitiful scrawl. I had to get a grip on my concentration problem.

COLLAPSED OVER THE BAR with Hank that evening, I let the ice melt into my rum and forgot how to fill my lungs. "Got the zorros over that test," I said tenuously, with what brittle breath I had left. A marlowbraid of doubt hitched a splice knot around my sternum.

"Cut the gas, flutter bum. That test is made in the shade." Hank took a swig of rum and shrugged.

"God gave me the royal shaft in the smarts department, Hank. I'm dumb as bricks."

"Smart ain't got nothing to do with school. Look, you just — you gotta find a way to stay in the room, to stay present. What's something that gets you in your skin?" He slid off the stool, corralled me over to the dart board.

"Lindy hop. Jive." I threw my missile, barely grazed the double ring.

"All right, well…get creative. There's gotta be a way to get as excited about ships as you do for dancing." Hank's turkey tail dart met the triple with a clear, secure thud.

"I am excited about the ships, all right? What I ain't too keen on is staring at a blackboard for hours."

Hank scratched his head. "What if —" He took another medicinal swig of rum. "What if you…Say, what if you had a themed jive for each ship?"

"You're a loon." I shook my head. The cat had stars for eyes.

"That may be, but it's worked for me so far. Now quit your gringies, ankle-biter, and finish your rum."

Hank polished off his drink and ordered another. I took my shot, hit the outer bull's eye.

ADMIRAL SPLICED THE ROOM with a loud belch, and my crewmates erupted in laughter. We were learning about different types of warships, and as always, arse-sweat sticking me to the chair, I couldn't stay focused.

I had overheard sailors telling tales of the places where two oceans meet — an ethereal line between the midnight blue of the Atlantic and the crystalline turquoise of the Pacific. I wanted to drag my hand through the split, swim smack-dab into the divide. That yearning was a stronger incentive to learn than the strap ever was, so I thought, *To hell with it, Hank.*

I coded each ship with a dance move: low-to-the-ground tranky doo, all thigh and rump, for U-boats; swizzlestick base, fluid and undulating in the torso, for submarines; a flighty half moon, high on the toes, energy pouring out the fingertips, for aircraft carriers. As the admiral carried on, I tapped my feet discreetly, scribbling out my cipher, pairing movement to meaning.

Charleston-swinging back to my sleeping quarters in the empty hallway that night, the marlowbraid around my sternum had loosened and I was filled with the strange enthusiasm of having created something, even if that something turned out to be no good. I closed my door and danced out my routine, emulating the ships' anatomy with my body, adding more detail and flair when something didn't feel right or an idea sparked.

And so I jived my way to a "Swell job, sailor ... Ronny, is it?" from the admiral when he placed my exam on the desk.

Draped in a cloak of pride, I rang Hank up to tell him about my aced exam. He ordered me to meet him outside the barracks, by the bay facing Mount Baker.

My face split into a smile at the sight of him, leaning

smugly over the wood rail. We walked along Stó:lō at the cusp of last light, staring into the flowing water painted a pale pink by the setting sun.

"You know this river is really called Stó:lō," I said.

"Who told you that? Far as I know, this is the Fraser River."

"I know. That's what everyone thinks."

"Stó:lō…hmm…that sounds nice."

"Yeah, I think so, too."

A feather of peace replaced the marlowbraid in the centre of my chest. It was a relief to hear Hank easily accept a different truth. We stood there in the dense silence, gazing out into the water as it faded from pink to silver, knowing that this, in all likelihood, was goodbye.

MIDWEEK, ON A WARM but drizzly day, I scraped a thin layer of skin off my neck while crawling under barbed wire. I flinched and lowered myself down, inhaling the moist black earth right up my nose. Rain lifted wriggling worms from the dirt. I felt like a damn worm myself as I writhed in the mud. A fly flew right into my gob at the same time as I felt someone's heat and friction to my right. I was quick, but the speediest recruit was a negro named Sam. On our sunrise five-mile runs, he'd wait until the last stretch, and then he'd launch past me. Just glide past me like air, as if he'd been politely holding back the whole time. Not trying to grandstand or nothing like that, so I didn't mind so much.

Sam was mesmerizing to look at. I'd never seen a face so full and symmetrical, nor skin so smooth. His skin wasn't tawny brown like Zenora's, or a freckly high yellow like Junior's. He wasn't redbone like Angel Man. His skin was ocean black. His eyes were big, dark pools, and his lips were round and full.

Sam's lithe body slithered right past me like he was being pulled. I dug my elbows in harder and heaved myself forward. The last stretch of the course was a run. I drove my heavy legs into the ground, eyes locked on Sam. But I suppose that was my problem. Sam had his eyes on the horizon. Like if he ran fast enough, he could fly. He finished a few yards ahead of me.

When he crossed the line, he went straight for water and I followed suit. Panting, I leaned against the wall, drinking the sweet coldness until it came out my toes. Nothing sweeter than cold water after training. Sam wiped the water off his lip with hands that made deep sea look pale and the admiral's hands frail.

"You writing a book or what?" he scoffed, then walked away.

—

MY FIRST TRIP WAS on the HMCS *Bonaventure*. I guess I had turned seventeen or eighteen by then, but without a birth date there was no way of knowing for sure. In the barracks, the night before boarding, the cinema in my mind played an endless loop of silver high seas. I threw my pillow on the ground, sat up at the foot of my bed drenched in anxious sweat, and accepted that sleep was not going to happen. Out the window, half the moon stared back, wrapping me in a celestial white glow.

I jived around the room, thinking of Angel Man and his music, Jagger and the rope swing. Of oolichan and the sobering coldness of the river. I thought of young Vince. Of Ray. My eyelids grew heavy, and I closed them briefly, falling into a wisp of sleep.

My thin slumber was disrupted by the blue light of morning, a grace note of a pastel sunrise before the sky turned back into Vancouver grey. I put on my new navy-blue slacks, white shirt, and navy peacoat. Feeling brand new, I stepped out into the drizzly morning looking crisp and clean. The faint rain felt nice on my tired skin, and the slight mist quelled my pounding headache.

Bonnie was the only remaining aircraft carrier in all of Canada. I stood a whole head above most of the crew. Though I was bigger and stronger than I'd been in my entire life, I was a reed compared to the rest of the men. Sizing the sailors up in order of physical superiority, my eyes, as did everyone's, landed on Sam. Everything about him was slick — tightly coiled hair trimmed to the scalp, smooth skin, broad shoulders, dense, muscular body.

After a meal of rubbery meat, creamed spinach, mashed potatoes, and a white roll with butter, we were shown to our sleeping quarters. Four grown men sardined into each room with barely enough oxygen to share. I was the first one in the tin can and used that advantage to swipe a top bunk. The bed was stiff as a plank of wood, and the sheets were paper thin, but I was relieved to have my own designated space. I lay down on the bed for a moment, let my muscles relax, and felt the weight of yesterday's sleepless night like stones on my eyelids.

"Oi!" A throaty voice split the air, ripped the insides of my ears.

My body felt groggy, like I hadn't used it for a year. I shuffled out from under the rag of a blanket, feeling hot and heavy, like I had sand for blood.

"Tot time, lads!" A stocky fella with flames for hair said he went by Torchie. Behind him came a fellow with an angular face and silky black hair who introduced himself as Tod.

"Shoot, you guys long-lost brothers?" Torchie scratched his head, pivoting between Tod and me.

"Huh?" I stared intently at Tod's knife-like cheekbones.

"I don't see it." Tod pursed his lips.

"Me neither." I shrugged.

"Where you from?" Tod asked.

"New West."

"Clan?"

"Uh…Clark Park gang." I laughed.

"Those zoot suit–wearing bastards?" Torchie rolled up his sleeves.

"Easy, I'm emancipated."

"We all are now," Tod said.

I could tell I was going to have a problem with this Torchie character straight away. Within five minutes he was telling us about his classy chassis back home and how he was distantly related to Sir Walter Torchie. I didn't know or care who that was.

"So this the lot of us, then?" Torchie chortled, revealing stained teeth.

Tod's resting face was a smile, so it was hard to tell how he felt about the whole situation.

"Don't look so disappointed. Colour don't matter so much these days," Torchie said, making eye contact with someone on the bunk below mine. "'Specially at sea."

I swung myself over the rails to find a muscular man with shellac-brown skin and stern eyes.

"With all due respect, what's that got to do with me?" Sam asked.

"Well, I mean, just to let you know that I'm not against…" Torchie stammered.

"About that rum…" I said.

Sam, Tod, Torchie, and I made our way on deck. The sound of thrashing waves was diluted by the clamour of sailors and the clank of shot glasses. We gathered around the holy rum tub, crafted of oak and reinforced with brass bands, draped with pastel lilacs and carnations of every colour. In brass letters, it read: *The Queen, God Bless Her.*

The rum ration consisted of one-eighth of an imperial pint of rum and was given out to every single sailor at midday. Senior ratings (petty officers and the like) received their rum neat. Us junior ratings got a watered-down ration — two parts water, three-eighths of an imperial pint of grog.

The captain, a lithe man with thick eyebrows white as snow, floated out on deck. "Sailors, look to your left and to your right."

I cast an eyeball at Torchie's big, dumb, grinning mug, then at Sam, cool as clouds.

"From this day forward, these are your brothers. *Bonnie*, our mother," the captain sang out.

"And the rum tub, our lover!" a petty officer joked.

We all laughed.

I took my inaugural tot and stared out into the infinite silk ocean, into its millions of colours, from silver to carbon to Majorelle. Its beauty overwhelmed me. In the pink glow of sunset, the seagulls looked like fluttering cherry blossom petals.

Sam leaned over the rail, staring out at the gulls.

"Guess you and I are brothers now." He turned to me and grinned, revealing large white teeth.

"Ain't that a bite." My chest ballooned with so much pride I nearly choked.

"Nah." He folded his arms.

The sweetness of the rum warmed my tongue, and I felt a sort of comfort, like a mother's embrace. The more I lingered by the water, the more I felt at home. In that moment, I decided that day would be my chosen birthday.

AN AMBER LIGHT POURED through the small oval window. I kneaded my stomach with the back of my hand. The taste of bile was fresh on my tongue and the smell of stomach acid hung sharp under my nostrils.

"Jesus, it ain't tot time yet?" Torchie complained.

The thought of more rum made me pick up my bucket again.

"Aw, what's wrong, landlubber?" he said at the queasy look on my face. "Sea leg growing pains?"

There were certain men, like Torchie, who were talkers. They boasted like no one I'd ever met, brandishing bar fights and dames they'd won. I knew they weren't that tough, learned to never be threatened by someone who had to honey their own reputation. That was why I held so much reverence for Sam. He never said too much of anything. He was a man of necessary words who worked hard and stayed humble.

"You good, Ronny boy?" Tod made the room colder as he entered, smelling like a crystal of salt.

"I'm fine," I snapped.

"He's...a little seasick," Sam said.

"I ain't."

"What are you then? Morning sick? You pregnant?" Torchie made me grind my teeth down to chalk sometimes. I could count on him to chirp something when I least needed it.

Tod laughed. "You really are an annoying son of a bitch."

When I was feeling more like myself, though, I didn't mind Torchie so much. Hell, there was even something consoling about him and his predictable motor-mouth antics. But right then he needed to bugger off.

The bell rang and a collective "Tots, lads!" echoed from the halls.

"Let's go then, boys," Tod said, fixing his cap. He had this low way of speaking, reminded me of the riverbed.

Torchie clambered out of the room, and Sam and Tod strode after him. I heaved into my bucket one last time, wiped my face with my sleeve, and took a long look at the ceiling before making my way out on deck.

My stomach settled on starboard. Water was there, in us and all around us — fluid, divine. As I watched the midnight-blue waves rise, sometimes as tall as the North Shore Mountains, the white foam brushing against the cloudline before crashing down, the ship, which looked so massive when we were on land, was a speck of dust. I was at the edge of the earth.

"Why's anyone think heaven is in the clouds?" I wondered.

"Careful, Ronny, you sound like a damn poet." Tod scruffed his hair. "You know, you look real familiar." His hooded eyes under long, dark eyelashes glinted in the light.

"Yeah, I'm your bunkmate," I shot back.

"Smart ass. No, you look like a friend of mine."

"Huh."

"You mixed?"

"No."

"Sure? You look it."

"Y'all ever see a coloured broad with blue eyes?" Torchie lurched between us, reeking of rancid sea cucumber, briny pit sweat, and rum breath.

"Can't say I have," I said.

"I have. Thought she was an angel." He sighed.

"You say that about every female you see, Torch." I looked deeply into the sea, swirls of pearl and azure.

"Beauty like that's enough to cure the world of racism."

"Sure thing, Torchie." Tod rolled his eyes.

Suddenly, Torch bolted upright, cupped his hands

over his ceaseless gob, and retched over the rail. The reek of hot, acidic vomit wafted up and turned my stomach. Torchie and the other talkers all seemed to flock together. They puffed out their chests, spouting stories of their grandeur:

The time I beat up a Yank at a jive.

The time I stole a Yank's girl, then crawled out the window.

The time I punched a shark in the face while we were stationed in the Bahamas… and later stole a Yank's girl.

Sam joked that there was so much bluster on board the ship that it was going to sink, but soon those same men ended up lurching over the rail and into buckets when we got to high seas. Somehow, the quiet sailors like Sam were less affected. As if resting their voices had given their bodies and minds time to adjust to their surroundings. I learned from them to lean into the swells, to be fully aware of my own insignificance. That way the realization that we were sloshing around in the Creator's belly didn't come as so much of a shock.

When my sea legs finally came in, I felt at peace, more stable than I'd ever felt on land. I liked knowing that the ocean could swallow me up at any moment, that it could just as easily swallow up the captain or the prime minister or the Queen of England.

MY FIRST JOB ABOARD SHIP was to control the Aldis lamp. With pulses of light, we sent messages in Morse code. Aiming the light at the recipient ship by turning a lever, the signalman opened and closed the shutter over the lamp. The receiver from the other ship would see the message through binoculars and reply in kind. The dits and the dahs of Morse code were a fresh slate of language. Instead of twenty-six different symbols, there were just a dash and a dot — symmetrical. If my brain flipped the symbols backwards, it didn't matter. I could tap out the grammar of Morse code with my movement, like dancing.

One night, I tapped Morse code on the steel rail of the ship to the glowing white orb above me.

.... . .-.. .-.. --- / -- --- --- -.

Hello, moon.

It reeled the ocean into itself, painting the deck in celestial light, making it easy for Sam and me to stay alert on night watch.

"I can't never sleep when the moon is ripe like this. That normal?" Sam's voice was muted by the echo of thrashing waves.

"Think so."

"Hungry all the time when I ain't asleep."

My stomach bleated. "Now that you say it." I started singing, "Beans and Cornbread."

Sam joined in with a liquid honey hum. "Damn, Ronny, where'd you learn Louis Jordan?"

"Why? You writing a book?"

Sam howled. We went back to singing and snapping. The melody wrapped around my heart like warm water. We were no Angel Hayes, but it did feel like I was back in Hogan's Alley. Just as we reached strawberries and shortcake, a godawful screeching pierced the air, followed by a violent banging, like atoms splitting or the kraken emerging from the sea.

Sam's mouth hung open.

I called over the bridge, "The hell's going on?"

"No sweat, sailor," chimed a bodiless voice. "We just ran over an airplane."

The catapult sling had broken while a plane was being ejected from the ship. It dropped over the side and got chewed up by the propellers.

Sam and I locked eyes and laughed. His white teeth illuminated the night.

SAM AND I CLICKED OVER TIME without needing to speak much, through humming, lamping, and standing guard. Some days, we all wanted to wring each other's chafed necks, but our annoyance dissipated the moment we docked in Hamburg.

The speed of the ground made me uneasy. It was deceptive — stalking and slow relative to the swift blade of air, light, or water. We wobbled down the wharf, an army of sea legs, feeling something like fish on sand.

Everyone said that German was a harsh language. Well, Torchie said so. But to me, there was something melodic about the guttural sounds and the smoky "ch" of Deutsch. The first German word I heard was "Himmlisch." As we stepped off the boat, a German officer exhaled it, staring up at the sky, a serene, rose blue full of cream-yellow cumulus. He was around my height, weak jawed. Hair about as dark as mine. He didn't look anything like the snow-blond, ice-blue, rectangular Aryans I expected.

With half our crew having last names like Zimmermann, Lehman, and Schwarz, the fact that German civilians looked more or less the same as we did shouldn't have been as striking as it was. There were also plenty of folks along the Rhine with the same dark complexion as Angel Man and Sam and every colour in between. Would you believe they even played jazz? As we meandered through the cobblestone streets, I heard Louis Armstrong playing, growing louder as I approached a small, dark child hanging linens on a line strung across fragments of brick. The apartment building had obviously been bombed.

"Schmetterling!" he called, tugging at his mother's currant-red petticoat and pointing to a brown moth.

The server at the small Biergarten we found where everything was made of wood was a tanned kraut with billowy black hair and sea-blue eyes. The three of us had to lift Torchie's fat jaw off the floor. She raised a bushy eyebrow at me. "Kann ich ihnen helfen?" Her elliptical eyes were prismatic swirls of blue and green framed by long, dark lashes. I shook my head and returned to my warm beer. It was the best ale I'd ever tasted. Oaty and dulcet.

"Einen schönen Tag noch," she said in a tone so bitter it sounded like it had been fermented in a barrel.

After a hot meal of red cabbage and rye bread, we wandered back to the strange calmness of the Innenstadt, where fragments of the old town came to a sharp halt in jaded edges of stone. The remnants of war hung over everything — not just in the rubble and ruins but in the eyes of the people. In the way they moved. In the air itself.

ITALY WAS AN ASSAULT on the senses. The stark slap of sewer stench suddenly intercepted by margherita pizza and pasta alfresco. The bellowing of bickering lovers and the soft accordion serenades at twilight. Genoa was a labyrinthine network of streets, with meat hanging in the windows of the butcher shops, the lads all buying heaps of salami. I saw these young Italian boys, tough and full of life, and I couldn't help but remember Vince and Micky.

It was in the busy port city streets of Genoa at the end of that trip that Torchie found the horse. A bay-coloured Calabrese.

"He's a stray! We gotta take him with us!" Torchie's pale, freckled face had turned redder than a ripe vine tomato.

"You're mad." Tod shook his head. "He's mad." He appealed to the rest of us.

"They eat horse meat here!" Torch made an erratic series of exasperated gestures, which, had it not been for his comedic sunburn, would have helped him pass for a local. He was right, though. Horse meat was everywhere, used in a variety of traditional recipes: a stew called pastissada, steaks, carpaccio, bresaola, simmered in tomato sauce in a terracotta dish and called pezzetti di cavallo. I'd unknowingly eaten thin strips of dried horse meat called sfilacci earlier that day.

"I swear to God, Torchie. Let the horse —" I began.

"His name is Edoardo, and he's coming with us."

"All right, then," said Sam.

Tod and I froze. Sam studied Edoardo, who snorted and whinnied.

"I dig horses, too." Sam shrugged, and that was that.

"If we're really going to do this, I need a drink." I closed my eyes and rubbed the back of my neck.

"That's the spirit," Torchie said, handing me his flask of gin.

I took a swig. It tasted like the whole region of Liguria, distilled — a tangle of Genovese basil, ripe, turning peaches, bustling cobblestone streets, lovers in moonlight, and echoey cathedrals.

"That's damn good," I said, taking another generous sip.

"Hey, hold your horses," Torchie said, reaching for the flask.

"*You* hold your horse." I stepped back and took yet another sip.

Bringing Edoardo on board the ship suddenly seemed both obvious and urgent. The horse neighed and huffed. His hooves clopped along the hard streets as we made our way down to the dock.

"What the hell you got there, Chief Petty?" Our lieutenant commander appeared out of thin air, his face mottled like salami.

"Just boarding ship, Lieutenant," Torchie said, tugging Edoardo towards *Bonnie* as if it were only natural. Edoardo neighed. Tod, Sam, and I followed suit.

"You drunk, sailors?"

"Affirmative, Lieutenant," I said.

"That has nothin' to do with it," Torchie insisted, trotting up the gangway, Edoardo whinnying behind him.

"Are you out of your damn mind?"

Torchie didn't answer.

"Let the horse go, sailor."

"With all due respect, Lieutenant — and I do respect you, sir — I can't do that."

"And why in God's name not?"

"Because…if I don't bring him on board, they're going to eat him."

"It's true." Tod nodded gravely. We all nodded in solidarity.

The lieutenant commander paused and studied Torchie's face, carved out by the white moonlight. "You eat meat, sailor?"

"I do, sir. But not horses," Torchie said, cavalier.

"And what makes a horse different than a cow?"

"Simple. A horse is a horse, and a cow is a cow."

Amid the banter, the commodore came out and berated Torchie, sent us all to bed. Told us to sober up and get rid of the horse, that if he even so much as heard the word *horse* again, we'd be setting ourselves up for an early discharge.

Torchie hung his head, clicked his tongue, and led Edoardo back into the cobblestone streets. When he came back, his eyes were red. He was gin-drunk, probably a little delusional, too, which can happen after being at sea for so long, but there was something real honest about his tears. He really cared about that goddamn horse.

That night, Tod, Sam, and I locked eyes in the bunk, bruised for Torchie. Suddenly, I was overcome by the urgent need to piss. I walked down the hallway, rubbing my eyes, asking myself if I was really living up to the creed by letting Torchie bring the horse near the ship in the first place.

Time elapsed. I got lost in the routine of Morse code and ship maintenance tasks. At around three in the morning, I was decoding a message when I could have sworn I heard hooves echoing in the ship corridor.

I locked eyes with Sam. "You hear that?"

He didn't say a word, didn't even blink. We rose from our seats, strode towards the quiet clopping in the hallway. Our spines stiffened as a loud neigh split the hush. We dashed out of the room like rockfish away from a speargun.

"What's wrong, Chief Petty, sir?" a young seaman on watch called down from the deck.

We ignored him and kept running, slipping in the freshly mopped halls as we swerved around a corner. Tod paced back and forth, studiously supervising the pettys.

"Where in Genoa's name is Torchie?" I asked.

"He's water king," Tod said in a low, serious whisper, ushering us away with stern eyes that said he didn't have time for our shenanigans, not now, not in front of the new recruits.

We straightened ourselves out, marched away with our heads up and shoulders back, until we were out of Tod's sight, then continued running. We made our way to the boiler room, where we found Torchie at work.

"Fess up, Torch, where's the horse?" I said.

"I don't know what you're talking about." He kept tending the boiler, didn't even lift his head.

We left Torch to scour the ship, went down to the cargo hold.

"Aw, shit!" Sam griped.

"What?" I said, taking another step and landing in something mushy. The stink wafted up and smacked me in the face with the memory of Tobias and the horse-whip. I shuddered, then looked down and saw the heap of horse-pie all over my shoe.

Lieutenant Commander came around the bend. "What're you doing down here? You're supposed to be lamping ship." He looked down at our shoes and the pile of dung.

Oh, Jesus, I thought, *this is it.* We were going to be blamed for the whole damn thing and discharged. Sweat pooled in my pits, streamed down the back of my neck, and dripped down my tailbone.

"Well…I suggest you get back to your station." Our lieutenant commander, uncharacteristically dismissive, waved us away with a pink, callused hand.

I quivered, tilted my head.

"Yes, sir." Sam saluted.

I followed suit, and we walked away, with shit-stained shoes and a thermal vent of questions. Every so often after that, late at night, a crew member would claim he heard what sounded like a horse neighing.

16

The Sea

W̱SÁNEĆ-ləkʷəŋən (Victoria, Canada), 1987–88

⸻

I submerged my calves in the jagged sea as the sky turned an aggressive shade of pink. New driftwood and broken shells scattered across the lagoon like calico confetti. The curved arbutus tree I'd held onto as I played *Tempest*, when I was Prospero, where I peeled the bark, had snapped in half from high seas and winter storms when I became Caliban. I picked up a perfect red crab shell, empty, and wondered where Rocky and Jill were. If they'd somehow drifted from the coast of Tamil Nadu to my parents' teardrop-shaped home of limes, peacocks, and elephants. Unsure who I was now, I was relieved by the boundlessness of who I could be.

High on our varsity scholarships and the rag-end of youth, Tony and I blasted Whitesnake and Blondie on the hour-long drive to Victoria. His folks owned a condo near campus we could move into. The soundness of Vathany's strategies, of her insistence on our proximity to white people, revealed itself more and more over time. Her monsoon steel heart withstood the hurricane of forced flight and settlement, while Appa's shattered like a peony in a mild storm — snapped stems, vibrant petals drained entirely of colour before releasing back into the earth they came from. The closer we drove towards the serrated Eocene sandstones and the hopeful purple tinge of the Olympic mountain range, the fainter my cutting thoughts of Appa's laboured breathing as he struggled to make his way down the stairs. It stressed me sudden and sick to see the wells around his eyes grow darker and deeper. Hugging him was like clasping air; he was dissolving into himself like the celery stalks Vathany let go limp in the fridge. By the time we were a few miles away from Nanaimo, I felt immense relief.

This reprieve was replaced by the ever-burn of two-a-day swim practices. A sneaker wave of soreness that turned shoulder and quad blood to blue fire and stomachs to ravenous black holes. My willpower to restrict food had slipped away in the night somewhere along with my acting dreams. Instead, I lined the dusty shelves in the condo with my algae powder, creatine, quick oats, and

birthday-cake-flavoured whey isolate, filled the fridge
with pounds of blanched spinach, pre-cut broccoli, liquid
egg whites, aspartame-sweetened peach yogurt.

"What's with you and food, dude?" Tony raised his
brows at my reduced-calorie cooking spray. I now ate
second, sometimes third, plates to satiety without much
guilt and didn't understand what he meant.

"What's with *you* and food?" I cringed at his Jolt soda
and midnight Hawaiian pizza habits in a tangle of disgust
and admiration.

I was a first-gen immigrant template on autopilot,
floundering through a general sciences degree, which
would lead to a career in medicine and, consequently,
a good income. This, Vathany prayed, would compensate for my dark hue. In my first few anatomy classes,
I learned that swimmers hold on to a layer of subcuta-
neous fat to protect them from the cold. We read a study
comparing the body fat levels of swimmers and runners
who expended and consumed the same amount of kilo-
joules; the swimmers all had more fat, which helped them
float, kept them warm. I ran my hands over my abdomen
and rib cage and considered quitting. Where I'd once
felt the swell of muscle and the hardness of bone was
a soft band of blubber. I couldn't glue my attention to
much else.

A constant hum of anxiety swirled inside me that
I could no longer out-swim or out-skate. I skated beneath

the canopy of turning maple trees, ollying over roots bursting through the pavement, carving chaotically past the rows and rows of people, the barefoot slackliners on the diamond, walking weightless on a low-tightrope between trees. Elevated cortisol levels — medspeak for sand fleas buzzing in my chest.

"Yo!" Tony said between bites of peanut butter toast, pulling a sweater over his wet blond hair.

"What?" I yawned, sprawled over our futon couch.

"You know that breaststroker, the one with the big hair who was on our swim team since we were kids? She's studying general sciences."

"Who?"

"Weird name. Sasha or Saskia or something. Think she's Russian."

Saoirse. Sounded like silk and a blade at the same time. I'd heard her name at a million swim meets and at least three times at the graduation awards ceremony. Got some big trophy from the Governor General.

"You gotta partner up with her, man, for real. That's a guaranteed A." Tony waved his toast at me for emphasis, flinging crumbs all over our grody floor.

"So what? Just, like, demand to be her partner?"

"C'mon, Chan, you're...you. Chan Juan, Electric Ladykiller...Let me call Paula, she's in the same dorm."

"Don't call Paula. She hates my guts." I lunged for the phone.

"You dog, ruined her for life. Once they go Black, they never go back."

SAOIRSE'S DORM WAS AT the top of a steep hill that led down to a small beach called Cadboro Bay. A pack of gazelle-legged track runners, shredded and shirtless, charged up the hill. Deep abs, not an ounce of fat on a single one of them. Pretty girls of all shapes and colours went in and out of their dorm rooms wrapped in towels or wearing pyjamas. I immediately realized two things: breaking up with Paula (and then Flossie) was a good choice, and living off-campus was a mistake.

I knocked on Saoirse's heavy, hollow door twice before it swung open. A face I thought I'd studied well but had never really seen before. Narrow, deep blue eyes, tendrils of wet black hair falling out of her towel turban.

"Hey, uh, I'm looking for Saoirse. Must have the wrong room," I said.

"Nope...that's me." Her hooded eyes, which vacillated between sad and stern, locked with mine. "We've been on the same swim team since we were, like, ten."

"I was kidding. Of course I know you. Backstroker with the hair..."

"Breaststroker."

Fantastic. "Yeah...So, uh..." Once again, I became aware of the way my body lied, of the corners where it hid truths, like my right fist, which kept clenching and unclenching. Like my eyes, which couldn't stop skirting around.

"So, you want to be my lab partner?" she asked.

"Shit, did Tony tell you that?"

"Yes."

"Ass." My knees buckled slightly, and I reached for the stability of the doorframe.

"You good? You light-headed?"

"Yeah, think so."

"You should eat something."

I stood in the hall for what felt like a semester.

"All right, sure. We can be partners," she said. "Only 'cause you're awkward and it's entertaining. I gotta go, though — looking for some wild thyme today." She shut the door.

I stood there in a confused daze. Took me an embarrassing length of time to collect myself and get out of there. I went the wrong way and bumped into a faceless blur of a girl holding a silver Walkman.

"Sorry."

She slid an apple-sized earphone off her ear. "What?"

Awkward? I darted down the stairs and out the door.

DAY AFTER DAY, I WAITED in line for my low-fat cappuccino, stirred in two packets of Sweet'N Low, and walked to class in a sea of students on their way to their respective lecture halls. Cute girls with heavily teased hair. Shredded rugby tanks, twiggy track boys, lanky surfers who slacklined between the trees. Lit nerds nestled against the tree trunks, slipping into other realms with their books. Campus was covered in trees: Garry oak, black cottonwood, rows and rows of maples. I hadn't noticed the differences until Saoirse started pointing them out. Over time, I started noticing the trees everywhere: the black oak, Sitka spruce, aspen, and balsam poplar. Pine cones hanging from my brain, I thought about the way their roots spoke to each other.

On our way to class, Saoirse bent down to pick up a bronze, fan-shaped leaf, then another, and another, following the trail to a leafless ginkgo tree. "Garry oaks are some of the most endangered ecosystems."

"Uh-huh…" I was trying to calculate how many calories I'd burned in practice that morning, if the oil-free, vegan carrot-flax muffin was cancelling out that brutal set of fly. Were muffins, including oil-free vegan ones, just cake, as the block-lettered headline of the university zine proclaimed?

"Yeah. They're more than just trees. They're, like, the veins of the ecosystem. Sharp-tailed snakes control the slug population, which control the flora. It's all connected — are you listening?"

"Huh? Yeah. Garry oaks and sharp-tailed snakes."

I combed my hand through my hair, stared at my reflection in the glint of the glass doors of the science building. I threw my unfinished muffin in the trash, just to be safe.

"You care too much what other people think about you."

My mouth hung open. "Listen, you don't know me."

"Weren't you voted most likely to fall in love with his own reflection?"

"Just because someone spends a lot of time analyzing themselves doesn't mean they like what they see." In fact, just the opposite.

Saoirse's half-moon eyes waxed. "Sorry."

"It's okay. I know what people think."

"No, you're right. I don't know you."

"But you'd like to." I winked, but the pang of her words clung to my ribs.

I walked into the stuffy lecture hall and took a sip of my coffee, searing my soft palate, the roof of my mouth reduced to ribbons. Tiny slits of windows were welded shut, the blinds drawn.

Saoirse sat next to me, a massive espresso cloud of hair. She pinned back the dark strands that had fallen in front of her face, revealing her narrow eyes and sharp cheekbones.

I looked around, concerned that people were staring at me and Saoirse. Her baggy red sweater, ill-fitting jeans, and dirty shoes. Except no one's head turned. There were two hundred other students in each of my classes. Nobody knew or cared who I was; they were all in their own little worlds. My shoulders eased.

Saoirse rarely talked about people, never talked about herself. She was all rock formations, ocean tides, the life cycles of plants, genomes, and collective consciousness. She didn't need to go to the water to feel peace because she saw divinity everywhere, crawling out of the ground, shrouding the buildings. First, it made me feel shallow. Then, it made me come back to myself.

"I love the way nature fights back. It's like it's protesting." Saoirse fingered a sprout of wood sorrel she'd pulled from a crack in the pavement on our way to class. "Hey, I'm going foraging this weekend. You want to come?"

"Foraging?"

"Yeah! Ever been to Mystic Vale?"

"No."

"Oh, then you have to come! It's way rad."

WE FOLLOWED THE QUIET crimson sway of October over the green velvet of the mossy glen. A few weeks ago, we'd spent hours here in the deep woods, collecting plump, trailing blackberries at peak ripeness. Saoirse had spotted the best ones, concealed under jagged green leaves, the slender hooked spines drooping under the weight of summer sumptuousness. My arms were long and my palms were tough and callused, making it easier for me to pluck them. But now, in the thicket, only shrivelled black cankers and naked stems were to be found on the canes... until we came across a patch of cantaloupe-coloured berries, the size of thimbleberries with blackberry-like drupelets.

"Are *these* salmonberries?" I asked.

Saoirse gasped, rushed towards the patch of amber berries. "Cloudberries!"

She picked one and placed it on her tongue, closed her eyes. I'd never seen someone eat that way. It was almost ceremonial, as if she was experiencing the berry with her entire body — the sensation of the amber fruit dissolving on her tongue, each drupelet breaking apart and releasing flavour into her taste buds, the juice travelling down into her guts and becoming energy in her cells.

"They're low-bush salmonberries, also known as aqpik!" She handed me a berry. "Eat it. Slowly."

I placed the berry on my tongue. It had the texture of yogurt and a dulcet peaches-and-cream flavour. Shockingly decadent. Everything around me snapped into focus. The soft hand-like lobes and branchless stalks. And the trees, all the trees. *Is this what eating should be? Is this what it could be like all of the time?* I wondered.

"Cloudberries aren't super common here. We must be near a bog... Maybe we'll see Seelkee..."

"What now?"

"A two-headed sea serpent. Maybe just a legend. Maybe not."

We topped off our blackberry buckets with the bounty of the cloudberry patch, leaving some for the birds or other foragers and thanking the earth before we left. Later, we went down to the beach to study. Saoirse talked about the Krebs cycle and I zoned out watching the waves.

"Do you even like this stuff?" she asked, closing her books and popping a cloudberry into her mouth.

"Yeah." I hesitated. "I mean, it's interesting."

"Yeah, so? I'm interested in dance. Doesn't mean I want to study it for four years."

I perked up, more intrigued than I'd been all study session. "You like dance?" I tried to envision Saoirse dancing, with her broad breaststroker shoulders, her stiff build, and her cold, serious face.

"It's like swimming on land. You have to learn how to work with the music. My dad was really into it. Like, really into it. Jive dancing, if you know what that is. Kinda old-fashioned, but it's the only time he ever seemed like himself."

"Your dad?" I laughed.

She shot a sharp look in my direction. I took a handful of bright orange cloudberries and popped them in my mouth all at once. A medley of tart and sweet.

"You know, ballet was invented by a man," Saoirse said.

"Really?"

"Mm-hm. Maybe if men danced more, the world would be a better place."

"Maybe." The air lulled, grew gelatinous with psyche-delic swirls of memory. "I miss acting. Think about it all the time."

"Oh yeah, I remember you were in that play at school. You weren't bad."

"You saw it?" I licked the sticky sweetness off my fingers and tried to sit up as straight as possible.

"I mean, I'm not into Shakespeare. Find his plays kind of overrated. And soooo long. Couldn't stand on a stage like that, no way. Must be awful."

"It's the best feeling in the world."

"With all those people staring at you?"

"It's not about that. To me, it feels more like I've escaped into another realm and there's less of an audience than there is when I'm offstage. Like that's the only time I'm not really performing."

Saoirse's dark blue eyes glinted in the autumnal sun, her nose and cheeks kissed with a cherrywood glow. "You ever think of changing your major?"

Something in me split and spread. A dull ache that went marrow-deep.

SAOIRSE AND I BLOOMED LIKE a violet webcap —
mycelial threads growing slowly under the soil and, when
the conditions were right, sprouting from the dirt to form
an unexpectedly alluring, velvety purple. Weaving time
between swim practice and cramming for bio, we foraged
for ourselves. Searching for black truffles at the base of
a Douglas fir and finding deadly galerina instead (Don't
touch!). Discovering a colony of honey mushrooms growing in a well of moss-covered deadwood. Saoirse pointed
out where the wild strawberries would freckle the forest
floor in June — everywhere.

At twilight in the cathedral of black cottonwood
and trembling aspen, a drop formed on a thin, white
branch, reaching, glistening in transient sparkle, begging to be held before releasing. Like a chorus, more
drips and drops joined in. Lips parted to taste heaven
on our tongues. Here, the line between land and water
was blurred, and the earth was sweet and wet. A sheath
of spring rain encrusted the lattice of heart-shaped leaves
on the forest floor in jewels of dew. Tresses of wild, dark
hair and Saoirse's short, dense eyelashes, too. The woods
are a place of reciprocity, of love. The trembling aspen's
pale bark, roots as thick as a swimmer's thighs, opened
wide. At first, foraging was plain hard work. Fingering
damp soft moss, parting the pale green leaves of catkins

that spread out like clouds, we searched for something we weren't sure we'd find in this shallow bed of fern. A tension vined through our bodies, pulsing. Soft wood became hard as an arrow. The sweat on our brows mixed with the rain and the dew and the sap and the salt thread of sea hovering in the spaces between pine, all lifting into a collective mist as we and the land became one. At the crest of desire, the final strokes before the flip turn, we ached with an athlete's refusal to quit and thrust and thrust all our last efforts into the parts that yield, and then, what started out as one unfurling pink blossom became another and another until what was once invasive, now naturalized, offered itself in vivid colour, moaning wild out of the earth. Releasing like water drops from a branch, floating in a lake of thyme.

I grew to love strange things about Saoirse, like the way she smiled and said, "Hi, air," whenever a sea breeze brushed against her skin. Nature went wild with colour when it made her face — the cherrywood tinge to her cheeks, pollen dust of deer-brown freckles, tangled mess of black hair, and ever-shifting blue-green eyes that scattered light like water. She wore baggy hockey sweaters, sometimes the same one for several days in a row, which, when removed, revealed a strong and tapered figure as sharp as her sarcasm. She swam as quick as her wit, and her keen, searching eyes clawed through the thorny brambles to see, plainly, what was at my core, and I had no choice but to be seen. It was a relief to be around someone who was more interested in the trees and the sky than social status. And as I fell for Saoirse, it became more and more apparent that I was not meant to be studying sciences.

As my first year of university came to a close, like a quicksilver dream, Olympic trials slipped further and further out of reach. My new coaches were not having my antics, reminding me, "You know that heavy feeling in your body? That's from carbon dioxide buildup in your lungs. I know, I know, breathing seems like a waste of time, but a swift, bilateral sip of oxygen is a water turbine. When you breathe properly, you're unstoppable." But my subpar technical habits were deeply rooted in muscle memory, difficult to unearth and correct. Swimming varsity was like brushing my teeth — mundane and habitual. Something I neither loved nor hated but had to do. I couldn't quit, clinging to the sport the way hours spent in water made my body cling to fat. I felt myself giving in to the undertow, swept up in a current of ambivalence.

Yet I can't say that the wandering sense of aimlessness was unpleasant, breathing out carbon dioxide for the wild ginger, arbutus, Pacific bleeding heart, sword fern, and Nootka rose rather than for faster swim times and accolades. My lungs, bronchi not unlike trees themselves, felt as though the precious air was theirs, and they alone would decide in what context it was gifted.

An act of reciprocity between the earth's alveoli and my own. Grounded by Saoirse and the land, I tried to trust the strange wild strawberry season I was in, a time of receiving abundance and pleasure.

WHEN I CAME HOME FOR the summer, Vathany had waxed with the strawberry moon, too. A serape of fat swaddled her lower abdomen and the backs of her arms. The black roots of her hair had grown in a few inches, and she hadn't bothered to dye them blond. She seemed calmer, kinder. Her extra padding acting as a buffer between her and the dolour of the external, softening not only her flesh but her heart. Appa wheezed as he stood up to greet Saoirse. His yellowed grin was contagious, had us all smiling from ear to ear.

"You have such beautiful eyes. So blue, or are they green?" Vathany leaned over the coffee table to scrutinize Saoirse's features, much closer than socially acceptable.

"It's actually a mutation." Saoirse laughed. "The third layer of my iris is translucent, so my eyes turn blue the same way that the sky and water do."

"Scattering light so that the blue reflects back out." Appa cupped his glass of lime water.

As I observed how Saoirse allowed herself to sink into the sofa rather than hovering primly on the edge, I thought of my first wave in Tofino, where Appa explained the elusive power of water's fluidity and ability to change states.

"And your parents? Did you grow up here?" Vathany asked.

"Born in Esquimalt as a navy brat." Saoirse shrugged. "Moved here when my dad stopped going to sea."

Vathany's bronze eyes sharpened. "But they are from here?"

Saoirse belted out a monosyllabic laugh. "No. Definitely not." She fidgeted, pulling at the sleeves of her shirt.

"And where are they from?" Vathany persisted.

Sweat pooled in my pits, trickled down my lower back.

Saoirse looked at me, her almond-shaped eyes, which appeared black in the dim light, widening as far as they could. "My mother is...Austrian, mainly. My dad, well, he says he was raised by a river. Foster kid, not really sure."

"Raised by a river." Appa broke into a soft laugh.

I stood up to pop Hendrix on the old record player. "Hey, what if we all went down to the lagoon? When's the last time you were there?"

"Pipers? Long time," Appa said.

"He's on leave, but he never *leaves*," Vathany tutted.

Appa whorled deeper into the sofa like a maple samara in autumn.

"Well, let's change that," I said.

"I don't know…," Appa said.

"Come on."

"All right. I guess."

Appa hesitated in the centre of the room as we swam around him. I tucked our swimsuits and towels into a duffle bag, Saoirse and Vathany piled an ice-cream pail full of fresh dosa wrapped in tinfoil, coconut buns, dried mango, Saoirse's plastic bag of wild strawberries, and salmon jerky, and we were off, the wind whip of the ocean slapping against the miraculously still-functioning Volkswagen van like welcoming applause.

A lilting calm draped over me as we pulled up to the turquoise, crystal blue, black, and green sea. Here, we shed the past years and got back to the way things were. Appa, whose pallor and posture matched the curved arbutus, refused my help once he saw the water. He hobbled down the beach, rickety joints ceasing to quiver once the invigorating jolt of ice-silk ocean washed over his calves, siphoning his spirit back into his old body. His sea-lion belly protruded from the skin of the sea like a rising sun before he flipped over with impressive grace, diving down into the algid liquid to retrieve his receding hairline, or a clamshell. Surfacing from a sparkle ribbon, he glided on his back again, lit by the glow of liquid platinum on the horizon, which smoothed out the lines in his face.

Saoirse held Vathany's frail hand, guiding her over the

hurdles of driftwood, down the beach of multicoloured shell shards, sea glass, and stone. Vathany flicked off her shoes and stuck her feet in, shrieking at the sensation of seaweed slime before relaxing into the muck.

I clasped Saoirse's feet as she floated, eyes serenely observing the moving clouds, the gulls, and the waning gibbous and the sun together in the sky at the same time. We laughed and laughed about something intangible until the sun scattered red light and bruised the sky purple, turning the sea and Saoirse's eyes to amethyst.

THE MORNING WAS UNNATURALLY BRIGHT. I rolled over to see Saoirse's mop of thick black hair and a stream of light pooling in the grooves of her pale back. I kissed her shoulder blade and sat up.

"Not yet," she groaned.

"Take it easy." I kissed her again, on the lips this time, and slid out of bed.

I went into the kitchen to make some coffee for Appa. As I was filling the coffee pot with water, a beam of sun struck the glass, sending glowing prisms all over the room. I paused, marvelling, then as I moved, the light splashed, sending droplets of gold everywhere.

I was sitting on the edge of my bed, folding towels into the same old duffle bag, when I heard a piercing shriek, so high-pitched it sounded like an otherworldly frequency.

I bolted out of the room, carried down the hallway as if by some magnetic force, following Vathany's seismic wails. Peering around the doorframe, I stiffened.

Appa's shell lay on the water bed, lips blue-black as a freshwater mussel. They say it feels like a fullness of the heart too great to bear. Pain and plaque accumulate in the arteries that bring blood to a muscle that men are taught to neglect. My knees buckled, and a sneaker wave of air pulled me to the earth's core. Vathany was curled up beside him, clutching onto his skin, wailing so high my ears bled.

Could I not be pulled back up to the surface of an earlier day by Appa's warm arms? His heart still light, still beating, my heart still open and full of wonder? Both of us, swimming, suspended in a liquescent lacuna, the possibility of healing that deep ache in him?

I crawled through the heavy air to the edge of the bed, touched Appa's cold flesh, and hoped he would enter his body again, scream awake like before. Vathany pulled me deeper into her current, digging her nails into my veins, praying in every tongue she knew, in dead languages to non-existent gods.

17

The River

kw'ótl'kwa, ləkʷəŋən
(from the sea to Esquimalt, Canada), 1960–65

Midnight ultramarine slated against a slab of scintillating translucent turquoise, as if the Creator had hand-painted a line right down the middle of the ocean. The Gulf of Alaska was the first place I saw a river meet the sea. I struggled to get the snug wetsuit over my newly thick and broad shoulders as Sam and I hummed a jambalaya of a tune we'd invented over our travels together — a blend of Nova Scotian sea shanty, Louisiana zydeco, and Genovese tarantella all wrapped up in a Bavarian oompah.

"Mother Nature's a damn artist." Sam shook his head.

"Amen to that," I said, breath caught paper thin in my chest.

Pigments of blue multiplied infinitely in the mesmeric waves, swirling hues of akoya pearl, Italian alkanet, late-August blackberry, azure, and jade moonlight. I looked intently into the inverted mirror of the water: cresting, breaking, vanishing.

"What do you reckon makes one ocean more blue than another?" Sam said.

"Different amounts of salt," I said, lifting lines I'd overheard from an admiral eons ago as a petty guppy, before being promoted to lieutenant.

"It's not two oceans." An eavesdropping commodore craned his head around. He was lithe and doe-eyed with deep-set acne scars, like lunar maria on his face. "In the summer, glacier rivers are like buzzsaws. They carve away the mountains and lift up all the crumbs of clay and rock — they call it glacial flour."

"The St — the Fraser River?"

"I mean, this definitely ain't it. Too far away. But sure, there's a Fraser River plume somewhere."

I rubbed the back of my neck with my slick gloved hand, suddenly reminded of my inferior education by this college kid. He went on to explain that once the glacial rivers poured out into the larger body of water, they were picked up by ocean currents and moved east to west, where they began to circulate.

Captain strode around the corner looking particularly pink and sun-chafed. "Well, don't you two look sharp."

We secured our oxygen tanks and took a quick look at the glaring white sky before diving into the reflected heavens. I was immediately shawled by glacial blue satin, a succulent coolness. Bubbles rose like streams of translucent pearls. Everything was fresh, crisp, surreally clear through the lens of my polished mask. I dolphin-kicked down, down, down, into the infinite crystal and stretched out into the blue cosmos. A loud underwater hum drummed in my ears, lifted all emotion. I was left with only wonder. This vastness, this liquid, it was made of the same things as I was: hydrogen and oxygen. That's all we were.

"Routine ship maintenance" sounds boring as hell, but it was meditative. Sam and I swam, effervescent, through the bright, pale turquoise. Sam looked over at me and nodded his head. I could tell he was humming our medley in his mind by the way his hips swayed. I nodded back and did a hallelujah, followed by a shim sham — under-the-sea lindy.

We grated the grime off the hull until our biceps burned and we could barely lift them anymore. I felt the gravitational pull of something swimming by and saw an albino sperm whale. Before I could say "Call me Ishmael," Moby-Dick shattered into pieces; it wasn't a whale at all but a school of white fish swimming right below us. Pausing to peer through the school of yellowfin croaker, fluttering by like snowflakes, I calmed my hastened pulse above the sky of another earth.

⌒

THE NEXT TIME I SAW a river plume was in the Gulf of Mexico. Translucent jade slate next to black-teal. The sun was oblong and pink, with serrated yellow rays, like a dragon fruit melting the equator. It left my skin pink and shredded like dried deep-sea chicory. Even Sam's skin blistered and chafed. We dove in for ship mainten- ance with an unrivalled eagerness and took our sweet time once we were in the water. Below our dangling feet we could see the coral reef, colourful and ornate as we scraped calcified barnacles off the boat twice over.

By the end, I was so hungry I thought my stomach would split open, but we didn't want to surface, not yet, not back out into the hellish heat. I was re-scrubbing an already sparkling patch of the boat when Sam nudged me, his eyes crescent moons. I turned around to see what looked like the long tail of a flamenco dress fluttering in the water, twirling with tantalizing grace. Hunger braided with reverie made me think of dancing with women.

The creature's spineless fuchsia body was so beauti- fully bright, and when it curled elegantly to look cinched and narrow at the waist, I began to feel a sort of way about a sea slug. I needed to eat solid food on sobering, solid ground. Give me a jaibas rellenas, a fresh, hot corn tortilla, and get my twitching toes onto a dance floor.

As I shook myself out of my daydream, something slithered towards me. At first I thought it was another Spanish dancer, but it was yellow. A thin, ribbon-like snake... Plenty of things in the ocean'll kill you — blue-ringed octopus, lionfish, box jellies, tiger sharks. But sea snakes were forged in the fires of hell. A king cobra can kill up to 160 people in half an hour. The venom of the faint-banded sea snake can kill a thousand men in the same amount of time. I looked around to see I was alone.

As the sea snake neared, it multiplied into a trio of yellow-bellied demons. I kicked, thrashing my legs as hard as I could. The gang of snakes swam with what seemed like vengeance. I pumped my legs and pulled with all my strength, but I was weak with hunger.

Two small daggers punctured my heel, and my entire body tensed. The lifeline descended into the water, and I clutched onto it, floating to the surface, shattering the barrier between water and air. I pried off my mask, shouting all sorts of curse words as Sam hauled me on deck. The strong taste of sea salt and the harsh Mexican heat were like sugary pan dulce compared to the piercing pain of the snakebite. A sharp blade had taken my tendons, braided them, and was now twisting and twisting until they'd all snap. My skin felt blue and bloated, and my heart was in a closed iron maiden. *This is it*, I thought, *this is the end*. Better here in the Gulf of Mexico than in the gutter or on the gallows of Vancouver.

The sparkling deck, glazed with water, blurred with the orange swirl of sky.

THE YEARS IN THE NAVY bled together, broken only by land and sea, but the snakebite had to have happened sometime in late February because Carnival burst out of the cracks of the confetti-dappled streets and crawled along the sides of buildings like neon weeds. As soon as I got out of the hospital, I bought eight churros from the first stand I passed and devoured every single one. The taste of fried bread, cinnamon, and sugar crystals took me back to Ray's boat. I looked around and saw him in the faces of the men selling fruit, strumming vihuelas, emerging from alleys in slick, pastel zoot suits. I rubbed my eyes with my dry, sea-salt-caked palms.

I came to a fruit stand piled with plump avocados the size of my fist, ripe red watermelon so juicy I was hydrated just from standing near it, parrot-coloured mangoes, kiwis, pineapple, white jicama. As I reached for a cup of cut watermelon, I noticed a small skull engraved in the wood. I looked up and saw small skeletons hanging from the top of the stand. As I limped down the street, swept up by the colour, the spices, the heat, I heard music. Mariachi — a tangle of fast-paced vihuela, trumpet, violin, and guitar. Suddenly, the parade engulfed me in cascades of colour — dancers in fuchsia, royal blue, neon green, and electric yellow; people dressed as pea-cocks; and mojigangas, giant puppets that needed three people to operate them.

A tall woman with a thick obsidian rope of hair floated past me, twirling the feathered tail of the fuchsia dress dangling off her dancing derrière. I turned around to get another glimpse of her mesmerizing backside when a giant green serpent the size of a small submarine came flying at me from the clouds. I shrieked and jumped into Sam's arms — well, I don't remember it that way, but Tod, Torchie, and a couple of straggling sailors insisted that's what I did. I could tell they were laughing only by their faces, because the sounds were sucked up by the parade.

AS WE SAILED OVER a sea of glittering paraiba topaz towards the big black smudge on the horizon, the over-powering boom-bahhh-bahhh-boom of the tariparau swelled like the glassy barrels offshore from Teahupo'o. Bronze-bodied men with shoulders carved out of bas-alt rowed towards us in their va'a, a wooden outrigger canoe. As they boarded the ship with their drums made of sharkskin membranes, the deck was engulfed in the rich, creamy smell of vanilla pods and hibiscus flowers.

I felt like a bud tightly wrapped in green sepals com-pared to the island in full bloom. First was the smell — a delightful tangle of vanilla, jasmine, coconut, and oleander that evoked such pleasure and contentment in me, I nearly wept. I wanted to slip out of my new commander's uniform and into a multicoloured pareo. The Tahitian way of dance looked like rhythmically peeling waves.

Our crew followed a trail of tiare flowers, white, star-like blossoms that freckled the lush green foliage. Hibiscus bloomed in a vivid palette of rich yellows, oranges, pinks, and reds. The petals had ruffled edges like the bottom of a frilly dress. As we wandered through the Ferme perlière Champon, the bustling black pearl market, I stopped at a woman's beading stall. She looked to be around sixty, with deep bronze skin, muscular arms, and wavy charcoal hair. She looked up at me with opalescent eyes, black jade like the pearls she was stringing into a bracelet.

"Vikings would have gone nuts for these." The sudden heat of Torchie standing behind me was jarring. He picked up a bracelet and held it to the light in a way that I felt was too careless for something so precious. So miraculously metallic and spherical. I had a crow-like impulse to snatch and pocket a handful of gems, but stealing pearls from a market woman was vastly different from purloining dough from gloating fat cats in the West End.

Sam joined us. "You've got a tan, Ronny. You fixing to shape-shift and stay here in paradise when we all get back on the boat?"

"Shoot, I'm seeing double," Torchie quipped, framing Sam and me with his sun-and-salt-worn hands, one thumb and nail black from a brawl with a high-seas storm.

"Please." I chuckled.

Torchie brought his bruised finger to his strawberry shred of a brow, then to where his upper lip should have been. "Where'd you say your parents were from, again?"

"Didn't say. Never knew 'em." I shrugged.

"Ah."

"It's all right, I don't know any different." I seemed to have sprouted up out of the ground without roots.

After the market, we toured a vanilla plantation. Tall, emerald-green leaves, fragrant vanilla orchids, and tropical fruit sugared the euphoria-inducing air. I sprinted through the Elysian grove as the sun set, splashing the sky with a dazzling array of colour that somehow rivalled the flora. We returned to our sleeping quarters just as night revealed its best jewellery — diamond dust, crystal constellations, and the pearl of Polaris.

The next day, Sam and I were on ship maintenance again. A mild ache still coated my arch and swelled with every limping step, but sorest of all were my nerves.

"There aren't any sea snakes in Ṭahiti, right?" I asked, pulling my wetsuit over my right arm.

The deck went cold and silent.

"Oh, goddammit, are you kidding me?" The sleeve of

my suit stuck to me like plastic wrap as I sought to yank it off. "No way in hell am I going back in there. Let me lamp ship. Hell, have me clean the toilets. I refuse."

Flicking my flippered feet gingerly, I glided through the glittering turquoise waters, scanning for sea snakes, lemon sharks, stingrays, and jellies. An intense fear geysered in me, but the water was clear, impossibly so. A shade of aqua so brilliant and crystalline it made me smile from inside my lungs. We scrubbed the boat to a sparkle in the company of damselfish, butterflyfish, and angelfish that emerged ethereally from an undersea Eden and a sunset of coral reef.

After we were through, we indulged in a little free-diving, scooping up oyster shells, pining for pearls.

A simple meal of poisson cru — raw fish marinated in lime juice and coconut — awaited us when we were dry. I looked around at the Tahitian naval crew speaking French, a dialect that sounded different from the language spoken by the people in the market and on the plantation.

I tilted my head. "Why do they speak French all the way over here?" The savoury taste of fish and sharp lime that coated my tongue became especially strong when I spoke.

"Same reason we speak English in Canada." Tod shrugged.

Sam, his cheeks bulging with food like a threatened

pufferfish, gestured his knife to Tod and nodded in agreement. We all turned to Torchie.

"What? My parents are Gaelic. My pasty arse is here to bash on the English as much as the rest of you!"

We all laughed.

"I speak some X̱aat Kíl," Tod said, so quiet he almost inhaled his words.

"What in the hell's Zat Kill?" I said.

"Language of my people, the Haida. Just a few words, though. It's technically illegal."

"How can a language be illegal?" I was incredulous.

"Not easy to steal someone's words," Sam said.

"They don't just steal words. They steal away kids so they don't even know what their words are," Tod said. "My sister even had her fingernails pulled out just for calling me by my real name. My parents were rebellious, though. They held on, taught us our language in secret." Tod's eyes glazed over in a way I was all too familiar with. Like the reel of a former life was playing in his head.

"Jesus," I said.

"Yeah, they taught us about him, too," he said.

"So, what's your real name?" I asked.

"You've got to earn the right to know that, man," Tod said.

That stung, because I thought I had.

I couldn't help but wonder what Tahiti would look like without all the French cathedrals, which were ornate and opulent, striking in their own way, but starkly out of place next to the towering palms, the vanilla groves, and the sunrise-coloured blossoms. And I wondered how many children were made motherless in the process of their construction, how many Tahitians were taken from their homes, had their long hair hacked off, their fingernails pulled out for speaking the land.

Perched on the dock as we prepared to pull out of paradise, I saw the black pearl woman from the market. She rowed in from the sea, docking her small fishing boat. From a distance, she looked like a child, but as she made her way up from the shore, the light pooled in the wrinkles and creases of her aging skin. She walked up the white sand, clutching her net of freshly caught black-lip oysters. Maybe, in another life, she was my mother.

MY FOOT HAD HEALED by the time we sailed over the Fraser River plume two solar spins later, but I still felt the phantom fangs as the glacial blue river reached for the dark cerulean sea. We docked in Esquimalt, on Vancouver Island, the shores lined with Sitka spruce. There was a dance at the naval base the night we arrived, and I was itching to jive. But I didn't want to go with Torchie as my wingman.

"Sorry, Ronny." Sam yawned. "I'm just not feeling it.

My legs are wobbling. Gonna take me some time before I can walk straight."

Tod clutched Sam's shoulder and grinned. "He just wants to ring his girl."

"That too." Sam smiled in a way that made me jealous. Like he was so happy he didn't want to talk about it because it would come off as bragging, so he just kept it inside. It leaked out like warm gold as he started humming, those white teeth blinding us all.

"You know I'm happy for you, you son of a bitch," I said. "You get the hell out of here and call that Yank Dorothy."

"Oh, holy hell, Sam's going with a Yankee girl?" Torchie crumpled his hat, squeezed a small whitehead near his ear.

"I can walk across the border from where I live," Sam said. "Borders ain't real."

"Amen to that," Tod said.

"Well, I'll tell you them borders are real as hell when it comes to the navy or going to war."

"All right, simmer down, Torch," Sam said.

"I need a feckin' drink," Torchie said and stomped off.

I shrugged. "Well, what's your excuse, Tod?"

"Tod's got a lady, too. You know that," Sam said.

"So bring her!"

"I think we just need some time, you know, to be alone."

"Well, what if I need some time to not be alone? Huh?"

"We ain't stopping you." Sam gleamed.

"Plus, there'll be dames there," Tod said.

But I didn't want dames. I wanted to tell Sam and Tod they were my best friends. Didn't know how to do that, though, so I just lingered awkwardly, looked down at my shoes.

Had I known we were going to split up, that we'd had our last sail together on ol' *Bonnie*, I would have said, *Hey, lads, y'all are like brothers to me. The things I love most in the whole world are you and this crew. We're all going to die one day, and life is short. I thought I was gonna get hung by the coppers or drown in a pool of my own blood in Hogan's Alley or poisoned by a sea snake bite, but here I am, so you both owe me a dance.*

WHEN IT WAS TIME to go to the dance, it was cold, wet, and already dark. The air had a bruised feeling, like all the pain in my life had been hovering around, an unkindness of ravenous ravens conspiring to latch onto me as soon as I stepped back on this land. I felt the melancholic dampness of the pavement in my soul, so I went with a few other sailors to the liquor store and got myself a bottle of Four Roses, gnawed on a tamarind candy I'd brought with me from Mexico. The tangy tamarind temporarily transported me back to the warm, colourful streets, and the Four Roses lit a fire in my belly, killing off the bad spirits, or at least shutting them up for a bit. Now that I had a nice warm buzz, I was ready to dance.

When I got to the hall a cold, blue light split the room, and that's when I first saw her. If looks could kill, that woman would have been hanged for murder. She had stern blue eyes, algid as the North Sea, and cheekbones sharper than a Swiss blade. She looked like Hamburg in female form — wounded, steely, oceanic.

"That one there." I pointed straight at the stone-cold fox. "I'm leaving here with her."

"Good luck." A petty officer called Ed chuckled. "Miss Lily there got herself a beau."

Torchie snapped his fingers to break my gaze, then cupped my neck. "Her father was an SS officer."

I lingered on it for a moment. "What?"

"Knock it off, Torchie," Ed said. "Her uncle was a Nazi. Her father would have been a Nazi, but he escaped. That's why she's here."

"I almost got killed by sea snakes," I said and brushed past them. "What's Hitler's niece?" The sailors chuckled.

"No sea too rough, no muff too tough."

"Thanks, Torch." I strode up to this Lily, the tang of hard liquor, ocean air, and perfume masking my sweat. "May I have this dance?"

Her lips curled, fighting a smile. She took my hand

and led me to the centre of the dance floor. I was surprised by how large and callused her hands were, with wrists as wide and weathered as mine.

"You in textiles or something?" I asked.

"Bullfighter." She flashed a cheeky smile. We rock-stepped over the freshly waxed linoleum. She kept good rhythm.

"I heard other rumours…" I studied her face, pupils dilated in the sepia light. Her hair was snow blond, her features severe, her red lips stern.

"All true."

Boy, could she move. Quick feet and swivelling hips. We danced together like we were caught in the same orbit. As we twirled and jived, she cracked open, erupting in a cosmic smile. Damn, this woman was glowing from the inside out.

"You're pretty for a kraut." I smirked, sliding my hand down her back.

Her face hardened, which I hadn't thought possible. "I'm Austrian."

"Get your hands off my girl." The meathead came lumbering up to me in an irrevocable state of drunkenness.

"Nope, don't think I will," I said, the phantom sting of the sea snake fangs sharp in my foot.

"You wanna take this outside, sea dog?" he hiccupped.

"Why not? Seems like a nice enough night."

Lily's icy, callused fingers dug into my skin, but she

didn't say a word. The woman merely watched the chaos unfold, a sick stroke of delight.

We tumbled out into the dark blue blur of the night. The crescent moon was a sharpened sickle and cast a silver shimmer over the glaze of rain on the pavement. The smell of damp cement and rust wafted up, made me think of Vince and the Italian kid. I twitched, the hairs on my body shot straight up, and my hearing sharpened. I didn't like that memory, not one bit. I didn't want to hurt this fellow bad, but before I knew it, he was grappling all over me, taking sloppy swings and kicking me in the shins. My reflexes took over. One knee to the gut, and then a sharp jab to the jaw, which knocked his lights right out.

I was so amped up I got my coat, up and left. As I was hobbling away, and sobering up, I remembered Lily. I stiffened and turned around. A gust of wind carried the ice-salt smell of winter sea with it. The wraith-like woman stood under the amber street light.

"You think you're pretty tough, huh?" Her thin red lips curled up in a mocking smile.

"Not as tough as you are."

She walked over, grabbed my face, and kissed me. Frosted hands, glacial lips, icicle tongue. She pulled me back into the hall, where Torchie swung his arm around me and offered me his beer. We jived past the dancers and slipped in through the shut doors of the deserted kitchen. Lily slid a mop between the handles of the wide doors. She turned around, saline river-mouth eyes nearly white under the fluorescence, and pulled me into her numbing permafrost.

LILY WAS ON THE ROOF AGAIN.

"C'mon down, Lil!" Warm bullets of summer rain dropped into my squinting eyes.

It was impressive the way she'd hauled herself up there at eight and a half months pregnant. Her globe of a belly blocked my view of the Mirabelle sun. I didn't know what I'd done this time, but hell if she was going to tell me. Lily punished me with silence.

Eventually, she came down, as she always did. She slid her swollen feet into her glittering, white leatherettes, teased her hair into a beehive, and mummified it with hairspray until we were both high from the fumes. Then we rolled out into the night, the sweet smell of pavement and stargazer lilies after rain, and walked down to the Lindy Hop Hall to swing dance.

"Hey, Ronny! Hey, Lil!" Tod gleamed. "Jesus, you're about to pop! You sure you should be out?"

"That's my business," she snarled. Lil glared at me and kept moving towards the dance floor. For the public good, I'd wanted to go to the dance alone. I didn't think it was a great idea for her to be out dancing — what with her being about to give birth any moment—but the promise of jive got her down off the roof.

All the rumours proved true. Lil's father was a hard man from a small village outside the foothills of Vienna. I met him once and nearly pissed myself because he reminded me of Tobias. He pulled me aside, poured me a finger of plum moonshine he'd made in his basement, and then calmly told me he'd never let a mongrel sea rat like me marry his Aryan daughter. Then he kicked his golden retriever right in the balls. It yelped, and I had to hold myself back from kicking the old man in the balls to see how much he liked it.

Her mother was withered and cold, but what else could be expected, tethered to a man like that. She just stared out the window, smoking like a chimney. Pining for elsewhere, I imagined.

"You're lucky you don't know your parents," Lil had said with a stiff upper lip. Holding two suitcases, one blue and one cream, she spat on the front step. "Good riddance."

I figured the pain over her Rabeneltern would fade, but she still carried it around with her like a cape, the way I still wondered about my own parents.

I checked our coats and took my place on the floor with Lil. We danced until we were drenched in sweat, and all the pain of our lives, which we'd thought we could escape through each other, poured out of the pores of our skin. Lil tilted her head back and laughed, that cruel, cosmic smile on her face. Pure laser beams and chaos. And, yes, there was love. She did have some love in her. Not for me, but for the first beat of the second triple when it fell on the first beat of the next measure, still faithful to the rhythm, married to that accent beat. There, and only there, were we in sync.

Lil stopped mid-swizzlestick, stumbling a bit. "I'm fine," she barked. She held her stomach and hobbled off to the ladies' room.

I wasn't about to hover in front of the bathroom door, so I boogied by myself. Soon, I felt a hand on my lower back, sliding along my hip bone. I turned around to see a woman by the name of Gertrude.

"How's about a dance, stud?" She was single and buxom.

I shrugged, took her hand, and we began twirling.

"You friends with that chug over there?"

"'Scuse me?"

"The Indian fella…First I've seen one at a jive."

"Mind your mouth. He's a sailor."

I let go of her as Lil emerged, menacing behind Gertrude like fog.

"Figures you'd side with that kind of scum. Married to an illiterate little kraut." Gertrude cackled.

Lil wore a steel-knife expression that could crack open an oyster shell. "Read this if you're so literate!" She struck

Gertrude so hard she nearly slapped the makeup off her face and onto the floor.

That's when Gertrude's brother, Mel, came lumbering up and shouted, "Get that scrappy shrew of yours out of here!"

When someone calls your pregnant wife a scrappy shrew, even when she's in the wrong, you're obligated to punch him out.

That wasn't the first time Lily and I limped out of the Lindy Hop Hall. Tod drove us home, wouldn't let me get behind the wheel because I was all rummed up.

"Where's Sam these days? I miss him." I tapped on the dashboard.

"Aw, jeez, you know how it is. It's harder out here for a —" Tod shrugged. "For a guy like him. Sam's got a family now, doesn't want any trouble. He's off the drink now, too."

But I sensed the real reason was because Sam felt he was better than me, and in that moment, it felt like Tod did, too. I grunted and looked out the window, couldn't see anything but black.

I SWAM AWAKE THROUGH the freezing waters of the Alaskan Gulf.

"Get up! My water broke!"

Wiping the ice water Lil had poured on my face from

my eyes, I scrambled up from the couch, my head pounding something awful. I tried to help Lily out the door, but she swatted at me. She nearly slipped on the front porch, and after taking a few laboured steps, she let me help her.

I opened my eyes as wide as I could while driving to Victoria General Hospital. The sun painted the sky coral, and the sea was a silver rim in my peripheral vision. I knew I had to be calm, to flow through this ordeal.

Lily didn't scream at all during labour, or so the nurses said. Later, Lil told me it didn't hurt, that all she felt was the shoulders. And then we had our son, our Kerry, our perfect baby boy. He had a full head of black hair and a healthy cry. My heavy heart released tears like a cloud releases rain, and I cried for the first time in a very long while. The gap that had gaped between Lily and me was sealed shut. A mother, a son, a father.

The entire crew came by with bouquets, beer, and a baby-sized sailor outfit.

I took a luxurious sip of a rich, barrel-aged porter, and a thick, warm hand pressed down on my shoulder. "Long time no see, Ronny."

I recognized that voice, that nectar-and-molasses melody. I leapt out of my seat to hug Sam, nearly spilling my porter on the sailor to my left. "Where the hell have you been? Huh?" He hadn't aged a damn day. I punched him firmly in the shoulder.

"Life on land, you know. It's different."

Didn't I know it, but it was a truth I simply refused to accept. I offered Sam an ale, a glass of Spanish wine, then my finest rum from the Caribbean, but he politely declined everything, electing for sugar water with maraschino cherries.

We braided together memories. "And how the hell did you scamps get the horse on the damn boat?"

"We didn't do it!" Sam, Tod, and I protested in unison before exploding into laughter. Then we all turned to Torchie.

"It wasn't me!" he insisted, cookie crumbs spilling out of his chapped lips, scattering over the chesterfield.

A hush fell over the room as Lil entered with Kerry. His porcelain face was surrounded by a halo of black curls.

18

The Sea

Snǝ'neɪmǝxʷ, 1988–89

———

Vathany said grief is like waiting for water to rise on the horizon, for a wave that never comes. It's an everlasting intermission before the final act, waiting with bated breath for the end of a civil war, for truth, for reconciliation.

My childhood home was suddenly full of ghosts. Coriander-and-cinnamon-scented strangers dressed entirely in white piled on my shoulders, smelling me, kissing me. A photo of Appa was placed in front of the rabbit-eared TV, draped in a funeral lei of white and red flowers. And then the wailing began. The death wail is an ancient keening art that only the island of my ancestors could produce, one of the few things that Eelam tribes maintained after genocide was their proudly savage grief. A white-linen wave of mourners crashed on our living room floor and lamented out loud, unleashing a torrent of lamentation that punctured dimensions. Saoirse and I stood, backs plastered against the wall, unable to wail, educated out of our own sacred heartache. Reduced to crusted eyes and leather skin stretched over parched bones like dry, cracked soil, I didn't have enough moisture in my mouth to speak, enough water in my brain for it to function. At the crescendo of the death wail, I collapsed.

That disintegration bled into my appetite, repelled by the ripe date and saffron sweetness of jaggery payasam, repulsed by coconut laddoo and lime-green bottle gourd halwa. Somehow, even a sip of tap water stacked up in my throat, and the thought of eating the life cycle made my stomach turn — fruit flowers before it ripens and rots; lettuce comes from the dirt, wilts to ochre death slime before returning to it. I became a shadow — thin and dark and looming. I subsisted off dreams, chewing on the rag-end of reverie and reluctant to enter reality, where only the dull ache of hunger could console me.

Saoirse leaned in to kiss my cheek before reeling back. "You need to shower."

I laughed at the sight of myself in the mirror. I had finally achieved the immaculate form — rope-like muscles from years of competitive swimming rippled under my cellophane leanness, the deep grooves of my abs and pelvic floor trenches unrivalled by anyone on the pool deck.

By the time the lakes grew skin, Saoirse too lost her warmth, as if she saw something familiar in the way I clung to my sorrow, something that scared her. She commuted back to Nanaimo on weekends, shoved mashed Cinderella pumpkin and fresh sockeye over black rice in my face between studying for midterms, slid thick slabs of homemade sourdough slathered in wild strawberry jam across the coffee table. I was on semester leave, stuck to the crusts of bread, eventually able to stomach small mouthfuls of unsalted rice and lemon water. Saoirse brewed me tea that tasted like pond and read me therapeutic passages from limnology books, dragged me on long winter walks in the woods, where I got lost in the mesmerizing frosted fern beds and their intricate lace of ice. Soon, outside was a death wail of bone-white snow, and when the sun slipped below the horizon, she encouraged me to sleep just as long. I looked at Saoirse with a snide and skeptical eye, wondering how she'd learned to care for someone so well. Love, I discovered, wasn't gentle and accommodating like television taught me. Love was, at times, a swift and forceful current, a tempest.

SNOW DELIQUESCED UNDER THE ever-reaching Garry
oak to reveal a dreamscape of purple Camassia and wild
hyacinth. As the coastal oak meadow bloomed, I started
eating again. With the return of my appetite came my
ever-thirsting mind, a mind that chugged back thoughts
like a sailor in a rum cellar. Greedy for alternative end-
ings and drunk on regret, never once stopping to say, *No
thank you, I've had enough*. Between stumbling spells of
reminiscence and blackout mirages of the future, I could
no longer sleep. Worse, I couldn't dream. To be guided by
the surge of a dream was to ride a wave; to sift through
conscious thought was to paddle against it.

After midnight, on a spring day hot enough to rival
an Okanagan summer, came the silent blade of white
lightning, which temporarily turned the night sky burgundy, then that periwinkle-blue at the heart of a flame.
Most other nights, blotches of midnight blue faded
slowly to a hazy black. Sometimes, though, right before
the sun split open the sky again at dawn, the heavens
would turn a deep mahogany. Watching the sky move
could pull me out of my mind's sleepless whirlpool and
tuck me into a few hours of slumber until true morning
came with the song of the starling and the gold-crowned
sparrow.

"Noisy little assholes. They're an invasive species from
Europe," Saoirse said, as I marvelled at the yellow-billed
starling's iridescent feathers, shining purple and emerald

in the sunlight, flecked with white stars like the sky had been just hours ago. Now the body of air was a soft blue, exploding into a gradient of lilac, magenta, and indigo. Tracing the violent neon-pink sashes as they swam slowly across the horizon, I jumped at a drumroll of knocking at the front door.

"I reached out to your cousins." Saoirse slurped some honeyed pond brew before handing it to me.

I sat up, cupping the soothingly warm ribbed mug, parched and angry at the loudness of the light. "I don't have any cousins."

Bagira and Moorthy stood on the doorstep, duffle bags swung over budding shoulders. Moorthy looked straight out of *Top Gun* in his Ray-Bans and leather jacket. Bagira's neon coral crop top made his mint-green eyes even more striking. In an accent that had faded only slightly, Bagira thanked me for teaching him to swim. Moorthy sounded like a local as he explained they'd joined a recreational swim club in Toronto. It was almost hard to look at them.

Found family is family. So it was according to Saoirse, who had no siblings and rarely spoke about her parents. Except to say that her mother was the most beautiful and terrifying woman alive, and her father was a fumbling old drunk who, despite being handsome in his youth, now resembled a bridge troll. He was soft as a molted feather and just as useless. That was the danger of not caring or healing or moving forward. That was the danger of dying before you were really dead.

"You turn into an algae-caked barnacle on a dead whale's ass," she said, gesturing to the barnacles on the tail of a dead pilot whale as the four of us walked over the rocky beach, Saoirse and I with our callused swimmer's feet. We preferred to walk barefoot, to feel the contrast of the sharp shells, the smooth sand, and the slimy kelp. Bagira and Moorthy laughed in pain, not yet adjusted to the jagged terrain of our beaches.

The satin shock of cold water washed over my calves, my torso, then my chest, and I felt the essence of Appa. We had scattered Appa's ashes into the lagoon so he could swim back to the white sand beaches of Ceylon. I was scared that the singed cells of his skin were as stagnant as his corpse had been, that he was still here, in this ocean. And perhaps part of him was. Bits of Appa in the Pacific, bits in a wisp of cloud sailing across a London sky, bits in the quartz sands of Gurubebila.

Something thawed in me, and I wept. I wept into a death wail that rivalled the song of the starling until the sea stacks shook and the water level rose to my ears. I gave in to my buckling knees and fell onto my back, unable to lift my aching heart to the sky. My body of grief too heavy to float. Liquid pooled into my caving chest and I eased into the sinking — yet I remained above water.

I opened my eyes to see Bagira, hovering above me as

he gently pushed my shoulders up towards the molecules of Appa in the clouds. Moorthy's knee was secured under the small of my back, swaying in the flow of Appa on his return to his homesands. Saoirse kissed the saltwater rivers running down the sides of my face before they met the parts of Appa in this sea.

I SWAM THROUGH MY GRIEF. Streamlining off the dock into the pine-nestled deep green of the water, I dolphin-kicked, underwater-pulled, and then flutter-kicked until the water turned black and my lungs felt like stones. When I broke the surface, before everything came clear again, I saw a flash of memory. Of Appa. I floated on my back, overwhelmed by the senseless beauty of the light dancing on the water's surface.

I swam at sunrise, at moonlight, when forest fires painted the Interior in a pink haze, when it rained, when the lightning came. I swam with Saoirse, with Tony, with Bagira and Moorthy, I swam alone. I swam with anger, sadness, and emotions I couldn't name, until I reached a ribbon of joy — or was it simply the absence of pain? I swam until I felt my limbs, until I re-entered my body and remembered that I was not a shadow.

"What do you think about open-water swimming?" Saoirse wrapped her legs around my waist, arching her torso out of the water and sculling to stay afloat.

"I haven't thought about it." I cupped the jade water in my palm and trickled it onto her forehead.

She flinched, launched off me. "I mean, what about competing in open water? You know, instead of the pool?"

My spine straightened. No blocks, no turns. "Like, trials?"

"Why not?"

"I haven't trained in months."

"You've *been* training for months."

"This isn't training."

"Just because you enjoy it, doesn't mean it isn't training."

STILL DAMP FROM A rainy morning swim, I stared out the window, sipping the harvested dandelion root coffee Saoirse had brewed. My appetite had returned and my strength with it. I'd eat poached eggs on a cakey slice of sourdough before cycling down to the water for a dip. No set distance, just swim until I felt like stopping. Appa's breathing lessons flooded in, and I thought of him with each inhale and exhale. Felt the strength of my limbs resurrecting with each stroke. Trials were in a little over three months and I had no idea where I was seeded.

The cold kiss of outside air flushed into the room, followed by a slam.

"Come on," Saoirse said, grabbing my arm and pulling me towards the door.

"Where are we going?"

"Whiskey Creek."

"What's in Whiskey Creek?"

"I want to make a grass pie."

"That sounds...terrible."

"Put your shoes on."

So I put my shoes on. Everything is more colourful after it rains, I thought, stepping out into a now brilliant, viridian June day. Under the yellow awning of sunlight, we searched through the deepest parts of the forest, sifting under the thickets, combing the base of trees until we found our trove. As we collected the nettles, I noticed just how impressive my wrists were; my hands, which I'd never fully appreciated. I raised them to the treeline, clenching and unclenching my palms, staring at the intricate network of lines.

At the sound of a hummingbird's buzz-whistle chip and twitter, I locked back into the moment. We were on the hunt for a wild weed, and I was determined. I moved forward over the soft crunch of leaves and the satisfying snap of brittle twigs. Eventually, I came to a towering redwood. I ran my hand over its bark. Smooth. A claret-umber with rivulets of cashew; it must have been hundreds of years old. Its nourishing life force surged into my palm, and I knew that I needed to keep eating. A tree would never deprive itself.

Just then, a ghost swooped over my left shoulder.

I traced its flight to the branches of an emerald balsam fir, where a strange opal bird with angel's wings, glacial blue eyes, and a snow-white beak perched. It cawed what sounded like a raven's song. Saoirse was metres behind, entrenched in foraging focus that only the startling call of a rare blue-eyed, white raven could break.

A halo of light refracted off the ghost bird's wingspan. It cawed again, launching into flight and swooping directly at my head. I ducked, palms pressed into the soft dirt, breathing slowly in time with the earth's pulse. At the disintegrating end of a fallen moss-covered tree trunk, horizontal in the forest's fern featherbed as if sleeping, was a cluster of alienesque fungi.

"Saoirse?"

"What?" She walked over with heavy, purposeful steps.

"What the hell are these?" They were bizarre — porous, sponge-like caps and curved stems.

She wiped the sweat off her brow and crouched down. "Oh my God! Oh my God!" Saoirse leapt up and down like an elated child, her face disappearing behind her mop of hair. "Morels! These are morels!"

I loved how excited she got over plants. Liked the way she talked about the land. How she pulled her sleeves over her hands before the words tumbled out. I'd heard Saoirse talk about morels before. About how they had a taste that captured the savoury richness of earth and the complexity of life. Sounded like hippie bullshit, but I drank dandelion coffee by choice now, so who was I to judge?

When we got home, we boiled the kettle and rinsed the mushrooms in the sink, plucking away microscopic insects and cleaning the dirt, moss, and tiny, tiny green worms from the stems and the intricate, honeycomb structures of the caps. I held one to my nose; it didn't smell like anything.

After the labour-intensive process of preparing the extra morels for drying, Saoirse instructed me to put a generous number in a pan with a clove of elephant garlic, a big glug of neon-yellow cold-pressed olive oil, and some slices of shallot that quickly sizzled to translucence. A rich, umami aroma enveloped the room. Saoirse took over, adding a dollop of fresh cream from local grass-fed cows and, finally, a generous splash of expensive Okanagan wine I'd gotten as a funeral gift. She served the morels over puréed sweet potatoes and steamed greens with a garnish of parsley and wood sorrel from the yard.

"Prepare to have your life changed forever," she said.

I sat on the edge of my seat, the warmth of the plate flooding over my face, and stuck my fork into a juicy morel.

"Wait! Wait!" she cried. "I almost forgot!" She rushed to the refrigerator, pulled out a hard chunk of Parmesan, and grated it over the steaming plate.

I bit into the morel's tender honeycomb flesh. It had

a gamey texture, rich and dark in flavour. The salty taste of earth and sun.

"That…," I said, sinking into the chair, contemplating the life of a mushroom — its complex, underground network of mycelial threads like veins — "…is good." I exhaled deeply, the tang of morel on my tongue, Saoirse's smiling eyes locked on me. This, all of it, was exactly what eating was supposed to be.

The phone rang, and Saoirse stood up to answer it. Instantly, the pitch of her voice changed, an unfamiliar weight to it. Her words became slower and fewer. I was curious, but not curious enough to stop eating the delicious morels. My plate was nearly polished off by the time she returned to the table.

"It was my dad." Her lively eyes had turned to stone. "He wants to meet you," she said.

"Oh." The silence was loud. "Does he know I'm Black?"

She rolled her eyes. "You're not really Black, you're Sri Lankan."

"I don't know if you're aware, but Black isn't a nationality. And I'm not Sri Lankan."

"Not everything is about colour."

Rocky had told me this, too. That colour blindness was the scapegoat of educated white folks, even the ones you loved.

We went back to the morels. Eating them all up. Followed by the rest of the sweet potato purée. I was full, satisfied, but Saoirse was gripped by an insatiable craving. She opened a box of water crackers and dipped them in red pepper jelly. Then she moved on to the pickled asparagus. To the olive tapenade and the sunflower butter. To plain goat-milk yogurt with honey, to the carnival rock candy and white nectarines.

Finally, she sighed, slumping next to me on the couch. For some people, having a father is as painful as losing one.

19

The River

lək^{w}əŋən, Snʊ'neɪməx^w, 1965–89

—

Our nights were fragmented and fitful. Waking up to quell Kerry's cries, I stitched together small blips of slumber. Sleepless yet serene, I was spellbound by the immeasurable harmony this tiny, tiny body had brought with it earthside. I smiled from twilight through dusk.

Then there was the night I was jolted awake by Lily, tugging viciously at my shoulder. "Ronny, Ronny, wake up."

"What?" I groaned, rolling over to flick on the lamp.

"Go check on him."

I didn't understand why we wouldn't enjoy a rare spell of sleep, but there was an urgency in her voice and she had hard hands.

Basking in a beam of moonlight was my son, curled up cold, hard, and purple as amethyst. Had I hollered at the boreal feel of death on his skin, or was it seismic waves, a moving body of air pulsing out from my trembling hands, that brought Lily into the room with me? I don't remember.

Lil had been pregnant when I left for Halifax to board ship, had Kerry a few days after my return to Esquimalt. Then he died. He was so small for such a big death. His nose bridge still non-existent. The tectonic grief split me in half.

EMPTY AND HARD AS the glass spirit bottles in the back of the liquor cabinet, I watched flickers of light, glimpses of the world passing through fogged-up green glass. I gave in to the bad spirits, and since I could no longer sleep, I drank to dream, crawling into the crystal cavern of the maple whiskey to mute the sticky, fermented rage.

One night, I stumbled home to find that Lil had locked me out.

"Oh, sweet Water Lily, let me in!" I tripped over a potted plant. Geraniums.

"You don't live here."

Oh, she was a scrappy woman.

"I do so, Water Lily. Now let me in, or I'll huff and I'll puff and I'll blow the house down."

"Why don't you just go back to the bar?"

"Huff." I clenched my fist. "Puff." And punched a hole through the window glass.

"Are you out of your goddamn mind?"

"Let me in, Lil, you Nazi bitch! I paid for this house."

Streams of hot blood coursed down my left hand. It looked kind of beautiful, I thought, as I passed out on the steps.

The next morning, Lil walked by me and what at first appeared to be a machination of light, the way glass can distort shape, was the first clear image I'd seen in months. When I saw her belly, full of new life, I felt nothing and stayed curled up at the bottom of the bottle.

"How can you know who you are if you don't even know where you come from, huh? There's a way to find out, to get ahold of those documents... He had the wrong name. I only called him Kerry because you said you were Irish."

"Ah, come off it already," I bleated.

Her words melted together with time itself, with the harsh sunlight and the boxes and boxes of things that had piled up in the living room. I'd wanted a neat life. Now I'd settle for a tidy space for my chaos to exist in. But after Kerry, Lil couldn't let go. Kept all the baby gowns, soothers, even held on to the cradle, though I'd wanted to throw it all into the fire.

Where was she now? I wondered as I got off my keister,

wading past the knitted booties that were never worn, rattles, obituaries with bleeding ink. With a head full of rocks I raided the cupboards and found nothing but expired pablum. I dragged my sorry sack of flesh over to the liquor cabinet. Empty. When was it? I had no memory of drinking all the rum or the schnapps or the bottles of peak-year Primitivo that I'd brought home from Italy to savour. Wasps had gotten into the caster sugar, the flour was rancid, but alas, there were no hidden bottles of eel juice to be found in the pantry. I tried my luck behind the cluttered chesterfield, the toilet tank, and the bags of cat litter, but it seemed I'd dug up and guzzled down every last drop in the place.

I couldn't find my wallet, but my naval card was still tucked away in the closet with my uniform. I pulled it out, took a long hard look at the lithe, handsome version of myself immortalized on the small piece of plastic. I slid the card into my pocket, then scavenged the couch for loose change, and staggered out into daylight.

The fresh air coated my skin like I'd just waded into thin water. It was cold and bright, a March day. Feeling like I'd been at sea for thirty years and forgotten how to walk on land, I made my way to the liquor store. My pants slid down past my ass, and when I reached back to pull them up, I felt my greasy oolichan of a lower back. I paced the aisles, the beer can labels looking impossibly red, glinting under the white fluorescent lights.

"Ron?"

I raised my head. It was Tod, holding a crystalline cask of expensive-looking rum. He'd gained weight — in the good way. His skin shone with health.

"Jesus, you look terrible."

"I've, ah — I'm sick," I said, not wanting to get into the particulars.

"Who you serving on these days?"

"I'm on leave, you know, after..."

"Ah, of course. I'm awful sorry about that, Ronny."

I grabbed a case of beer, not the brand I wanted, and headed to the till. "Tot time?"

"Nah, not for me. I don't drink. It's for Torchie, you know, it's his birthday," Tod said, and I groaned on the inside. "Hey, you have time to join us? We're all getting together at Cara Bay. I'm sure Sam and the boys would love to see you."

I found that hard to believe, seeing as I hadn't heard a word from Sam since Kerry died, when I needed him most. "I've got plans."

"Oh, yeah? What kinda plans you got?"

"I'm...have to...boil a ham."

"Do you now?"

"Yes."

"You're boiling a ham at nine in the morning?"

"Yes."

"What for?"

"That's my business."

I slid the coins across the counter, collected my change along with my shame and resentment, and stormed out of there. As I walked down the street, the image of the silver sea kept stabbing me in the brain, and so I went down to it.

When I got to the water's edge, the first thing I saw was shells, so many shells, all clean and white. Some remained perfectly intact, others shattered. I found one clam, still alive, only a chipped edge. I picked it up, felt the grooves and the cluster of sand collected on the top. Then I chucked it back into the sea.

I looked out into the vast expanse of water, put my fingers in. Tiny needles of ice prickled all over my skin. I searched for the Stó:lō twined with the Pacific, the way you search for a person's ancestry in their bone structure and skin. I swore I could feel it, its pace, rushing. Its story.

Leaning against a piece of driftwood, dry as bone, I thought seriously about getting sober before remembering, vividly, the salt-in-the-wound sting of not hearing from Sam or Tod or Torchie after I lost my son, and cracked open a beer instead. It tasted like cow piss but took the edge off. Beer after beer, I receded with the tide: *tschkkk* went the tab, and on went life, the days, the years, the decades.

THAT FIRST DRY MONTH stung like sea snake venom. Toxins twisting around tendons, thick tongue, blurred vision, vomiting up lung and memory for half a solar spin.

And then, like the first hit from an oxygen tank, a clearing opened in my mind. My files. I wanted to get my files back, to know where I came from. To finally put that flapping thing in me to rest. Morning undressed itself, aurelian and soft, the kind of dazzling purity that mocks you, makes you sore with unworthiness. I looked down and recognized my striated canyons, swollen red with river, the now less-callused crests where finger meets paleolithic palm. I, water, cupped a body of air in clarity, felt firm in my fluidity. With this lucidity came the torrential mourning, came the cascading memory reel, came thawed time tumbling out my eye sockets. Curled up on a rain cloud of shag carpet, for those five moons, I could only weep.

"Oh, join the club," Lil said in an atomic tone so tremorous and unforgiving it could split the earth's crust. She put on a record to drown me out. Dizzy Gillespie. The honey-like notes oozed into the room, painting everything with an ochre light.

I stopped my snivelling and looked up, saw Jagger, Vince, Kerry. My mother. Transparent wraiths, dancing. I threw my head back, skin tight from dried tears, and laughed. I got to my feet and shimmied in the cluttered living room.

Lil leaned against the chesterfield suffocating under

boxes of memorabilia, magazine clippings, leaving no place for someone to sit. "Madman."

"I prefer 'sailor man,' thank you."

"Ain't no difference."

"The difference is the sea."

I shuffled towards her through the disarray, my aged joints clicking like I was made of tin. I took her hand and pulled her into the middle of the room, where we jived together for the first time in years, surrounded by the swinging spirits and dusty belongings of our dead.

The record scratched to a halt, sending the marigold light out the window, and Jagger, Vince, Kerry, and my mother evaporated with it. When the quiet came, we were drenched in sweat.

Lil tucked her hair behind her ears and stepped back. "I better start supper." Her large pupils were dilated in her glacial eyes. Borderless blue-grey swirled around like high seas in the dim light. The hairline wrinkles that framed her permanent frown hadn't settled yet, suggestions of age more than age itself.

"Nah, Lil, let me make it. Roasted tomato sandwiches with poached eggs?" I held out my arms, widened my eyes in a way that would have charmed her twenty years ago.

"It's really no bother, Ron." She was already moving towards the kitchen.

I snatched her arm, ham-handedly twirled her around. "C'mon."

"You're a lousy cook."

"Sheesh," I said. "Kick a man when he's down."

"You're the most up I've seen you since we met."

She continued into the kitchen, and I, slapped steady by her words, lunged for the phone. Some drinkers say they can sense it's the sickness their wives really hate — the bottle, not the man — but I wasn't so sure. Still, Lil was the one to remind me of my mother, of my files, of the time I still had that I was willingly whittling away in a drunken stupor. My hands trembled as I dialled the rotary.

"Saoirse speaking."

"Hi. How's school?"

"Good."

"All *A*s for awful?"

Silence. Was this trembling all nerves or the withdrawal?

"When you coming home, kiddo?"

"Depends. When are you going to stop drinking?"

"Haven't drank since Christmas."

"Three months?"

"Two and a bit."

"I've been seeing a boy."

"Huh… pregnant already?"

"I'm hanging up now —"

"No, wait. You, uh, why don't you bring him over for Easter dinner?"

"Since when do we celebrate Easter?"

"Since now."

"You in one of those Christian rehab cults?"

"Not yet."

"All right, I'll ask."

Saoirse hadn't spoken to me since I missed her high school graduation. A drunk sack of trash wallowing on the couch while his daughter was awarded a full-ride scholarship to the Faculty of Science and a Governor General's Award for the highest grade-point average in the school. That dumb part of me liked to think she chose to live two hours away in Victoria because our few good memories were ledged there, near the Esquimalt navy base. The lucid part knew it was because I was a terrible father.

By the time the knotted pain in my chest when I thought about Kerry had untangled itself somewhat, Saoirse had already reached double digits. I still couldn't pronounce her name right — *Seer-sha*, a Celtic name. Lil's idea because I'd panicked when she asked about my heritage and told her I was Irish. A memory clear as the Indian Ocean: at Saoirse's tenth or eleventh birthday party I was already halfway through a bottle of Four Roses when she begged me to take her to the bathtub race. She had an impressively firm grip and weight for a little girl, a stubbornness and quick tongue matched only by her mother's. Thing was, even when I was sober, the bronze anchor in my chest, dense and fouled, laden over my barely beating heart, fastened me to the seabed of the hell I'd made.

At least I managed to take her to watch the salmon spawning upriver, hoisted high on my broad diver's shoulders to pick the ripest blackberries. Showed her how yellow chanterelles, which smelled faintly of apricot, concealed their false gold gills beneath fern and ground cedar. Told her to go down to the water when she yearned for what there were no right words for. That was all I did, and it was nothing the earth wouldn't have revealed to her on its own. But now I'd been off the drink for some 160 consecutive days and was inspired to make amends, or at least try.

The Walkman helped. That newfangled tape player that Lily had gotten Saoirse for the Christmas she didn't come home allowed me to carry Angel Man's alley with me. The music soul-stepped into my ears, doo-wopping me back into my body until I was lifting my knees, rocking my hips, and twisting around the jail where I worked. I had transferred there from the navy in the early eighties. There, I was known as a soft guard, a gentle giant. In truth, I was in a perpetual state of hangover and heartbreak. I felt like I was locking up past versions of myself or the gang every time I ushered some scared-shitless kid into a cell for stealing or dealing.

But that Supreme Saturday morning was all "You Can't Hurry Love" and "Love Child" after speaking with

333

Saoirse, even as I fingerprinted a sallow Sc'ianew kid who was caught shooting up in the skate park. I clocked out and stared into all the hours I had left of my day. Directionless and at the mercy of the rhythm in my head, I lindy-hopped across the paved parking lot, towards the opposite of what appealed to me.

I always liked the smell and look of libraries but felt like a fish on land when I stepped into one. At the back shelves a jewel-toned rainbow of engraved leatherbound spines beckoned. Here was an endless sea of story that I wanted to dive into. I pulled a burgundy book off the shelf with a title I could comprehend — *The Clansman*, which I reckoned would grapple with what I craved most: family and belonging. But the words were printed so small that my eyes burned and my brain cramped just trying to read a sentence.

"Hey."

I snapped the gold-gilded pages shut and jolted around to see a pale, aquiline man with hardened eyes and familiar ferret-like features. A quiet co-worker of mine named Clay that I'd never paid much mind to. He had an uninviting grey pallor, frail hands gone yellow at the fingertips.

Clay waved a thin, navy-blue book in my face. "Shit is enlightening." He pulled a leaflet out of his pocket, slipped it into the book, and slapped the thing against my chest. "We're having a cookout at Whiskey Creek tonight. You should stop on by," he said, before wisping away like a streak of mist.

I returned the leatherbound book to its place before sleeving the leaflet out of Clay's book and placing it in my pocket.

The librarian winced at the sight of the title, gave me the old up-down. "We don't have the print version of this, but we do have a bundle of three contemporary audio collections of this nature. Excuse me . . . but, well, I have to ask what it is you do for work before I lend you these materials. They're pretty controversial these days."

"I work at the jail."

"Ah." She settled back into her chair, looking relieved. "So you're . . . conducting research, then? On this kind of group?"

"Something like that."

IT WAS A MISERABLE, humid spring; the cloudless afternoon swelter turned the idle morning raindrops to steam. I crossed the street for shade and pressed Play. The narrator's smooth voice eased the dead anchor from my sternum. I walked, limp and languid, until the lightly salted breeze became pure brine.

The narrator asked me if I'd ever felt shunned by society. He asked me if I'd been wandering the earth half asleep, with a thicket of despair in my chest. He said that men like me were in grave danger. Brainwashed by a communist society that was trying to convince us there was no such thing as a natural order. I didn't know what communism was exactly — something about not owning a toothbrush — but I sensed that it was a bad, bad thing. The narrator explained that it was a denial of the dominance hierarchy that allowed inferior races to get ahead while white men were left in the gutter. Where did I, with my unclear origins, fit into that? *White*, affirmed the voice, which wormed into my head.

I walked back up from the port, through the meandering alleys of inner Nanaimo. Now, while I was not fully latching onto any ideas, I was cordial to anything offering me a seat at the table, even if that table was covered in bird shit and moss in the ass crack of Whiskey Creek.

THE LEAFLET LED ME to the yellow ferns and unpaved roads where a rare white raven had been spotted just days ago. Fresh black bear tracks in mud paired with the anaemic twang of insipid elevator country music would have been enough to repel me if not for the hook of ambrosia and sunrise salad and the line of brotherhood spooled around salted meat sizzling in oil that reeled me in like a white perch born yesterday.

Save for the pewter pendants around their necks, the Odinists at the Whiskey Creek cookout looked ordinary enough. Inches above Thor's engraved hammer was a familiar face from the liquor store, the post office, the prison, the butcher. I was about halfway into my second venison burger when "Hound Dog" started playing on the boombox. "Here we go!" I howled, rocking to the beat. A memory flash of Vince and Angel Man, of jumping trains and jiving until beads of spirit leaked out through my pores, coated my skin in soul and made me feel real. I dug into my dissolving lime and strawberry marshmallow swamp, dotted with maraschino cherries, canned mandarins, and whipped cream. Not half bad.

"Ronny, glad you turned up." Clay leaned his slight frame over the stone picnic table. "You like the King?" He yawned, revealing mercury molars and a snow-white tongue that didn't look right.

"Huh?"

"Elvis."

"He's the king, hey? How come? Because he died on the throne?"

Clay's stern, mayonnaise and Jell-O-speckled face remained unflinching.

"You know, because Elvis died on the toilet and all..."

"I know, a tragedy. Those Jews in Hollywood had their way with him. He's the king of rock and roll."

"Says who?"

Windless silence. Stubbornly still, the western white pine's rapier-like needles pointed me back to the conversation.

"He's all right." I swayed. "I prefer the original by Big Mama Thornton. Anything's better than that mopey racket y'all had on before — no offence."

Clay squinted, shoved his rolled blue sleeves farther up his arms than they wanted to go. "Big Mama Thornton, eh? Sounds like a coon name."

I stiffened. "Does colour matter when it comes to music? Wasn't Elvis part Cherokee? Morning White Dove...heard that somewhere."

"'Spose if I can appreciate the stag I hunt for their swiftness and beauty, I can appreciate the pipes of the coloured. Those monkeys have lungs, I'll give 'em that. But like deer to a venison burger, we all have our place. Dancing and singing is one thing, walking alongside us as equals is another...Imagine a deer on its hind legs, working at the prison with us!" Clay's laugh was a wet cough, all cigarette and ground meat.

I inched my tailbone as far back on the cold stone bench as I could without him noticing. The artificial lime tang and tasteless maraschino cherry bulge on my tongue turned to a sickening, saliva-softened bayou of sugar. Clay reached across the table to wipe the pink blob I'd let drop from my fork with his napkin.

At that moment, the ringleader of this circus started on about his Vikingry, about the white raven sighting being an omen of Odin. Hail, Odin! Whose hammer we must slam down on the tent city accumulating on the island, on the crackheads, the Natives, the Pacific Islander rugby club, the Underground Railroad afterbirth that had "infested" Salt Spring Island. The spiteful drawl from the man at the invisible podium loomed like the briny deep. Frozen in this freak show, I found I'd lost my sea legs. How was I going to extract myself from a helping of mayonnaise-sopping potato and egg salad on a paper plate, offered by the Frigg-infatuated husband of a bank teller? Well, I did it politely, and then slipped away towards the restroom before bolting the hell out of there.

I lone-wolfed to where emerald moss and glow-worm-green laces of lichen draped stones veined with quartz. The dense forest behind the lagoon, where fluted trunks emerged from the earth on either side of the cascading waterfall, webbing out like a spider's silk. I was drawn to a scarred shore pine with a tapered strip of missing bark on its left side, where it had significantly larger branches. I sat down to remove my mud-covered boot and empty out the water, but the liquid stayed collected in the heel.

Over the two-toned sea in Alaska, Tod had told me about Raven. The raven is a trickster, a shape-shifter, changing form at will. According to the Tlingit, Raven, Kit-ka'ositiyi-qa-yit, was originally the colour of fresh snow. Pure, white t'aagaaw. In my favourite story, Raven let water stolen from an everlasting spring drop from his mouth to create the Nass, Stikine, Taku, Chilkat, and Alsek Rivers. He spat out small salmon creeks and brought daylight to the people fishing oolichan in the dark.

I stood up and hobbled along the pavement into sunrise, determined to walk my aching and aged body back to youth.

I HADN'T THE GUTS to return the Odinist audiobooks to the library before Easter. They remained scattered somewhere in the house with the rest of my vagrant shame. To stay off the drink, to prove it to Saoirse, I was trying my old southpaw at a bathtub boat. Well, I had a few sketches and a daydream.

"What's this?" Hot rollers in, thin red lips ajar at the sight of me, Lily pulled my rough tub templates from under my pen; a long line of blue ink streaked across the scribbles. "That supposed to be a boat?" Before I could part my lips to answer, she turned her gaze to my blackened toast. "Breakfast? You're eating breakfast?" The whole kitchen smelled like singed bread and hair.

"I showered, too." I licked the stream of yolk that ran down my fork, pointing the silver prongs at her.

"My stars, who are you and what have you done with my husband?"

I had scrubbed the entire house down like it was *Bonnie* in the Gulf of Mexico, dusted the fish tank and the bookshelves until everything glittered. Then I made my squash supreme, grilled tomatoes, roasted ham and pineapple, rice, and bannock. I could show Saoirse and her new beau who I really was underneath these smoke-stained feathers, the man I'd been at sea.

The doorbell rang, and my heart banged like a naval ship running over an aircraft. I looked around for my ghosts before opening the door, on the other side of which was a new world. I reached for the brass handle, pulled it towards me, and choked on my own tongue as the wooden panel swung open.

There, on my front step, stood the darkest-skinned human being I'd seen in my life.

20

The Sea

Snʊ'neɪmɑxʷ, 1989

⌒

Saoirse's father had cheekbones that could cut glass and eyes the same narrow shape and river blue as his daughter's. His hair was sablefish black, contrasted by rogue silvery-white strands that sprouted from the base of his scalp, ears, and nostrils like the invasive weeds that had overthrown his front lawn. He had the comedically pink, bulbous nose and slalom buoy gut of a man who drank too much. The green pillows beneath his eyes indicated some form of nutrient deficiency. Even so, it was clear he had been a handsome man in his youth.

"Hi there, uh —" Mr. Young's lips capered over the words. He looked down at his shaking palm before extending it to me, his trepidation clear as a spring brook.

I reached out for Saoirse, who veered away from my touch. She brushed my persistent arm off her sundress-exposed shoulder. Her tear troughs had turned velella from sleeplessness. Since the phone call, she'd been an everlasting spring of nerves, waking up dozens of times to relieve herself throughout the night, an unhealthy frequency she maintained during the day. She ate stale toaster strudels from a vending machine and let the lamb's lettuce wilt in the fridge. She cried at small things, like stuck zippers, crystallized honey in a plastic squeeze bottle that just wouldn't give, and lost socks.

Now, she looked through me with a vacant gaze, and I, the stranger, was once again made to know myself through another's eyes. She should have listened to me, should have warned them. Because now it was too late. Man overboard. Her parents had capsized at the sight of my skin, and it was up to me to swim us all back to the shallows.

"Chandra," I introduced myself. "Pleasure to meet you."

Mr. Young forced a smile before leading us unsteadily through the dining room. The place was laden with naval insignia, a helm clock, and other maritime relics.

"I'm Lily." Saoirse's mother was straight off the silver screen, though she wasn't wearing any makeup. Her snow-blond hair glimmered in a beehive, and her eyes were ice — nearly white, with no outer ring.

I shook her hand, which was strikingly broad and callused, fine blue veins running down her muscular forearms. Saoirse'd said her mom worked in the cowshed growing up, but she must have built it bare-handed.

Out on the back porch, a weathered mint-green patio umbrella provided unnecessary shade from a frail sun whose pale blades were muted by a dense thicket of cloud. We took our seats and sipped over-sweetened iced tea. My eyes darted around. Who was growing lobelia in a pair of rain boots? What was all the blue tarp for? Was the clover-covered vessel draped in vine and drooping sunflowers once a rowboat? I peered down at my fork, too dull to refract or reflect, then at the glazed ham, encircled by a sodden moat of limp baked pineapple rings. And then my focus returned to Mr. Young, leaning forward, his unruly thistles for brows dangling above the wary eye he inspected me with.

Overhead, an unkindness of ravens swooped down from some unseen perch, an onyx omniscience. The ravens spread their batting black wings over the moment before cawing in a short, shrill chain and plummeting towards the sweating ham. At the very last moment, so close I could feel the ripple of air from their wings, the four birds whipped around in a swift, balletic reversal.

"Tricksters," Mr. Young scoffed, strangely unfazed compared to the three of us, who clutched the edges of our plastic garden chairs in stunned stillness.

"Sorry?" I braced myself.

"Them ravens." Mr. Young sat back and smiled, a real smile.

This was a relief. "We saw the white one."

"Did you?"

"Yep. Out in the woods."

"Wild. So, Chandra, what do you do?"

"I, uh, I'm a student. Bachelor's of science…and a swimmer. Same as Saoirse," I said.

"A swimmer, eh? That's…real great. You sail?"

"No, but I surf."

"Ah." He sat back. "You dive?"

"No."

"Fish?"

"He's vegetarian," Saoirse cut in, though I wished she hadn't. I stared at the scintillating grooves in the Waterford crystal and poured myself another glass of tea-hinted sugar water.

"Ah, well, good thing I made all this rice."

"Chandra doesn't care for white rice."

Mr. Young's elbows hit the table, and I noticed the thin streak of cloud stretching out into nothingness along the horizon to reveal the most puzzling pigment, a strange shade between orange and indigo. Being Black, or being in the realm of it, means something different to everyone. It gets thrust on you at some point and over time you grow into it, make it your own — or at least try.

But I'll wager for most of us it has, at one point, meant this: being plucked out of the present moment, being told what you are by someone else on sight. You learn to read subtext like a wave pattern. You can feel it in the way the air changes like before a storm, grows thick and sickly warm with tension. Mr. Young tilted his head and launched in me the acid tongue and tight throat usually reserved for pre-race jitters in marshalling. I wanted to tell him what I am, but he wouldn't be satisfied. I wanted to tell him what I am, but I didn't know. You learn to live outside your skin, live with it, never settling in.

I dragged my fingertips against the swell of my biceps, felt the mass and thickness of my thighs. "That's not true, I don't mind white rice," I lied.

"Really? Because whenever I cook it, you go berserk and say without the husk it's just refined starch."

I pulled over the bowl of rice, which looked buttered, and piled my plate high before bringing the fork swiftly to my lips in a heaping, calorific mouthful. Though I couldn't place where I knew it from, the plate of golden bread beside it looked and smelled specific, familiar, and much more appetizing.

"You ever been in a bathtub race?" Mr. Young asked.

Before I could string together a response, I was struck by a familiar piano chord, muffled and distant, but those mid-high quarter notes were still tangible.

"Someone playing the Supremes around here?"

You'd have thought I was fresh out of the asylum by the look Lily and Saoirse shot my way, but Mr. Young fumbled and grumbled in his seat. He reached for something in his back pocket as a flurry of spring pollen made me sneeze up a lung. "Shoot, must've sat on my Walkman." He chuckled.

"No apologies needed," I said raspily between coughs. "You have good taste."

"Yeah? You a music lover?"

"Yes, sir." I held my nostrils shut as the spores billowed up into the atmosphere, sounding more nasally than Bob Dylan. "Though, shoot, now that you bring it up, my guitar's been collecting dust for the past two years."

"I know how that goes. Hey, if you're interested, I'm building a little collection inside. Buddies from the navy... well, I don't see them all that often, but they send me music from time to time. Some records, some tapes, too."

Defiant auric rays punctured the cloud mass, making the glaze on the ham glimmer even more unappetizingly. But I felt good, for a moment, before a coat of frost formed over my shoulder where Lily lingered. "Where'd you get that Walkman?" she demanded.

Her icy expression was mirrored in Mr. Young's panic-stricken pupils. "That was for Saoirse." A guttural partition was drawn between each equally punctuated word. Mr. Young's face went crimson, and he hung his head sheepishly before sliding the Walkman across the table.

Saoirse got up from the table with a clang, splitting the awkward lull. "No, no, Dad, you keep it. I've already got one." She clutched her stomach, a plum tinge to her tired face. "Sorry, excuse me." She bashed her hip against the table before disappearing into the house.

"Saoirse?" Mr. Young stood up, whacking his knee on the opposite corner of the table, then his elbow on the doorframe as he went in after her.

I was left with Lily, whose bewitching eyes landed on me, dropping my basal temperature by several degrees. Chillingly beautiful, the woman looked like she could slit my throat and then eat a biscuit.

"You know, *I* never had any problem with coloureds."

Here we go. I took a bite of grilled tomato. Tasted like a sour foot. Tried the squash to wash the taste down. Also terrible.

"My father did," Lily went on. "But he was a Schweinhund, pardon my Deutsch."

I forced a smile and an airy laugh. Was I meant to be thankful for this weirdly cordial white supremacy? I poured myself yet another glass of tea. "My parents are actually from Sri Lanka. I wasn't born there but —"

"Where now? Tree Munkah?"

"Sri Lanka. I don't know if I'm even pronouncing it

right, to be honest. It's a . . . an island. I think it's technically in South Asia."

"Ach so, I'm not so good with geography. Didn't finish
school. Neither did Ronny. You must think we're dumb."

"No, I don't think that. No one knows where it is. I've
never even been there myself."

"Mmm. You know, you should ask Ronny, though.
He's sailed around the whole world. All over the world."

"Really?" I'd always dreamed of taking off somewhere
tropical.

"Mm-hm, all over the whole world. Didn't Saoirse
tell you?" Lily took a long drag from her cigarette. "Ach,
nei, I guess I can see why not. We . . . we are not perfect
parents. Or people." She exhaled a smoke cloud with an
agonal sigh.

"I . . . I think I'll go check on that music collection,"
I said, feeling my bladder full to the brim with iced tea.
Feeling the tingle of melanocytes. Feeling so dark.

Lily nodded, flashed a smile. "Go right ahead."

The house creaked strangely, with the sudden trills
and sliding pitch of a crooner's voice. Smelled of moth-
balls and cobwebs steeping in a whiskey marinade. Beside
the helm clock, the wooden steering wheel of a ship, an
unplugged rotary phone, and some sort of medal, I found
the music stash. Good stuff. Mainly jive, swing, and soul.
Bite of blues, and a dapple of doo-wop and Motown.
Heaps of Dizzy Gillespie, who I was embarrassed to say

I'd never heard of. Here was an archival evolution of sorts, from Billie Holiday, Chuck Berry, and B. B. King to Otis Redding, then Aretha and the Supremes. While I figured it could have used a psychedelic rock album or two, Mr. Young's collection was upbeat and bright. Jams that would make even a narbo with two left feet get up and bust a move.

A laceration of dread replaced the peace in my chest when I realized the last tapes on the shelf weren't music but a series of the most peculiar books. I pressed my back to the wall, and that is how I caught the voices echoing from the bathroom.

"So you're serious, then?"

"Maybe."

"Are you ready for the world? How they'll see you two together? You sure you want all that?"

"You know, maybe I do prefer you when you're drunk and passed out."

A wordless cry ricocheted off the glass sliding door, growing louder from the long hallway. I glided over the shag carpet, nearly knocking over a vase holding a wilted bouquet before I exited the house and sat back down at the table, holding my breath. I poured myself a seventh glass of iced tea, heart thumping fast.

"You all right?" Lily slid towards the edge of her seat wearing a concerned expression.

"Mm-hm," I lied, suffocating in a swarm of sand fleas.

Folks of my shade have incarnations of this experience every second of every day, all over the world. I supposed a man like Mr. Young was white wherever he went, but my identity was a shape-shifter. My colour always evoking curiosity, always a tilt of the head. Sometimes the interrogations were plain funny, other times perplexing. Sometimes the statements were strange, absurd, upsetting. Every once in a while, I was lashed by a torrent so haunting, I realized that even my bones would never be white enough.

Not all of us are called, or call ourselves, Black. But I do. Maybe it's because my roots were tangled before they were severed clean off. Black is a moving identity. Black is slippery, has no borders, no one culture, no one nationality. And that's why, for all its evasiveness, I made a home in my Blackness. Being Black meant that, even when all alone at a table full of white people, I had a past, present, and future's worth of backup.

So I stood back up, tall.

Saoirse returned with a gravid expression. Mr. Young forced his way out onto the porch behind her and spoke in a nervous falsetto. "Back to that bathtub race in July." He extended his arm like an auctioneer, failing to mask his shame.

My gut sank and twisted with sugar water and caffeine. "I hate bathtubs!" I blurted. My hip thudded against the table with an inelegance I might have apologized for in other circumstances.

Saoirse lifted an eyebrow above a swollen, red eye.

"What's your angle, old man?" I turned to Saoirse. "I can deal with a drunk, but a neo-Nazi?" I pulled the audiobooks from my jacket, tossing them across the table Frisbee-style.

"Oh, no, those aren't what they look like…a friend gave…I am no Nazi," Mr. Young sputtered.

I hadn't expected his sad blue eyes to dazzle in the sunlight in a way that both reminded me of Saoirse's and irritated me beyond measure. Nor was I prepared to see a half moon so peach and spectacular, sharing a sky that had stealthily gone clear with the sun.

"My apologies, an Odinist."

"What's an Odinist?" Saoirse asked.

"Just neo-Nazism for Viking nerds. They're on the news all the time for hate crimes."

The cutlery on the table trembled as I thundered out of the house and we split.

IT WAS STILL BRIGHT when we got back to Saoirse's dorm, but now, as stars hatched in the burnt-umber night, Saoirse remained curled up on the sofa with her shoes on.

Forget him and forget bathtub races. I paced under the clothesline of drying herbs and lavender, breaking off a sprig to smell. That helped somewhat. I flicked the kettle on and washed a few peppermint leaves. While the water came to a boil, I opened the fridge and pulled out a half-eaten bucket of tart cherries, strong and sour. I dusted the glistening, ruby fruit with bitter cocoa and cinnamon before placing the bowl on the desk that doubled as a coffee table in front of Saoirse, who was spiralling into herself like a nautilus shell.

"Chocolate cherries?" I offered.

She rubbed her pink eyes and tucked her hair behind her sweet elf-like ears before reaching for the crimson abundance. A strange look passed over her face. "And your dad, he was the nicest man I've ever met." She laughed and that broke open the waterworks. Big belly guffaws punctured the membrane, releasing the storm-tossed melancholy, the overdue sorrow.

Saoirse reached out to me with chocolatey fingertips, placed my hand on her lower abdomen. "It doesn't matter what my idiot dad, or anyone, thinks. We have each other, and our baby."

"Yeah... Wait, what?"

She popped a cocoa-dusted cherry into her mouth and smiled, tears caught in the wells of her eyes. "I'm pregnant," Saoirse said, chipmunk cheeks full of tart cherries.

I went limp with laughter and felt her wrap around me. Soft, like a cushion between my body and all the celestial grief. A drop of laughter can hold as much pain, as much multiplicity, as a tear. We laughed a river, welling up and overflowing onto the floor until we were wading knee-deep in it all: the beauty and the ugliness.

21

The River

Snʊˈneɪməxʷ; xʷməθkʷəy̓əm, səlilwətaɫ, Sḵwx̱wú7mesh;
qiqéyt; Stó:lō (Mathexwi-Semá:th)
(from Nanaimo to Vancouver and New Westminster to
between Matsqui Prairie and Sumas Mountain), 1989

Mind cluttered as our kitchen sink, I tossed and turned
on the couch in the damp heat, starlight spilling through
the curtains. Each tick of the helm clock walloped deeper
and deeper into my skull. I flung the itchy blanket off and
sat up, not exactly hungry but hankering for something.
I flicked the light on in the kitchen, opened the fridge,
and lost my appetite when I saw the leftovers from a meal
that was meant to feed four.

These college kids and their air of superiority made
me grit my teeth. Kids who didn't like white rice and
thought that just because they could spin fat, frou-frou
words into apple butter, they had it made in the shade.
Well, some things you simply can't learn in a classroom.

Like how savage the world is to alley mutts and half-breeds. Their roofs were leaking if they thought it was a wise idea to bring a kid like that, half-Black and half-mess, into chaos like this. Witless, we all want to bring our child into a world that makes sense. And that world doesn't exist. There was no good future for an out-of-wedlock mulatto kid with a genetic predisposition for bad spirits and left-handedness.

Lil had sure let me have it when she discovered I'd been listening to "Gefährlicher Gestapo garbage." Kept whipping my thigh with the tea towel while I sulked at the table and then banished me from the bedroom.

"I didn't know!" I protested, ashamed to admit that I'd been duped, that I'd driven all the way up to Whiskey Creek and eaten not one but two Odinist venison burgers. "Excuse me for daring to think differently."

That stopped her right in her tracks. "Herr. Why not think differently in the way that invents a cure for cancer, or a clone wife that can fill in and have Scheiß conversations like this for me?"

"Ah, shut up, you old hag," I grumbled, chewing a cold slab of rubbery ham before resigning to swallow it down in chunks. That almost sent her back onto the roof.

What she didn't understand was that, for the briefest moment, I was offered what I had thought was a life raft, a vessel to blame for my ails. What haunts me to this day is the hard fact that, had I not known the friendship of

Sam, Tod, Angel Man, or Ray, had my own origins not been so obscure, I might have leapt into it.

Sure, I knew the way I was thinking wasn't right, the way a kid slipping through log booms ain't right. The way a kid can be taken from his own mother without a trace, a name, or a birth date and try his best to have a family, only to have it crumble in his own hands. It ain't right.

Saoirse wouldn't return my calls and Lil blamed me, which was only half fair. I'd caused the quarrel, sure, but Saoirse had inherited her mother's bone to pick, that same venom that sent Lil huffing and puffing down to the red brick public library to blow all the Gestapo garbage off its shelves in one breath. Or at least she tried. Even made the local paper. They ripped select books from the spine of the library's Dewey decimal system, but it turned out that kind of thinking was a disease; many of the most revered books and their authors, and even language itself, had been infected by it. Still, a line was drawn somewhere, between the coveted "classics" and well-meaning "fictions," and books like the ones given to me, which were considered knowingly bad and intended to incite hate. I wasn't so sure this was the solution, but afterwards, Lil regained some sleep and my thigh some relief from the tea towel.

The voracious urge to drink made my skin itch, but even in exile, some senseless part of me held on to hope that Saoirse would come back to me, and that kept me sober. I had no choice but to sit and unpack the cobweb-covered suitcases in the den of my memory. When Lil'd first suggested I go back to Vancouver to collect my files from Children's Aid, I'd snapped at her to quit pestering me. I wasn't ready for the finality of knowing. But now the only thing I could think to do was to go back. To go down to the water.

I was a navy recruit all over again, leaping through hoop after bureaucratic hoop, biting my tongue over the phone, dragging myself through the mud of Children's Aid as I ducked beneath judicial barbed wire before being thrown on a drenched deck in a high-seas tempest. Requesting my records was no five-knot wind or mild swell, and at first it seemed out of reach. But I held firm to my mast of grit as I weathered the ministry's gusts. Somewhere among the merciless litany of phone calls and faxes, they realized this sailor wouldn't let up until they agreed to give him back his past.

THE FERRY RIDE OVER to the mainland quelled my nerves some. The sea was blue-black and tempting, reminding me how small I was. Nothing more or less than a water droplet. My problems weren't as big as they seemed, so long as I was alive and kept flowing forward. I inhaled the sharp, briny air and leaned over the rail. Two orcas spy-hopped a few metres away from the boat before disappearing into the horizon. As the ocean air whipped my face, I closed my eyes. I wanted to dive into the infinite darkness and dissolve.

Silver skyscrapers blocked out the sky and newfangled automobiles zoomed over the streets in the ever-shifting mask called "Vancouver," which now looked and smelled like it had been coated in lacquer, suffocating ancient moss and stone. Bussing through downtown, the sight of the Georgia Viaduct made my stomach turn. Squalor beyond salvation is what they wrote of it, a derelict district of undesirables between Prior and Union and Main and Jackson. Always a racket out there, they said, and the buildings were in need of renewal. By buildings, they meant their residents. By squalor, they meant Black. A Black community thriving all threateningly like that... Well, that's a racket even in its reticence. That's a boisterous provocation even when it doesn't make a sound.

So Angel Man's alley was demolished, displaced for a bridge, and all the light it held was now scattered throughout the city — pockets of wild grass pushing up through cracks in the newly paved sidewalk.

I couldn't picture my music or my people in the places they'd once lived. I passed the boarded-up joint that used to be the China Pheasant, heard a phantom chatter of Italian. Even the smallest embers of my history were being scraped off and sanitized. I didn't have so much as a birth certificate to prove my entry into the world, and now all the places I'd known, all the evidence of my life, was flaking away like chipped paint in Chinatown.

I got off the tram, turned left, and neared Children's Aid, which was outside downtown's new dazzling nucleus. There I saw a threadbare cluster of people I recognized as my own, shells of themselves all sloughed to the gutters. I entered the building, which was now a shade of mellowing piss yellow, the climbing vine enveloping the majority of the edifice. The tired woman at the front desk was long gone, but the secretary in her place shared the same listless demeanour. With a manicured hand, she slid my file across the counter.

"This is it?" I flipped through the obscenely thin stack of pages encased in a new manilla envelope. "I'm sure it was five times this size." Might have lost a few brain cells from the drink, might have failed to remember many things as they were, but I was certain about the enormity of that file.

The secretary pursed her non-existent lips and clicked her pen in rhythmless agitation. "Some things were confidential. Some things government policy wouldn't legally allow us to hand over to you."

"It's my life. It shouldn't be confidential to me."

"Other lives go into lives." She yawned, waving me away like I was nothing.

I tipped my hat, but on the inside, I was flipping the bird to that broad and everything she represented. How was it easier to access Odinist audiobooks than the details of my own life?

I went down to Stó:lō. The trams were gone and the buses were numbered all different, but I eventually got down to the quay. Ray's boat was nowhere to be seen. Everywhere I turned was a depressing ash-grey tapestry of demolishing and drilling. The aggressive sights and sounds of lush green being replaced by hideous concrete. My stars, New Westminster was all ritz and glitz. Far too upscale for left-handed foster hoodlums.

I sat down on a bench beside a strategically placed palm tree. Despite being out of place, it was a fine tree, and it consoled me with its quiet sway. The whir of the river was the same, at least. The consistent pace of the rushing current carried me as I sifted through the scraps of my life. Page by page, I uncovered fragments. First, familiar stories stitched together and summarized in smudged ink over yellowed paper — the dog leash, Mrs. Belyea's severed finger, the BB pellet in Gordon's ass, the pitchfork in the kraut's foot, and reports of gang affiliation.

By the fifth page, I uncovered new things. Things that altered and anchored my history, my reality. I was a whole two years older than I'd been told, according to some unofficial birth certificate that had labelled me a "papoose" before someone crossed it off as a mistake. There was no information about my father, apart from the fact that "A Father" had brought me to the orphanage. Before she became "unknown," my mother was a woman named Emily Abrahams. There was no contact information, but there was a number written beside her name, barcode-like, as if she were a scannable can of soup. She was, it said, a fifteen-year-old student at St. Mary's boarding school.

BEFORE CHECKING INTO MY dingy motel room, I bought a fillet of maple smoked salmon, a fresh honey bun, and a gallon of pink lemonade. I licked the glaze off my sugar-and-salt-caked fingertips as I flipped through the phone book, scanning for St. Mary's, struggling to find the listing in the area code. I held the phone away from my ear at the sound of the dull, robotic dial tone.

"Operator."

"Hello, ma'am, I'm looking for Saint Mary's?"

"Saint what now?"

"The, uh…boarding school."

"Let me check."

Seconds stretched across the pink motel room, which reeked of cigarettes and had a perplexing greenish stain where the walls met.

"Sir?"

I swallowed down a large sip of lemonade so fast I felt ill. "Yes?"

"I have on record that Saint Mary's was one of them schools for Indians. Closed down several years ago. Building is, uh, still standing, from what I know, but it's way upriver. Not sure if anyone's still there."

The earth split open to the renewed sound of the dial tone. I stood up, light-headed, my blood heavy and tired. I burst out of the building with my files tucked loosely under my armpit and collapsed on the edge of the metal steps in a cold-sweat daze. The melon sky stared at me with an intensity I couldn't match, burning my eyes. Defeated, I looked down at my feet, where an uninvited squall of memories began to thunder. Comments the Children's Aid wraiths had made about my skin that turned the colour of terracotta in the summer, about my ever-elusive origins. I didn't want to know how a fifteen-year-old Native girl ended up pregnant with a blue-eyed baby while attending boarding school.

When the sky became a dense tangerine, I went back inside to make another call. The phone rang faster than normal.

"Evening, you have Tod —"

I slammed the receiver down. What the hell was I thinking? I hadn't talked to Tod in ages. How was he supposed to help me? I was too white and too late to be Native.

But was my mom alive? How old would she be now? Would she even want to see a child with the eyes of someone who hurt her? The questions made my brain twist.

I went back down to the river, guzzling a cold bottle of Four Roses, barely letting the whiskey touch my tongue. The sky was honeymoon blue now, bright with black clouds, the white sun and white moon like mirrors of each other. Then came the stars. I felt a deranged anger towards the beauty of it all. The world had put its hands around my neck and strangled any sliver of optimism out of me. This angry alley mutt, this alcoholic asshole, was all that was left.

But that scorching anger dissolved in the river's thunderous whir. I looked out into the water and felt my mother's spirit, cooling the third-degree burn on my soul.

THE VAST, LUSH FIELD leading up to the building where stolen children were forced to forget was dotted with dandelion skeletons and clearings of ghostberry. To my right, the scintillating river whipped by, leading me to an edifice that looked like it was made of cardboard.

A brown face popped out of a cracked window. "Yo, you the one who called?"

"Ray?" I lit up, ran towards him.

"Ray? No, name's Tawahum."

Ray's face turned into someone else's entirely, some-one much paler, taller, and younger. Someone with angular features, whorls of elliptical wolves tattooed on their spindly arms, and long, box-dyed hair fastened into a knotty braid.

"Do you, uh — I'm looking for my mother?"

"Right. Tod said she was sent here."

It took me eons to ring Tod up without ducking for the dial tone when I heard his voice. He wasn't from anywhere near the pit-house-filled prairie where St. Mary's stood, but he went out of his way to help me find someone who was. Put me in touch with some tech-savvy Cree kid who called me brother when I asked him why he was willing to help me. Caught my pain through the phone, he said. Wouldn't rest until my spirit could. I told him he was angling for eternal insomnia with a condition like that.

Now the trees were louder than they'd ever been, and Stó:lō started flowing from my eyes.

"Most people who know about it won't come near this place," Tawahum said. "Especially if they were forced here. There are sick places like this all over Turtle Island."

I followed Tawahum to their truck as fat berries of spring rain dropped from ripe clouds.

"My ancestors pushed a school to close in Saddle Lake way back in the sixties," Tawahum continued, fiddling with the radio. "Each victory sparks hope in some young fighter — or, shoot, maybe even an old fighter, somewhere. That's what got me here. But by the looks of you, no offence, man, I couldn't take you in that building. Place needs to be smudged from the inside out. Or maybe just torn down." Tawahum laughed, and the raindrops changed shape, became auriculate as they arrowed against the car. A swirl of seagulls circled and called, and if I'd chosen to ignore the Creator's message, I might not have looked up, might not have seen the arc of violet, indigo, blue, green, yellow, orange, and red that spilled into the roadside river.

"Woo!" Tawahum cheered. "Yeah, yeah, we see you, Creator."

The crescent of colour held every pigment I'd ever seen, from Tahitian waters to amethyst, moss green to Sitka, allamanda blossom, sea snake, and Italian lemon. From cloudberry and flame to sockeye and wild heart berry. The rainbow was so vibrant and surprising, it reduced me to tears again.

"You, uh, seem like you could use some sage or a sweat yourself," Tawahum said.

We drove past marshlands of blue heron for seven songs on the radio until we reached a secluded place on the river's edge where two older women sat on a large granite stone. One had kind eyes and a round, radiant face like the sun; the other had cheekbones as sharp as mountain ridges and silver-streaked hair that flowed down her torso. Tawahum and I crouched by a cedar totem that scraped the sky. I put my hands in the damp hair of the earth and realized it'd been a long time since I'd felt grass.

The sun Elder held an abalone shell filled with burning sage, a smell that transported me to Ray's boat. She brushed the smoke over me, saying words I didn't understand, as the other Elder handed me a coffee and a paper towel to wipe my streaming face. Shame geysered in me like a hydrothermal vent. I faced Tawahum and the Elders. "What exactly happened in this place?"

"Learned us to forget," the sharp-faced woman said.

"Tried to kill us, body, mind, and spirit." The kind-eyed Elder rested the burning sage beside my thigh.

"What for?" I asked.

"Land." Tawahum placed their deep bronze forearm on mine, pale and liver-spot spackled. Our struggles, though linked, had been different. For all my heartache, the relative whiteness of my skin, the elusiveness of where I came from, as much as I resented it, allowed me to flow more freely through the world.

They hadn't heard of my Emily but told me that stories of missing mothers and stolen children were as regular as rain in November and sockeye in spring. Told me that babies were thrown into the furnace and sometimes built into the walls. Told me it was a miracle I'd made it out alive. My survival gave them hope for all the others who never came back.

"So women and children just go missing and no one cares?"

Three firm hands pressed into my back. "The ones in

power took our tongues. People care plenty, once they know," Tawahum said.

We sat there for some time, embers of sage glowing sunstone and whispering gypsum up into the atmosphere.

"What if I got it all wrong? What if I'm not from here?"

The Elders knelt down on either side of the rock where I was perched. "You're here now."

The four of us turned our faces to the river.

22

The Sea

Snʊ'neɪmǝxʷ, 1989

⁓

You ever been held by a day? The deliriously beautiful way light spills through ribbons of red alder, ripples across feather beds of fern. When its honeyed light bends around pine cones, cascades through canopies of cedar, splashes across the dew-covered black earth that matches your skin. Among the tangle of ancient moss and the marshmallow-like fungi blooming out of decaying deciduous, find a place of velvet earth. At the base of the towering grandmother pines of the forest, linear time is rendered obsolete and a single moment can stretch out for eons, just like the light itself. Breathing in late July, all sea breeze and sugar, the gold body of August ripens on your tongue, and you hope it'll sweeten you the way it does the blackberries.

Clawing out of the salmonberry bramble so fermented I could get drunk on it, I placed my hoodie and scuffed-up skateboard deck in the driftwood. A soft whip of wind coated my skin with goosebumps. And then the sun ascended over the Sitka-framed mountain ridge, dappling the surface of the lake and, finally, my entire body with morning's glitter. I slipped into the water like I did a dream, gliding through with as much ease. Swimming like this hollowed and hallowed me. In this liminal liquid space, I could swim to the shores of Ceylon, to other timelines and states of consciousness. With each stroke, I rehearsed what I was going to say during the phone call I planned to make.

After the dip I dried off on a large boulder, solar-charging for the skate home. Vathany was outside talking to herself in the kale beds as I made sautéed morels on buttered sourdough and sipped unsweetened swamp water by the kitchen window. The ashwagandha, turkey tail, and anise concoction still tasted like a pond to me, but it did wonders for my nerves. It was peculiar — to feel nourished and rooted in my own flesh without paying much mind to how it looked.

I rocked back and forth on my heels, the ringing phone vibrating against my cheek. A contralto voice soared through the receiver. "Mo Sitka speaking."

"Hello —"

"Chandra."

I swallowed the piece of anise I was chewing on to keep calm. "How did you kn —"

"Caller ID."

I stroked the sides of my throat.

"I remember you from my good friend Sparky's production of *The Tempest* two years back. Never forget a great voice like yours. I'm afraid it's a little late to join the Phoenix, though…"

"Oh, yeah, that's why I called. I figured —"

"But we do have a seaside production coming up. A new stage play by two local playwrights."

THAT SUMMER, SAOIRSE AND I stayed home and helped Vathany finally sift through Appa's things as I swam his lake loop. I inherited his white Volkswagen van; cigarette smoke clung to the seats as resolute as his memory, but the thing was still kicking. Tony and I took it out to surf Jordan River one weekend, snagging long rides where the river mouth tumbled into the ocean. In the evenings, I dropped Vathany off at Kingdom Hall before driving up to catch the sunset at Sugarloaf Mountain, Neck Point, or Benson, where I ran lines for my audition. The play was a surreal little piece about a half-human, half-orca named Qeyqeyx̱elósem, evading settlers who razed the land and the sea with avarice, leaving Qeyqey to live in the in-between, in the splintered remains.

Saoirse stood ankle-deep in Green Lake, long coral dress gathered in her hands. She'd been eating watermelons by the pound as her pregnant belly swelled to a comparable size. A ray of sun fell on her right cheek, and she released the bunched fabric to stroke her globe of a belly in a spell of sun-drunkenness. As her skirt darkened slowly at the hem, she looked up and said, "Handsome boy."

That stopped me in my tracks. The first time Saoirse had complimented my appearance.

Her face froze over like a midwinter tidal pool. "Shoot, I said that out loud."

"Handsome, hey? Like, for a dark guy?"

"No, for an annoying guy," she scoffed, a black seed wedged between her pink-tinged incisors. "What does your skin have to do with anything?"

I chewed my lip, didn't know where to begin. She pulled my face to hers with her sweet, sticky hands. I kneeled on the rocks, held her angular cheeks, kissed her watermelon-flavoured mouth, kissed her firm belly.

"Can I say something?" she asked.

"I don't know, can you?" I rested my head on her stomach briefly before jolting back. "I felt a kick! I felt a kick!"

THAT NIGHT, THE BLUE-SKINNED GODDESS rose from a gentle opal-jade slate of sea. She twisted from the bright water and smiled as her arms turned into rivers. Her current propelled my chipped pink bathtub boat forward to the rocky black surf. The liquid bronze hem of the horizon unravelled into the water with resplendence. Beholding it felt like Appa.

The transient energy of the sea was working with me, and I was sailing effortlessly towards Appa's amber light, when my bathtub came to an abrupt halt. Algid black water sloshed in as a pair of beige arms hoisted themselves over the lip of the boat. Mr. Young was sinking my damn tub! I tried to pry his arms off the rim, but he wouldn't let go. The tub tilted, inundating the boat with brine until we sank deeper and deeper into a murky tangle of seaweed.

I woke covered in cold sweat, scanning my surroundings before daring to touch the floor, and spent the rest of the day suspicious of the ground. For the following weeks, Mr. Young tormented my dreams, sinking my bathtub every night with his ham-coloured forearms. The days bled together and my audition came and went as quickly as a receding tide.

Despite my sleep deprivation, I won the supporting role of the Seelkee. When I got my script, freshly bound, I tipped the title page in Saoirse's direction to show her the names of the playwrights.

"No way ... *the* Rocky and Jill?" she asked.

"*The* Rocky and Jill."

⌣

IT WAS MIDDAY, BUT the moon was out at the lagoon, glowing and full in the periwinkle sky. I hadn't wanted to wake Saoirse, who was napping on the couch after a nasty spell of morning sickness, so I'd decided to go spend some time with Appa and run over my monologue. Teal waves glittered and rolled as I scrabbled for footing on the driftwood.

"Chandra?" A familiar gruff voice cut the air.

I toppled, scraping my shin. Behind me stood Mr. Young, looming against the arbutus, rocks, and beach debris like a shadow.

"Been meaning to call you," he said, followed by an inaudible mutter and a sip of beer.

You've been trying to drown me in my dreams, I thought.

He grumbled again, avoiding eye contact. "I'm, ah, I'm sorry for everything," he said, still staring at the sea. "I'm not in a good way."

"Look, don't apologize to me. I'm used to it."

"I know." He exhaled a searing breath. "Saoirse. I'm ashamed, to be honest, don't know where to begin."

I softened. "Quit drinking. Start dancing again."

"How'd you know I danced?"

"How do you think?"

"Huh. Well, why do you care, anyways? I was an

asshole to you. You think you'll never become what you hate, kid, and then it creeps up on you like a sea snake. And get this, hey, turns out I'm not even all the way white."

I took a step back, considered Mr. Young. A bit of colour to his skin, sure, but a pair of baby-blue peepers like that are enough to change your whole life. "You look pretty white to me, Mr. Young."

"Well, things are complicated. And call me Ronny." He clasped his cheap beer to his lips.

I snatched the beer can away with a conviction that surprised me. "Cycles gotta stop somewhere, Ronny."

He looked down at his empty hands, out to the crashing waves, then back at me. "Give me my beer back, son."

"No." I leapt up to an elevated piece of driftwood, leaning into the surf of my own chaotic trickery.

"Give it here." Ronny clawed towards me.

I dodged. "No."

Ronny wrapped his leathery limbs around me, grappling for the beer can.

"It's killing you!" I crumpled the can, tossed it far into the fungal sea stack thicket.

"Hey! That's bad for the environment!" Ronny clamoured at me, digging his fingers into my ribs.

"Shit... Saoirse's going to be so mad." I ran my fingers over my scalp.

We stopped. I looked down at Ronny, arms still

sheathed around my waist, his face rippling into laughter. We planted our butts in the rocky sand, laughing until it turned to tears.

"What are you doing down here anyway?" I asked.

"Oh, you know, sorting through my thoughts... My son's ashes were scattered here."

"You had a son?" I looked into Ronny's eyes, the same stoic watery blue as Saoirse's. "My app — my father's ashes were scattered here, too."

Ronny placed his hand on my shoulder, and we watched the tide reach out for the aurelian horizon.

WE STOPPED IN AT a dingy old pub near the naval base for grub. Ronny opted for fried halibut, chips, and mushy peas. I stuck to lemon water and crudités — open-water trials were coming up.

"Ain't no Vie's," Ronny grumbled.

"Ron? How in Odin's name are ya?" An otter of a man with a blond ponytail and a weak jaw leaned over the bar. He saw me, celery stick half-masticated in my mouth, and stiffened. "What you gaping at, boy?"

"That's my son... in-law, er, my daughter's beau."

Otter retracted his thick, callused hand from Ronny's shoulder, leaned in, and whispered in his ear, "Rather my daughter be a whore."

Ronny took a deep, anguished breath. By the time

I realized he'd risen to his feet, he'd already decked the discount-bin Viking square in the jaw. Punched him right into a pirouette, an immaculate spin beneath the verdigris light illuminating the faded leather of his Sons of Odin vest before he crumpled into an empty barstool.

Ronny turned to me and shrugged. "I'm left-handed."

My eyes bulged out of my skull, the acrid taste of celery coming back up. "What does that have to do with anything?"

"Bad spirits," he said, downing a stranger's abandoned glass of ice-diluted whiskey.

This man was an even bigger basket case than I was. We tossed cash onto the bar, hopped into the Volkswagen, and blitzed out of there into the warm and windless night before anyone could memorize our faces.

"You smoke, kid?"

"Nah, my old man did."

I drove us to a hidden cove outside the naval base where the sky and sea had melted together into infinite charred indigo. We trudged calf-deep into the water before looking out into indefinite space. The ocean was chameleonic — white star clouds freckled the opalescent swell.

"Look." Ronny skimmed the water with his hand and a ribbon of sparkling blue-green light danced after it. Living light. We glided over constellations, over Andromeda's galaxy. Over Appa. "What do you believe in, son?"

"Nothing," I said. "Everything. You?"

He laughed. "I think I've decided not to decide...but there's something about water. Water and jive and folks that are kind."

"Yeah, I hear that."

I splashed the heel of my hand in Andromeda's pancake-shaped speck of a galaxy. Neon-blue embers glittered for a moment, then disappeared. I tilted my head back and breathed out. No one ever told me about the clarity that darkness brings. The divine beauty in the blackest night. When we're taught to fear something, we never spend enough time near it to discover its splendour. Cloaked in the infinite obsidian, Ronny's face was impossible to make out, but I saw him in more detail now than I had in broad daylight.

"WHADDYA THINK?" RONNY EXTENDED his arm in glee to reveal a hideous bathtub stained Serratia orange that had been abandoned on the side of the road and now sat in his backyard. He claimed to have scrubbed it as "clean as *Bonnie* in Tahiti," yet the thing remained spackled suspiciously pink.

When it comes to bathtub racing, alignment is critical for handling, as is precise measurement. Ronny and I were two cliffs of the same offshore sediment—a dancing diver and a thespian swimmer with no shred of attention span for precision. I had a sudden respect for the artistry of surfboard shapers and mechanics. The old man and I got our thrills adapting to turbulence — the art of rolling with the punches — rather than the careful calculation this work required. A tub's hull can be made by several different methods, but all the ones Ronny and I came up with would sink us.

Saoirse, looking like a planet, took over, unable to abide our painstaking grasp of physics. She was here, she said, to build a bathtub boat, not a relationship with her father, though she'd find herself equally invested in both projects.

"Don't trust your eyes, Dad. You have to actually measure things, you know? An engine four hundred feet underwater won't win you any races." She sent us to collect wood and filler.

Lily laughed. "Not to mention it'll create a big old hole in the back of your boat."

Lily was much better at rolling out the bubbles and wrinkles on the resin-wet E-glass, her hands as large as mine and twice as tough. And then Lily and Saoirse made sure the aluminum-made transom was as well built and strong as they were.

Somewhere between constructing the tub and the hull, Vathany stopped by with a batch of homemade lavender lemonade. By some miracle, my mother intuited the perfect technique for bringing the two separate bodies together with fibreglass strips, knowing how critical it was that everything was well reinforced.

"It's not perfect, but it will sail," she said with a grin, turning to the empty pitcher. "I should have made more lemonade."

I helped Ronny hand-paint three tentacles on each side, carve the suction cups off an old bath mat, and super-glue them onto our boat: the *Hexapus*.

On race day, the four of us crammed into the old Volkswagen to pick Ronny up from AA.

"I'm all for getting sober, but could they spare me the religious stuff?" His gruff voice billowed like Appa's phantom cigarette smoke as he hoisted himself into the passenger seat.

Vathany raised an artfully threaded brow. "Religion anchors some people."

"Didn't mean to offend," Ronny said.

With that, our parents spiralled into a discussion about the nature of the universe, sounding like a couple of college roommates on shrooms.

"In the book I'm reading — well, trying to read — it says some people come from the sky, some from the mountains..."

Saoirse rolled her eyes. "That's just basic evolution, Dad."

"What about the sea?" I asked, staring into Ronny's scowling reflection in the side-view mirror.

"From there, too. There's a local story that orcas swam in a circle here, transforming into sea wolves and, eventually, into people."

"Not to be a broken record, but that's evolution," Saoirse repeated.

"Well, that just shows how we're all raindrops," Vathany quipped. "Chandra came from the sea. His father, a rice paddy floodplain. And me? The mud."

The rest of us laughed and laughed and laughed.

"What? Why are you laughing?" she protested. "Like a lotus!"

When we got to the beach, Ronny and I dragged the bathtub towards the shoreline before Lil and Vathany split off to collect sea glass and Saoirse said she had a hankering for cotton candy. By the time our *Hexapus* was docked, Saoirse returned with Tony, a big, blue balloon, and a Black pirate. I lifted my head with a smile to fist-bump Tony and collect my belated balloon.

"Ahoy there, Moon."

"No damn way." I wrapped my arms around Rocky, pressing him into a pearl. "You're so much smaller than I remember!"

"Heard ye be starring in our new play." My lips parted to respond as Rocky raised an open palm towards the rainbow arch of boats at the water's lapping edge. "But we don't have time for all that now." He reached down to retrieve his megaphone. "All tubbers to their tubs!"

I sat in the *Hexapus*, met by the same sand-flea heart hum of the diving blocks. The boat rocked in the ebb tide. When the starting pistol pierced the air, sea foam frothed at the tub's base and I was launched from the sand by Ronny's brawny sea dog arms. With a thump, a splash, and a large glut of salt sea, Ronny heaved himself over the side. Our sail was oceanspray, laughter, and the shadows of loved ones on the sand. We were so focused on staying afloat, we didn't realize, or care, that we came in dead last.

FRESH WATER ON THEIR MINDS, silver coho ran up through the very estuaries they'd entered the sea through for the first time. Saoirse propped her swollen feet on the dashboard as we drove up to Skaha Lake for open-water trials. Tony's tanned forearms, now thick and covered in blond hair, gripped the steering wheel of Appa's Volkswagen. The scented air fresheners did little to tackle the third-hand smoke, but the radio man was on my side with his hit parade, and I had the backseat and the whole world to myself. Tone told me to close my eyes and conserve my energy, but I spent the drive observing the way the crimson-clementine-chanterelle day held these two people under its arbour of changing leaves. People who had chosen me, who cheered me on from my childhood driveway in Nanaimo all the way until I stood on this wooden dock, suited up in Lycra.

The Cascade mountains lined the horizon, the air was rich and redolent with autumn, and the water was inviting. Ponderosa pine, alder, and cedar teemed along a sash of cerulean sky that matched Saoirse's irises. I looked intently into the rippling lake, where rings of the past stretched out in a shimmer to encircle the present, framed and clear. But it was in Saoirse's eyes, which had flashed up to meet mine in the rear-view mirror as we made way for an unrelenting tree root, that I saw my future.

At the sound of the gun, we were in. We swimmers slipped over each other like silver smolt reaching for the mint-green Gulf of Alaska, like a single body made of droplets, like water itself. No lanes. No turns. No red line to follow. No fear of the other side. Had it not been for the photos to prove it, I wouldn't have believed how early I towed myself into a generous lead. A steady heartbeat thrummed in my ears as I kicked, pulled, breathed.

∞

From the River to the Sea

shxwtelí —
where you come from

———

You roared like an earthquake when you took your first breath, an éy swayel to the world. My í:meth — is that right? A little cinnamon baby with a full head of Tahitian-pearl hair, beads of water on your skin, streaming out of your eyes and mouth. I held you, and everything snapped together. The room flooded with the warmth of the Mexican sun, with the whirr of the river current, with the pulse of jive music, and I realized this whole time it was not my mother but you who was calling to me.

As you grew, your grey eyes turned amber — round and kind like your father's, who liked to put his gold medal around your neck. You had your mother's wild black hair and love for the land, and my cheekbones, sarcastic smirk, and inability to stay stagnant. When you started showing a preference for your left hand, I panicked, thinking I'd passed my bad spirits on to you. But your mother told me being left-handed means you're creative. A storyteller. Must be why you're such a pain in the arse, always asking so many damn questions. Hell, can't help but imagine who I'd be, had I been told my bad spirits were creative spirits instead.

This land entered me and it's my home. But I don't know what Nation I'm from, if I'm from any, and it wouldn't be right to pretend that I do. Even though you look the way you do, blood isn't the same as belonging. It's important to speak clearly about these things. I'm learning the language of this land because the land shaped it, out of respect for those of this land who had their words stolen from them, in the hope that one day someone will pick up the loose threads I leave behind, and just maybe they will lead them home.

I myself speak only for the alley mutts. st'éxem. For those of us who must learn the details of our ancestry in fragments, carving out communities for ourselves in the aftermath of all this separation. It was the river that raised me. I was saved by the givers, by human beings with searching hearts, by the sea. They will always be my kin.

Pain sometimes creates a fog over the lens we view the world through, blotting out all the beauty. Clear that off, chóxw, mí:lthet, and seek the good, because it's there. It's the space between everything. It's love. stl'ítl'el. It's art. sqw'eyílex; shxwi'atl'qels; t'í:lem.

It's water. qó.

Even when things seem rigid or isolated, they're not. Everything, everyone continues to flow infinitely, like the clouds into the river into the sea.

Acknowledgements

Gin 'waadluuwaan gud ahl ḵwaagiidang (Everything is connected to everything else).

Yalh yexw kw'es hoy (Thank you for what you have done).

Thank you to the Matsqui and Semá:th nations of the Stó:lō Nation, on whose beautiful territory I was born and raised. Thank you to my mother, Shalegh, for teaching me to love the land and all living things, and for cautioning me to always be precise with my words, no matter how tedious that can be. Thank you to my three younger sisters, Tiahna, Katrina, and Emily, for always listening to my stories. Thank you to my best friend and soulmate, Ali Taylor, for making me a better human being.

Thank you to my chosen life companion and lover, David Mäder, for supporting me tirelessly throughout this process. Thank you, Senica Maltese, for being a superb and generous first reader. Háw'aa Jaskwaan Bedard for being the embodiment of joyful activism, and for reminding me that Indigenous languages are not and never have been "lost," as they are embedded in the land itself. Kw'es hoy Kwilosintun (Brandon) for the fish. Thank you to my agent, mentor, and literary inspiration Chelene Knight, for believing in me and in this book. Thank you, Shirarose, for taking such good care of this story.

To Nadia, Elissa, Kayla, Jeremy, Grace, Isabel, and Mayu — thank you for your friendship, which makes life worth living.

RACHAEL MOORTHY is a writer of mixed heritage who still hasn't figured out how to answer the question "Where are you from?" She is passionate about telling stories from the perspectives of people who, like her, have complex and tangled roots (namely, melanated, diasporic, and displaced Indigenous identities). She hopes to carve out a community of belonging for the aporia caught in the liminal aftermath of colonialism, whose ancestral and cultural connections have been fractured because of foster care, adoption, and genocide. She believes she is best able to remain humble as an advocate in the dialogue surrounding Indigenous sovereignty by standing firm in her fluidity as a multi-ethnic person raised in a Eurocentric, assimilated context. Rachael has a bachelor's of writing from the University of Victoria and is pursuing a master's in multi/interlingual literary studies at the University of Basel. She was shortlisted for the 2020 Far Horizons Award for Poetry, and her fiction has appeared in publications such as *PRISM international*, *SAD Magazine*, and *Revue Zinc*. Born in Matsqui, British Columbia, she lives in Switzerland.